By XAVIER MAYNE

NOVELS

BRANDT AND DONNELLY CAPERS
Frat House Troopers
Wrestling Demons

Husband Material

NOVELLAS
The Accidental Cupid

Published by DREAMSPINNER PRESS
http://www.dreamspinnerpress.com

# WRESTLING DEMONS

## XAVIER MAYNE

*Dreamspinner Press*

Published by
Dreamspinner Press
5032 Capital Circle SW
Suite 2, PMB# 279
Tallahassee, FL 32305-7886
USA
http://www.dreamspinnerpress.com/

Wrestling Demons
© 2014 Xavier Mayne.

Cover Art
© 2014 L.C. Chase.
http://www.lcchase.com
Cover content is for illustrative purposes only and any person depicted on the cover is a model.

ISBN: 978-1-62798-625-0
Digital ISBN: 978-1-62798-626-7

Printed in the United States of America
First Edition
April 2014

*For J, always and forever*

# ACKNOWLEDGMENTS

I'd like to thank all of the readers on Literotica who read the early version of the original book in the series, *Frat House Troopers*. Your feedback gave me the confidence to seek a publisher, and the success of the book encouraged me to continue the story of Brandt and Donnelly into a series. Thank you for reading, and I look forward to bringing you more adventures.

# CHAPTER ONE
## DEBUT

THE VIDEO was grainy; there was no sound, but the subject of the video was clear. A row of lockers occupied the frame and seemed to extend beyond it both left and right; in front of the middle locker stood a young man with a towel around his waist. The locker door was open, and he was busily engaged in taking out and replacing various articles that could not be made out clearly. Several times other men walked through the frame, and each exchanged a greeting with the central subject of the film. With several he conversed for a moment or two while continuing to tend to his locker. Finally, he picked up a bottle of some kind, closed his locker, and walked out of the frame to the right, where each of his interlocutors had also gone.

There was a sudden cut in the video, and the man walked back into the frame from the right. His dark, short hair was wet, standing in crazy spikes all over his head—a condition he intensified by rapidly shaking his head several times. He faced away from the camera, opened his locker, and replaced the bottle he had taken with him. Again, several others walked through the frame, from right to left this time, and he exchanged words with them as they passed and had more extended conversation with a couple.

Finally, he turned his back to the camera and brought his hands to his waist; he loosened the towel that was tucked tightly there. It opened, and it began to drop from his body.

The frame froze, the towel a blur of motion. The young man's modesty was preserved, but only just.

"Oh no you didn't!" shrieked Bryce. "You get that finger off the pause button or I will twist it so badly, when you hail a cab it'll stop on the other side of the street!"

"But, my love," soothed Nestor, his voice a humid breeze of old Havana, "we are out of the popped corn. You love the popped corn on the movie night. Please, let me make you more." He slid the popcorn bowl from Bryce's grip, kissing him on the cheek as he did so. "I will return, to fill your mouth with my salty goodness." Nestor slid out from the sheets and strode out of the bedroom.

Bryce turned to watch Nestor go, and his fit of pique over the pause button seemed to evaporate under the influence of nudity. He watched the door for Nestor's return, for the front of him was as fine as the rear.

A few minutes later, Nestor came back into the room with a full bowl of popcorn. He settled in next to Bryce and fed him the first few fluffy kernels.

"Thank you, doll. All is forgiven," Bryce murmured between mouthfuls. "Now, can we get back to our feature presentation?"

Nestor nodded and pressed the pause button once again. Down at the foot of the bed, the screen jolted to life, and the towel succumbed to gravity. Down it fell, out of the frame.

Bryce gasped, his hand at his throat. "Oh my heavens—what a work of art is man!" His wide eyes were focused on the screen like an eagle's when it spies plump, slow-moving prey. "Pause it! Pause it!"

Nestor rolled his eyes and hit the pause button. "Before you no like pause…," he muttered.

"Hush! Now, look at that. Is it not a wonder? All that bunched muscle, that flawless skin, not a mark on it. Oh, what I wouldn't give to have an ass like that."

"But my love, your *culo* is just as pretty as that one on the film."

"I don't want to *have* an ass like that—what would I use all that muscle for? But if I had an ass like that right here in bed with me—oh, the things I would do to it…." His eyes grew unfocused and dreamy. Then he snapped back to the moment. "I would share it with you, of course," he said to Nestor. "Like when we split that pizza delivery man last week."

"Mmm," Nestor purred at the recollection. "Spicy, with extra sausage."

"You know, we should order from them again. I think next time I'll go for an additional topping."

Nestor nodded his agreement.

"Now, though, let's see what develops with our athlete here. If I know my locker-spy porn—and you know I do—I suspect he's about to turn around and reveal the extent of his musculature. My guess is"—he cocked his head at the screen—"a soft five, or a semi six."

Nestor pushed the pause button.

On the screen, the athlete reached up into his locker and pulled out a pair of underwear. They were boxers, in a faded plaid material, and even with the low quality of the video, signs of wear on the waistband were apparent. He stepped into them one leg at a time, not bending over enough to afford Bryce a view of the other sight he was looking forward to. The boxers bunched up under his rounded buttocks, and he slid his thumbs into the waistband and pulled them up, obscuring the view. The rest of the film consisted of the same athlete applying deodorant, pulling on his shirt, jeans, and shoes, and then finally donning a sweatshirt before slinging a backpack over his shoulder and slamming his locker shut.

"But... but...!" was all Bryce could manage to get out. He turned his crestfallen face to Nestor. "But... that's it? That's all we get?"

Nestor picked up the keyboard and searched the site for additional videos from the same user, but he found nothing. He shook his head, and shrugged at Bryce.

"Well, that's certainly not up to the standards I have come to expect from DudesCaughtNudeintheLockerRoom.com! Really—all that buildup and not even a glimpse of the goods. I may have to compose a strongly worded e-mail."

"Please, let this not ruin movie night," murmured Nestor. "We have popped corn, and I bring a bottle of your favorite."

"The strawberry kind? That stays slippery for hours?" Bryce asked through pouting lips.

Nestor nodded.

"All right," Bryce said with a small, dignified huff. "Let's see if there's anything new in the way of drunk college boys." He took a large handful of popcorn as Nestor's fingers flew over the keys. "How terribly boring spring break must have been before smartphones and two-dollar margaritas."

They sat back against their pillows as a conga line of naked men—half of them wearing backward baseball caps—jostled past the camera to the appreciative hoots of an assembly of bikini-clad women.

Bryce turned to Nestor and kissed him on the nose. "I love movie night."

THE PHONE on his desk blipped, jolting him from his concentration on the report he was writing. The phone so rarely rang anymore—most communication came through e-mail or messaging—that every time it did, he jumped in surprise. It usually meant someone outside of his usual contacts was trying to reach him as everyone in his division knew how to reach him electronically.

"Brandt," he said into the receiver.

"Officer Brandt, good. This is Chief Powell up in Woodley. Got a little issue here I hoped I might get your help on. Your chief said it was okay to contact you directly."

Ethan Brandt had gotten used to this kind of call over the past six months. He and his partner Gabriel Donnelly were the first officers in the state police to be fully out as gay men, and the publicity around their mission last year investigating a sex-cam website had attracted the attention of police departments across the state. The calls for help generally involved one of two things: violations of the state's statutes protecting gays and lesbians or people being filmed in compromising sexual situations. Come to think of it, Brandt reflected, most calls involved both of these things.

"How can I help you, Chief Powell?"

"We got ourselves a situation involving one of those cell-phone videos. Shows one of our high school students in… ah… well, in an intimate setting."

Brandt sat up in his chair. Woodley… yes, he'd heard of this case. "Is this the video of the girl at that party?"

There was a pause on the other end of the phone. "Ah, no. This is a new one."

"I don't mean to cut you off, chief, but I need to know—is the subject of this new one of age?" All he knew about the earlier case was that the girl whose image had been captured in the scandal was under eighteen. The state police had a unit for dealing with underage videos, and Brandt would involve them from the beginning if needed.

"Yes, yes...." There was a long pause. "He's eighteen."

"Wait, did you say *he*?" Brandt had definitely not heard of this case—in fact, he hadn't heard of any such case in the state.

"Ah... yes. It's also a matter of some delicacy in the community, Officer Brandt. Do you think you might be able to come up to Woodley for a meeting, help us figure out how to proceed?"

"Yes, of course," Brandt replied immediately. He pulled up his calendar app. "My partner and I can be there tomorrow morning at... say, ten?"

"Oh, right, your 'partner.'" The chief sighed. "I still can't get used to...," he muttered, then seemed to stop himself from going any further. "Anyway, tomorrow would be fine. I appreciate your help, Brandt." He clicked off the line.

"Donnelly!" Brandt called two desks over to where his partner worked. "How do you feel about a field trip tomorrow?"

"Where we going? Someplace glamorous?"

"Yeah, not so much. Heading to Woodley."

"Oh."

Brandt got up and walked over to his partner's desk. "I can tell from your tone you are less than thrilled with my choice of destination."

"You're a mind reader, you are." Donnelly grinned, looking up at his partner with eyes that sparkled with mischief but clearly showed he was very much in love. "What's the occasion?"

"The chief there says they have a video of a high school kid, and they aren't sure how to handle it."

"Well, they could hardly do worse than they did with that one a few months back."

Brandt squinted at his partner. "I didn't know you kept up on the goings-on in Woodley, of all places."

Donnelly rolled his eyes. "Ugh—that place. I grew up near there. Remember those great stories I've told you about my hometown? Well, Woodley's even worse. Batshit conservative top to bottom. In high school we used to wrestle against them. You've never seen a town so fixated on sports, and on wrestling in particular. They always had some pastor come out and say a prayer before meets, but their true religion is wrestling."

"Their public high school has prayers before wrestling meets?"

Donnelly nodded. "Yep. It's that kind of place. So, thanks for the chance to go back and visit—it'll be awesome."

"Your job satisfaction, as always, is my primary concern," cracked Brandt as he walked back to his desk.

THAT NIGHT, as Brandt pulled back the covers and slipped into bed next to Donnelly, he was already running scenarios on their trip to Woodley. "Today, when you said Woodley had fucked up the video case six months ago, what did you mean?"

Donnelly set down his e-book. "It was a classic case," he replied. "Girl goes to a party at a friend's house after the winter formal, ends up getting frisky in one of the bedrooms."

"May be a parent's worst nightmare, but I imagine it happens all the time."

"Except this time, someone got video of it on their smartphone camera."

"Again, probably happens all the time. Jeesh, kids today." Brandt sighed at the decadence of youth—a neat trick, given that he was only twenty-five years old himself.

"Here's where it gets more interesting. The video was taken—and posted online—by one of the people in the room with her."

"Wait, one of the people with her? How many were in there?"

"Two besides her, apparently. You know, best buds doing some male bonding."

"Oh. That's a bit more… unusual. How did they handle it once the video got around?"

"Badly. Everyone ganged up on the girl. It was about the most intense slut-shaming you can imagine. Even some of her own family blamed her for embarrassing everyone."

"But she wasn't the only one there, and she certainly didn't film it and forward it to her friends, right?" Brandt felt himself getting angry. "Didn't the guys get some of the blame?"

"Yeah, not so much. The guy with the camera was pretty careful not to get their faces in the shot, so there's no hard evidence on who it was. But that really doesn't matter."

"It should. It damn well should!"

"I mean, it doesn't matter in Woodley. She was in the video having sex, so she's the slut. They didn't even work very hard on finding out who the guys were. She claimed that it was two stars of the wrestling team, but no one believed her."

"Why not? She's the one who would know."

"Yes. But you missed the part about their being stars—on the wrestling team. Wrestling is like a religion in Woodley, remember? They would do anything to avoid those guys getting in trouble."

"Well, that sucks."

"Indeed it does. But it sucks the most for the real victim. She and her mom basically had to leave town. Went out west somewhere, I think, to live with relatives."

"Hmm." Brandt was reconsidering the nature of their meeting in Woodley tomorrow. "This Powell guy said he wanted to talk to us because this new video is a sensitive matter in the community. And it's a video of a guy. I wonder if the two situations are related."

"Look at you, already on the case," Donnelly said, shaking his head. "Can you take a few minutes away from your work to do something for me?"

"Sure. What do you need me to do?"

"Me, if it's not too much trouble." Donnelly set his e-book on the nightstand and threw off the covers, revealing the porcelain skin and powerful musculature that Brandt loved so much.

"I think I can work you in," growled Brandt.

"Hey, it's my turn," Donnelly replied. His delighted expression clearly conveyed he was up for anything Brandt might want to do.

"We'll just have to see about that," Brandt said with a sly grin as he launched himself atop his willing partner, and all thoughts of the scandal in Woodley left his mind.

WOODLEY LAY two hours to the north of the city. Brandt prided himself on never being late, so he had dragged Donnelly out of bed and gotten on the road by seven thirty.

"Can we stop for coffee?" groaned Donnelly.

"You haven't finished the one I made you before we left the house!"

"Yeah, but by the time you find a place to get more I'll have finished it." He turned his sleepy eyes to Brandt. "I'm just trying to be efficient. You know, planning ahead."

"If we make good time, we can stop on the outskirts of town."

"We're going to Woodley. There are no outskirts. Once you're there, you're there."

"Then we'll hit the Starbucks in town. Happy now?"

"Not so much. The Starbucks in Woodley closed last year. They were driven out of town by a group pissed off about the company giving domestic partner benefits."

Brandt turned a disbelieving look on Donnelly. "Are you serious? Who does that?"

"The good people of Woodley, that's who. When are you going to stop being surprised by that?"

"I guess I've just been sheltered. We live in a pretty great city, and almost all our friends and family have been completely supportive of us. I kind of thought the world was getting better all over."

"I recommend you dial back your expectations, buddy. Woodley's like a little chunk of 1958 that got lodged in the throat of time."

"That's one of your less appetizing similes, I have to say."

"Sorry. It's the caffeine deprivation. It's all starting to get fuzzy…."

"Hold out for three minutes, drama queen. There's a truck stop next exit that promises 'top-quality expresso.' Sounds yummy, right?"

"Spelling it with an *x* means it's automatically going to be horrible. But as long as it has caffeine, I'm not going to quibble. Wake me when we're there."

"I told you it's only three minutes," Brandt began, but was stopped by Donnelly's histrionic snoring. "Fine. I'll wake you," he grumbled.

THE POLICE department was, like the rest of Woodley, severe and old-fashioned. It inhabited a low-slung building in the middle of downtown, which it shared with the other municipal offices. Brandt drove slowly by but kept going so as to take in the whole town—and find a place to get decent coffee. The truck-stop "expresso" tasted like the by-product of a motor-oil recycling program, and they were both eager for a drinkable cup. They found a tiny storefront on the edge of downtown with a cheery sign out front and a wheezing monster of an espresso maker inside. Fortified, they decided to walk the four or five blocks back to the station.

"Did that barista wink at you?" Brandt asked as they walked.

"Are you asking me as a police officer, or as your boyfriend?" Donnelly asked. "I need to know whether I'm obligated to give evidence or to spare your feelings."

"I thought so." Brandt smiled. "Did you think he was cute?"

"Couldn't really tell. There was so much steam from that pre-Mussolini espresso maker that I could hardly see his muscles and charm."

"Nice. I take it we'll be stopping back in to grab a little something to take home?" Brandt asked with a chuckle.

Donnelly stopped suddenly. "Do you think he'd come with us? We haven't really talked about this—it's all so sudden!" Brandt gaped at him, and he burst out laughing.

"Keep it moving, Officer Donnelly," Brandt scolded. "We've got a job to do."

They walked into the police department and presented their badges at the front desk. They were shown into a conference room and left with an assurance that the chief would be in shortly. They admired the photos of pastoral landscapes that decorated one wall of the conference room and the photos of various sporting events that decorated the other three.

"I see what you mean about this place and sports," Brandt muttered.

"There's no pride like Woodchuck pride," Donnelly replied with a roll of his eyes.

"Woodchucks? Really?"

"Yep. I remember when I was in high school there was talk about updating the mascot. But in the end the forces of tradition won out. They always do around here."

With a heavy foot, Chief Powell lumbered into the room. "Officer Brandt?" He was an energetic man of about sixty with a prodigious belly and a booming voice. He set the laptop he was carrying down on the table and shook Brandt's hand vigorously. "Thank you for coming."

"Chief Powell, this is my partner, Officer Gabriel Donnelly."

Powell held out his hand with perhaps less vigor than he had shown Brandt. "Officer," he said with an almost grudging undertone.

Donnelly simply nodded.

"Please, sit," Powell said, taking the chair at the head of the table.

Brandt and Donnelly sat down on either side of him.

"Now, you're aware of the incident we had back in the fall." The officers nodded. "Damn shame that was—almost derailed our wrestling season before it even began."

"Yes, that would have been a hardship," Donnelly said, his voice low and even.

"But once that girl finally came to her senses and left town, things settled down. That's why this latest development… well, I just want to make it go away as quickly and quietly as possible."

"Perhaps you can give us some details on what's happened?" Brandt asked. Before leaving work yesterday, he had checked on whether any recent news had come from Woodley about a video scandal and had come up with nothing.

"About a week ago, one of the kids at the high school came to the school counselor about a video that was being passed around. Good kid, but she wouldn't say who had passed it to her. Anyway, the counselor watched it and notified us right away."

"And what does this video contain?" Brandt prompted.

"I'll show it to you. As I mentioned, the person in the video is eighteen, but it's still shocking. Of course, what shocks you city people may be different from what riles us country folks...." He cast a wary look at Donnelly, as if he suspected the officer from the city liked to watch videos of a depraved nature over his organic bulgur-flax granola in the morning. He opened his laptop and stabbed at the keyboard with fat, certain fingers; he spun it around to show them once the video window opened. "Here you go."

The video showed a locker room and a young man in a towel.

WHEN THE video concluded, the chief shut the laptop and looked from Brandt to Donnelly. "Well, I think you can see why we're so upset."

Brandt looked across the table at Donnelly, who gave the smallest shrug, and then at the chief. "I assume you've interviewed him?"

"We brought him in right away, and his parents as well. They were beside themselves, naturally."

"He had no idea the video had been made?"

"None at all," the chief replied. "And if you're going to ask next whether we found the camera, the answer is no. We searched the locker where it seems from the video that it was located, and all of the others on that row, and came up with nothing. No sign of anything having been there at all."

Brandt took a deep breath, let it out. "Chief, I'm sure this has been embarrassing for the boy, and for his family, but I'm not sure how we can help."

The chief leaned in, a deep scowl on his face. "Officer Brandt, I'm sure you appreciate that we cannot have a pervert on the loose taking video of innocent athletes. They have a reasonable expectation of privacy in the locker room, and that has been violated. And if this video is being passed around the high school, then it is only a matter of time before it finds its way onto the Internet and this young man's future is over."

Brandt had had enough. "Chief Powell, with all due respect, this video—while it certainly is a violation of this man's privacy—would get a PG-13 rating if it were in a movie. If we're going to have a manhunt every time a high school boy's butt is displayed to the public, you're going to have to make mooning a felony."

Powell's eyes narrowed to slits. "Perhaps I have not made myself clear, Officer Brandt. Someone has violated this young man, and they can destroy him with a click of a button. It is our duty to keep that from happening." He turned to Donnelly as if giving up on Brandt altogether. "You see, Mr. Jonah Fischer is one of our top wrestlers, and as a senior he is currently being recruited by some of the top college programs in the country. This video could end all of that."

"Pardon me, chief, but why would a recruiter pull an offer because Mr. Fischer was recorded without his permission?"

"You never wrestled, did you, son?" the chief replied, shaking his head at Brandt.

"No sir, I—"

"I did," blurted Donnelly. "I understand the problem, chief." He turned to Brandt. "Wrestling is different, Ethan. Most sports have their homophobic aspects, mainly as a defense against the idea that football players piling on top of each other or basketball players covering each other closely is in any way erotic." The chief bristled at the word. "But in wrestling, all you have is contact. It's two superfit guys in skintight singlets writhing around on a mat grabbing and holding, each trying to be the first one to climb on top of the other."

The chief shook his head, clearly distressed at this characterization. But Donnelly was undaunted.

"That's why wrestlers can sometimes be the most homophobic athletes—it's kind of a natural response to the fact that everything they do to beat a competitor is exactly what they would do to make out with him. They need the deniability that homophobia provides."

Brandt looked at the chief. "Does that about sum it up?"

The chief sighed and studied the tabletop for a moment before answering. "That isn't it at all. Wrestling is one of the oldest sports, and one of the most pure. It's the perversion of our modern world that makes it seem to some people—" He looked with obvious disgust at Donnelly, then resumed with a snarl. "—*erotic*. That's why we have to stand strong against perversion in all of its forms. Whoever made this video wanted to turn the purity of athletics into something dirty, to expose this poor boy to the sick desires of deviants. No wrestling program is going to want to be associated with that."

"Which is basically what I said," Donnelly added. "That doesn't mean it's right, chief. There are gay wrestlers, just like there are gay football players and gay basketball players. And they compete and win just like the straight ones. Wrestling is a great sport, and it will get even better once it shakes off its homophobic baggage. There are surely some university wrestling recruiters who won't care about the video, but until the entire sport comes around to that view,"—he looked to Brandt—"it could be a pretty big deal. If we can help this kid out by finding out who did this and stopping it from going any further, we should."

Brandt nodded. "All right, we'll see what we can do. Can we talk to this Jonah?"

The chief's expression lightened. "I hoped you would want to do that. I've asked his parents to bring him in this afternoon when school is over. That'll be at two thirty."

"Good enough," Brandt replied. "We'll come back then. Do you mind if we head over to the high school and take a look at the locker room?"

"Like I said, we've gone over the place pretty thoroughly. But it wouldn't hurt for you to take a look as well. I'll let the wrestling coach know you're coming by."

"Thanks." Brandt and Donnelly rose. "We'll see you at two thirty."

They shook hands, and the officers walked back to their car.

"Well, that was fun," Brandt said as they strolled. "Thank goodness I had a native speaker of wrestling to translate for me. Otherwise I would have been completely lost."

Donnelly shook his head and looked into the distance. "What amazed me is how he cannot see the similarities between these two video cases. Being filmed completely ruined that girl's life, but he didn't give a crap about her. This boy's ass, though, gets him all worked up."

"What do you think the odds are that this video is going to end up on a website?"

"Are you kidding me? Did you have your eyes closed when we watched it? Even setting aside those who watch hidden camera videos just because they're hidden camera videos, there would still be a whole lot of people in the world who would watch that. He's as well built as any of those guys Nick manages back at the frat house."

"Dude, we're supposed to be professionals here."

"I'm giving you my professional opinion that our Mr. Fischer is definitely going to go viral, if he hasn't already."

Brandt shrugged. "Yeah, you're probably right. I've learned to respect your taste in asses."

"Speaking of which, how about another cup of coffee?"

Even Brandt slapping the back of his head couldn't keep Donnelly from having a good laugh at his own juvenile humor.

BRANDT AND Donnelly were shown into the coaches' offices while a noisy group of phys ed students shouted and jostled their way through the locker room. They sat at the wrestling coach's desk and awaited his arrival.

The athletic complex was, predictably, out of all scale compared to the rest of the high school campus. The facilities rivaled those of the university Brandt had attended and looked to be no more than five years old. The locker rooms were built in an elliptical shape, with the offices for the coaching staff in the center. They were raised up a half flight of stairs from the floor level in the locker room, and windows all around the offices commanded a view into all of the areas of lockers below. Underneath the offices, a half flight lower than floor level, were showers.

Once the din of high schoolers bound for the fields had died away, a fit and wiry man in his thirties sprang up the stairs into the room full of desks and strode over to meet the officers. According to the embroidery on his slick polo shirt, his name was Coach Woody.

"Ah, you must be here to see me," he said as he extended his hand to the men. "I'm Woodrow Gustafson, the wrestling coach. Please, call me Woody."

Brandt nodded. "I'm Officer Brandt, and this is Officer Donnelly. Chief Powell asked us to gather some information about the video of Jonah Fischer."

Coach Woody grew immediately serious. "I'm so glad you're here to help. I just hate the idea of anything happening to Jonah's chances of getting a ride to college. Kid's parents work so hard, but they've had some setbacks, and the only way he's going to get a shot in life is a wrestling scholarship. Otherwise, it's community college for him, and probably a welding job over at the works in Somerville. Now, don't get me wrong—metalworking is what built this whole region, but Jonah's far too smart for that. A good education and the sky's the limit for him."

"We all have the same goal, Woody. Can you take us to where Jonah's locker is located? We'd like to see it for ourselves."

"Oh, sure! Follow me." Coach Woody turned and walked to the stairs on the far side of the office. The officers followed him down the stairs and around to a bank of lockers they immediately recognized from the video. "This is Jonah's locker, here," Woody said, stopping suddenly and pointing to his left. "Chief Powell figured the camera must have been mounted here." He pointed to the locker opposite Jonah's.

"No one's using this one?" Brandt asked, peering through the mesh door into the empty locker.

"Not now. It had been used by another wrestler, but he left Woodley a couple of months ago. It's been empty since."

Donnelly opened the locker and ran his hand around the inside. "Wow, these are sure nicer than the ones my school had. No holes, no rusty vents. And nowhere to run wires."

Coach Woody stood up straighter, clearly proud of the facilities. "Yep, these are state of the art. Solid, high-impact plastics, impervious to mold and mildew and fully vented on the front. Thanks to donors in the community, our wrestlers get the best."

Brandt, who had been surveying sight lines up and down the row of lockers, turned to the coach. "What can you tell us about Jonah? Popular kid? Anyone who might have a grudge?"

"Oh gosh, no. Everyone loves Jonah. He's the all-around good kid. Gets good grades, always on time for practice, volunteers with his church group. I can't think of anyone who's ever had anything bad to say about Jonah."

Brandt nodded, his brow furrowed.

"I do have a question for you, though," Woody ventured.

"Sure—ask away."

"Why do people do this kind of thing?"

"What do you mean?" Donnelly asked.

"Take video like this?" the coach continued. "Who would want to see video of a guy changing his clothes?"

"The likeliest explanation is that someone wanted to embarrass him for some reason. Just about all high school students carry a device these days that allows them to take pictures or video of other kids doing stupid things—or everyday things that aren't meant to be recorded or shared. Just kids being kids, not aware of the harm they may cause."

"I get that part," the coach said, nodding. "When I was in high school a standard prank was to shove some poor kid out into the hall in the middle of changing his clothes. Everyone would have a good laugh at his naked butt and life goes on."

Donnelly nodded. "These days, in a lot of places that would be treated as a sexual assault. Times have changed."

"I guess the Internet is the new hallway," Woody said, shaking his head. "The video has kind of run its course around here. All the kids have seen it, and most seem to think it's no big deal. But the police say they're concerned about it getting posted online and more people seeing it. So that's my question—who would want to see that?"

"That's the magic of the Internet," Brandt said. "There's something out there for everybody, and there's somebody out there for anything people might post."

The coach shook his head. "I just don't get it. I'm surrounded by kids changing clothes every day, and there's just nothing"—he lowered his voice to a whisper and leaned close—"sexy"—he looked sheepish, then stepped back and continued—"about it."

Donnelly seemed up to the challenge of explaining further. "Would you say the same thing about a hidden camera in the women's locker room?"

The coach gulped. "Well… I… um, I'd have to say that… um…."

"Yeah, it's like that," Donnelly said, mercifully interrupting the coach's embarrassed stuttering. "There are some people who wouldn't mind seeing women athletes changing clothes, and there are other people who enjoy watching the men."

"Huh," the coach grunted. "So there are perverts out there who look at my wrestlers like normal guys would look at women?"

"I don't think the labels 'pervert' and 'normal' are really helpful here," Brandt said. "Let's just say we'd like to make sure it doesn't get posted online in the first place."

Woody shook his head again. "That poor kid."


BRANDT AND Donnelly stopped for lunch at a small, old-fashioned diner in the middle of town, where they were served what could charitably be termed "comfort food," involving heavy plates of meat and gravy.

"Whew," groaned Donnelly, pushing his half-full plate away from him. "It's a wonder everyone in this town doesn't weigh three hundred pounds."

Brandt chuckled. "Most of the people I've seen are well on their way. Coach Woody seems like a notable exception."

"So there's a homophobe with sixty good years left in him. Yay."

"Well, aren't we cynical today?" Brandt winked at his partner while he took a sip of his iced tea.

"Sorry. It's being back in this damn town. Every person we meet manages to work in some gay-hate without even seeming to be aware of it. It's kind of toxic."

"Given that, I appreciate how thoughtful you've been about Jonah the wrestler. You and Powell came at it from different sides, but your conclusion is pretty much the same."

Donnelly grunted. "Huh. Much as I hate to agree with that guy about anything, he's right that this video could pretty much screw the kid's chances. Another ten years, it won't matter. But for now, if we can help him, we should."

Brandt looked at his watch. "We'd better get back to the station. Jonah and his parents will be there soon."

They walked across the street to the police station and were back in the conference room by two fifteen to await the arrival of the Fischers. Promptly at two thirty, they were brought in by Chief Powell.

"Mr. and Mrs. Fischer, Jonah, this is Officer Brandt and Officer Donnelly. They've come here to help us get a handle on this situation."

"We were so relieved when Chief Powell said the State Police would be coming to help," Mr. Fischer said, energetically pumping Brandt's hand and then Donnelly's. "Thank you."

The family shook hands all around and then sat down at the conference table. Powell retained his seat at the head of the table.

"We're pleased to meet you, Jonah," began Brandt. "I'm sorry it has to be under these circumstances."

"It's not the way I imagined my senior year going, that's for sure," Jonah replied, the corner of his mouth tucked up in what was likely intended to be a stoic grin.

"Do you have any idea who might have taken the video of you?"

Jonah sighed as if he'd been asked this question a million times. He shrugged and said, "I don't. And it seems like a really weird thing to do. I mean, I get that it's supposed to be embarrassing and stuff, but it's not like I was doing anything weird. I'm not actually sure why everyone's making such a big deal out of it."

"Because it's sick and wrong," announced Powell. "It would be terrible if this kept you from getting a scholarship for wrestling, now wouldn't it?"

Both Fischer parents nodded emphatically.

"I know, I know. It's just really… awkward. I mean, I'm missing practice so we can all sit around talking about my butt being on the Internet."

"Now, we don't have any evidence that it's on the Internet, buddy," said Mr. Fischer in a fatherly "buck-up" voice. "That's what we're trying to avoid."

Jonah replied to his dad with a voice that clearly conveyed how little he thought his dad understood how the Internet worked. "There's not really anything we can do about that, is there? People post stuff like this all the time. So what if it shows up on someone's Tumblr? It's not like I'm some celebrity who's going to get reposted all over the place."

"Young man," boomed Powell, "you have to understand that no university wrestling coach is going to take on a new athlete who's got something like this hanging over him. They just won't want to deal with the scandal and bad publicity."

"Well, then," Jonah replied, "maybe I don't want to go to a university that sees it that way."

Powell shook his head and emitted short bursts of mirthless laughter. "They all do, son, they all do."

"We're supposed to meet with the wrestling coach from State next Wednesday," Mrs. Fischer broke in. "What are we supposed to tell him? Do we say something about the video, or do we keep it a secret and hope he never finds out about it?"

"Mrs. Fischer, I understand your concern," Donnelly replied. "How about this: give us a few days to do some investigating, and we'll be able to evaluate what the risks are. How about we meet next Tuesday and talk about what we've found, and then you'll have a better idea how to handle the coach from State?"

The Fischers looked at each other, conferring wordlessly. Mr. Fischer nodded to his wife.

"All right," he said. "We can do that. Until then, we won't say anything and just pray this all goes away."

"And we'll be working on finding out who was responsible for recording the video," Brandt said. "If we can do that, we can keep them from circulating it any further."

They all rose from the table and moved toward the door.

"Thanks for your help," Jonah said. "And I really have no idea who might have done this. I've thought about it a lot over the last few days, and I can't come up with anything. I've always tried to be nice to everybody."

"I'm sure you have, buddy," said Donnelly, clapping his hand on Jonah's shoulder. "Don't lose any sleep over this. We'll take care of it."

Jonah smiled for the first time during the meeting and then followed his parents out of the conference room.

Once the Fischers had disappeared down the hall, Brandt turned to Powell. "Chief, you said the student who brought the video to the school counselor wouldn't say who had sent it to her, right?"

"That's right." Powell shook his head. "She's a good kid— probably scared to point the finger at whatever deviant did this."

"It might be helpful if the school counselor could explain to her what the stakes are for Jonah. She may be willing to help out. If we can trace the chain back, it would bring us a lot closer to the origin."

"I'll talk with the counselor. See if she can draw her out."

"Great. In the meantime, we'll start working the other end of this. If it's hit the web, we need to know." Brandt turned to Donnelly. "Shall we head back to the city, consult our sources?"

Donnelly nodded. "Let's roll."

They walked out of the police station and up the street to where they had parked their cruiser.

"Last chance for coffee," Brandt teased as they neared the cafe.

"You read my mind," Donnelly said with a wink.

The cafe was empty, given the midafternoon hour. Behind the counter, tending to the enormous brass espresso machine, was the same barista who had seen to their needs in the morning. He turned when the bell jingled on the door.

"Can I—oh, welcome back!" he called, once he saw who had entered.

"You remember us?" Donnelly replied with a coyness in his voice that Brandt had never heard before. He wasn't sure he liked it.

"Not often we get strangers through here. Especially not... like you." The barista gave the officers a quick glance up and down. "What can I get started for you?"

"I'll have a short skim latte with an extra shot, and my partner here"—Donnelly jerked a thumb over his shoulder—"would like a tall Americano."

"Wouldn't we all," cracked the barista as he turned to prepare their drinks.

"God, you're so embarrassing," Brandt muttered to Donnelly.

"What? I'm just being friendly."

"You know, less than a year ago the idea of two men being together made you crazy. You would have given Chief Powell a run for his money. But now look at you, throwing yourself at baristas. I guess we'll call this progress."

"Is it wrong for me to feel more comfortable with my sexuality?" Donnelly whispered. "And why are we having this conversation in a cafe?"

"Because this is where you decided to start flirting like a bead-deprived sorority girl at Mardi Gras."

Donnelly rolled his eyes in exasperation.

"Here's the latte for you." The barista handed a cup to Donnelly. "And a tall Americano for your partner. Anything else I can get you?" He rang up the sale on the register.

"Now that you mention it," Donnelly said as he fished in his pocket for change, "I do have a question for you."

"Yes?" asked the barista, leaning forward in expectation.

Brandt groaned and looked away as he took a drink of his coffee.

"Why the hell are you in this town?" Donnelly asked.

"What?" The barista seemed completely flummoxed by the question.

"This is the most backward, traditional, and dare I say homophobic burg on the map. It must be awful living here. I've been here five hours and I'm going nuts. The next person who utters a thinly veiled bigotry—I swear to God I'm going to kick him in the throat."

The barista was stunned by this outburst, and his eyes flashed to Brandt, who simply shrugged. Then he burst out laughing. "Five hours! Ha—you should try twenty-five years! I tell ya, I'd be outta here already if I hadn't inherited this place from my dad a couple years ago. He put his blood, sweat, and tears into it, so I can't really walk away from it. So I'm stuck here serving sweet, fatty drinks to blue-haired church ladies who drove my only competition out of town a year ago and want me to be grateful for it. Imagine my delight at having homophobia prop up my business." He took a breath, a bit winded from his tirade. "Sorry, it's been a long day—they all are. You two have been the highlight. Name's Malcolm, by the way." He held out his hand.

Donnelly blushed. "Well, you're in luck, Malcolm. We'll be back next Tuesday for more fun in Woodley. I'm Gabriel, and this is Ethan."

"Nice to meet you both, and I'll look forward to your return," Malcolm replied with a wink.

"Well, sorry to drink and run, but we've gotta hit the road," Brandt announced. "Can I have my partner back now?" he asked with a grin, but with a warning in his voice.

"Oh—oh, sorry. When you said 'partner' before, I thought you meant, like, in the police sense, given the car you're driving. But you meant.... Oh." Malcolm stepped back from the counter, hands waving in an alarmed gesture of distancing himself from Donnelly.

"Don't worry about him." Donnelly jerked his head toward Brandt. "He's just a jealous boyfriend with a short temper and a big gun." He winked at Malcolm, who managed a weak smile. "We'll see you Tuesday," he said as he and Brandt exited the cafe.

Malcolm waved after them.

"What was that about?" Brandt asked as he guided the cruiser down the main street toward the highway.

Donnelly looked at Brandt as if the answer should be obvious. "Think about it. What has Powell gotten himself so worked up about?"

"He's afraid some gay Internet mafia is going to get its hooks into Jonah's ass."

"Exactly. And the best way to find out if that's what's going on is to get tapped into the gay population of the town. And now we know he's named Malcolm." Donnelly looked askance at his partner. "It's called police work, officer."

"And here I thought you were just flirting." Brandt grinned at his boyfriend. "It kind of made me crazy."

Donnelly smiled. "Good. Keep you on your toes."

"Bastard," Brandt muttered. But he reached over and stroked Donnelly's hard, flat belly before straying down lower for a quick feel.

"Hands on the wheel, mister." Donnelly's mood seemed to brighten with every mile that opened up between him and Woodley. "So, where we heading?"

"Figured we'd go to the person who knows the most about Internet porn—get some expert perspective on where to start looking."

"Nick?"

"Yep. We can drop by the house on our way into town."

Nick worked at the frat-themed sex-cam house they had investigated the year before. The business he helped manage was as ethically run as any porn shop could be. Brandt hoped he could help them narrow down the sites where Jonah's video might be posted.

About ninety minutes later, they pulled up in front of the house. It was just another mansion in a development of mansions, with no outward indication of the exuberant nudity that was the lifeblood of the business.

Brandt knocked at the front door, and a few seconds later, Nick opened it.

"Jason!" he called, pulling Brandt into a bear hug. Jason had been Brandt's cover name when he posed as an employee of the house for his investigation. Nick still used it sometimes to recall the time that they had worked together. "It's great to see you!" He turned to Donnelly. "Gabriel, how are you, man?" he asked as he pulled Donnelly, too, into a bear hug.

"We called ahead and still you answer the door naked?" Brandt asked as they entered the house.

"I wasn't naked when you called," Nick said with a laugh. "I just like to do it for old time's sake. Can I get you guys something to drink?"

"Nah, I'm good," Brandt replied, and Donnelly shook his head as well. "We've got a case we could use your expert help with." He took a seat on the leather couch in the living room.

"Happy to help. What's up?" Nick sat on the other end of the same couch, seemingly oblivious to his own nudity.

"There's a case upstate we've been called in on. Kid on the wrestling team got videoed in the locker room. Just being passed around among the students right now, but we're worried about it getting posted online. He's looking for a wrestling scholarship, and the video could blow it for him. We were hoping you might be able to give us some ideas about which sites to monitor so we can do damage control if it does show up."

Nick's brow furrowed. "Kid's under or over?"

"Over, luckily. There's one problem we're not having to deal with."

Nick nodded. "Well, you know we don't deal with hidden camera stuff. The other sites I have contact with don't either. There are sites that do a great business in it, but a lot of it is fake. You know, they film a pro pretending to be caught on tape." Nick pondered Brandt's question for a moment. "You know who might know about this kind of stuff—Andy. Remember, the guy I sent you to when you needed to buy a jockstrap for the private show? Because he's in sporting goods, it's possible he has some contacts in the locker room genre. I would pay him a visit—he's still at Sporting Wood on Alta Avenue—and see if he has some leads for you."

"Excellent," Brandt said, standing up. "Thanks for your time, Nick."

"Always a pleasure, Ethan," Nick said, shaking his hand.

Brandt pulled him into an embrace, and they shared a laugh along with the hug.

Nick reached out and hugged Donnelly as well.

"You know," Donnelly said as they embraced, "it's our turn to have you and Pete over for dinner."

"That would be awesome. Anything to get more of your home cooking," he said with a wink at Donnelly. "Love you guys."

"Love you too, Nick," the officers said in unison.

Nick, being naked, didn't see them all the way to their car.

"Grab some dinner?" Donnelly asked as they pulled out of the driveway. "I'm beat from all this driving."

"Sounds good. Get something light, and we can hit the sack early. Play a little 'the barista and the tough customer'?"

Donnelly socked him on the arm and laughed giddily.

# CHAPTER TWO
# ACT II

"SWEETIE, IT'S not movie night again already!" Bryce was flustered by Nestor's insistence that he join him in looking at the computer screen.

"But I have found something that will bring you joy in your pants," Nestor assured him, clicking with elegant speed at the keyboard. "One moment...."

Bryce rolled his eyes but complained no further.

"There," Nestor said and sat back to view the video along with Bryce.

"Oh! Oh! It's our locker room tease from last night. You found another video, you lovely man, you."

"Yesterday there was no video, and today there it is. I bring it to you as soon as I find."

On the screen, the same young man stood in front of the same locker, being filmed from the same angle. This time, however, when he returned from the shower, he didn't simply drop his towel and slip on his boxers; instead, he dried himself very thoroughly, spending a great deal of time patting and rubbing himself all over. And then, in one moment of delicious suspense for Bryce and Nestor, he turned around to face the camera.

"Aiiee," shrieked Bryce, causing Nester to flinch away instinctively. "Look at that. It's the most beautiful thing I've ever seen. It's perfect!"

Nestor studied the screen, and, finally, nodded his agreement. "It is a poem written in meat," he said simply.

"I couldn't have said it better myself," Bryce whispered, awestruck.

The video ended shortly after the exposure of the masterpiece of genital beauty.

"More! More!" Bryce extended his hands imploringly toward the screen.

"They cannot hear you, I think," Nestor said soothingly, patting Bryce's arm.

"I know," Bryce whimpered, his hands clapped to his mouth in despair. "I know."

THE NEXT morning Brandt and Donnelly sated their need for caffeine—with some breakfast on the side—by stopping in at their favorite diner on Alta Avenue. On this stretch of downtown boulevard, a straight barista would have been as rare as a gay one in Woodley.

Having finished their repast, they walked the three blocks to Sporting Wood, the athletics-themed store where Nick's friend Andy worked. They found him at the front of the store, slipping new jockstraps onto mannequins that were rather shocking in their anatomical correctness.

"Hey, Andy!" Brandt called as they entered the store.

"Brandt—good to see ya, bro." He left the last mannequin with a bright red jock around its knees and came over to grip Brandt's hand. "And Donnelly, you been working out more? Looking pretty hot there."

"You're looking pretty good yourself, there, Andy. For a straight guy, I mean," Donnelly replied with a grin.

"The ladies don't complain," Andy said with a modest flex of his bicep. "How can I help you gentlemen today?"

"We're looking for some information Nick thought you might be able to help us with," Brandt said.

"Always a pleasure to help out my local law enforcement. What is it?" Andy asked as he returned to tugging the red jockstrap up the mannequin's muscular legs.

"It's a kind of spy-cam situation," Donnelly explained. "High school kid filmed in the locker room."

Andy stopped what he was doing. "Look, I don't know anything about underage stuff, if that's what you're getting at. Couple years ago I was a high school kid in a locker room—that kind of stuff creeps me out."

"But you work in a place where you model jockstraps for men," Brandt said, recalling that this had been precisely how he'd met Andy last year.

"Totally different thing. I'm legal, I'm paid for it, and if it gets creepy I can get the hell out of the dressing room."

"Well, this guy is legal too. That's not the issue," Donnelly continued. "In fact, the video is pretty tame. And right now it's only being passed around among the students at the school. But if it gets posted online, it could really damage his chances of a wrestling scholarship, so we're trying to gather a list of sites that specialize in that kind of thing. That way if it gets posted, we have a shot at trying to get it taken down before too many people see it."

Andy nodded. "Gotcha. Well, you're right that a lot of my clientele are into those sites. Thing is I couldn't really give you a list of them. Honestly, I kind of tune out when they talk about them. But I do know a couple of people who would be able to point you in the right direction—and I think you do too. I saw them at your party last year, the one that Nick's company threw for you as a thank-you?"

Brandt and Donnelly exchanged a look and then burst out laughing. "Bryce and Nestor," they said together.

"They're your guys," Andy said, joining in their laughter. "Those two are like savants of porn. They'd know where you should look."

"Thanks, Andy. You've been a big help," Brandt said as they turned to go.

"Anytime. Good to see you guys," Andy said as he picked up another jockstrap.

"Why didn't we think of Bryce and Nestor right off?" Brandt asked his partner as they headed up the street.

"Maybe because it's so exhausting just to be in the same room with them?" Donnelly replied with a smile. "They're like a glitter whirlwind, those boys."

A FEW minutes later, the officers stopped at Grindstone, the clothing store where Bryce and Nestor plied their trade, giving workplace fashion advice and measuring inseams. They were very thorough in this latter pursuit.

"Ready?" Brandt asked, hand on the door.

"Ready."

He pulled open the door, and they stepped inside.

"In 3…2…1…," Brandt counted down.

"Ooh! Troopers!" squealed Bryce, quickstepping his way to the front of the store. "It's been far too long, my dears. You clearly can't be bothered to pick up a phone, though it looks like you've been picking up your share of heavy things in the gym. But all is forgiven, my darlings, because you are finally here!" He gave air kisses to both men, engulfing them in a cloud of perfume while simultaneously managing to cop a quick feel of both sets of firm buttocks. "Now, tell me, how can I service you today?"

Brandt tried to adopt a serious expression after being subjected to Hurricane Bryce. "What we need is some—"

"Of those!" called Donnelly, who had caught sight of some new boxer briefs in a shimmery palette of technical fabrics.

"Your taste is as tasty as ever," hooted Bryce as he dashed over to the display. "We've just this week gotten these in, and they are simply astonishing. They stay cool, stretch while remaining skintight, and they are almost impossible to rip off." He leaned in conspiratorially. "If I hadn't had a nail file handy, I might never have gotten in there!" He cackled gleefully. "Now, would you like to try them on?" Bryce was almost twitching with excitement at this prospect.

"We didn't come here for new underwear, did we, partner?" Brandt looked scoldingly at Donnelly.

Donnelly shook his head in contrition but flashed a glance at Bryce, who set aside a pair in Donnelly's size.

"We're hoping to draw upon some particular expertise that only you and Nestor have among our entire acquaintance."

"Ooh," said Bryce, his eyes wide. "For official police business?"

Brandt chuckled. "Why yes, it is for a case we're working."

Bryce jumped up and down, making tiny clapping motions. "Oh! Oh! Oh! How exciting! Now, tell me, officer, will I be required to go undercover? Perhaps insert myself into the lair of a burly eastern European gangster and tease secrets out of his crew of hardened, sweat-kissed criminals?"

Brandt was by this point laughing so hard that Donnelly had to take over. "Nothing like that, at least at the moment. But there is something we would like to show you—can we find someplace with a little privacy?"

"Now you're talking!" Bryce hustled down the main aisle of the store and turned abruptly when he reached the dressing rooms. He opened a door in the wall the men hadn't noticed before—it was unmarked and positioned between two racks of clothing so that its frame was obscured.

Inside was a small office, surrounded by what seemed to be windows into other small rooms. In the middle of the room sat Nestor, who was sipping coffee and had no other visible occupation.

"Nestor, darling, I brought goodies!" Bryce bustled through the door and stepped aside so Brandt and Donnelly could step in after him. He pulled the door shut, and the room grew dim and close.

Nestor rose and extended a limp but graceful hand to the officers. "To see you is to breathe again," he murmured.

"As always, Nestor, you speak in poetry," replied Donnelly with a genuine smile.

Brandt was looking around the room. "What is—oh, I see." Through one of the windows they could see a man taking off his pants. "You can sit here and spy on all of the dressing rooms?"

"It's called loss prevention," sniffed Bryce, whose professionalism had clearly been challenged. "All of your major retailers do it."

Nestor backed him up. "We must prevent the loss of such sights as this," he said, pointing to the window through which they could see the man standing in his underwear in front of the dressing room mirror, flexing his quadriceps. Then he turned to appraise the view from behind. Both Bryce and Nestor tipped their head to the right, as if studying a painting.

"I do love working in retail," sighed Bryce. He turned to the officers. "Now how can we help you with your investigation thingy?"

"There's a video of a young man going around a high school upstate, a video that was taken without his permission with a spy cam, and we'd like to be sure it hasn't been posted online. We thought you two might be familiar with sites that post such material."

Bryce seemed genuinely shocked. "Officer Brandt, surely you aren't implying that I seek out videos of high school boys."

"Oh, no, that's not it at all. He's eighteen. Besides," Brandt said with a wink, "I picture you with a real man."

"So do I, honey, so do I," sighed Bryce, the return of the arch in his eyebrow a sign that no lasting offense had been taken. "From your lips to Daniel Craig's ear."

"Will you show us this filming, so that we may be helping you?" asked Nestor.

"Of course," said Donnelly, who pulled a laptop out of his briefcase and set it on the table. Movement in one of the dressing rooms caught his eye as he did so; two customers had entered one of the rooms and were immediately clinched in a passionate embrace. "Umm...?" he said, pointing to the happy couple.

Bryce glanced over. "Oh, that's just the pastor from that new evangelical church on the south side of town. Don't worry about him shoplifting—he's not even going to try on the clothes he's brought in there with him. The only thing he ever slips into is his parishioners. Please, proceed."

"Ah... yes, here we go...." Donnelly fiddled with the laptop, clearly distracted by the sight of the church outreach happening on the other side of the glass. "Now, this is not something that has been circulated to the general public, so we'd appreciate it if you—"

"Darling, we are the souls of discretion! Are we not, Nestor?"

"I shall wrap my lips around your private matters and never let go," Nestor solemnly swore.

"All right, then," said Brandt as he pushed the play button. The scene opened on the Woodley locker room.

The dramatic gasping that followed has only seen its equal during royal weddings when the ladies of the realm premiere extravagant new hats, or when Olympic divers slip into the water and their suits do not.

"What? What is it?" called Brandt over the din of Bryce and Nestor hyperventilating.

"That's... but that's...!" stuttered Bryce, flailing his hands at the screen. He returned to gasping.

Donnelly turned to Nestor for help. "Why are you...?"

Nestor took a calming breath and laid a hand on Bryce's shoulder in an attempt to bring him to ground as well. "We... have seen this video before."

"Oh, shit," Brandt and Donnelly said in unison.

"I am so sorry, boys," tutted Bryce. "But, on the plus side, he gets very high ratings."

"I'm sure that will be a comfort to him and his family," Brandt said sharply.

"Ethan, calm down. We don't know how bad it is yet." Donnelly turned to Bryce. "Can you show us where the video is posted?"

"Nestor can. He's a whiz with all of this technology."

"May I?" Nestor asked, pointing at the laptop.

"Yes, please," Donnelly replied. He turned the laptop over to Nestor.

Nestor opened a browser window and typed a long string of letters. He then leaned close and read from the screen. "It say you violate the terms of the service."

"Work laptop—forgot about that. Here." Donnelly reached over Nestor and typed an authorization code.

"They gave you a code to get around the porn filter?" Brandt asked indignantly.

"Remember, I had to use it to watch your performances, dear," Donnelly replied and kissed him on the cheek. This elicited an appreciative sigh from Bryce.

"Here is the site," Nestor announced, pointing at the screen.

Brandt had never seen DudesCaughtNudeintheLockerRoom.com, but he was familiar with the genre. The site existed solely to sell ad space, to which it drew eyeballs by placing marketing messages next to scandalous videos submitted by random and often anonymous videographers.

"Well, shit," Brandt muttered. "This cat's out of the bag."

"It says it was posted four months ago. And"—Donnelly squinted at the screen—"over 12,000 people have viewed it." He looked at Brandt. "Well, at least we know it can't get any worse."

"Would you like to see the part two?" asked Nestor brightly.

Brandt stopped breathing. "There's another video? Of the same guy?"

"It show up last night. I watch for it, to make my Bryce happy." He cast a loving look at Bryce, who blew him a kiss in return. A few keystrokes and he brought up the video to show the officers.

Both men's mouths dropped open as they watched the video— Donnelly even went so far as to call out "No!" when Jonah began to turn around to face the camera. But turn he did.

Brandt grunted. "Just got worse, didn't it?"

"'Fraid so, buddy," Donnelly commiserated.

Brandt snapped upright, as if his commanding officer had entered the room. "Thank you, gentlemen," he said to Bryce and Nestor. "You've been a great help, as usual. We'll leave you to your work now, and we must go do ours." He turned and opened the hidden door.

"Thanks, guys," said Donnelly as Brandt stepped out into the store. "We'll see you soon, I'm sure."

"If there's a medal involved, I'm using my platinum jewelry for spring!" Bryce called after them.

BRANDT WAS furious, gripping the steering wheel with white knuckles. "Life just got a lot worse for Jonah," he fumed. "Kids shooting video, sending it to their friends, without any idea that it could show up on a site like that."

"I think we have to admit the possibility that whoever shot it fully intended it to end up on a site like that. The question is why."

"You think someone's doing this on purpose? Obviously someone uploaded it to that site on purpose, but was it the intention of the person who captured the video to make it public like this?"

"We won't know that until we find out who posted it. Won't be easy," Donnelly said as he typed at his laptop in the passenger seat. "Says here the site is hosted in Springfield, and that means we're not getting anything from them. If he were under eighteen at the time, that would allow us to get a subpoena…."

"And probably get some misguided sophomore branded a sex offender for life. Not sure that's the best way to handle it."

"Well, I'll get the takedown order drafted, and I'll contact the site to see if they can give us anything—IP logs, video file metadata, whatever might leave a trace. Want to tell the Fischers now, or wait until we have more info?"

"Let's see what we can come up with today, and then we'll decide."


BY THE end of the day, they had secured the site's agreement to take down both videos of Jonah—the mention of a high schooler's image being on the site got their attention quickly—but the officers made no progress on developing any other information. The site was unable to give them an IP address of the person who uploaded the video. In fact, their inability to do so is what made the site so popular among uploaders of questionable content. All they had was a username: Whistlepig.

"Well, that's pretty much a tip-off right there," mused Donnelly.

"How so?" asked Brandt, who was reviewing their research to draft a preliminary report for Powell.

"Whistle pig. It's another name for the woodchuck." He smiled. "And that's your biology lesson for today."

"So if the uploader was making a joke about the name of the team…," Brandt thought aloud.

"They must have known that Jonah was a Wrestling Woodchuck," continued Donnelly.

"But there's no indication of that in the videos, is there?"

"Not that I recall. There's nothing on his sweatshirt, nothing on the wall, nothing in the lockers...," Donnelly replied, eyes closed in concentration.

"Looks like we have a pretty strong indication that the person who posted this online is from Woodley."

"Or nearby. Remember the wrestling team has a pretty high profile in that area. There are people in a dozen towns around there who would recognize him from the video."

Brandt turned to his partner. "But why would someone from the community want to post a video like that?"

"Competitive advantage, for one thing. Distract the wrestling team with a minor scandal, put them off their training."

"They really do take this shit seriously up there, don't they?"

"What else have they got?" Donnelly asked in response. "The economy dried up the local industries—the few that managed to survive after all of the manufacturing went overseas. This is the kind of thing people cling to when they're trying to keep a community together."

"You sound like you're running for a spot on the Woodley Chamber of Commerce."

"I didn't say it's objectively worth saving, did I? I'd be happy if they evacuated all the people and gave the land back to the woodchucks."

"Yeah, I think fewer people would want to watch videos of actual woodchucks in the locker room," Brandt said. "Well, I guess I should call Powell, let him know what's up. Got anything on your calendar for tomorrow? He may want us to meet with the parents about what we've found."

Donnelly flipped to his calendar. "Nope, all clear for a road trip to the paradise on earth we call Woodley. I'll bring rope so I can restrain myself from paroxysms of joy."

"Yeah, I might want some of that myself," Brandt said with an insinuating chuckle. He dialed the direct number Powell had given him.

"Chief Powell," the gruff voice answered.

"It's Brandt, sir. We have some new developments I think you should know about."

THE NEXT morning found Brandt and Donnelly on the road again, driving north to Woodley. Powell had asked them to come up so they could meet with the family—more recruiter visits were starting to be scheduled, and they would soon have to decide how to handle any questions about the video.

"It really is pretty out here, isn't it?" said Donnelly as they drove.

"It is, especially in early spring." Brandt scanned the pastoral horizon, taking in the trees beginning to bud and farmers getting their fields ready for planting. "I have to say you're in a much better mood on this trip, which is amazing considering we had to leave even earlier this time." Powell had asked them to meet at nine so they could get the local police up to speed as soon as possible.

"As much as I hate Woodley, seeing what Jonah's up against has made me want to figure this the hell out. I guess good ol' boy Chief Powell and I really are on the same team. Ick—I kind of grossed myself out saying that aloud."

They pulled into Woodley a good fifteen minutes before their appointment with Powell.

"Grab a coffee before we go in?" Brandt asked as he parked the cruiser.

"Oh, sure, if you need to," said Donnelly with badly faked disinterest. He made a beeline for the cafe at the end of the street. The door jangled to announce their entrance.

"Is it Tuesday already?" a voice from behind the counter called.

"You remembered," replied Donnelly, peering behind the pastry case to where Malcolm crouched, restocking scones.

"Listen to yourself," Brandt whispered. He rolled his eyes and stepped back when Donnelly made a shushing motion at him.

"I told ya you were the highlight of my day. You can see what my usual customer base offers." He tipped his head to the tables, about half of which were occupied by the womenfolk of the town. "The average age in here was approaching triple digits before you guys walked in."

"Glad we could help."

"Can I get you the usual?" Malcolm asked, stepping toward the monstrous espresso maker.

"That would be great, thanks," Donnelly replied, pulling out his wallet.

"Hey, Mal, I got all the trays clean, and the mixer's been wiped down. Anything else before I get going?" A teenage boy wearing an apron came out from the back of the cafe.

"No, that's great, Casey. You better head out now or you'll be late for math."

Casey took off his apron and hung it on a hook behind the kitchen door, grabbing his backpack on his way. After he ducked under the counter, he turned back to Malcolm. "I may be a little late this afternoon—Coach Woody says he might want some extra time to get ready for the meet tomorrow."

"No problem. Come when you can—the work will be here!"

Casey nodded to the officers as he passed by and out the door.

"Here's your coffee, gentlemen," Malcolm said as he passed over two cups.

As Donnelly paid, he asked, "So, you've got some help running the place?"

"Oh, Casey? Yeah, good kid. He helps me get the baking done in the morning, and then after school and practice he comes back to help me close up and get ready for the next day."

"Wrestler, right?" Donnelly asked, his voice casual.

Malcolm looked toward the door through which Casey had just left. "You could tell that just by looking at him? Wow, you're hardcore, man." He laughed and shook his head.

"Actually, we met with the wrestling coach yesterday on some police business. Does Casey ever mention Jonah Fischer?"

Malcolm grew immediately serious. "They're best friends, as far as I know." Then a realization seemed to dawn on the barista. "Oh, I get it. You guys are here about the video, right?"

Donnelly nodded.

"I really feel for Jonah. Casey says he's hangin' in, but it's gotta be tough." Then Malcolm brightened a bit. "So, you guys are some kinda ninja counterespionage hired guns they brought in, right?" he asked with a tease in his voice.

"You got us," Donnelly replied, all fake modesty. "In fact, we're due at the police chief's office right now for a briefing. Please excuse us, lives are at stake."

"It's an honor to serve you." Malcolm snapped to a smart salute, then began giggling.

"Good lord, why am I being tested this way?" Brandt groaned as they left the cafe.

"And that's how it's done, Officer Brandt," Donnelly said to his partner once they were halfway down the block.

"You are the luckiest cop in the world," Brandt replied. "Every time you are about to embarrass yourself with your flirting, you accidentally do some police work."

"I'll take that as a compliment," Donnelly said through a sweet smile. "I think we might want to swing back by the cafe at the end of the day."

"So you can watch Malcolm ply his steamy trade?"

"Also, we could have a chat with Casey. See if we can get some context on Jonah's situation. A best friend will know things that a parent or teacher won't."

"Wouldn't know about that," Brandt said breezily as they crossed the street. "My best friend's being kind of a pain in the ass right now."

"You sweet talker, you." Donnelly followed Brandt through the front doors of the police department.

They were waved down the hall by the officer at the desk and arrived at the conference room to find the Fischers and Chief Powell already sitting at the table.

"Officers Brandt and Donnelly, thank you for coming." Powell stood and shook their hands, as did Mr. Fischer.

"Mr. and Mrs. Fischer, Jonah," said Brandt and Donnelly as they made their way to open seats on the other side of the table.

"I have to say, we're a little concerned about what you have to tell us," Mr. Fischer began. "Chief Powell recommended we take Jonah out of class to be here, and that's got us a little worried."

"I'm afraid what we have to share isn't very good news," Brandt said. "First, we found that the video making its way around the school has also been posted online."

Mrs. Fischer gasped as if she'd touched a hot stove. Her husband put his arm around her and turned a brave face to Brandt. Jonah stared out the window, blankly.

"Is there anything we can do about it?" Jonah's dad asked.

"We've gotten the site to take it down, and as of this morning, it's no longer available."

"Oh, thank God," Mrs. Fischer said with a deflating sigh.

"Unfortunately, it was on the site for much longer than we'd thought," Donnelly continued. "It was posted nearly four months ago. There's a very good chance that during that time it was downloaded and shared on other sites. There's no way for us to know if it's still available online."

The Fischers exchanged a woeful look.

"There's more bad news, I'm sorry to say," Brandt said. "A second video was posted this week."

"What?" Mr. Fischer said, in a tone of voice just short of a shout. "Another video of Jonah?"

"I'm afraid so," Brandt answered with a consolatory shake of his head.

"Can I see it?" Jonah asked. It was the first thing he'd said this morning.

Brandt turned to Donnelly. They exchanged a nod.

"I have it here," Donnelly said to Jonah. "Since you're an adult, Jonah, I'll show it to you, and you can decide whether you want your parents to see it."

"Just show it to everyone. If it's already out there, who cares who sees it?"

Donnelly nodded and opened his laptop. He turned the screen to face the other side of the table and started the video. Mrs. Fischer's face told the tale—she was curious, then angry, then shocked. Finally she looked away, burying her face in her hands.

"This video has also been taken down. And because it was online for a much shorter period of time, there's less chance that it was mirrored to other sites. Again, there's no way to know for certain how widely it's been viewed."

Jonah returned to looking out the window, a look of resignation on his face. "It's over, isn't it?" he said quietly.

"What, honey?" asked his mom.

"My chances of getting a scholarship. I guess I can kiss that goodbye."

"No, son. We can't give up yet," said his dad.

"I agree with you, Mr. Fischer," Donnelly said. "I think you should go ahead and meet with the recruiters, and if they somehow find out about the video, you can explain to them that it's the subject of a police investigation. They should see Jonah's done nothing wrong."

"I need to get some air," Jonah said suddenly and rose from the table. He strode from the room before his parents had a chance to say anything.

"I'll go," said Brandt. He turned to the Fischers as he walked around the table to the door. "I'm sure you understand it may be awkward for him to talk about this with his parents." They nodded as he left the room.

Brandt found Jonah sitting on a bench under a tree outside the police department. The spring wind was chilly, but the sun was bright. Brandt sat down next to him, and waited. It was several long minutes before the silence was broken.

"Why is someone doing this to me?" Jonah asked in a quiet voice.

"I don't know, Jonah," Brandt replied. "We have a theory that it's someone who knows you, or at least knows of you. Donnelly thinks it could be someone on an opposing team who wants to get an advantage—like if you're distracted by this from your training, you might not wrestle as well."

Jonah turned to look at Brandt. "And posting naked videos of me is what they came up with as a distraction?" He shook his head. "That just doesn't seem...." He sighed bleakly. "I do plenty of dumb stuff. Last year my friend Casey got a video of me after taco night ripping the biggest fart you've ever heard. Why not put up something like that if they wanted to throw me off?"

"They did it because it works. Because our society is so hung up on sex that a naked video seems like the worst thing in the world. But it's not, and you can't let them get into your head."

"Easy for you to say. You've never had a naked video of you posted online."

Brandt pondered how to respond. "Actually, I have. It was pretty awful. But I put it behind me, and you can too." And my video was a whole lot worse than just standing naked in a locker room, he didn't add.

Jonah was clearly shocked by this revelation, but he seemed to think better of asking for details. "I just hope it's over now," he said.

"I do as well. But I need you to really think, Jonah, about who might want to embarrass you—for any reason. Anyone who doesn't like you or something you are involved with, or someone you are close to? Any possibilities like that would be really helpful to us."

Jonah shook his head despondently. "No, I still can't think of anything that would help. I honestly have tried to be nice to everybody."

"I'm sure you have. Here's my card, though, if you think of anything that might be worth looking into. Text me anytime."

Jonah took the card, studied it. "Thanks. I will."

"Now, we should probably get back in there before your parents think you've run away from home."

"Believe me, I've thought about it. But you can't run from the Internet, right?" Jonah's voice had a less dismal undertone for the first time.

They began to walk back into the police department.

"So, this video of you—" Jonah began as Brandt opened the door.

"Sorry. Classified police business," Brandt interrupted. He gave the kid a grin to show him he wasn't offended by the question.

They entered the conference room just as the others were standing to leave.

"I've been showing the rest of our research," Donnelly said to Brandt. "They had a few questions about the technical aspects of the investigation into the website and some other stuff they can bring up when talking to recruiters." He turned to the Fischers, now joined by Jonah. "Do you have any other questions?"

"Not right now," Mr. Fischer said, extending his hand. "You've been such a help, Officer Donnelly. I don't know how we can thank you."

"All part of the job," he said. "Please don't hesitate to get in touch if there's anything else you need."

The Fischers departed, and Brandt turned to Powell.

"Chief, do you think you can get us a schedule of the Woodchucks' upcoming wrestling meets?"

"Sure. I've got one on the board in my office. Let me grab it." Powell strode out of the room and down the hall.

"Working the competitive angle?" Donnelly asked.

"Worth a shot. We don't have much else to go on."

Powell came back in with a sheet of paper that he handed to Brandt. "Made a copy for you."

"Thanks," Brandt said, somewhat absently. He was studying the schedule closely. "So, if I'm reading this correctly, this is the final week of regular competition, and then next week starts the regional meets?"

"That's right. The schools in the area compete for the next three weeks, and then they face the top teams in neighboring leagues. State finals are next month."

"Hmm," grunted Brandt.

"What are you thinking, Ethan?" asked Donnelly.

"That this is the only thing I've found so far that lines up. The first video was posted four months ago, just as the season was getting underway. The second one shows up right before regionals. The timing seems intended to shake Jonah's focus."

"Chief," Donnelly said, "can you get us a list of wrestling coaches at the schools that Woodley competes against during the regular season? I think it might be useful for us to talk with them."

"Coach Woody would have that. I'll have him fax it over." Powell hurried back to his office.

"Can you believe that guy?" Donnelly said once he was gone. "Who faxes things anymore?"

"Remember, we're in 1958. Faxing is completely cutting edge here."

Powell returned shortly with another sheet of paper to hand to Brandt.

"All right, we're going to pay some calls on coaches," Brandt said as he folded the paper and put it in his pocket. "Anything else you need from us right now, chief?"

"No. You two are doing some great work. I'm really glad I called to ask for your help."

Brandt nodded the compliment away. "We'll be in touch when we have more to share." He walked out of the conference room, Donnelly following right behind.

When they reached their car, Brandt handed Donnelly the paper. "Get us a route?" he asked. Donnelly pulled up a map showing all of the high schools in the area. He picked them off in the most efficient order, then nodded to Brandt which direction they should head out.

Brandt pulled onto the highway heading west out of town, and Donnelly began calling the schools to arrange meetings with the wrestling coaches.

They spent the better part of the day making the rounds of all competing schools, where they heard the same story over and over again—Woodley was the team to beat, but certainly no one on their own team had anything but the purest motives of competition and sportsmanship. The officers were careful not to mention the reason for their visit, only that they were looking into (in the intentionally vague terminology of law enforcement) a "situation involving Jonah Fischer." Jonah was clearly well known to all of the coaches, but they had, to a man, only good things to say about him. After a half-dozen calls of this nature, they had come up with no earth-shattering revelations.

"So, I guess it's back to Woodley, then?" Donnelly said with a yawn. It was late afternoon, and they'd been in the car for most of the day, even eating lunch between towns as they drove.

"Fancy a coffee?" Brandt said, his voice all insinuation.

"Wouldn't turn one down," Donnelly said with a saucy wink to his partner.

"Back again!" called Malcolm when Brandt and Donnelly entered the cafe just before its posted closing time. "This is my lucky day."

"We'll have the usual, barkeep," blustered Donnelly, grinning broadly.

"I should get a coffee card started for you," Malcolm said, reaching under the counter. "Since you're turning into my best customers." He picked up his hole punch and clicked it eight times. "There ya go. Two more and I'll give you anything you want." He winked as he handed the card over to Donnelly. "From the menu."

"Damn. That's some pretty serious bait and switch there," Donnelly grumbled as Malcolm turned to make the drinks.

Brandt rolled his eyes and wandered away from the counter, taking in the artwork hanging on the walls. Motion on the edge of his vision attracted his attention, and he turned to find Casey wiping down the tables.

"You're Casey, right?" Brandt asked, taking a couple of steps toward the young man in the apron.

"Yes, sir," Casey replied.

"I'm Officer Brandt from the State Police." He nodded to Donnelly at the counter. "We're here to look into this situation with Jonah Fischer. I believe he's a friend of yours?"

Casey seemed surprised. "Wow, you're good."

Brandt smiled. "Can we sit for a minute? I'd like to get your thoughts on what's going on with Jonah."

Casey looked nervously over to Malcolm behind the counter. "Mal, can I have a minute to talk with...." He tipped his head to Brandt.

"Sure," replied Malcolm. "They're here to help Jonah, so go ahead."

Casey sat at the table he had just wiped clean. Streaks still shone on its surface. Brandt pulled out a chair and joined him.

"Known Jonah long?" he asked.

"Just about all my life," Casey replied. "Friends since before kindergarten."

"Would you say you were close friends?"

"The closest. It's killing me to see him so torn up about this video thing. He told me about the second video during lunch today. We walked out back behind the cafeteria, and he was crying. He just sobbed until he could hardly breathe. He's so...." Casey's voice failed as tears welled in his eyes. He didn't even seem to notice them, and they made wet tracks down his cheeks.

"It must be really hard to see your friend like that," Brandt said gently. "Can you think of anyone who would want to do this, to embarrass him this way?"

Casey's eyes snapped up to Brandt's. "If I knew who did this, I would have done something already." His voice had a sudden steely edge that surprised Brandt. "You have to understand who Jonah is, sir. He's the best person I know." He wiped away the tears and took a calming breath. He looked down at his hands as he continued in a soft, low voice. "When we were in middle school, I got leukemia."

"I'm sorry to hear that, Casey."

"I'm fine now, thanks. But when I was sick with it, really sick, I was helpless. The chemo worked on the cancer, but it just about killed me. Between treatments, I couldn't go to school—couldn't even walk on my own. Jonah stayed with me the whole time. He got my assignments from class, and he practically taught me the whole seventh grade. Some nights he slept in the chair by my bed because I was crazy with the pain and the drugs." The tears were flowing again. Casey wiped them with the back of his hand, but still they came. "He carried me to the bathroom—the fucking bathroom!—and he wiped my ass when I was done shitting out my guts." Two sobs interrupted his story. He took a deep breath and continued. "Sorry for the language, sir. I get kinda crazy when I talk about it."

"I understand. Sounds like a really tough time, and he's a great friend."

"He's more than that. Do you know anyone who would carry you to the crapper and then mop you up when you're done shitting all over the place? And still smile when he'd gotten you back to bed? That's the kind of person Jonah is. I can never repay him for that, but if I could have five minutes alone with whoever took that fucking video, I'd make a start at it." The fire had returned to Casey's eyes, burning the tears away.

"I promise you, we will do everything we can to find whoever's responsible and make sure they are punished."

"Thank you, sir. I'm glad you're helping him." Casey looked around the empty cafe. "I should get back to work, if there's nothing else...?"

"Sure. Thanks for talking."

Casey nodded and picked up his rag.

Brandt joined Donnelly at the counter.

"Well, that sounded intense," Donnelly whispered.

"It was. Good kid, though. And I think we can probably cross personal vengeance off the list of motives—our Jonah seems like a saint."

Donnelly nodded. "We should get going, I guess?"

"If you're done here," Brandt said with a grin, nodding at Malcolm.

"Oh, I won't be done until I get my card fully punched," Donnelly answered with a laugh, and Malcolm joined in.

"See you guys," Malcolm called as they left the cafe.

"I'm sure you will," rejoined Brandt.


"THANKS FOR coming, man." Jonah handed Casey a mug of cocoa and kept one for himself. They were sitting on the back porch of Jonah's house, overlooking the woods that lay beyond the backyard with its bird feeders and dormant garden plot.

"Anytime." Casey sat back on the porch swing and took a long slurp of cocoa. Jonah's mom still put marshmallows on the top, and sometimes drinking around them was a challenge. There was a chill in the air, and Casey zipped his sweatshirt to the top.

They rocked on the swing in silence for a few minutes while the twilight darkened over the woods.

"I talked to the cops today," Casey said, eyes on the horizon.

Jonah nodded.

"They seem nice."

"Yeah," Jonah replied.

"I wonder if they're going to be able to find out anything."

Jonah shook his head. "I don't think anything they do is going to help," he said miserably.

"You don't know that," Casey said, turning to look at his friend. "Maybe they can figure out who posted the videos, and whoever it was will stop putting them up."

"Nothing ever gets taken off the Internet, you know that," Jonah replied wearily. He'd clearly been through this line of thought himself. "I just wish I knew why this is happening."

"Well, there's only one explanation I can think of," Casey said.

"What?" Jonah asked with a start. He turned to Casey expectantly.

"Someone figures that the entire world needs to see Jonah Fischer's amazing wang."

Jonah fixed his friend with a glare but could only hold it for a second or two before bursting into laughter. "Thanks, man," he was finally able to say. "I really needed that."

"Like the world needs your wang," Casey replied and then burst into laughter again.

They settled down and sipped their cocoa again.

"I'm really sorry about all this," Casey said after another few minutes of silence.

"Everyone's been great about it. No one's made a big deal about it, or teased me or anything."

"Coach Woody kind of laid it out for us this afternoon. Said we can't let whoever did this mess with our heads. He also said it could have happened to anyone on the team. I didn't really agree with that part, because no one has a wang like Jonah Fischer's."

"Shut up, doofus," Jonah said with a punch on Casey's shoulder. Once their laughter had died down, he grew more serious. "Thanks for being there for me," he said in a quiet voice.

Casey turned to him, his own voice just as low and serious. "I will always be here for you, Jonah. Always. I love you, man."

"You just want my wang," Jonah said.

"What's so funny out there?" called Jonah's mom from the kitchen. "It's getting dark out there. You two should come in."

"We should probably do what she says. She's kind of in super-overprotective mode right now." Jonah rose from the swing.

"You gonna be okay?" Casey asked as he, too, stood.

"Yeah. Not like it could get any worse, right?"

# CHAPTER THREE
# A HARDER PROBLEM

NESTOR WAS compiling a playlist for his and Bryce's Saturday evening viewing pleasure when a notification popped up on the app he used for monitoring their favorite porn sites. He tapped on it, and the window opened to DudesCaughtNudeintheLockerRoom.com. He drew in a sharp breath.

"Bryce, my darling, can you be coming here?" he called. "Making quick, please?" Nestor's already tenuous grasp of English diction came undone in moments of stress.

"I'll be right there, dearest. Just finishing up drinkies," Bryce answered from the kitchen. Soon his footsteps came clicking down the hall. "All done. You are going to love love love this. I went completely retro and made us fuzzy navels! Of course we didn't have orange juice or lemonade, and that left the peach schnapps—and we didn't have that either, so I just used vodka." He handed a tall glass of the clear liquid to Nestor. "So, what did you want to show me?"

Nestor pointed to the computer screen, where the video was cued up.

Bryce shrieked and staggered back, hand on his chest (he didn't spill a drop of his drink). "Oh, my stars and garters," he panted. "Is that what I think it is?"

Nestor nodded gravely.

"Well, should we watch it, or should we call them right away?"

"It is very late on the Saturday night," Nestor mused. "They would be making the sex now."

"Oh, let's hope so. They work so hard. They deserve a little time to themselves, to relax, perhaps read a book, and thrust madly into each other like thoroughbreds." Bryce gave a little sigh and then returned to the issue at hand. "I guess it wouldn't hurt to take a little peek."

Nestor hit the play button.

IT WAS two minutes later that Brandt's phone rang. It was nearly midnight, and he and Donnelly had gone to bed two hours earlier. They had gone to sleep fifteen minutes ago.

"Mmm—hello?" Brandt said groggily into the phone.

"Oh, honey, it's bad. Very bad," the voice on the other end darkly dramatized.

"Who is it?" asked Donnelly.

"It's Bryce," Brandt replied.

"Why yes it is, how thoughtful of you to recognize my voice," Bryce twittered in flattered tones. Then he seemed to recall he was the bearer of bad tidings. "Oh, honey, I have the most dreadful news."

"What is it? What's wrong?" Brandt demanded.

Bryce paused, likely to intensify the effect. It had the desired impact on Brandt, whose pulse was rising with every second of silence. He sat bolt upright and gripped his phone in an iron clench.

"There's another video," Bryce said in an exhalation of despair mixed with the thrill of revelation.

"Oh, shit."

"You're going to want to see this one right away," Bryce continued, "There's some additional… material."

"Is it on the same site as the last two?" he asked and then signaled for Donnelly to grab his laptop, which was in his briefcase by the dresser.

Donnelly brought up the web browser and picked the site from the history menu. He did a search for Whistlepig, and just one video came up—posted earlier in the evening.

"Thanks, Bryce. We appreciate your help." He listened for a moment and then turned to Donnelly with a roll of his eyes. "Nothing," he said. "Any other questions? All right, thanks again."

"Nothing what?" asked Donnelly as the video loaded.

"He asked what you were wearing," Brandt said. Some informants required cash, but Bryce seemed content with details of Brandt and Donnelly's intimate life. It was cheaper that way, overall.

The video buffered sufficiently to start playing, and for the third time the camera showed the now-familiar row in the Woodley locker room. There was no one in the frame at first, and then Jonah arrived from the right side, obviously fresh from the shower. He dried off, front and back, revealing his entire body to the camera. As teammates passed by, Jonah wrapped the towel around his waist. Then one person sat on the bench next to Jonah.

"Is that...?" Donnelly asked.

"Yep, that's Casey." Brandt replied. He had gotten a closer look at Casey than had Donnelly, during their conversation back at the cafe two days ago.

With no sound they didn't know what the two young men said to each other, but they talked for nearly a full minute, far longer than the greetings Jonah had exchanged with other teammates. Then Casey rose, and Jonah was alone—no more traffic of teammates down the aisle. Jonah looked both up and down the row and then loosened the towel from his waist. As he turned to step into his boxers, the camera captured a full-length side view.

"Whoa!" both Brandt and Donnelly said, recoiling from the screen. Brandt leaned forward, not wanting to have seen what he thought he saw. But a second look confirmed it.

Jonah was fully erect.

It was with difficulty that he stuffed his hard-on into his boxers, which remained obscenely tented. He quickly pulled his jeans up, just as Casey reentered the frame. He turned abruptly away, obviously desperate to hide his condition. He hurried the rest of his clothes on and then slammed his locker. He and Casey walked out of the frame together.

Teasers for other videos appeared over the final frame as Brandt and Donnelly sat back in shock.

"So... um... Jonah," said Donnelly.

"Yeah, it kind of seems like... yeah."

"He was… totally boned, right? And he wasn't before he started talking to Casey, right?" Donnelly clearly hoped Brandt would disagree with his assessment.

"That about nails it. Shit." Brandt rubbed his eyes with both hands. "I don't know about high school kids today, but I can't think of anything as toxic as a boner in the locker room."

"When I was growing up," Donnelly said, "a kid sprung a stiffy in the dressing room at the town pool. Fourth grade, it was. We were still teasing him about it when we graduated from high school. That"— he pointed at the screen— "will never go away."

"Can you dash off a quick takedown notice?" Brandt asked.

"On it. They gave me a direct e-mail contact after the last one, but I'm not sure anyone's going to be available to take it down on a Sunday at 1:00 a.m." He typed away with blinding speed.

Brandt considered what to do next. Jonah needed to know about this, but it wasn't really the kind of thing he could roll out in front of his parents. He would have to figure out how to get him on his own without panicking the Fischers.

"Done," announced Donnelly as he clicked a final key and shut his laptop. "I also opened a support ticket, sent a direct e-mail, and clicked the 'Flag this video' icon. If anyone's home, they've now heard from me."

"Nicely done. Now, what do we do about Jonah?"

"That really depends. If that boner was a result of him being eighteen and charged up all the damn time, then it's embarrassing and he'll be teased about it at the their twentieth reunion. But if Casey did that to him, then he's facing a much steeper road."

Brandt turned to his partner. "Anything like that ever happen to you?"

"Inconvenient erections? Twelve times a day when you're around," Donnelly replied with a rakishly cocked eyebrow.

"You are such a romantic. But what about in high school?"

Donnelly shook his head. "Not even once. Of course, I wasn't gay back then. At least, I didn't think I was. You did this to me," he said, poking Brandt in the chest with an accusing finger.

"And if I had it all to do again, I would." He kissed Donnelly on the nose. "But we need to figure out what to do about Jonah."

"What we need is to know what they were talking about. That should give us a clearer picture of what may have inspired little Jonah to pop up that way. If Casey was talking about a skin flick he caught on cable the night before, then we have our answer."

"Got it," Brandt said. "We'll get Walters to take a look. He's a whiz at lip reading."

"I'll invite us over to Chris's house for Sunday brunch. Walters practically lives there these days."

"Perfect." Brandt took a deep breath and settled back in bed while Donnelly put his laptop away. Brandt watched his partner move gracefully across the room. "Speaking of inconvenient boners...," Brandt wheedled.

"Seems pretty convenient to me," Donnelly replied cheerfully and turned out the light before pouncing.


"GABRIEL! ETHAN! So glad you could invite yourselves over," called Chris from the porch of her house as the men climbed the steps. She kissed her brother and then Brandt. "Just kidding. I've been meaning to have you over, and it's a beautiful morning for the first patio brunch of the year."

The sun had broken out in full force this Sunday morning, and it was a happy foursome that gathered on the small concrete patio behind Chris's house. She and Jimmy Walters—colleague to Brandt and Donnelly, and Chris's boyfriend of six months—made pancakes and bacon while the men arranged the fresh fruit and flowers they had brought. After the meal, they drank coffee and chatted.

"So, you have a video you need my help with?" Walters asked.

"If it's not too much trouble," Brandt said.

"No, not at all. Happy to help."

Donnelly pulled his laptop out of his briefcase and set it on the table. He had downloaded the video and edited a version of it that showed only the conversation between Casey and Jonah. "What we're interested in," he explained, "is the conversation between these two boys. The video has no sound at all."

"Okay, let me see it," Walters said, maneuvering the laptop so the screen was shaded and he could see clearly. He watched the video once through and then rewound to the beginning. He watched it several more times, his lips moving along with the images on the screen. Finally, he looked up and nodded. "Got it," he said confidently.

"What are they saying?" Brandt asked.

"I'll voice it for you as it plays," Walters said, returning the video to its first frame and pressing play. "The guy on the left says—"

"Casey," Donnelly said. "The guy on the left is Casey, and the guy on the right is Jonah."

"Gotcha. So, Casey says, 'Coach says we gotta be there by five for the bus.' Then Jonah says, 'That sucks.' High schoolers, right?"

They all nodded.

"You may be more interested in what comes next. Casey: My mom has to open tomorrow. She could drive us. Jonah: Yeah, if I spend the night at your house. Casey: Want to? Jonah: Why not spend the night at my house? At least I have two beds. Casey: But then my mom wouldn't be able to drive us, and one of your parents would have to get up early. Jonah: That's true. Casey: What's wrong, you don't want to sleep with me? I promise I'll keep my hands to myself. Unless you don't want me to. Jonah: Shut up, you pervert. Casey: So, you'll come over? Jonah: Sounds good. I'll text my mom and make sure it's okay. Casey: Awesome. I'll go pick out my prettiest nightie. Jonah: Fuck you."

Brandt stared at the screen, lost in thought.

"Thanks, Jimmy." Donnelly said. "That's exactly what we needed."

"What kind of case is this?" Chris asked, but her tone clearly said she didn't expect an answer.

"Nice try, sis," Donnelly said with a chuckle. "Can't really give you the details right now."

"Flirty trash talk is one thing, but a boner doesn't lie," murmured Brandt, lost in thought.

"It's always about sex with you guys, isn't it?" Chris said with a chuckle.

"I guess it's kind of our specialty," Donnelly replied with a grin. "Stick with what you're good at, right?"

"Ewwww," cried both Chris and Walters together.

"Well, aren't we being a little homophobic?" Donnelly groused.

"Gabriel, you're my little brother. The idea of you and sex is always going to make me go 'Ewww.' Get over yourself."

Brandt slugged back his coffee, and stood abruptly. "Chris, thanks so much for hosting us today—and on such short notice. Walters, thanks for your help. You are the best tech on the force." He bowed to each of them in turn. "Now, partner, I think we have a call to make."

"Well, we're all business suddenly," Donnelly said as he too rose. He hugged his sister, shook Walters's hand, and stepped to Brandt's side. "Next time brunch at our house, okay?" Chris and Jimmy nodded good-naturedly.

As they drove toward home, Donnelly said, "Seems like you got the answers you were looking for."

"It seems pretty clear what was going on in that video, once we found out what they were saying."

"What's your take on it?"

"Bottom line? Casey was poking fun, like boys do in the locker room. Jonah, on the other hand, well… like I said, boners don't lie."

"You think he's into Casey?" Donnelly mused.

"Seems logical to me. Before Casey, little Jonah is floppy. Casey comes by to talk about how he wants them to sleep together, little Jonah is suddenly not floppy and not so little."

"I know, right?" Donnelly muttered sheepishly. "He's a grower."

"So now I have to find a way to break it to him that not only is his secret no longer secret, but he's probably lost his best friend to boot."

"Think Casey would freak out? He seemed to really have Jonah's back."

Brandt sighed. "It's not Jonah's back that's going to cause him a problem. I mean, really, what's worse—getting a boner in the locker room, or causing a boner in the locker room? Casey's going to have a tough time sticking with him if this video gets around like the previous two have."

"So, should we call him this morning and let him know about it?"

"We have to," Brandt said glumly. "Otherwise he might run into it at school tomorrow, and that would be the worst day ever."

Donnelly pulled out his phone and tapped away at it. "Looks like the video is down already. I guess we got them to see the urgency of the situation."

"That's the one piece of good news we've had on this case lately. Good work, Officer Donnelly."

"Thank you, Officer Brandt. Now comes the hard part."


"HEY, IT'S Jonah."

"Jonah, it's Officer Brandt. How's it going today?"

"It was going okay, but I don't think you'd call me on a Sunday morning with good news, so now I'm not so sure." Jonah gave a half-hearted chuckle.

"Do you have plans for the day? There's some stuff I need to talk over with you, and it would be a lot easier to do it in person."

"No, not really. My parents are at church, and they'll be there all day helping with some big picnic fundraiser thing. I was going to go fishing with Casey, but other than that, I didn't have anything planned."

"Great. How about I come up, and we can get a late lunch or something. Maybe around two?"

There was a pause on the other end of the line. "How about if I came down there? I never have a chance to get out of this town for anything except wrestling meets. Casey and I were just going to drive out to the lake anyway. Would it be okay if he came along? He has a car."

Brandt looked wildly at Donnelly, who was listening to the call as it was piped through the car's stereo. Brandt had no idea if Casey being there was a good idea or a terrible one, but Donnelly nodded emphatically.

"Yeah, that would be great, if he's up for it," Brandt answered, taking his direction from Donnelly without knowing why.

"Okay. Where should we meet you?"

Brandt knew it was the wrong thing to do, but in this case the wrong thing might turn out to be right. "Let's meet at my house. I'll text you the address."

"Sounds good. I'll see you in a couple of hours."

Brandt clicked the phone off. The men looked at each other.

It was Donnelly's turn to play the skeptic. "Do you think having them come to our house is a good idea?" he asked.

"What about you—do you think having Casey come along is a good idea?" Brandt asked in return.

"Having Casey there will help, because if he freaks out we'll be able to help calm things down. If Casey abandons Jonah, I don't see how he survives this."

Brandt nodded thoughtfully. "Okay, I see your point. Good thinking. Now, as far as meeting at our house, I think it would be a whole lot better there than in a police office—too cold and impersonal for such a private thing. And I'll admit what we haven't said: it can only help to have two men who are partners there to show Jonah that if he is gay, he'll be okay."

Donnelly nodded. "All right, I guess we're on the same page. Now I believe we have to get the house ready for company."

"I'll make lunch if you vacuum," Brandt said teasingly. He knew Donnelly hated the vacuum and would do anything to avoid having to use it.

"Yeah, not a deal," Donnelly said with a smile.


IT WAS just over two hours later when the doorbell rang. Brandt opened the door and found a rather serious-looking Jonah with an equally pensive Casey behind him.

"Jonah, Casey, you found us! Come on in." Brandt stepped aside and waved them into the house. "Can we get you something to drink? Tea, coffee, water?"

Jonah shook his head, but Casey said, "Coffee? If it's not too much trouble some coffee would be great. I usually drink it when I'm working at Mal's, and on my days off I sometimes get a headache."

"No trouble at all," Donnelly called from the kitchen. "How do you take it?"

Casey seemed a little startled at hearing a man's voice coming from the kitchen, but he covered it quickly. "Uh, black, ton of sugar? Thank you."

"Please, sit," Brandt said, pointing them to the sofa.

Donnelly hustled into the room. "All right, black, three sugars," he said as he handed Casey a steaming mug.

Casey did a double take when he saw Donnelly. "Oh, do police partners have to live together too?" he asked.

"No," Brandt replied with a smile. "Officer Donnelly—Gabriel—and I are partners in the sense of working together as well as in the sense of being in love."

"Oh," Casey said, almost inaudibly, his coffee cup suspended in midair.

"You know, I think I would like some water," Jonah blurted.

"Be right back," Donnelly said, stepping quickly to the kitchen.

"Now, Jonah, you're probably wondering why I asked to see you today," Brandt said, turning serious.

"Like I said on the phone, I figured it wasn't good news," Jonah replied. "How bad is it?"

Brandt took a deep breath. "It's not good. Last night another video was posted online."

"Here," Donnelly said, holding out the glass of water. The young man, his face a frozen mask of pain, didn't move to take it from him. Instead, he looked down at the coffee table in front of him and stared at it as if it perhaps contained the answers he sought. Finally, he heaved a great sigh that was almost a sob, and he looked up at Brandt.

"Show it to me," he croaked.

"Of course," Brandt replied softly. "But I think you should see it alone first. It shows something a little more... intimate than the first two."

Jonah clapped his hands to his face, and this time he couldn't choke back the sobs. Casey set his coffee down and put his arm around his best friend. Donnelly sighed sympathetically as he sat on the arm of Brandt's chair and put his arm around his partner's shoulder.

"It's okay, buddy," Casey murmured in Jonah's ear. "We'll get through this."

Brandt gave Jonah some time to recover, and then asked him if he would like to go into another room to watch the video alone.

"Is it another locker room video?" he asked.

"Yes, it is," Brandt replied.

"Well, then, it wasn't filmed in private. Anything I did in the locker room I did in front of other people, so it can't be that bad." He turned to Casey, who nodded in support. "Let's go ahead and see it."

"Jonah," Donnelly said, gently but emphatically, "I think it really would be best if you saw it alone, at least the first time."

"Then you don't know Casey," Jonah said, a strength in his voice that had been absent before. "He's the strongest person I know, and he can handle anything."

Donnelly looked at Brandt, eyebrows raised in question. Brandt shrugged slightly and then nodded. Donnelly opened the laptop and brought up the video. He looked at the two young men, and they nodded once more in unison. Donnelly started the video.

"There's our star," Casey said exuberantly when Jonah walked into the frame. He was clearly trying to buck Jonah up, and it seemed to be working—he looked less desolate as the video played. "And there's the real star, Jonah's wang!" Jonah managed a giggle at this. "Ooh! I'm in this one!" Casey called out as he saw himself enter the frame.

Brandt was studying Jonah's reaction as it appeared to dawn on him what he was watching, and what he was about to see. He stopped chuckling at Casey's ebullient commentary, and the smile faded from his face. He paled and seemed to be holding his breath as he looked from side to side, desperation on his face.

"Oh, whoa!" shouted Casey, jumping up from the sofa at the moment Jonah's erection bounced into view. "What the fuck, dude?"

"I think I'm going to be sick," Jonah said in a weak voice, and he stood unsteadily.

Donnelly took him by the arm and guided him to the bathroom down the hall. He waited a few moments outside the door before returning to the living room.

"Casey—Casey, calm down," Brandt was saying to the frantically pacing young man. "How's Jonah?" he asked Donnelly when he returned from the hall.

"He's throwing up. Kind of a lot, actually." Donnelly's eyes followed Casey up and down the room several times. "I take it we're not doing much better out here?"

"Can't tell yet." Brandt turned to Casey once again. "Casey, look. You need to stop pacing and sit. You need to talk about this."

Casey stopped suddenly in the middle of the room. "How is talking supposed to help? Will that somehow magically make it so my best friend didn't pop a boner in the locker room while talking to me? Will it make all of this go away?" Tears welled up in his eyes. "I just want this all to go away," he pleaded, his voice hollow. Then, finally, he collapsed onto the couch.

"I know this looks weird," Brandt said in a calm voice, "but just because this happened once in the locker room, it doesn't mean—"

"I think I know what it means, Officer. I think I know exactly what the fuck it means." Casey's face was red now, as if embarrassment and anger had joined up with betrayal and shock to completely demolish his emotional state.

"I'd better check on Jonah," Donnelly said, returning down the hall.

"Casey, take a deep breath and let's be rational about this," Brandt said, in his best "now, put the gun down" voice.

He was interrupted by Donnelly's heavy tread as he ran back into the living room.

"Jonah's gone," he said as he ran out the front door.

"He must have gone through the window," Brandt said, bolting upright. "Don't go anywhere, Casey. We'll go find him. Just sit tight."

"The hell I will," Casey said, jumping up from the sofa and following Brandt out the door.

Donnelly and Brandt dashed around the side of the house to the alley that ran behind the houses in their 1940s-era neighborhood. With the wordless communication of longtime partners, Donnelly ran at top speed up the alley, while Brandt headed down.

CASEY WATCHED until the officers disappeared down the block in opposite directions.

*Where you heading, Jonah?* Casey thought to himself as he stood in the alley. He knew better than to run off randomly. If he could take a minute and think like Jonah would have thought, he would know which way to go.

He imagined having climbed through the window in the bathroom and then stumbling out into the alley, stomach still convulsing, tears streaming. What would he think as he stood here in a strange neighborhood, in a strange city, in a cloud of shame and embarrassment? *Think!*

Casey looked up the street and down, and then he heard it—the long, hollow wail of a train laboring its way through the city. He knew where Jonah had gone. He turned his head, triangulating the sound, and then took off at a run. He was going to find him.

BRANDT AND Donnelly executed a textbook-perfect search of the neighborhood, crisscrossing streets in an expanding pattern from their house. They crossed paths several times and kept in touch with quick text messages when they were not in sight of each other. Brandt hadn't expected Jonah would go far, but their search turned up nothing. They were a half dozen blocks from home now, and their search pattern was so diffuse that it couldn't possibly be effective with just the two of them.

"Let's regroup down by the deli," Brandt texted to Donnelly. "He may have ducked into a shop or cafe."

Five minutes later the two men jogged up to their local deli from opposite directions.

"Okay, so you're eighteen, freaked out, and want to get away," Brandt said, breathing hard. "Where would you go?"

"Remember where I grew up. I could run for five minutes and be in the middle of a cow pasture. Having alone time wasn't really a problem out there."

"Let's scan the windows and see if he decided to hide out along here somewhere. If we haven't found him by the time we hit the tracks, we'll figure out where to go next."

They strode purposefully along the avenue, looking into windows on both sides, coming up empty-handed. Two blocks of this ended them up at a terrace overlooking the commuter rail tracks below.

"Which way, you think?" Brandt asked. They could cross over to the other side of the tracks on a footbridge, or they could walk along the overlook in one direction or the other. The problem was that no direction seemed to have any advantage over the others.

"No clue," Donnelly said, clearly frustrated. "I guess we should have given him the bad news in a locked room."

Brandt's reply was drowned out by the horn of an approaching train. The service on Sunday was less frequent than on weekdays, but the trains ran faster through this part of town, bearing families and tourists on express trains from downtown out to the city's new zoo and aquarium complex. The train, traveling at least sixty miles an hour, blasted its horn again, this time in a succession of short bursts.

"Oh, God!" shouted Donnelly, and he was a blur of motion toward the stairs that led down to the rail station below.

Brandt followed instantly, but had no idea what his partner had seen; then, as they hit the first landing in the long, concrete stairs, he turned and saw a lone figure on the tracks in front of the approaching train.

There was no way they would get there in time.

"Jonah! Jonah, move!" screamed Brandt. He raced down the stairs two and three at a time, right on Donnelly's heels.

They weren't going to make it.

"Jonah! No!" Donnelly bellowed, racing now across the side tracks.

The train, honking and with brakes shrieking, sparks shooting from its wheels as they struggled for purchase on the steel rails, would not stop in time.

It was close now—Brandt could feel the rumble every time his feet hit the ground. Jonah turned toward the train, stared it down, arms by his side as if he had given up completely. The impact sent him flying.

But it wasn't the train that hit him, knocking him off the tracks. It was Casey. He had slammed into Jonah from the side. They rolled across the gravel track bed, coming to rest against a barrier that separated the opposite-direction tracks from each other. Brandt and Donnelly, trapped on the other side of the still-braking train from the young men, couldn't see or hear them. They kept running, and finally they rounded the last car as the train lurched to a halt.

"Jonah, Casey! Are you okay?" Brandt yelled as they approached. They were crumpled together at the base of a short concrete wall, and they weren't moving. Donnelly looked them over carefully before touching them, to avoid jostling any severe injuries. But they sprang to life as he and Brandt crouched next to them.

Casey rolled off of Jonah, and tried to get up. He got as far as kneeling and stopped to catch his breath. Jonah lay moaning, but then he too sat up. There was a scrape on his cheek where he had hit the gravel, but neither boy seemed injured.

"You bastard!" Casey screamed suddenly. He lunged at Jonah and gripped him around the shoulders. He shook him violently. "You fucking bastard!" he howled again. He pulled Jonah to him and held him tightly. Then he broke down completely, sobbing into Jonah's shoulder. "Oh God, Jonah," he repeated over and over. Then, as his tears ran freely, his voice softened to a plaintive moan. "I almost lost you, almost lost you," he said again and again as he rocked Jonah back and forth.

"Casey… Casey, I'm sorry," blubbered Jonah, finally finding his voice.

"No. No. No," Casey replied, still crying. "You're okay. You're all right. It doesn't mean anything. Nothing does. You're okay."

Donnelly got to his feet to intercept the conductor of the train, who was storming over to the scene playing out by the concrete barrier. He pulled out his badge, which checked the conductor in his fury, and he walked with him back to the train.

"You guys okay to walk?" Brandt asked. He didn't want to rush them, but they couldn't stay tangled miserably by the side of the tracks much longer without attracting even more attention.

"Yeah," Casey said, and he rose and helped Jonah to his feet.

"Jonah, do we need to get you to the hospital?" Brandt asked. If he were to go by the book, he should have taken both young men directly to the hospital, and then to the police department to be booked for interfering with the operation of a passenger train. But that's not what they needed right now, and for once Brandt was going to throw out the rule book if it threatened to do more harm than good.

The three of them were most of the way back up the stairs to street level when Donnelly caught up with them.

"They're relieved you're okay. Pissed that you were there in the first place, but that poor engineer has pasted six people in the last five years, and he's happy enough to not have you be number seven. I promised him you would be cited, but I seem to have misplaced the paperwork." Donnelly, at least in Brandt's view, had always been the more flexible one when it came to rules and procedure.

"Let's get these guys home," Brandt said.

Casey and Jonah still clung to each other, so Brandt put his arm around Jonah, and Donnelly took up station on Casey's side, and the four of them walked the six blocks back to the house.

"YOU GUYS just sit down and take a deep breath," Donnelly said as they entered the living room. "Do you need some water or something?"

"Maybe in a minute," Casey said. His voice was hoarse from crying. He turned and pressed his face right against the side of his friend's head and spoke directly into his ear, softly. "Jonah, you okay?"

Jonah blinked hard, twice, and then nodded, imperceptibly at first but then more surely.

"Jonah, we're all glad you're not injured, but walking in front of a train is pretty serious stuff. You should talk to someone. We can call your pastor, and we have social workers in the department we can call...."

Jonah shook his head without looking up.

"It's really important that you have someone to talk to," Brandt continued, his voice gentle but definite.

"That's me," Casey said, turning to Brandt. "We talk about everything." He turned back to Jonah. "Well, I guess there was one thing we haven't talked about," he said, his voice lightly teasing. But then he grew serious again. "There's nothing that Jonah can't talk to me about. Nothing."

Jonah closed his eyes again, squeezing yet more tears from them. "I can't," he croaked.

"Yes, you can," Casey replied. "It doesn't matter what it is. Even if it scares the crap out of you, you can talk to me."

"Not about this," Jonah murmured miserably.

"Even about this, whatever this is," Casey said, his voice growing stronger. "You wiped my shitty ass, man, when I was too weak to do it. This is a whole lot easier to deal with than that."

"But I don't even know what's wrong with me—that's the problem. I don't know why it happened, and I don't know what it means, and I don't want everyone staring at me while I try to figure it out!" Jonah buried his face in his hands again.

Donnelly touched Brandt on the shoulder and motioned to the kitchen. Brandt followed his partner out of the living room.

"That poor kid," Donnelly said as he pulled sandwich makings out of the fridge. "He's lucky to have such a good friend."

Brandt nodded. "I don't know what we should do."

"First we remember that they are high school wrestlers and haven't eaten anything for hours. They'll be in better shape once they eat something."

"Gabriel Donnelly, you are going to make an amazing mother," Brandt said with a laugh he desperately needed; it had been an overwhelming afternoon.

But Donnelly knit his brows into an expression of purest desolation. "I'm starting to think it's never going to happen for us," he said. "We keep trying and trying—why, last night we tried twice." Donnelly winked at Brandt and continued with his lunch preparations.

"But seriously, we have an obligation to report Jonah's attempt."

Donnelly set down the knife he was using to slice bread. "Really? Do you think that's the best thing for him? Or does he need the love and support of a good friend?"

"Gabriel, you know as well as I do what the law is," Brandt scolded. "We have to report this."

"Let's say we do. Then Jonah gets locked in a hospital room on an evaluation hold, and everyone back in Woodley finds out, and then the video comes along to provide the reason for it, and now his life is basically over. Plus, at the end of the seventy-two hours he can, as an adult, refuse treatment. So after three days spent enjoying the hospitality of the state, his life is no better, and actually is a whole lot worse than it would have been if we'd just said nothing."

Brandt sighed. He knew he was on the right, but losing, side. "I see your point. But you know how I am about rules."

"Honey, look at it this way. Jonah has no history of suicide threats that we know of. Certainly nothing has shown up in any of the interviews we've done or the files we've reviewed. We know why he did this—because his secret came out suddenly, and he panicked. The crisis has passed. He's got some shit to work through, and it won't be easy, but it really doesn't look like he's a danger to himself."

Brandt grumbled but then nodded and took Donnelly's hand. "You're right. Of course you're right." He looked out through the doorway to the living room, where Casey and Jonah remained huddled together on the couch. "Let's give them some time to process what's happened—and eat Mrs. Donnelly's delicious lunch—and then they can head back home. And hopefully we got the latest video down before anyone was able to grab it."

"You're a rebel, you are," Donnelly said as he began assembling sandwiches. "Now, be a useful rebel and scrub up some carrots."

It was fifteen minutes later when Brandt and Donnelly emerged from the kitchen with lunch, and during that time Jonah and Casey had remained right where they were, clutched together on the couch. It seemed to Brandt that Casey simply didn't want to let go of his friend in case anything else came along to threaten him; Jonah appeared content to shelter in his friend's protection.

"All right, guys, have some lunch," Donnelly called as he set the trays in front of them.

Casey reached for a sandwich. "Thanks, Officer—"

"Gabriel. Please, call me Gabriel."

"Thanks, Gabriel," Casey said with an almost sheepish grin.

"Ethan and I were just talking in the kitchen, and we've agreed not to say anything about what happened this afternoon."

"Thanks," Jonah replied. "I appreciate it."

"But you need to promise us that you aren't going to try anything like that again, and that you will seek help if you need it."

Jonah raised his eyes to meet Donnelly's for the first time. "You don't have to worry. I won't. I was just really freaked out. I thought Casey would hate me. But I think I'm going to be okay."

Casey picked up a sandwich and handed it to Jonah, nudging him on the shoulder to take it. When he did and took a bite from it, Casey looked to Brandt. "So what are the odds that when we get to school tomorrow, this new video is going to be all over the place?"

"I don't know. We haven't seen the second video being sent around, so perhaps—"

"I have," Casey interrupted.

"What?" all three men said at once.

"I didn't want to say anything, but someone on the team sent it to me last night. Said he had heard a bunch of people talking about it in his math class on Friday."

Jonah set his sandwich down.

"Hey, it's not that bad. He said that the girls in his class were impressed, so that's a plus, right?" Then Casey winced. "Unless that's not what... I mean... oh, shit. Sorry."

Brandt tried to save him by redirecting the conversation. "I think we have to assume the video is going to get out. And it's going to be hard."

Donnelly slapped his knee and mouthed, "Really?"

"I mean," Brandt blurted, "it's going to be difficult—to deal with—at least at first. There's no getting around it. But you have friends who will stick with you, and I'm sure your parents will be supportive, and Coach Woody."

Jonah shook his head miserably. "I don't know about my parents. They've been great so far, but this might be too much for them."

"They may surprise you," Donnelly offered.

Jonah shrugged as if his parents' support would indeed be a surprise.

"If things get rough, I want you to know you can always count on us," Brandt said. "If there's anything we can do to help, we'd be happy to."

Jonah seemed about to shrug again, but then snapped out of it, as if he'd remembered his manners. "Thank you. I really appreciate everything you've done for me."

They ate lunch in long moments of silence between half-hearted small talk. It was getting on toward four o'clock when Casey announced that they should get going.

"You're right—I forgot it's a school night," Brandt said in his best "it'll all be swell!" voice. "You should let your parents know you're on your way home."

"If we were up at the lake fishing, we'd be back pretty late, so they're not going to be worried," Casey said. He and Jonah rose to go.

Jonah held out his hand to Brandt. "Thank you for everything," he said.

He repeated this gesture with Donnelly, who held his hand a little longer than is customary. "We're here for you, Jonah, no matter what. Anything you need, I want you to get in touch, okay? We've got your back."

Jonah nodded, and his eyes reddened instantly. "Thank you," he was able to eke out in a hoarse whisper.

"Casey, you're a great friend," Brandt said, shaking the young man's hand.

"Thank you, sir. I learned from the best," he said with a grin and a glance at Jonah. The latter managed a weak smile. He shook hands with Donnelly. "All right, buddy," he said to Jonah. "Let's hit the road."

Jonah nodded, and they walked down the steps and out to Casey's car.

"I feel like we're sending them off to war," Brandt said as he put his arm around Donnelly's waist.

"They'll be okay. It may not be easy, but they'll be okay."

The men turned and went back into the house.

CASEY PUNCHED the go home button on the GPS stuck to his windshield and pulled away from the curb in front of Brandt and Donnelly's house.

"I really don't want to go home," Jonah said.

"We're not," replied Casey in a chipper tone.

"We're not?"

"Nope. I have a better idea. The parents think we're up at the lake anyway, so let's just go there. I loaded up the car before you called and said we were coming here, so I have everything we need. The ice is probably all melted in the cooler, but other than that we're good to go." He looked over at Jonah, hoping this new plan would lighten his mood.

It seemed to be working. Jonah looked at Casey for a long moment and then out the window. "I still can't believe you're okay with all of this."

"I figure we don't even know what 'all of this' is, and until we do, there's no sense freaking out."

"But there's a video out there where you... and then I...." Jonah closed his eyes, a pained furrow on his brow.

"Dude, chill. Relax about the whole video thing. Just kick back and rest until we get there. You've been through kind of a lot today. We can talk more when we're at the lake and we have a nice fire going. You know that's the best place for working through shit."

"Okay," Jonah said, his voice already heavy with exhaustion. He turned a sleepy look to Casey. "Thanks, man. I don't know what I would—"

"Shh. Don't. Just rest."

Jonah cranked back the seat and closed his eyes.

Casey focused on the road because thinking about that video would make him crazy. He was clinging as hard as he could to the memory of how great a friend Jonah had always been. That was the only thing getting him through.

THEY ARRIVED at the lake as the sun dipped toward the hills. This was a plot of land Casey's family had held for several generations until they fell on hard times; Casey's uncle had finally sold it to finance his gambling addiction. The current owner, who farmed the land all around the area, liked Casey and allowed him to keep coming here to fish and camp out by the side of the small spring-fed lake. Casey was navigating the bumpy dirt road when Jonah awakened.

"Crashed pretty hard there, bud," Casey said as he parked the car. He set the brake and hopped out, popping the trunk release as he did.

Jonah joined him, shaking the nap out of his limbs. He didn't meet Casey's eye as they unloaded the small cache of camping supplies Casey had brought: blankets, some simple food, and a cooler with drinks floating in icy water. These things they carried a few hundred yards to the small clearing Casey had used for a campsite since his scouting days. He and Jonah had come here hundreds of times over the years. Often in the summer, his uncle would drop them off here first thing in the morning and not return for them until after dark. They would spend the entire day skinny dipping, catching and eating fish, and lolling about the lakeshore, talking and laughing and napping. Casey felt more at home here than anywhere else in the world, and he hoped Jonah felt the same.

They laid out a couple of blankets on the cool, flat ground near the fire ring, and without speaking both of them fell into a routine of long standing—gather firewood, fill the big iron pot with fresh water from the spring where it ran into the lake, cut branches for roasting hot dogs. Casey soon had a fire blazing in the ring, its flames reaching several feet into the chill air of the spring evening, crackling with a primal rhythm of life. The boys sat down on the blanket near the fire, its warmth breaking over them in waves.

Casey opened the cooler and spoke the first words since they had gotten out of the car: "Here." He handed Jonah a can of beer.

Jonah looked at it with a start.

"It's okay. I just took a couple. She'll never notice two missing. You look like you could use a beer." Casey had always wanted to say that, but would gladly have foregone the pleasure not to have those videos hanging over them.

Jonah shrugged and nodded, and then opened the beer and took a drink. Casey mirrored his actions.

"You know," Jonah said, "we signed a pledge not to drink during the season."

Casey could recite the same lecture as Jonah—Coach Woody had drummed it into their heads a million times. Since wrestlers work hard to keep their weight down during the season, they have less mass for absorbing alcohol and are particularly susceptible to its effects. "I just brought two. And I think we have bigger issues to deal with than a stupid pledge." Casey tipped up his beer as if doing so won the argument.

Jonah grunted his agreement and killed off his beer as well.

The first stars twinkled into view as the purple sky of sunset darkened above them. Off in the distance, a mallard couple nibbled in the mud for a last meal before turning in for the night. There were no other sounds.

Casey broke the silence. "I can't get that video out of my head," he said quietly.

Jonah stared into the fire with an intensity that unsettled his friend.

"I'm not mad, if that's what you're worried about." Casey's voice was gentle.

Jonah shook his head. "You should be," he replied. "You shouldn't ever want to be near me again."

"I'm not going anywhere. I… I just don't understand it, that's all."

"I don't either," Jonah said miserably. "I can't explain it, and I hate that it happens to me."

"Wait, this has happened before?" Casey's voice was hollow.

Jonah stared into the fire, wiping his eyes as tears ran down his face. Finally, seeming to break under Casey's stare, he nodded.

"Shit, man. I don't know what to say."

Jonah closed his eyes. "There's nothing you can say to me I haven't said to myself a hundred times. I'm broken. I'm"—he wiped his cheeks with a violent motion—"just... broken." He sobbed silently, clutching his knees to his chest.

"Jonah, listen to me," Casey said in a voice that surprised him with its force. "Are you listening?" He waited for a feeble nod and then continued. "There is nothing wrong with you. Nothing."

"Then why does this happen to me?" Jonah was crying freely now. "It's not normal."

"Fuck normal."

"What?" Jonah's eyes flew open, and he turned to Casey in disbelief.

"I said fuck normal. Who gets to decide what's normal?"

"But what happens to me isn't right. It isn't what happens to you, or to anyone else I know."

"Dude, listen to yourself. You make it sound like you caught a disease or something. What is on that video isn't something that happened to you—it's you, and it's what your body does. You can try to deny it, you can tell yourself you're sick or broken, but the fact is that your body is going to do what it's going to do, and that's normal for you."

"But it's not right! You're not supposed to get a boner for your best friend. You're supposed to get one when you touch a girl's hair, or when you're slow dancing, or when you watch lesbian porn."

"Yes, yes, and oh hell yeah. But that's just me. If those things don't float your boat, then whatever."

"Whatever? Whatever? The only thing that makes my stupid fucking dick stiffen up is my best friend, and that's whatever? Is it whatever when we're running drills and the way you smell makes my stomach hurt? Is it whatever when I sleep over at your house and I lie awake all night because I'm afraid I'll roll over and you'll know I'm boned up?" Jonah was choking out the words now, sobbing and sniffing and nearly shouting. "Is it whatever when I have to hide every fucking day that my stupid fucking body only wants you?"

"It can't just be me."

"It is," Jonah whispered. "It always has been."

Casey stared into the fire for a minute. "Jonah, do you think you might... be...?"

"Go ahead and say it."

"Do you think you're... gay?"

Jonah's voice could hardly be heard, though the only other sound was the fire crackling. "I don't know." The firelight danced on his face as searched for words. "I don't want to be," he finally said.

"Maybe what you want doesn't matter. Maybe you don't get a choice."

Jonah heaved a great sigh. "All I ever wanted was to fall in love, and get married, and have a family who would be happy to see me at the end of the day when I come home from work."

"Okay, so?"

"So, I don't get to have any of that because of my stupid dick? Seriously? How pathetic is that? Everything I ever expected to have in life gets thrown out because I get hard at the wrong times?" Jonah turned suddenly to Casey, his eyes flashing. "I can't be gay. I'm not what those... people... are."

Casey smiled and shook his head. "Gabriel and Ethan are those people."

"They're not like other gay people. How many gay people have you ever seen who were like that?"

"Like what?"

"Like them—regular guys. They don't act like gays."

"Neither does Malcolm," Casey said.

Jonah's mouth dropped open. "Wait—Malcolm's... gay?"

Casey nodded. "Yeah."

"Then why do you work for him? Does he hit on you all the time?"

"I work for him because he's nice, and he pays well. I didn't even know he was gay until I saw him flirting with Gabriel. And he's never laid a finger on me. Just because someone's gay doesn't mean he runs around with his dick out. I overheard Gabriel and Ethan today in the kitchen. They broke the rules to protect you. They really care about you."

"But think how stupid this all is," Jonah said. "I'm supposed to change my entire life because of when my dick gets hard?"

Casey looked at his friend, wondering how to help him. "Can I ask you something kind of awkward?"

Jonah rolled his eyes. "I think we're way beyond awkward."

Casey thought carefully about how to ask this question. "What is it about me?"

"I don't…?"

"That makes you, um… react… the way you do?"

"You don't really want to have this conversation."

"I really do. You'll see why."

Jonah frowned. "This is going to sound stupid."

"I'm your best friend. If it sounds stupid, I'll let you know. But I don't think it will."

"It started with your hands."

"My hands?"

"Yeah. The way they move. The way you spin your pencil in math class when you get impatient with whoever's at the board working a problem and screwing it up. The way they feel when we're sparring at practice and you run them along my sides, trying to get leverage. You have amazing hands."

"Okay, hands. What else?"

"Your eyes," Jonah replied immediately. He was clearly warming to his subject now. "There have been times when I think I only exist when you're looking at me. Your eyes are so wide and truthful. It's like they knew my secret all along. I've watched you sleep just to see how beautiful your eyes are when they're closed."

"Uh-huh," Casey said, nodding. "I'm just going to make an observation, okay? You said you didn't want your dick making life decisions for you, right?"

Jonah nodded.

"But nothing you've said is in any way dick-related. Looking at someone's hands? Watching them sleep, but not touching them? I don't think I'd get boned up about a girl that way."

"It's not just that. There's other stuff too," Jonah offered.

Casey swallowed, not sure he wanted to know more than he already did. "Like what?"

Jonah opened his mouth to answer but then made a kind of choking noise and fell silent. He cast a helpless glance at Casey, as if begging him to be let off the hook.

"Tell me. Whatever it is, I promise I will not be mad."

Jonah took a shaky breath and huffed it out without speaking. Then he took another and tried to find his voice. "Last month, before that Saturday morning scrimmage with Somerville? When I spent the night at your house?"

Casey nodded encouragingly. He really didn't want to hear what Jonah would say next, but he tried to look as though he did.

"You'd been asleep for a while, and you rolled over onto your back. And I—"

"Oh, dude, no," Casey said before he could stop himself.

"No! It wasn't anything like you're thinking. I wouldn't do that to you."

"I'm sorry. I know you wouldn't." Casey closed his eyes, took a deep breath, and then focused on Jonah again. "Go on, tell me what happened."

"You lifted your arm up so it was on the pillow between your head and the wall. And I... I laid my head on your chest. Just for a minute. I figured if you woke up I would pretend I had rolled over in my sleep. But you didn't wake up. And so I just lay there for a while."

"Then what?"

Jonah looked desperately into the fire.

"Come on, man, tell me everything. You'll feel better."

Jonah looked up from the fire, right into Casey's eyes. "I imagined what it would be like to be able to do that every night. To feel your heartbeat, and your breathing, and to feel safe right there because everything that's fucked up about me would be normal if we could just be like that every night, together." The tears he'd been holding back broke free, catching the firelight in tiny sparkling rivers down his cheeks. "I don't want to be gay," he sobbed. "I only want to be with you."

Casey was silent for a moment, letting the worst of the grief work its way through his friend. Finally, the sobbing slowed down to a sniffling echo of itself. "We're together all the time."

"But not like that," Jonah replied, his voice thick with crying.

Casey came to a decision. He stood up and grabbed one of the sleeping bags he had brought for extra padding on the ground. He unrolled it and plopped down on it. "C'mere," he said to Jonah. He patted the sleeping bag next to him.

"No," Jonah said, clearly shocked.

"Why the hell not? You're beating yourself up because you don't know what you want. One way to figure that out, man. Get your ass over here and find out."

"But it's not what you want," Jonah replied.

"This isn't about what I want. This is about you, and I can't stand to see you like this. If I can do something that might make you happy, fuck yeah I'm going to do it. Come here right now." He pointed emphatically to his side.

"This is pretty fucked up," Jonah said, but despite that he got to his feet.

"Don't care about the fuckedupness," Casey said. "Don't care at all. Get over here."

Jonah approached awkwardly and then sat next to Casey.

"Good. Now...." Casey reached over, picked up the other sleeping bag he had brought along, and placed it, still rolled up, on the one he'd laid out. He then lay back, resting his head on it like a pillow. "Is this right?" he asked as he lifted his arm above his head.

Jonah looked at him, stretched out on the sleeping bag, and then closed his eyes. He nodded, his face a study in stoic shame. He opened them again, as if agreeing with them closed didn't really count.

"Then c'mere," Casey said, tipping his head in a beckoning gesture.

"You don't really want to do this," Jonah murmured.

"I really really do. I want you to do this. Who's it going to hurt? No one ever has to know. We're all alone out here. Who gives a fuck what we do?" He lay his other hand across his chest right over his nipple, and patted the spot he wanted Jonah to take. "Come on, right here."

"Are you sure?"

"Jonah Fischer, I swear I have never worked half this hard to get a *girl* to lie down with me! Now get over here."

Jonah blushed at Casey's mention of girls, but he nodded sheepishly. He scooted over a bit so their hips nearly touched, and then he lay back, his head coming to rest in exactly the spot Casey had patted.

Casey could feel the tension in Jonah's body—it was like he was keeping every muscle tight to minimize the contact between them. "Relax, man. Just let go. This is okay, and we're okay. Take a deep breath and de-stress."

Little by little Jonah's body relented in its clenching, and Casey could feel a softer contact between them.

"That's better, isn't it?" he asked. He could feel Jonah nod. "Good," he whispered.

They lay there for a long while, watching the smoke from their fire rise into the sky and make the stars flicker. Casey lifted the arm that was raised up and brought it around Jonah, coming to rest with his fingers on Jonah's chest. He felt Jonah startle.

"Sorry, my hand was falling asleep. Is it okay if I rest it there?"

Jonah nodded.

"Dude, your heart is pounding," Casey said. He could feel Jonah's pulse, strong and rapid, through his fingertips.

"Sorry. I'm just kind of—" Jonah started to sit up, but Casey held firm with the arm he had draped around him.

"Shh. Stay. This is really nice." Casey felt the tension in Jonah's body, which had spiked when he began to sit up, flow slowly out of it again.

"How can you say it's nice? This isn't what you wanted."

"It's what you wanted, and that's good enough for me."

They lay silently for a few minutes more.

"Thank you," Jonah whispered.

"I love you, you know," Casey said in a soft voice. "No matter what happens with the video, no matter what people say, I will always love you."

Jonah was quiet but began shaking.

"Are you crying?" Casey asked, and then he felt dampness on his shirt, so he knew Jonah was. "Jonah, stop. What's wrong?"

Jonah sniffed. "This is too perfect. This is everything I wanted, and it's you and it's perfect and once we leave here I'll never have this again and I'll be alone and—" A sob cut off his frantic ramble.

"Honest to God, you can be so thickheaded," Casey scolded. "We can do this anytime you want. We can do it every damn day if you want to. As long as you take a shower once in a while, I'm up for it." He held Jonah tightly with the arm he had slung around him. "You will *never* be alone."

Jonah turned his face toward Casey's chest and cried, and Casey just held him and held him until the fire waned and night settled in all around them.

AN HOUR later Casey pulled his car up in front of the Fischer home. During the ride from the lake, they had finally managed to have something approaching normal conversation, about the upcoming regional competition and the essay for American literature that neither of them had yet started.

Jonah opened the door and then turned back to Casey. "I will never—never—be able to thank you for what you did today."

"We're friends. That's what friends do."

Jonah shook his head, but smiled and punched Casey on the arm. Then he stepped out of the car before leaning back in. "See you tomorrow?"

"How could I live without calculus?" Casey answered with a chuckle.

Jonah nodded and rolled his eyes and then shut the door and walked to his front door.

Casey watched him go and then pointed his car home. He had a lot to think about.

# Chapter FOUR
## An Outing

CASEY WAS turning out the dough for scones when he heard his phone vibrate. No one ever texted him at 5:00 a.m., so he was in the habit of putting his phone on a shelf near the kitchen door to avoid a repeat of the flour accident that had claimed the life of his previous phone. He ignored the buzzing and went on with his work, lining up dough for plain, raspberry, and ginger scones.

His phone buzzed again. And then again and again.

"Crap," he muttered and wiped the slightly sticky dough off his hands as he walked over to where his phone was. He looked at the display and saw texts piling up from a large (and growing) number of people he knew from school. They all asked variations of the same thing—did Casey know he was in the latest Jonah video?

"Fuck," he said.

"What's wrong, Casey?" called Malcolm from the other side of the kitchen. "You sound like you just got punched in the stomach."

"Nothing," he said and started to put his phone down. It buzzed three more times before he had even set it on the shelf. "Shut up," he growled at it.

"What is it?" Malcolm asked, coming over to Casey's side of the kitchen. "Get some bad news?"

Casey rolled his eyes. "You could say that." He typed out a terse text message to Brandt's number and then switched his phone off so that it could buzz no more. He slammed it down on the shelf and returned to his scones with a renewed vigor.

"Is it about Jonah?" Malcolm asked.

Casey startled. "Why would you think that?"

"Just a hunch." Malcolm waited for Casey to say something, but the young man remained silent. "You know, if you need to talk to someone about what's going on, I'd be happy to—"

"I promised Jonah I wouldn't." But then, the video was clearly out in the open, so it wouldn't harm anything if he were to say something about it to Malcolm. "There's another video," he said quietly.

"Oh, no," replied Malcolm, sounding truly devastated. "That poor guy."

"Yeah, well, I'm in this one too," said Casey with a groan.

"Wait, so it's not personal with Jonah? Someone's just filming random people in the locker room?"

Casey pondered how to explain this to Malcolm. "No, it's not really random—it's still mainly Jonah. But...." Casey paused uncertainly. He was trying to figure out where the boundaries were between his secrets and Jonah's, and how much of what they had shared he was ready to think about, much less talk about.

"Casey, if you were filmed as well, you need to let the police know right away so they can be aware of that in their investigation."

Casey nodded. "I texted Ethan just now."

Malcolm stopped and fixed Casey with a quizzical look. "Ethan? You're on a first-name basis with the police?"

Casey felt the blush and looked quickly away, hoping to hide his reaction. "Yeah, I guess. They seem really nice—like they want to help."

"Seriously, are you okay?" Malcolm asked, stepping closer to Casey. "If you need to talk, I'm a good listener."

Casey shook his head. "I'm just trying to figure out what it's going to be like at school today, suddenly being a video star and all."

"A wise old man once said that in the future everyone will be famous for fifteen minutes. I guess that should be updated—nowadays everyone's naked on the Internet for fifteen minutes. And then, through the magic of technology, forever." He shook his head. "What a world."

"You're telling me," Casey said with a sigh.

THE FIRST thing Casey did upon arriving at school was look for Jonah. They normally met up before math class in the quad area at the front of the school, but this morning he was nowhere to be found. Casey made the rounds of all of their usual haunts but could not locate his friend. Finally, just as the tardy bell was ringing, Jonah rounded the corner of the building, looking very much like he was trying to slip in unnoticed.

Casey met him in front of the classroom door. When Jonah reached for the handle, Casey grabbed his wrist.

"Can we talk for a sec?" Casey asked.

Jonah looked puzzled, and then he paled visibly as the seriousness of Casey's expression sunk in. "What happened?"

"Let's go to my car."

"Shit, Case, you're scaring me. What's up?"

Casey just shook his head and walked out to the parking lot. He opened the doors and slid into the driver's seat. Jonah did the same on the passenger side, and they sat in silence for just a moment. Casey knew what he had to say would be devastating for Jonah, so he tried to give him a last minute of peace.

"They got the new one," he said, knowing Jonah would jump to the right conclusion about who had what.

Jonah turned to Casey, his mouth open. He looked absolutely bereft. He turned back to the windshield and gave a little moan. That was his only reaction.

"Jonah, did you hear me?" Casey asked. Jonah's lack of reaction was more alarming to him than screaming would have been.

Jonah nodded, still saying nothing.

"You okay?" Casey prodded, fishing for a response—of any kind.

Jonah shook his head slowly, as if he was trying to say "no" to the entire situation. Then, finally, he found some words. "I can't go in there."

Casey nodded. "Yeah, I thought you might feel that way."

"Can we just drive, just get away from here?"

"Sure," Casey said and started up the car. Once the tardy bell had rung, the custodian was supposed to put up the chain closing off the parking lot, but he was running late this morning, and they were able to drive out and down the street without anyone seeing them.

Casey looked over at his friend as they drove down the main street. Tears streaked his cheeks—again. Jonah had cried more in the last few days than he probably had in his life. Certainly more than Casey had ever known him to.

As soon as they pulled away from Woodley on the highway, Jonah's funk seemed to lift. He wiped his cheeks and blew his nose on a tissue he pulled out of Casey's glove box.

"Most fucked-up senior year ever," he said, looking at his hands resting in his lap. "So, who let you know the video was out?"

"Everybody. Got texts from everybody."

"What did they say?"

"They all wanted to know if I knew I was in it," Casey answered. "I guess they all figured they were doing a public service by informing me of my Internet debut."

"I'm so sorry," Jonah said miserably.

"We covered this," Casey said definitively. "You have nothing to be sorry about."

Jonah snorted a pained laugh. "Do you think they would be passing this shit around if I didn't? Before, it was just poor Jonah in the locker room. Now it's going to be Jonah's boner all day every day until I die."

"And I'm right there next to you, don't forget. We're in this together."

"No. We aren't. You don't have to take this on. All you need to do is tell everyone you had no idea that I was such a pervert, and as soon as you saw the video, you told me to fuck off and you're never going to even talk to me again. You do that, and this video isn't a problem for you anymore."

"The hell I will," Casey snapped. "I'm starting to think you have a hearing problem, my friend. I keep telling you I'm not going anywhere, and you keep not hearing me. The only thing I would ever say about that video is Jonah is my best friend, and if he gets wood being near me, then he's going to be hard all the damn time because we are together a lot."

"They're going to think you're gay."

"They can think whatever they want. Fuck 'em." Casey thought he saw a shadow of a smile cross Jonah's face. This was progress.

They drove in silence for a while.

"Where are we going?" Jonah asked finally.

"I figure Woodley's the last place you'd want to be today, so I thought we'd head back to the city for a while. I did some research last night, and apparently there's a whole neighborhood that's mostly... well, it's where a lot of... so it's kind of—"

"Gay? You mean a gay neighborhood?"

Casey nodded, scared of the reaction that word might provoke.

"Shit," Jonah said and turned to look out the window. "Look, I don't even know if that's what I am. In case you didn't get the message yesterday, I'm pretty confused right now."

"And that's exactly why we should go. You can try it out for a day—see what it's like?"

"Being gay? You want me to try being gay for a day?"

"No! I mean, well... yeah, I guess. That sounds weird, doesn't it?"

"You make it sound like I would be trying on a new kind of running shoe or something. I don't think gay is something I can just pretend to be for a day, see if I like it."

"No, but you can get a feel for what it's like for the people there, if you think you could see yourself there someday. You know, once you get this all figured out." Casey looked at his friend, who seemed to be coming around to his way of thinking. "And look at it this way—no one there knows you. No one there has seen the video. And no one there has ever even heard of Woodchuck Wrestling. Even if you hate being there, it beats the hell out of spending the day in fucking Woodley, right?"

Jonah considered this. "You make a good point," he said with a nod. "All right, let's give it a try. But if it's too weird, we'll just leave, okay?"

"This is your big gay adventure, buddy. I'm just along for the ride."

"Yeah, let's never call it that, okay?" Jonah said with a chuckle.

Casey was glad to see some sign of his friend underneath all of the misery.

NEARLY TWO hours later, Casey pulled his car into the first parking spot he found on Alta Avenue, right where the rather prim map he'd consulted online last night told him the "alternative district" began. He put the car in park and shut off the engine.

"So, this is it," he said to Jonah, who was surveying the street through the passenger window.

"It's not what I expected," Jonah replied.

"What did you expect?"

"Well, every time you see gay people on the news, they're wearing dresses with feathers or dancing in speedos on floats." Jonah peered through the windshield.

Casey burst into giggles. "That would be pretty fucked up, man. Think about the traffic around here if they all traveled on floats."

Jonah laughed, though he sounded a bit more anxious than his friend. "You sure you want to do this?"

"It's what we came for. No one here knows us, and no one will ever find out we were here." Casey nodded encouragingly and opened his door. Jonah did the same, and they stepped out of the car.

"I gotta put some money in the meter," Casey said, patting his pockets. "Did you bring any gay money?" He winked at Jonah, who rolled his eyes and handed Casey all of the straight coins he had in his pocket.

"There. We can be gay for"—Casey squinted at the meter— "exactly two hours." He turned to Jonah. "If you feel the need to be gayer than that, we can always come back and feed the meter."

"Are you going to keep doing that?" Jonah asked. "Because I might have to kill you."

"Sorry, man. Just having a little fun. You know, feeling kinda happy and gay." Casey saw the glare Jonah was sending his way and recoiled, genuinely startled. "Okay, no more jokes. Got it."

Jonah grinned. "Well, maybe a few more. You're awesome to do this with me."

Casey smiled, pleased to see his friend's mood lighten for the first time in days. "So, our first stop should be right up here." He pointed to the other side of the street on the next block up.

"Wait, you planned this out? Like an itinerary?"

Casey nodded, uncertain whether this was something Jonah might view as an intrusion on his prerogative as a sexually questioning individual. "I thought it might be helpful. I didn't know we'd end up here so soon, though, so I hadn't really gotten it all nailed down. I mean, do you like gay Thai food or gay Indian food?"

Jonah closed his eyes and shook his head. Then, without warning, he threw his arm around Casey's shoulder and pulled him into a sudden hug. "Best best friend ever," he whispered.

"Save it for the float, bro," Casey replied, deeply thrilled to have made his friend happy. "Onward!" he called, and they walked to their first destination.

They soon found themselves in front of a large bookstore called, as Casey had discovered in his research, Pen is Mighty.

"Look how they repeated the name and ran the letters all together," Casey said to Jonah as they looked at the front of the bookstore. "See how it looks like it says Mighty Penis? Hah! How gay is that?"

Jonah looked at him, eyes bugged out. "Casey, you can't just say that, especially not here!"

"I didn't mean gay like stupid, stupid. I meant it like 'appropriate considering the target market and neighborhood demographic.' Jeez, you need to lighten up." Casey shook his head scoldingly at his friend.

Jonah rolled his eyes and sighed. "Let's just go in, okay?"

They walked through the door and stood in the two-story atrium with blonde-wood shelves reaching from floor to ceiling.

"You know, I don't think I've ever been in a bookstore—even a straight one," Casey said as they took in the scale of the place.

"Let's try not to look like farm boys, okay?" Jonah pointed toward the center of the store. "This way?"

"Your call, chief." Casey smiled and followed along.

They walked into the center of the store, from which two stories of shelves radiated like spokes. They stood and looked around and had no idea where to start.

Casey was undaunted. He marched up to the information desk and waited for the young man with the Clark Kent glasses to finish consulting the computer about the book he held in his hand. Finally he looked up, and did a double take when his eyes landed on Casey.

"Well, hell-lo," he said, sliding along the counter on his rolling stool until he was directly opposite Casey. "How may I be of service, sir?"

Casey had never understood what people meant when they said someone had "undressed me with his eyes." Now he did. The clerk looked him up and down, lingering over areas Casey suddenly felt his clothes were inadequate to cover. He shook off his insecurity and forged ahead with his question.

"Where is your how-to section?" he asked.

"How to what, then?" the clerk replied.

"Um, how to be gay, I guess? It's for my friend over there." Casey tipped his head over to Jonah, who was still turning slowly around, absorbing the size and complexity of the place.

"Riiiiiight, your friend," the clerk said with a smile. "Okay, let's get your friend the information he seeks. Follow along, cutie." He came around the side of the information counter and gave Casey another once-over. "Hmm. Sure it's just for your friend?"

"Oh, about 99.9 percent sure. But thanks for the creepy look," he said with a sunny smile that clearly intended no offense.

"We'll see," said the clerk with a wink. He headed across the hub of the store, tapping Jonah on the shoulder when he reached him, signaling Jonah to follow. The three of them climbed the staircase to the second level and arrived shortly at a section of the store where several rows of shelves radiated out from some conversationally arranged couches.

"Now this is the sexualities section. Here we have lesbian, gay, bisexual, asexual, polyamorous, cisgender, transgender, and, well, other." He pointed to the shelves on the left and then moved his hand, making chopping motions, as he swiveled to the right. "So moving into the gay section, we begin with 'Am I gay?' then on to 'Why am I gay?' to 'Hell yeah, I'm fucking gay so deal with it!' down there at the end. Then on this shelf we have 'What kind of gay am I?' to 'How do I have gay sex?' and finally 'Why does no one want to have gay sex with me?', which honestly, you two are not going to have to worry about for many many years. With me so far?"

Casey, eyes spinning a bit, nodded gamely. Jonah seemed hardly to be breathing.

"Great. Now next row over we have the coming out section. Coming out to Mom is this shelf—and those four over there. Coming out to Dad is on the next two shelves, and then on down through grandparents and second cousins, and finally rich uncles who might cut you out of their will if you're gay. Got that?"

The boys nodded helplessly.

"Then finally, we have gay culture, gay cooking, gay travel, and gay automobile maintenance. We used to have a gay fashion section, but now that's just basically the fashion section on the lower level. It's fabulous. Any questions?"

Casey could only shake his head. Jonah was reading titles on the shelves with increasing alarm.

"Okay, so…," the clerk said, trying to catch Jonah's attention.

"Jonah," Casey said. "His name's Jonah."

"Okay, Jonah. There's really only one question you need to ask yourself, and the answer will help you more than all of these books. You know the feeling you get in your tummy when you look at your friend here?"

Jonah looked at him quizzically.

"Hang on, let's get this right. Here, you…." He pointed at Casey.

"My name's Casey."

"Casey, great. Okay, Casey, take your shirt off."

"What?"

"Do you want to help Jonah, or not?" the clerk demanded. He crossed his arms and tapped his foot imperiously.

"Yeah, I do. He's my best friend."

"Then off with it. Just for a sec."

"But...," Casey stammered, looking around. There were no other patrons in the section, but still.

"Take it off! Now!" ordered the clerk, in a commanding tone Coach Woody could never hope to attain.

Casey crossed his arms and whipped his shirt off.

"Oh, fuck me," the clerk whispered under his breath. He shook it off and turned to Jonah. "Now, Jonah. You know the feeling you get in your belly when you look at Casey? Be honest now, you know what I'm talking about, don't you?"

Jonah looked at Casey, the friend of his entire life, and his eyes slowly ran down the lithe musculature honed by years of wrestling. He nodded. "Yeah, I know," he said in a small, pained voice.

The clerk smiled warmly. "Thank you, Casey. If you insist on being fully clothed, which is, I assure you, a loss to humanity, you may put your shirt back on." He turned back to Jonah. "I know you're confused and anxious because you don't understand what's inside you. That feeling is the truth, Jonah. No straight man could have answered that question in the affirmative. But you felt it, just like I felt it, just like most of the men here would have felt it."

Jonah looked at the clerk, panic in his eyes.

The clerk continued, his voice low and gentle. "It wasn't put there by the left-wing media, and it wasn't put there by Satan to lead you astray. It wasn't put there by your mom loving you too much or your dad being distant. It didn't come from anywhere—it's a part of you. It's the most 'you' thing that's in you. It will always be there, just like it's always been there. You can try to ignore it and tamp it down and hide it, but that won't make it go away. You will be happier, and healthier, if you listen to it and accept it as part of your life. You know this about yourself, Jonah. You know it."

Jonah's eyes welled up as he shook his head slowly under the onslaught of the clerk's monologue. The clerk matched his cadence with nodding, and he laid a hand on Jonah's arm. That seemed to be the last straw. With a stifled sob, Jonah slumped as if the head-shaking refusal had exhausted him. He closed his eyes, forcing tears from them, and then nodded slowly. He looked over at Casey. "I'm sorry," he said.

Casey came to Jonah and pulled him into a hug. "No. You're Jonah. Never be sorry to be who you are."

"I'll give you two a moment," the clerk whispered, a tear running down his cheek as well. He backed away and walked off down an adjacent aisle.

"Happy now?" Jonah muttered into Casey's ear.

"Gay now?" Casey muttered back. Then he broke into giggles.

Jonah slapped him on the back of the head but then held him tighter. "Thank you," he said. "I keep saying that, but I can't say it enough. I can't believe you did this."

Casey gripped his best friend more tightly. "I love you, man. I want you to be happy, and to be happy you need to be yourself."

Jonah took a deep breath and released his hold. The friends stepped apart and wiped their eyes.

"You know, I don't think I need any of these books," Jonah said.

Casey's eyebrows shot up. "Really?"

"Nah. If I get lost, all I have to do is ask you to take your shirt off. Apparently, that's the only guide I need." He grinned.

"Think what you'll learn when I take my pants off," Casey replied with a wink.

"Let's save that for when we're someplace a little more private, okay?" Jonah said with a laugh.

"Deal. Now can we get some gay lunch, please?"

"You got it. Let's go."

They walked back down the stairs to the main floor of the bookstore and stopped at the information counter where the clerk was beaming at them from his stool.

"Thank you," Jonah said, extending his hand.

The clerk took it and shook it gently. "People say that coming out is the most difficult thing they've ever had to do, Jonah," he said with a smile. "But you've done the hardest part—you came out to yourself. And to your best friend. Nothing will ever be as hard as what you've already done. You're home, Jonah. Your new life—your real life—starts today."

"Yeah, happy gay birthday, buddy!" cheered Casey with a wink. He slung his arm around his friend and they walked out of the store together.

THE BOYS stepped back onto the street, blinking in the bright sunshine, and walked farther up the block. They didn't have far to go before coming across an eatery that looked perfect for lunch, a hot dog place called Sausage Fest. They found an outdoor table, facing the sidewalk, at which to eat their foot-long meals (this was the only size on the menu).

"Oh, crap," Jonah said suddenly, before he'd taken the first bite of his hot dog.

"What is it?" Casey asked.

"We're skipping class."

Casey looked around, as if it was just dawning on him that they were not, in fact, in fourth-hour biology. "You know, you're right."

"When you skip class, they call your parents to check up on you."

Neither Casey nor Jonah had skipped class much, given that perfect attendance was a basic requirement of being on the wrestling team. "Oh, crap," Casey said. Then he thought about what would happen if the school called his house: his mom was working today, as she did pretty much every day of the week, and she wasn't allowed to carry a personal cell phone on the job. "I guess it won't matter much for me, but your mom's home, right?"

Jonah nodded. "I don't have my phone with me. I turned it off and left it in your car. Can I use yours to call my mom?"

Casey handed over his phone and went back to eating his lunch.

Jonah flicked to "favorite numbers" on Casey's phone, and of course his home phone was entry #2, right after his mobile number. He tapped it, and the phone began to ring.

"Hey, Mom." Jonah was silent for a couple of seconds. "Yeah, I know. I'm with Casey." He drew a deep breath. "You know about it?"

He closed his eyes. "Casey told me this morning. That's why we left." Suddenly, he sat bolt upright in his chair. "Mom, no! No, that's not what—Wait! No, don't put him—" Jonah looked pleadingly at Casey, who had no idea what was going on, much less how he could help. "Hi, Dad." Jonah's voice was tiny. "Dad, it's not what you—No, he's not—" Jonah's face froze in an expression of pure terror, and he was silent for a long while. "Dad, why would you say that? You're not actually saying that I can't—" He shook his head, a look of bewilderment on his face. "No, I can't tell you that because I don't— Dad? ... Dad?"

Jonah handed the phone back to Casey, then stared out into the street, unfocused.

"What happened? What was all that about?" Casey asked. "I didn't get what they were—"

"They saw the third video." Jonah heaved a deep breath, let it out slowly. "Someone at my dad's work told him about it and then forwarded it to him."

"Oh, man, that really sucks. I'm sorry."

"He said he was shocked and disappointed, and that his only hope was that you were the one to blame for what happened to me in the video. When I told him it wasn't you, he went kind of insane and started screaming at me."

"What did he say?"

"He said that he had defended me, but now that I turned out to be some kind of pervert, he couldn't do it anymore. He said that no son of his is going to be a deviant in the locker room. He said I had to tell him, right then, that I wasn't gay. I couldn't do it."

"What the actual fuck? He can't be serious—you and your dad have always been great."

"He said I can't come home. He doesn't want me to be around Sam."

"Wait, what? What does your little brother have to do with what's going on with you?"

"I don't know. He just said he couldn't risk having me anywhere near Sam and not to come home."

Casey shook his head. He couldn't believe what he was hearing. The Fischers had always been loving parents. "I don't get it. They've been so supportive all along, through all of this video crap. What changed them?"

"I guess the video of me getting a boner from being near you in the locker room is what changed them."

"And now he thinks that if you're gay, you're going to molest your twelve-year-old brother? That's toxic."

Jonah closed his eyes. "The whole thing is toxic. Where am I supposed to live? How long before I can go home? And what gives him the fucking right to call me an incestuous child molester just because I'm gay?"

Casey looked at his friend and smiled broadly. "I am so proud of you."

"What? You're proud... of what?"

"You. The first time you get challenged on being gay—less than a half hour since you first admitted it to yourself—you stand your ground. Against your dad of all people. You, sir, are a hero." Casey lifted his glass of soda to Jonah in salute.

"I don't feel like it," Jonah said quietly. "I feel homeless."

"You're not homeless. You can come stay with me while your parents cool down."

"My dad didn't sound like he'd be cooling down anytime soon."

"Then you can stay with me as long as it takes."

"No."

Casey looked at his friend, confused. He waited for elaboration.

Jonah's voice had taken on a calm that was perhaps more unnerving than his initial devastation. "I'm not going back to fucking Woodley. If I'm not welcomed there by my own fucking family, then why would I go back at all?" He shook his head disgustedly and returned to looking out onto the street.

"So what are we going to do?"

"What do you mean 'we'? You're going to go back to Woodley. You have a job and wrestling practice and classes and stuff."

"So do you. If you're not going back, I'm not going back." Casey realized this sounded much braver than he actually felt, but it seemed to him that bravery was what was called for in this case, so he went with it.

Jonah turned his previous question back on him. "So what are we going to do?"

"Eat a good lunch, because after this I'm pretty much out of money."

Jonah seemed to find his appetite and reduced his foot-long to less than eight inches in a single bite.

Casey picked up his phone and texted Malcolm that he wouldn't be coming in this afternoon. About five seconds after he hit the send button, his phone rang. It was Malcolm.

"Old people," Casey said. "Using phones for talking." He put the phone to his head. "Hey, Mal. No, we're fine. Just didn't want to be around today as the latest video production starring Jonah and me made its way around school." He winked at Jonah. Then he suddenly grew serious. "What? He did?" He held the phone aside and said to Jonah, "Your dad just called Mal to ask if he knew where I was."

"He thinks we've run off together," Jonah said with a grim chuckle.

"Tell him not to bother looking—we're not in Woodley," Casey said into the phone. "Would it be okay if we kind of played my work schedule by ear for a few days? I'm not sure if it's a good idea for us to be there while the video burns its way through everyone's in-box." He listened and nodded. "You're awesome, Mal. Thank you so much for understanding. Yeah, I'll tell him."

Casey set his phone down and picked up his soda. "Mal says he hopes you're doing okay, and he's sorry this happened."

"He's really nice to let you out of work."

"Like I said, he's a good guy. Maybe once you—"

Casey was interrupted by his phone buzzing on the table. He picked it up and read. "It's from Gabriel." He looked at Jonah with a frustrated roll of his eyes. "Your dad called him, said we were missing." Casey started tapping out a reply.

"Wait—don't," Jonah said, putting his hand on Casey's phone.

"Why not?"

"I just… I need some time away from all of that. If we tell him and Ethan where we are, they're going to tell my parents, and then we'll get dragged back up there—though what good that would do anyone I have no idea, since my folks have basically thrown me out of the house." He closed his eyes, and took a deep breath. "Can we just go off the radar for a day?"

Casey nodded. "Yep." He put his phone in his pocket. "I need to take a leak. If I'm not back in five minutes, come in after me, okay?" He laughed and went into the restaurant.

In the hallway outside the restroom, he took his phone out of his pocket. "We're fine. Taking a day away from fucking Woodley. Please don't tell parents." He sent the reply to Gabriel before going into the bathroom.

When he returned to the table, Jonah had found his appetite—his lunch was gone, and Casey thought there might be a bite missing from his own dog. He smiled at his friend's spirits returning.

"So now what?" he asked as he sat down.

"I need to figure out what to do next," Jonah said, his voice dead serious.

"You mean, like, today? Or are you talking big picture?" Casey suspected from his tone of voice that he might well mean the latter.

Jonah looked him in the eye, his gaze unwavering. "My family doesn't want me back. That Powell guy said if more videos showed up, I'd be damaged goods to the recruiters, so it looks like my wrestling days are done, and my scholarship chances. Everything I've worked for over the last six years since I first started wrestling in middle school is pretty much out the window." He looked down at the remains of his lunch. "I'm starting from scratch, man, and I got nothing."

Casey reached out and put his hands on top of Jonah's. "I'm not nothing," he said, in a strong and low voice. The intimacy of the gesture surprised him, and it seemed to shock Jonah as well. But Casey was going purely on instinct, and it had served him well so far. "We'll figure this out together."

Jonah smiled but shook his head. "I appreciate the thought, man, I really do. But if I'm going to end up in some shelter for wayward boys, I can't expect you to be there with me. You have a home, and a mom who would probably be thrilled to have you bring home a boyfriend because she could get tips on how to liven up her living room with new window treatments. But she doesn't have to worry about that, because she got the normal son." He grunted out a mirthless chuckle. "Sorry, I know I shouldn't say that—makes me sound all pitiful and bitter. But my life is pretty fucking different all of a sudden, and yours can pick up again in a week or so, when people get tired of the video."

"What did I tell you last night at the lake? You will never be alone. Better get used to that."

Jonah's eyes welled up at his friend's unwavering support. They sat, silent, hands clasped, for several long moments.

Suddenly Casey's eyes darted to the sidewalk. "Wait, did that guy just take a picture of us? What the hell?"

Jonah turned to look at a couple of men who had turned around and walked quickly off the way they had apparently come. Casey bolted upright and, in one lightning motion, vaulted over the decorative iron railing that marked out the restaurant's outdoor seating area. In two strides he caught up with the men.

"Hey, dude, did you just take a picture of us?" Casey's angry tone was part defensiveness on behalf of his friend and part anxiety over the conspiracy theories running in his head involving parents, the police, and whoever planted that damn spy cam. If he could confront any part of that dark network, he would do it. "What the fuck?"

"I don't know what you're talking about," sniffed the taller of the two men, summoning all of the dignity he could under the circumstances.

"Then why is your phone still in camera mode?" Casey pointed to the phone in the man's hand.

"He was taking the pictures of… flowers. So lovely, no?" the other man asked, in exotically accented, lilting tones.

"What flowers?" Casey pointed out the complete lack of greenery along the entire block. "Come on, tell me why you were taking pictures of us. Do you work for the police or something?" Casey's voice was getting louder as he questioned the men, and his fists were balled up, ready to strike if needed.

The taller man stepped toward Casey. "Perhaps we can join you at your table?"

"Why would we want to do that?" Casey retorted.

"Because," the man leaned close to utter confidentially, "we have seen your videos."

"What?" Casey whispered. His knees felt weak, and his head spun a bit.

"Can we sit and have a little chat, now?"

Casey nodded only because he had no idea what else to do. He reentered the restaurant's fenced area by a gate at the corner and led the way to the table where Jonah sat watching their approach, his mouth gaping.

"Who are…?" he managed to utter.

"Sit, I guess," Casey said to the men, motioning to the two extra seats at the table.

"Thank you. Now, I know this must be strange for you, but please let me introduce myself. I'm Bryce, and this is Nestor, and we… well, we are acquainted with your video work."

"Oh, fuck," said Jonah, visibly paling, his face a devastated grimace.

"No, no, please don't! It would be criminal to wrinkle that darling face." Bryce smiled but seemed to sense immediately that his compliment had gone unappreciated. "Anyway, you have nothing to worry about from us." He leaned in and whispered conspiratorially. "We've been involved in the investigation."

"What?" the young men said in unison.

"Oh, yes. The officers came to us for help in locating the videos. We're sort of confidential informants." Bryce practically vibrated with the excitement of his contribution to law enforcement.

"And what are these officers' names?" Casey asked. He wanted to see how much this Bryce knew.

Bryce looked around like he was about to deliver state secrets. "Brandt and Donnelly," he whispered.

Casey laughed and leaned back in his chair. "Oh, so you know Gabriel and Ethan? Small world, right?"

Nestor looked confused, Bryce crestfallen, and Jonah aghast.

"It's all right," he said to Jonah. "We're all friends here. I'm Casey, and this is Jonah."

Introductions seemed to cheer Bryce up no end—he clearly wanted very much to be friends with the locker-room video stars. "Well, then, what brings you to our fair city? I thought you were from… where was it? I know it had 'wood' in it."

"Woodley," Casey answered, as Jonah had still not found his voice.

"Right, right. Such nice lockers they have there." Bryce sighed at the vision in his head. "Anyway, isn't today a school day? And yet we find you here stuffing sausages into your lovely, lovely faces?"

"You may have seen our latest video? The one with the…." Casey lifted his index finger straight up.

"Oh, my, yes," Bryce gasped. "You have nothing to be ashamed of, my dear," he assured Jonah. "I've seen many videos—of celebrities, even—who don't measure up to your screen presence."

"Um, thanks? I guess?" Jonah managed to say.

"We of course alerted the officers when we found that video. Called them right away, even though it was very very late and they were very very naked in bed. When I think of those fine men and their dedication to duty, well…." He fanned himself delicately.

"Well, I guess we have to thank you for finding it. I just wish we'd been able to keep everyone at school from getting a copy of it."

"People are passing it around? Like you were some common tramp, or"—he shuddered—"a Kardashian? Oh, the very idea makes me furious."

"Well, how did you come across it?" Casey asked, a grin playing on his lips.

"Oh, that's entirely different," Bryce blustered. "We are connoisseurs of fine cinematography, seekers of revelatory aesthetic experience!"

"As long as the guys get naked at some point, right?" Casey said.

"What would be the point if they always wore the clothes?" Nestor said, as if this concept should have been obvious.

Jonah suddenly snapped to life. He turned to Bryce. "Do you think… would you be able to… help us?"

Bryce sucked in a great breath of excitement. "Help you? Oh my goodness yes, we would do anything to be of service to you, my dears. And I do mean anything." He looked at Casey intently. "Any-thing."

"My parents found out about the boner video," Jonah began.

"Oh, what earthy parlance!" hooted Bryce, clapping his hands. "Did you hear that, Nestor? Boner video! I can hardly wait to use that one—they'll simply spit their tea at our next discussion group."

"Wait, you guys have groups where you discuss videos?" Casey said with a startled chuckle. "Oh, man, this is a whole different world."

"And you are welcome in it, my darlings. Now, you were saying about your parents and the… boner video," Bryce said with a giggle, clearly enjoying wrapping his lips around this new phrase.

"They kicked me out of the house. I have nowhere to stay. I've been gay for a total of"—he glanced at his watch—"an hour, and I'm already homeless. So, do you know of any shelters or anything I could look into?"

"Oh, oh, honey, I'm so sorry! What a terrible thing for someone so muscular to have to go through." Bryce shook his head and made tut-tutting noises until he seemed to realize something. "But where are my manners? Did you say that you've been gay for an hour?"

Jonah nodded.

"How wonderful for you. And you?" he nodded to Casey.

"Still straight. Just happy to be along for the ride."

Bryce nodded sagely, as if he had heard such protestations before and had learned not to put much store by them. "To you, Jonah dear, I say welcome. You have come home. To you, Casey, I say thank you. Any young gay man would be lucky to have an ally like you. And to you, Nestor, I say you owe me five dollars."

"But he say he was no gay before!"

"We'll settle this later." Bryce turned back to Jonah. "Now, to your problem. I know what it is to be thrown out of one's home. My father sent me away the very first time he saw me in a dress. I told him he had to accept me for who I was, and that I wasn't willing to be less fabulous to be more acceptable."

"Did you have to move out on your own?" Jonah asked.

"Oh no, dear, I was only six. He sent me to a strict military boarding school. Where, by the way, the sex was a-maz-ing. Everywhere, all the time." He sighed and looked into the middle distance.

"My love, we try to help?" Nestor prompted.

"Oh, yes, of course. Now put aside all of this nonsense about a shelter. How dreadful to be packed in with all of those young, outcast, desperate...." Bryce grew unfocused again, until Nestor elbowed him. "Right, sorry. No shelters for you, my dear boy. You must come home with us." Bryce held his hand up. "Now, I expect nothing in return, nor shall I accept anything you might see fit to offer." This declaration clearly cost him, but he plowed ahead. "We have a guest room, and you are welcome to it for as long as you have need."

Jonah looked at Casey. "What do you think?"

"One condition," Casey replied. "We have to check with Gabriel and Ethan. I know you didn't want to let them know where we are, but we're adults, and if we tell them not to say anything, they won't. They didn't tell our parents about yesterday, right?"

Jonah nodded.

Casey pulled his phone out of his pocket and tapped out a message to Gabriel: "Met Bryce and Nestor. Offered to put us up for the night. Okay? Don't tell Woodley." Within thirty seconds, the reply buzzed in: "Yes. We won't tell. Breakfast tomorrow?" Casey replied in the affirmative.

"Gabriel says it's fine," Casey said to Jonah, putting his phone away again.

"Ooh!" Bryce jumped in his chair and pulled out his own buzzing phone. He read the message and laughed. "It's from Ethan. 'Lay one finger on either of them and I will....'" His eyes widened and his mouth gaped; he made a noise like a surprised kitten before finding his voice again. "Well, the rest isn't terribly interesting...." Bryce put his phone down gingerly, as if it contained explosives.

"Will you be our guests?" Nestor asked, his smile brilliant.

Casey nodded to Jonah.

"Thank you so much," Jonah said to Bryce and Nestor.

"Perfect perfect perfect!" called out Bryce, clapping merrily. "Now, we do have to finish our day's labors, as we are simple working stiffs. But we finish at six, and then you will be our guests for dinner. Meet us at Grindstone"—he placed a card on the table with the store's information on it—"and we will whisk you away for the night. How does that sound, darlings?"

Jonah laughed, clearly overwhelmed by Bryce. "Sounds great, thanks."

"Now, you two have fun exploring the avenue. If anyone accosts you—men here can be so forward!—simply mention casually that you are playing hooky from high school and whoosh! Good as pepper spray."

"Thanks for the advice," Casey said with a laugh. "We'll see you at six."

"It is all I will be thinking about," said Bryce as he rose from his seat. "So nice to have met you in the flesh." He shook their hands, as did Nestor, and the pair made their way out of the restaurant.

"So now you're not homeless," Casey said brightly.

"At least for one night," Jonah replied. "It's a start."


THE YOUNG men whiled away the rest of the afternoon window-shopping and people watching. They spent the last of their money on the parking meter and the rich gelato they ate on a bench in a little park midway along the avenue.

"So, what do you think?" Casey asked.

"I think you can't really go wrong with 'double double chocolate,'" replied Jonah.

"No, I mean about all of this—about your big gay adventure in the city?"

"I think being gay is more than shopping and eating, as amazing as this stuff is."

"Yeah, I guess at a certain point there's going to need to be something more… physical."

Jonah shivered. "Not sure I'm ready to even think about that, to be honest. What if I don't like it?"

"Don't like what?" Casey asked.

"You know," Jonah replied. Then, under his breath, "Sex."

"Who doesn't like sex?" Casey asked, shaking his head in confusion. "I thought that was pretty much hardwired."

"Yeah, I guess. But the thing is you spend eighteen years thinking you're supposed to be interested in sex with girls, and then suddenly your life changes direction. All of the movies and TV you've seen, all of the stuff you hear in church, all the jokes people tell—everything points you toward girls. But I honestly have no idea what it would be like with… a guy. What if that's not what I want after all?"

"I think the odds of that are pretty small," Casey said. "It's not all that different, really, is it? You still kiss and make out and touch and stuff."

Jonah squinted at his friend. "You're kind of creeping me out talking about this."

"But you need to talk about this stuff," Casey replied. "It's like you said—no one talks about it, and that makes it scary and unknown and weird. But it probably isn't, once you do it."

Jonah shook his head. "I don't know, man. It's a pretty big change."

"Then take it slow, and don't stress about it. You're going to have your pick of guys when you're ready, by the way. Have you seen how they all look at you?"

"They've been looking pretty hard at you too, you know."

"Yeah," Casey laughed. "How great is that?"

"It doesn't bother you?" Jonah asked.

"Why should it? I can't help being beautiful," Casey said, tossing his head like a model and laughing even harder.

"You are such a freak," Jonah said. "That's why I love you."

Casey blew him a kiss. "Ready to go? Got another hour to kill before meeting up with Bryce and Nestor. Let's break more hearts on the avenue."

"Sounds like a blast." They got up from their bench and continued up the street.

SHORTLY BEFORE six they arrived at Grindstone.

"There are my darling boys!" cried Bryce as he rushed to greet them. "Did you enjoy your day? See the sights? No one accosted you, unless you wanted them to, which you shouldn't, but of course who would blame anyone for taking a second look at such beauty? Are you positively famished? You athletic types are legendary for your appetites, which I should be only too happy to indulge—by which I mean food, of course, only that, and not anything more than that, certainly."

Jonah and Casey stood gaping, overwhelmed.

"Nestor, darling! Our guests are here." He turned back to the boys. "We have such a treat planned for you two. Nestor will be preparing the specialties of his homeland, which he never gets to do because honestly, who can eat when one is required to be a beacon of fashion and taste? Those Cuban bean-and-rice things are great for feeding peasant farmers, but—oh, Nestor, there you are! Well, shall we?"

The four of them left the store and walked down the block to an apartment building on the corner.

"After dinner, you can park your car here." Bryce pointed to a spot in the alley next to the building. "We don't drive, but we keep the parking space. You never know when you might want to offer the pizza delivery man a spot to squeeze into."

Casey chuckled and shook his head. He had come to the conclusion that he should just let Bryce be Bryce and enjoy it. He was a little concerned about Jonah, though. He seemed to regard Bryce with something between ironic enjoyment and outright horror. Casey got the sense Jonah was trying to find his future as a gay man and had decidedly mixed feelings about Bryce as a role model.

They climbed three flights of stairs to the top floor of the building, where Bryce and Nestor's apartment occupied the back half. Bryce deftly opened half a dozen locks, then pushed the door open and swept his arm grandly into the space.

"Welcome to our humble home," he said with a bow.

Jonah and Casey stepped into the apartment, which was small and rather dark. Bryce remedied this latter condition by switching on what seemed to be a hundred strings of white, pink, and purple twinkling lights. They crisscrossed the ceiling and hung down in sweeping swags of sparkling, glowing light. The cracks in the plaster barely showed.

"Wow, it's beautiful," Casey said.

"Oh, my, well," Bryce said, launched into an orbit of flattered excitement, "thank you for saying so! Now, let me show you to the guest room." He led them down the hall to a small room next to the kitchen, in which Nestor had begun to busy himself. Bryce opened the guest room door, and switched on the light.

Casey and Jonah stepped into the room, and looked around. There was almost enough room for the three of them and the furniture. A queen-size bed took up most of the floor space. A small nightstand on the side of the bed held a lamp, and there was a shallow armoire next to the foot of the bed.

"This is really nice, thank you," Jonah said—it was the first substantive thing he'd said to Bryce since they'd met up at the store.

"It is the least we can do, darling. It is a special treat to be able to provide succor to one taking his first baby steps, even if he is taking them with such strong, long legs." Bryce sighed and then continued his tour. "Now, the bed has fresh sheets, and there's a drawer here that contains necessities should you require them." He opened the top drawer of the nightstand, which appeared to contain three different kinds of lube and a gross of condoms in a kaleidoscopic array, at which Casey and Jonah stared wide-eyed. Bryce slid the drawer smartly shut. "Now, let's have an aperitif while Nestor gets his Havana on, shall we?"

"You know we're not legal—for drinking," Casey said, impishly.

"Honey, you are legal for everything that I hold dear in life—not that it matters, as we are under strict police orders. But we will be whipping up virgin mojitos for you tonight. Nestor's muddler is a thing of beauty!"

Bryce led the way into the kitchen, where Nestor had lined up four mason jars full of mint, lime, and sparkle. Steam was already rising from the tiny stove, and the aroma of the island filled the kitchen. Bryce handed the jars out and then raised his high. "To Jonah, on his first night. May your journey bring everything you wanted, and a few things you didn't know to wish for."

They cheered and shared a joyous drink.

"MAN, THAT Nestor knows how to cook," Casey said, closing the guest room door behind him.

"Right? I have no idea what most of that stuff was, but it was amazing!" Jonah replied.

The boys had decided to turn in soon after dinner, as they suspected tomorrow would be another trying day. Bryce had provisioned toothbrushes and other toiletries for them, and had collected their clothes for laundering when each had taken a shower. They now wore robes Bryce had supplied, apologizing profusely that he had nothing else in his closet that would fit over their "bulging, lovely muscles."

Jonah sat on the bed, and Casey plopped down next to him.

"They're so nice to do this for us," Jonah said, shaking his head.

"It's funny, isn't it? Your parents kick you out because of who you are, and now we find these wonderful people who want to help you for the same reason. They aren't family, but they do care about you, and that's kind of awesome."

Jonah nodded. "When that video showed up, I felt more alone than I ever have in my life. I figured I'd lost you forever, and my parents… well, I kinda knew how that was going to go. But you're still here, and there's this whole world I didn't even know existed."

"See? It's like I said—this is your big gay adventure."

Jonah laughed. "Well, I guess we should turn in. I don't know what time Gabriel and Ethan will be here in the morning, and who knows what the hell happens after that."

"No matter what happens, you're going to be okay," Casey said.

"I hope you're right. I'm just kind of pessimistic about my family right now."

"Give them time. They'll come around. Once they see that being gay doesn't make you breathe purple fire."

Jonah laughed. "Now there's a superpower I could really use."

Casey stood. "Should I turn out the light?"

"Sure," Jonah answered.

Casey clicked off the lamp, leaving the room dark except for the halo of pink light that slipped in through the gap all around the door. He took off his robe and laid it at the foot of the bed, and as he pulled back the duvet, he could see Jonah in silhouette doing the same. He slid under the comforter and felt the bed sag as Jonah joined him.

They lay in silence a long while.

"So," Casey said, finally. "Big day."

"Yeah, kinda," Jonah said with a chuckle.

More silence.

This time Jonah broke it. "I couldn't have done any of this without you, you know. If you hadn't gotten me out of Woodley, I don't think I would have made it through the day. But instead of this being the worst day of my life, it was the best. And Bryce's corny toast was pretty much right on—I'm starting a whole new life."

"That's awesome," Casey replied out of the dimness.

"Thank you for being the best friend ever in the history of everything," Jonah said, in a low and serious voice.

"It's nothing you wouldn't do for me, and I know that for a fact."

"We been through some shit, haven't we?" Jonah said with a laugh.

"Hells yeah," Casey replied. "Wouldn't change a thing. Well, except for the cancer. I could probably skip that and still be fine."

"No, don't say that," Jonah said, turning to his side and propping his head on his elbow. "You beat the crap out of leu-fucking-kemia, buddy, and that's something not everyone can say. Plus, it gave me a chance to rack up some amazing best-friend points I've been cashing in on by running in front of trains and getting awkward boners on video."

Casey giggled delightedly throughout this monologue. "That's the spirit! Fuck cancer! Fuck homophobia! We make our own rules!"

They shared a round of giddy laughter before settling down again.

"Seriously, though, I owe you my life," Jonah said. "Not in the figure-of-speech way, but in the real-deal, I'd-be-dead way. I will never forget that."

Casey looked at the outline of his friend on the bed next to him. "Come here," he murmured.

Jonah startled. "What?"

"Come here," Casey repeated. His voice was stronger, but just as low.

"I don't understand. We're in the same bed already."

"Just come here," Casey said again. He patted his chest, the way he had by the fire last night.

He could hear Jonah take several deep breaths.

"No, I can't."

"Yes, you can. I want you to."

"But... we're naked," Jonah whispered, as if suddenly scandalized by being in this state.

"I don't care. I want you to come here."

"But I don't want you to feel—"

"This isn't about what you want. This is what I want." Casey's voice was insistent, almost a growl.

"But you're not... I mean, we're not...."

"Jonah, I've watched you all day as your entire life has been turned upside down, and you've been amazing through it all. I told you we could do this every day, and I meant it. I meant it for me, not just you."

"It's really okay?"

"Yes, it's really okay. It's more than okay. It's what I want." Casey patted his chest again. "Now, come here."

Jonah lifted the covers and scooted closer to his friend. He lay his head where it had lain the night before, but this time the back of his neck touched Casey's bare chest.

"There. Isn't that better?" Casey asked. This time he didn't wait before bringing his arm down around Jonah's shoulder. This time he felt them touch, skin on skin, the warmth of their contact tingling up his arm.

"It's… yes," Jonah whispered.

They lay quietly for a moment or two, feeling the rise and fall of their breath.

"This would be so easy," Casey murmured, his cheek pressed against the top of Jonah's head. His hand began to move in small, slow circles on Jonah's chest.

"What would be easy?" Jonah asked, his voice a little higher than usual. Goose bumps began to rise on his chest.

"Just this. What if the world out there didn't exist, and we had no families to worry about, no scholarships to stress over, no Internet stalkers making trouble for us. What if it was just us?"

Jonah swallowed hard.

"I've been with a couple of girls," Casey said, his voice continuing soft and low, his lips brushing Jonah's short, spiky hair. "And it was never this easy. You can't just lie there, talking and then not talking, like we can. You're always worried about where your arm is, and are you sweaty and gross, and what happens if your stomach growls or you need to fart, or whatever."

"Dude, you fart and I am outta here," Jonah said with a laugh.

"Oh, I know that's not true," Casey replied, giggling at his own juvenile humor. In the silence that followed, his fingers found Jonah's right nipple and brushed over it absentmindedly. "I could lay here all night like this."

"I think people might talk. And by people, I mean God's gift to gossip out there in the next room."

"Let 'em talk. Honest to God, Jonah, if this is what being gay meant, I would totally be on board."

Jonah lifted his head from Casey's chest and turned to look him in the eye. "Um, Case? Two guys naked in bed, touching like this? I think that's pretty much the definition of gay."

Casey's response was to strengthen his grip, pulling Jonah to him even more tightly. Jonah's face was smashed against his chest, and Casey felt hot breath rush over his skin.

"Stop it," Jonah said playfully and pulled himself off. But he settled back down onto Casey's chest and began to run his fingers up and down his forearm, gently and slowly, brushing against the fine hairs.

"Mmm, that's nice," murmured Casey. He was so happy, with nothing between him and his best friend, that he put out of his mind entirely what anyone outside this room might think of what they were doing.

"I love you, Casey," Jonah whispered, so quietly he may well have expected not to be heard.

But he was. "I love you too," Casey whispered back, and kissed the top of Jonah's head.

CASEY, USED to a job that started at 4:30 a.m., awoke early—though not as early as he would have on a work day. Light was beginning to filter through the small window in the corner, and he guessed it might be 6:00 a.m. or so. He looked around the room, replaying the previous day's events in his mind. He smiled when he got to the part about how they'd said good-night; there was a tiny twinge in the back of his head that suggested he should be ashamed of wanting so badly to be close to Jonah, but that voice was easily dismissed. He rolled over and watched Jonah sleep.

*Get a good rest,* he thought. *You'll need your strength.* He lay for a long while, watching the rise and fall of Jonah's breath, the twist and tension of the muscles in his back. Casey knew all of those muscles, and what function they served, having wrestled Jonah every single day in practice for the last four years. Now, though, they seemed softer, warmer. They were still powerful, but there was a beauty in their power he had never noticed.

Finally, when the better part of an hour had passed, Casey scooted closer to Jonah, until his chest was up against Jonah's back. He put his arm around his friend, and they lay there, breathing in effortless unison, for some time. Then Casey felt Jonah's breath grow more shallow, and he began to stir.

"Morning, sleepyhead," Casey murmured from behind, his head sharing Jonah's pillow.

"This is amazing," Jonah replied.

"What is?"

"I wake up every morning for eighteen years all alone, and the day after I finally figure out I'm gay, I wake up with the man of my dreams spooning me. Whatever fairy dust got sprinkled on me yesterday is the shit."

"Man of your dreams," snorted Casey. "You need better dreams, bud." He wrapped his arm tightly around Jonah and hugged him hard. "We should get up. Our police escorts will probably be here soon."

Jonah sat up, and Casey joined him. The bathrobes they had left at the foot of the bed the night before were gone, replaced by two stacks of neatly folded clothes. Bryce had laundered everything they had come to the city wearing and sometime in the night had brought it to them.

"Bryce is unbelievable," Jonah said.

"Yeah, I think if we tried to explain what he's like to the people back in Woodley, they wouldn't believe us. He's like a big gay unicorn—no one would think he actually exists."

"Guess we should get dressed." Jonah said. "You first."

"Why, so you can perv on me like in that video you're famous for?"

"Actually, the wake-up spooning kinda did it to me already," Jonah said sheepishly. "If you go first, it'll give me time to… recover."

"I don't think that will help," Casey replied with a laugh.

"Why not?

"Because if lying near me did that to you, just think what this will do!" He threw back the covers and sprang naked from the bed. He struck an antic series of impromptu poses, some sculptural and some obscene, before reaching for his underwear and beginning to get dressed.

"You are so weird," Jonah said, when he recovered from his laughter. "Hot, but weird."

"That's the winning combination I'm going for," Casey replied, hopping as he tried to get his other leg into his pants.

The boys were dressed and ready in short order and ventured into the quiet of the apartment to see if their hosts were awake. They found

Bryce in the kitchen, pushing buttons randomly on the coffeemaker. "Oh, good morning, my darling boys! Did you sleep well? Are your clothes satisfactory? Do you require coffee? Nestor's not awake yet, and I have no idea how he coaxes espresso from this fiendishly complicated machine. It was a gift from a delightfully generous older gentleman who imports coffee. He found that our dear Nestor's tongue is quite talented—for tasting coffees, you see."

"May I try my hand at it?" Casey asked. "I've been working in a cafe, and I think I can pull a shot or two."

"You may try your hand at pulling anything you like, dear boy. Anything you like."

Bryce stepped aside, and soon Casey was handing around steaming demitasses of espresso. Nestor appeared shortly after the aroma of coffee began to waft through the apartment.

"You have the gift," he murmured as he took in the steam from the cup Casey handed him. He slurped noisily, as a professional taster would. "Ai, this is very heaven!" He leaned over and kissed Casey on the cheek.

Casey beamed, pleased to have compensated his hosts in some small way for their hospitality.

The group was interrupted in their caffeine-induced swoon by the buzzing of the building intercom.

"Yes?" said Bryce into the tarnished brass faceplate of the device.

"It's Gabriel," the speaker crackled. "Have we come too early?"

"Oh dear, no! You are welcome to come any time you like. Third floor and enter at the rear, darlings." He pressed the button to open the door and then hurried off toward his bedroom. "Nestor! We must make ourselves presentable. One cannot entertain officers of the law with one's hair in disarray." The two men skittered off to the bedroom.

A knock at the door a moment later announced the arrival of Brandt and Donnelly. Casey worked out the locks and opened the door for them.

"Casey! Good to see you," Donnelly said as he stepped in. Brandt followed closely behind. All four exchanged greetings and handshakes.

"So this is Bryce and Nestor's palace," Brandt mused, looking about the tastefully fabulous space.

"They have been so nice to us," Jonah said. "They brought us here, fed us amazing food, and tucked us into bed. They have single-handedly restored my faith in humanity."

"That sounds like them," Brandt replied with a chuckle. "Always a helping hand for their fellow man."

"So how was your day?" asked Donnelly.

"It started out horrifying, but it got better once we got out of fucking Woodley," Jonah said. "By the end, it was amazing." He glanced at Casey, then back to Donnelly.

"Our boy here is the amazing one," Casey said proudly. "His dad was an absolute shit to him on the phone, and he stood his ground. We're here, he's queer, get used to it!"

"Sounds like you had an exciting day," Brandt said to Jonah.

"It was kind of epic, but it's mostly a blur. I think I'll be sorting it out for a while. But Casey has been amazing through it all." He beamed at his friend, who blushed to be praised so extravagantly.

"Stop in the name of the law!" Bryce flung open the bedroom door. He and Nestor emerged, perfectly coiffed and looking like they'd just stepped out of a magazine. "Always wanted to say that," he hooted as he embraced and air-kissed the officers.

"Thank you both for taking good care of Jonah and Casey," Brandt said.

"The pleasure was ours, of course," Bryce replied. "It does my heart good to see two such upstanding young men, supporting each other, snuggled so tightly together all night...." His voice trailed off dreamily. He was brought back to reality by the fierce stare of the police officers. "Oh, I simply delivered their laundry and happened to catch a glimpse of them... together."

Jonah studied the floor, while Casey blushed and looked sheepishly at Brandt and Donnelly. Gabriel raised an eyebrow, an amused smirk on his face, but said nothing.

"We should get these boys going," Brandt said. "Lots to get figured out today, right?"

Jonah nodded with a resigned sigh.

"Of course, of course," twittered Bryce. "Now, you"—he took both of Jonah's hands in his—"be strong, be fabulous, and above all be yourself." He looked into Jonah's eyes until the young man nodded. Then Bryce turned to Casey. "You are simply the best friend ever, and it thrills me to see how deeply you care. You have a journey ahead of you as well, take my word for it. Remember who you are."

"As always, you are dramatic and eloquent," Donnelly said with a laugh.

"And right, darling. I'm always right." Bryce winked at Casey.

"My people have a saying," Nestor said solemnly. "To be, one must first become." He looked at the confused faces surrounding him. "Perhaps it is clearer in my mother tongue." He shrugged and then smiled placidly.

"Thanks again, guys. We'll see you soon, I'm sure," Brandt said, opening the apartment door.

"You shall, you shall!" called Bryce as they made their way down the hall.


BRANDT HELD open the door of the diner for the other men to enter.

"Morning… officers…," breathed the elderly man at the first table. He was hooked up to an oxygen tank but wore a broad smile as he greeted Brandt and Donnelly like old friends.

"Good morning, Sarge," Donnelly replied. He stepped closer to the man's table. "How did it go yesterday?"

"Oh… you know… doctors…," the man wheezed. "But… I'll… live."

"Glad to hear it." Donnelly walked down the main aisle of the diner, which was long and narrow, with booths on one side next to railroad-style windows and a counter on the other. "Okay if we grab our usual, Shirley?"

"All yours, hon," the waitress called back.

The four settled into the booth, Casey and Jonah next to the windows with Brant and Donnelly, protectively, on the aisle side. Shirley brought two mugs and a pot of coffee to the table.

"You two want coffee?" she asked Casey and Jonah as she poured for Brandt and Donnelly.

"Yes, please," answered Casey.

"Just water for me, thanks," Jonah replied. Once Shirley had departed, he looked at Casey. "You already had that super strong espresso at Bryce and Nestor's, and now you're having more? You're an addict, buddy."

Casey shrugged. "There are worse things to be addicted to."

Shirley brought a mug for Casey, filled it with strong black coffee, and set a glass of water in front of Jonah. "Menu's up there," she said, jabbing a thumb behind her at the chalkboard above the counter. "I'll be back to take your order." She smiled at the men and walked to refill coffee cups around the diner.

"Nice place," Casey said as he reviewed the menu options.

"I kinda figured we'd be going somewhere on Alta Avenue," Jonah observed. "Isn't that where all the... friendly places are?"

Brandt and Donnelly shared a chuckle at the memory of how unfriendly this diner had been to them once upon a time.

"You know," Brandt answered, "places like Alta Avenue are great, especially when you're first coming to terms with being gay. But unless you decide to live your entire life in that one neighborhood, you're going to have to figure out how to make your way in the larger world."

"Ethan and I came here the first morning after we—" He looked at Brandt, seeming to search for the right word. "—began to redefine our relationship. It was awful. Everyone seemed to be looking at us, judging us, and some of them were downright rude. We thought we'd never come back. But after a while, I got angry that there were places we couldn't go as a couple, and we decided to try again. It wasn't the most welcoming place at first, but that's mostly because the folks here didn't think they knew any gay people. Once they saw we were just regular guys who happened to be together, they came around."

"The best way to win a gay-rights argument is simply to be out to the people in your life," Brandt said. "I know this sounds like a public-service announcement, but it should at least give you some hope. Even the most homophobic people can change if someone they know comes out to them."

Jonah nodded. It seemed a lot to take in.

"I just have one question," Casey said.

Gabriel smiled across the table at him. "You can ask us anything."

"Is it better to get bacon on the side or as part of the combo plate?"

The entire table broke into laughter, and they began to discuss the finer points of the diner's menu.

Once their breakfasts had been laid in front of them, and Casey and Jonah had tucked in the way eighteen-year-old athletes do, Brandt brought up the topic they all knew they needed to address.

"So, in the last twenty-four hours, we've been in contact with what I think is the entire population of Woodley." He looked at the young men. "Everyone's very worried about you two."

"Huh," Jonah said around a mouthful of waffle. He finished chewing and continued. "I didn't think my parents sounded all that worried."

"They have some issues to work through, that's obvious," Brandt replied. "But parents will always worry. And your mom"—he turned to Casey, next to him—"seemed to already know what an amazing friend you are, because nothing we told her seemed to surprise her in the least."

Casey shrugged his thanks at the compliment and continued demolishing his scrambled-egg platter.

"Also, Malcolm says he's struggling along without his baker, but he's getting by. And finally…." Brandt looked over at Jonah. "Coach Woody says you can take the week off practice if you need it, but he's got to have you back Monday in order for you to qualify for regionals."

Jonah set down his fork. "What?"

"He says you need to be back in practice next week, or you won't be able to compete at regionals."

"I thought…." Jonah looked around the table, confused. "Does he not know about the latest video?"

"Oh, he knows," said Donnelly. "He was pissed. He seemed such an even-keel kind of guy, but he was furious."

"Then why does he still want me on the team?"

"He's not mad at you, Jonah," replied Donnelly. "He's angry about the videos. He sounded ready to kill whoever's responsible."

Jonah sat, stunned. Casey took up the conversation.

"Did he see the video? Did he see my boner?" Casey asked.

"It was my boner, remember?" Jonah said, the expression of confusion deepening on his face.

"Technically, it was," Casey replied, a hint of a grin playing on his face. "But I caused it, so I'm just going to call it mine."

Jonah rolled his eyes.

"Yes, he's seen all three videos," Brandt said. "We made sure he did, just in case he might see anything in them that would help us figure out who made them."

"And he still wants Jonah on the team?"

"Says that the team's chances for a state championship depend on him," Donnelly answered.

Casey nodded and mulled over this new information. "Okay, so here's what we're going to do."

"This should be good," Jonah said with a tinge of sarcasm that was softened by a smile.

"We head back to Woodley, and you come stay at my house. Take the week off from school and practice and let the video thing die down. Then you walk into that school on Monday morning, and anyone who wants to give you shit can fuck the fuck off. Sound like a plan?"

Jonah considered this. "Not sure it's worth it, especially if I'm not really up for scholarships anymore. Why wrestle if it's not going to get me to college?"

Brandt took this one. "You don't know how the recruiters are going to react. They could ignore it like everyone else is probably going to. You may just need to wait it out for a week or two."

Jonah looked around the table, from face to face. "I can't believe this," he said, softly. "I thought my life was over—that everything I was and was going to be was over." He wiped his eyes. "But now, all of you have put the pieces back together. Aside from my dad being an asshole, life can almost get back to the way it was. That's... well, that's just fucking amazing is what that is."

Casey reached across the table and took Jonah's hand. "Not everything is the way it was," he said, reminding Jonah with that simple phrase of how very much his life had changed.

Jonah beamed at his friend. "Thank you," he whispered.

"Perhaps you should ask your mom if the plan is okay with her," Donnelly suggested to Casey.

"Oh, I already did. Texted her this morning while I brushed my teeth. She's totally on board." He turned to Jonah. "She just loves Jonah, and the idea of stealing him out from under his churchy parents is a bonus."

"It's a plan, then," said Brandt. "And we'll continue to investigate the source of the videos. If we can just keep any more from coming out, we can give you guys the room to pull your lives back together."

"I for one would be happy to never appear in another video," Jonah said as he mopped the syrup off his plate with a last bite of waffle. He pointed at Donnelly's plate. "Gonna eat that sausage?"

"All yours, chief," Donnelly said with a laugh as he pushed his plate across the table.

# CHAPTER FIVE
# BACK TO WOODLEY

AFTER BREAKFAST the officers dropped the boys off at Casey's car outside Bryce and Nestor's apartment.

"Call us if you need anything," Brandt said as they stood by Casey's car.

"Anything," Donnelly emphasized, and he pulled Jonah into a hug that appeared to surprise them both. But Jonah closed his eyes and seemed to soak in the security of the officer's embrace.

"Thank you," Jonah said after Donnelly had opened his arms.

Donnelly nodded, a simple gesture that communicated a great deal.

"Let's saddle up," Casey called, unlocking his car doors. They climbed in and were soon driving out of the city and through its northern suburbs.

"Didn't think we'd be heading back to Woodley so soon. I kind of thought my life there was over," Jonah said.

"Sometimes it can seem like everything's changed, but when you have a chance to take a breath, turns out it's not all that different after all."

"There's a lot about Woodley I think should be different, though," Jonah mused, looking out the window at the landscape sliding by.

"Like what?"

"Like how they cancelled the prom last year because that girl wanted to bring her girlfriend from another school as her date."

"Yeah, that wasn't Woodley High's finest moment," Casey agreed.

"Or that ridiculous sex-ed thing they inflict on us every year—where they invite local churches to send in their abstinence troops? Not only do they never even use the word 'condom,' they keep saying sex is a gift from God that only a married man and woman can open. Kinda leaves me out, doesn't it?"

"I guess we're on our own to figure out the gay-sex thing, right?"

"We?"

Casey giggled. "You, I mean. Sorry."

"Yeah, me too," Jonah said, quietly.

They pulled into Woodley around noon.

"Can we stop by my house and see if anyone's home?" Jonah asked. "Maybe I can pick up some clothes and stuff."

"Sure. Do you want me to drive past and we'll check the driveway for cars?"

"Sounds good."

They turned into Jonah's neighborhood, where it seemed that every other house was for sale or already foreclosed. Jonah's street was one of the nicer ones, near the golf course, but it was not immune from the effects of the downturn; there were several empty houses with overgrown lawns along their route. Casey slowed as they neared his friend's home.

They had hoped to find an empty driveway, but instead they saw both his father's work truck and his mother's hatchback, as well as another car they didn't recognize—a large maroon sedan.

Casey drove smoothly past. "Who was that, you think?"

"I don't know. But it must be pretty important if they're home in the middle of the day." Jonah seemed lost in thought for a moment. "I wonder if it's a recruiter from one of the universities."

"You might want to check your phone, see if they've tried to get in touch." Casey had been trying to find a way to suggest this all morning.

Jonah shrugged and then opened the glove box and pulled out his phone.

"Still have battery?" Casey asked.

"Yeah. I turned it off yesterday. Didn't want them tracking me. I'm on their rate plan, so they can use that family finder thing to locate me if they want to. Now that we're back in Woodley, I guess it doesn't matter." He switched the phone on and waited for messages to come in. "Holy fuck," he said under his breath.

"What is it?"

Jonah held up his phone. "Can you believe every single one of these people thought I would want to know there was a video of me going around? I must have gotten texts from like a hundred different people."

"Is that a good thing or a bad thing?"

Jonah chuckled grimly. "I think when someone's texting you that there's a boner video of you going around, it doesn't really matter whether they throw in a happy face or a sad one—your boner's still on their damn phone."

Casey laughed at his friend's black humor. It seemed like a good sign.

"Okay, so, we'll go to my place. We'll get you settled, and then I really should go help Mal out."

Jonah nodded, and Casey headed across town, a trip that took three minutes. Casey's family had been Woodley's version of old money, but they had long since fallen on hard times. His dad left when he was young, and it was just his mom and him now in the tiny cottage that used to be the boathouse on the estate. The old mansion had been turned into a lawyer's office and the rest of the property sold off in pieces. The boathouse and its small lake frontage was the last remnant of the family's holdings. His mom worked exhausting hours managing the drugstore out by the highway to make ends meet, and Casey helped out by contributing most of his money from the job at Mal's cafe. She insisted that he keep enough to buy gas and insurance on his car, which she viewed as an essential expense in a town this small and remote.

"*Mi casa es su casa*," Casey said as they walked up the steps to the door of the boathouse. He opened it, and they stepped in. Jonah had been here hundreds of times, of course, but this time felt different. It wasn't just his friend's house, it was his refuge. He took a deep breath of the still and slightly damp air of the snug bungalow.

"Lunch?" Casey asked, swinging open the fridge door and peering inside.

"Nah. Not really hungry, thanks." Jonah sat on the small sofa that faced the television in the tiny living room.

Casey came and sat down next to him. When no more words were forthcoming, he nudged Jonah with his shoulder. Still nothing. "What's up, buddy?"

"You're all I've got," Jonah replied quietly. "All I have in the world."

"That's not true," Casey said gently. "You are still on the team, and that means you still have a great shot at a scholarship. Full ride to college and whatever the hell you want after that. You've got a huge future, man!"

Jonah shook his head. "All of that is pretty far away. When I look at what I have, right now, in my entire life, it's you. I don't even have a toothbrush to call my own."

"Mom's going to pick up some stuff for you tonight from the drugstore. You'll be all set."

"Thanks. You and your mom are awesome to do this."

They sat in silence for a long moment. Finally, Jonah turned to face Casey, look in his eyes. "You are... everything to me," he whispered.

"Shh," Casey replied. He leaned toward his friend, thinking he would put an arm around him, jostle his spirits up, but instead he found himself leaning farther, farther, until finally his lips met Jonah's. They kissed.

Jonah gasped and pulled back. Casey sat back on his side of the sofa, desperately confused about what he had just done.

"Um," he said. "I—I should get going. I'm sure Mal needs me." He bolted up but then walked haltingly to the door. "I'll be home before dinner. Just, um, make yourself, um, comfortable." Casey stood at the door, stealing quick glances at the shocked and silent Jonah. "Okay," he said, in response to what he wasn't sure, and he walked out of the house.

*What the fuck was that?* Casey sat in the car for a long moment, unable to answer this question. He drove toward the road, shaking his head in confusion.

"WELL, YOU'RE here early!" called Malcolm when he saw Casey come through the door. "Shouldn't you still be in school?"

"Yeah, kind of skipped that again today. But I wanted to make it up to you, being gone yesterday and this morning."

Malcolm rang up his last lunch customer and tossed Casey an apron. "Good to see you. How's Jonah?"

Casey knew he should have been ready for this question, but it somehow blindsided him. "He's... good? I think? He's been through a lot, but I think he's going to be okay. I guess." He looked around the cafe. "Where should I start?"

"You can start by sitting down and letting me make you a coffee. You're looking kind of dazed."

Casey grunted. "Heh. I guess I am a little stressed right now. Thanks," he said as he pulled out a chair and sank into it.

Malcolm brought over two mugs of steaming black liquid. "Four sugars, like you like it," he said with a grin as he set one of the mugs in front of Casey. "So, want to talk about it?"

Casey took a long, thoughtful sip of his coffee. He set it down and looked at Malcolm. "How did you know you were gay?"

Malcolm nearly spit out his mouthful of coffee. He swallowed the burning liquid, squinting at the discomfort, and then took a ragged breath. "Oh, okay. So. Um.... Well...." He looked at Casey, with a look of confusion on his face. "Why do you ask?"

"It sounds stupid for me to say I have a friend who's figured out he's gay, but I really do." He leaned close, in case any of the elderly clientele might have their hearing aids turned up to "eavesdrop" level. "It's Jonah," he whispered.

Malcolm nodded. "I see. Wow, when he has a crisis, he really goes all out, doesn't he?"

Casey chuckled, relieved to have Mal take this news so easily. "Yup. Internet boner video, parents throw him out of the house, might as well be gay, right? Why not?" Casey sipped his coffee and shook his head. "How did you do it?"

"Well, I knew from a really early age. All of the classic signs—loved musicals and dress-up, played with girls rather than boys, definitely Team Jacob." He laughed. "When I came out no one was really surprised. Except my girlfriend."

It was Casey's turn to nearly spit his coffee. "Your what, now?" he asked.

"Yes, I had a girlfriend. It was high school—I'm sure you understand as well as anyone the pressures you're under in those years."

"So, even though you knew you were gay, you still had a girlfriend?" Casey shook his head. "What was up with that?"

"You can know something inside yourself, but not know how to live it on the outside. This sounds crazy, I know, but I convinced myself that what I knew about myself wasn't what I really was, and if I lived the way people expected me to, then I would actually be like other people, and this difference I felt inside would go away." He shrugged. "Humans are pretty fucked up when it comes to sex."

"So what Jonah's doing is trying to figure out how to make his outsides match his insides?"

Malcolm nodded. "That sounds about right," he said.

"Like, before he can be, he needs to become."

Malcolm smiled and nodded again. "That's very profound, Casey."

"A friend of mine said it, and I had no idea what it meant. Now I think I see." He slugged back his coffee and stood. "Thanks, Mal. This helps a lot. Now, what can I do before I need to leave for practice?"


IT WAS after six o'clock by the time Casey pulled into the driveway of the boathouse. His mom was home already, and the smell of dinner cooking wafted out to greet the returning wrestler.

"Hey, guys!" Casey called as he threw the door open and barreled into the living room. "Mom, that smells amazing."

"Wanted to make something special, to mark the occasion," she said, smiling warmly at her son.

"Where's the guest of honor?" Casey asked. Jonah's absence worried him after the way they had parted earlier.

"He's in your bedroom. He came out to help me unload the car, but then asked if he could go lie down. Poor fella. Looks like he's really been through a lot."

"He's not through it yet, either. But I have a feeling things are going to turn around for him soon." Casey kissed his mother on the cheek. "Thanks for letting him stay with us."

"It's no trouble at all," she replied, kissing him on the cheek in return. "He's such a good kid, and I know how much he means to you."

Casey stopped to consider this. "Do you?"

"I do." She tipped her head at him in that knowing way moms have. "Do you?"

He laughed but then saw how serious she was. He looked down at his hands, which clasped and unclasped nervously and without purpose. "I think I do," he said softly.

She smiled at him—the kind of smile he expected when he won a match or aced a test. "Good." She kissed him again, this time on the forehead. "Go be with him. I'll call you for dinner."

"Thanks, Mom." He walked to the bedroom door and knocked. "Jonah?"

"Come on in, it's your room," Jonah replied.

Casey entered, closing the door behind him. Jonah lay on the bed, looking out the windows at the lake. Casey sat down on the other side of the bed. They were silent for a long moment.

"Mom's making something amazing for dinner," Casey said, not knowing how else to break the silence.

"That's great," Jonah said, without perceptible emotion in his voice.

"Jonah, what's wrong?"

Jonah finally looked away from the lake, turning his eyes to Casey without really focusing on him. "You kissed me."

Casey's cheeks were instantly on fire, his mouth parched. He had no idea what to say, assuming he could even make a noise at all.

"Is what I'm going through a joke to you all of a sudden?" Jonah asked, his voice haunted, hurt.

"No!" Casey shook his head violently. "Why would you even say that?"

"I'm trying to figure out what this all means, and ever since that boner video, you've been all over me. That lying together stuff at the lake was nice and all, but then again last night, when we were naked? And then snuggling up this morning? And as if I'm not confused enough by the whole thing, then you kiss me? It's like you're rubbing it in my face that I got wood from being near you. Like you have this power over me, and you're going to remind me every chance you get that you can make me do what you want because of it. I thought you were being supportive, but now it looks like you're just being cruel."

Casey gaped and stammered. "I... I have no idea what you're talking about."

"I'll tell you what I'm talking about." Jonah's voice was choked with misery. He sat up and turned a tearful face toward Casey. "I'm talking about you taking advantage of the fact that I'm in love with you."

"You're... what?"

"In love. With you. And now that you know... you're just teasing me. Do you get some kind of thrill out of making me crazy? Fooling me into thinking you might feel the same way? That's fucked up, man, that's what that is."

Jonah stopped his halting monologue to look fiercely into Casey's face. He recoiled. "What the fuck? Why are you smiling?"

"You got that from a kiss? That I'm bent on destroying you, now I know your secret? That I'm a tease who gets turned on because you want me, but will never let you have me? You got all of that out of a kiss?"

"What else could I get out of it? Why else would you do it?"

Casey shrugged. "I did it because I wanted to do it, I guess. Didn't even know I was going to do it until I did it. And honestly, I wasn't thinking at all about how you would react to it. I did it for me. Just like I did all of those other things—for me. Because I wanted to be close to you. Because I needed you to know that even though your life has kind of gone to crap lately, I am here, and I will always be here. I tried to tell you that, but I couldn't be sure you would hear me. So I showed you instead. I wasn't teasing you. Everything I did I did because I love you."

Jonah closed his eyes as if he'd heard nails on a chalkboard. Tears squeezed out, running down his cheeks. "But you don't love me the way I love you."

"How can you say that?"

"Because of who we are. I'm not who I was a week ago, looking at you and hoping you don't notice. I know who I am now, and that's pretty much fucked up everything else in my life, except for you. Only you. But I have to live every day knowing you can never love me the way I love you." He paused to wipe the tears from his eyes. "I want what Ethan and Gabriel have. I want a friend and a partner and a lover, and I want them all to be the same person. I want them all to be you. And the one thing I want more than anything in life, I can't have."

"Why? Why can't you have it?"

"Because you're straight, Casey."

Casey shook his head in frustration. "I'm just going to say this once. I love you. And when I say I love you, what I mean is I love you. That's it. I don't care what you or anyone thinks it means—to me it's dead simple. I. Love. You. I would take a bullet for you. I would run in front of a train for you. I would do anything for you. Because nothing means anything to me unless you are okay. I know you're going through some shit right now, and I'm trying my hardest to help. But please for God's sake don't push me away because you think my love for you is the wrong kind. I don't believe there is such a thing, and neither should you." He concluded his tirade, and sat, panting slightly, looking at Jonah.

"Casey? Jonah? Dinner!" Casey's mother called from the kitchen.

"Coming, Mom!" Casey called back. "Now," he said to Jonah. "I want you to stop this moping around about who loves who and how.

Chill the fuck out and enjoy the fact that even when your stupid family can't see how amazing you are, I can. And so can my mom, which counts for double because she's old and she knows things. Now let's go have some dinner, okay?" He sprang up from the bed and held the door open.

Jonah got up from the bed and managed a smile as he passed Casey on the way to the kitchen.

"WELL, IT'S nice to see that in all of the chaos that's been inflicted on you, your appetites remain intact," Casey's mother observed as she surveyed the aftermath of dinner.

"That was delicious, as always," Jonah said.

"And it was a pleasure to share it with you, as always," she replied. "Now, you boys have missed two days of school, so you should probably hit the books, right?"

Jonah sighed. "All of my books are at my... my parents' house."

"Too bad we can't share," Casey said with a frowny face. "It's not like we're in all of the same classes or anything."

"Well, you two shouldn't stay up too late knocking your heads together over your textbooks," Casey's mom said with a laugh as she began to clear the table.

"No, let us do that," Jonah said, rising quickly and taking the plates from her hand.

"Us?" Casey cried. "Nice of you to enlist me in your chivalry."

"I'll even let you choose wash or dry," Jonah replied as he took the three steps from the table to the kitchen sink.

"So generous, you are." Casey picked up a towel and took up his station at the counter. Then he snapped Jonah's backside with it. "Get a move on, you! I'm waiting to dry things!"

Jonah danced out of range of Casey's snapping towel and continued to stack the dinner dishes on the counter. Both boys laughed boisterously as the washing up began in earnest.

"I'm going to turn in," Casey's mom said. "I have to open the store at six tomorrow." She kissed Casey's cheek and then kissed Jonah as well.

"Good-night, Mom," the boys said in unison.

She chuckled at them and retired to her bedroom for the night.

After washing and drying the dishes, Casey and Jonah broke out the books at the kitchen table. Though they hadn't been in school for two days, they had several projects underway that they could continue working on. They applied themselves to it for two hours, until Casey yawned noisily.

"I should turn in. Gotta be at the cafe by four thirty."

"I don't know how you do it," Jonah replied. "I have a hard enough time getting up at seven to get to school on time."

"How about I wake you up at four, and you can experience the magic?"

"Good luck with that. I've slept through alarm clocks louder than any sound you know how to make."

"There are ways I could get you up," Casey said with a wink as he stood and gathered up his work. They stowed his books and laptop on the shelves in his room.

"Let me show you where everything is in the bathroom," Casey said, motioning for Jonah to follow. One of the great luxuries of this tiny home was that each of the bedrooms, occupying opposite ends of the house, had its own bathroom. Casey's wasn't directly connected to his bedroom, but it was just next door. This way it could be used for guests as well as his own purposes.

"Here's a toothbrush, that weird toothpaste you like, and here's soap for your face. The rest of the stuff you already know. Towels are back here"—he pointed to a shelf over the toilet— "and soap, shampoo, and conditioner are in the shower."

"Where's the drawer with all the lube and condoms?" Jonah asked with a barely contained giggle.

"Yeah, I'll add that to Mom's shopping list for tomorrow," Casey replied with a roll of his eyes.

Jonah started brushing his teeth; it wasn't until he spat and looked in the mirror that he saw Casey stripping off his clothes behind him. "Dude, what the hell?"

"I'm gonna grab a quick shower. There's not enough time in the morning to do it before I race out of here for Mal's." He reached in and turned on the water and then slipped his boxers to the floor before stepping in. He noticed Jonah staring at him in the mirror. "What?"

"Casey, you're naked."

"That's how most people shower, buddy. Or maybe you weren't aware of that." Casey smacked himself upside the head. "Oh, that's right, I've seen your videos—you know all about being naked." He swiped the shower curtain shut with a manic flourish.

Jonah went back to brushing his teeth while his friend splashed and sang on the other side of the curtain.

"I just realized—I don't have anything to wear," Jonah said over the din of the water.

Casey pulled the curtain open at the end of the tub and poked his head out. "We share clothes all the time. You can wear anything you find in my room. Oh, I have an idea! Come here and I'll tell you." He motioned for Jonah to come closer.

"What is—hey," Jonah yelled. "What are you doing? Stop that!"

Casey had grabbed his arm and was pulling him into the shower. Jonah fell awkwardly against the tub, but Casey wasn't letting go, so he stepped clumsily over the tall tub's side and into the water so he wouldn't fall over completely. He tried to step back out, but Casey had a strong grip on him and wasn't letting go. Finally Jonah gave up and flopped into the tub. Casey was laughing raucously.

"What the fuck?" Jonah demanded. The shower spray was soaking through his clothes as he struggled to get to his feet.

"Up ya go," Casey said, helping Jonah to his feet. "There. All better."

"Except for the part where my clothes are completely soaked and stuck to me. What the hell?"

"You know, you're right," Casey said, as if this hadn't occurred to him. "We'd better fix that." He pulled at the hem of Jonah's shirt, and by the time he had it halfway off, Jonah was so tangled in the wet fabric that he could no longer struggle to keep Casey from taking it off. "Good. Looks like you've got the shirt under control. I'll take care of the rest." Casey unbuttoned Jonah's jeans, unzipped them, pulled them open, and pulled them down. All the while Jonah wrestled to free himself of the wet shirt, which had become a straitjacket.

"Stop that!" he demanded, turning away from Casey so he couldn't reach the front of Jonah's jeans anymore. It was too late to do any good, of course, and Casey simply shucked them the rest of the way to his ankles.

"And these have to go, of course," Casey said, slipping his thumbs into the waistband of Jonah's soaking-wet boxer shorts. With a giddy hoot, he slid them down Jonah's muscled legs to join his jeans around his ankles. Casey bent down and tugged at Jonah's left foot. "Lift," he said, and Jonah, just now beginning to fight his way out of his shirt, couldn't resist when Casey nudged him to the side, threatening to tip him over. "And lift," Casey said, tugging the jeans and boxers off his other foot. He grabbed the shirt as soon as Jonah wrestled free of it, and with a wet sloppy plop, the clothes met the bathroom floor.

"There. That's better, right?" Casey said cheerily.

"What. The fuck. Are you doing?" Jonah asked, his voice deadly.

"I'm taking a shower. You were worried about your clothes, so now they're halfway to being clean, right? And I was worried about sharing a bed with a smelly wrestler, and so both of our problems have been solved." He paused, waiting for a reaction. He got none. "You're welcome."

Jonah shook his head. "Can I get out now?" he asked, his voice angry.

"But you haven't washed up. Come here, I'll step aside, and you can have the water."

"I'm not going to turn around."

"Why not? The whole point of a shower is to get under the water."

"It would not be a good idea for me to turn around right now." Jonah bit off each word distinctly, with ferocious calm.

"Jonah," Casey replied, suddenly serious. "I know why you don't want to turn around. And I'm telling you, you can."

"I don't want you to see me this way," Jonah replied, a plaintive tone making itself heard in his voice.

"It's nothing you won't see too, if you turn around."

Jonah froze. He seemed to Casey to not even be breathing. Slowly he began to turn, his eyes closed. Casey saw what he expected, and what Jonah dreaded. Jonah was fully erect from Casey's shower play. But when Jonah opened his eyes, he saw Casey was telling the truth when he said Jonah would see the same.

In the steam and spray, they faced each other, their erections already nearly vertical. As the young men stared at each other's comprehensive nudity, their penises, bobbing slightly with each pounding pulse of their hearts, rose to point directly to the ceiling as if they drew strength from each other.

"Dude," Jonah exhaled, looking from Casey's wide and surprised eyes to his cock and back again.

Casey did the only thing he could think of to do. He opened his arms and said the words that had become an incantation over the last two days: "Come here."

This time, Jonah didn't argue. He didn't even seem to think about it. This time, Jonah came.

They embraced, feeling for the first time the full contact of their bodies, knees and hips and pectorals and penises, and lips to neck and then lips to cheeks and then lips to lips and they were joined.

Casey brought his hands up to Jonah's neck and felt the strong muscles he knew so well. The entire landscape of Jonah's body he knew better than anyone, probably better than Jonah himself, but at this moment it all felt new, completely undiscovered. And hot. And wet. He suddenly felt light in the head.

"Oh my God," he gasped when he pulled his lips from Jonah's.

"Casey, why are you doing this?" Jonah asked, his voice rough and thick.

Casey laid his hands on the side of Jonah's head, holding him in place so he could drive this meaning into him, by force if necessary. "Because I love you. I love you because you're my best friend, and I love you because it feels fucking amazing to be right here with you, holding you, pressed up against you. I love you because our dicks agree with each other that this is what they want, and why argue with biology?"

Jonah closed his eyes and pressed his head into Casey's hand, as if he were trying to convince himself this was really happening. "I never knew it could be like this," he murmured.

"Seriously? I thought every gay man in the world dreamed about being in the shower with me. I'm not sure you're doing it right if you never knew it could be like this."

Jonah smiled and opened his eyes. "I'm being serious. Everyone makes coming out seem like this huge deal, like everything in your life is going to change. But it's just this. We've showered next to each other for years, and now we're three feet closer together. Boom—easy as that. You're a fucking miracle worker, you know that?"

"Wait till you see what comes next," Casey said with a laugh, and he reached down to pick up a bottle of body wash. He flipped open the lid and squirted a fat bead of the pearly liquid all over them. He set the bottle down and then began a primitive but effective dance of obscene friction, rubbing the front of his body up and down Jonah's, building up a stiff head of froth between them. The packed muscle of their torsos slid and slurped against each other while their cocks jousted in their slick frenzy. Casey's hands slid down Jonah's strong back until they reached his buttocks; honed from years of wrestling, these compact globes of muscle fit almost entirely within Casey's hands. He squeezed and pulled, bringing Jonah into even more forceful contact with his own body.

"Fuck," Jonah huffed, bracing himself against the wall behind Casey to keep from toppling completely over. He lunged at Casey's mouth, their tongues writhing, battling each other for dominance. Finally they broke, panting.

"I've had my hands on every inch of your body, but it was never like this," Casey growled.

"We've never been wet and soapy like this before. Plus, kissing. That automatically makes it awesome." Jonah's smile was broad and genuine and like nothing Casey had seen for more than a week.

Casey looked his friend in the eye. "I want you. In my bed. Right now."

"Try and stop me," Jonah growled back, and he began to sluice the soap off of his body, and Casey's body, and all of the places where their bodies touched.

"This is my lucky day," Casey said with a giggle. "That line never works with chicks."

Jonah kissed him again. "Yeah, can't imagine what's up with that. But it's what I've been waiting to hear for more years than I can count."

Casey froze and looked at his friend with the peaked eyebrows of flattery mixed with empathy. "You've really wanted this, all that time? Wanted me?"

"You're the only one I've ever wanted," Jonah replied, his low voice just above a whisper.

"That is both the sweetest and the sexiest thing I've ever heard," Casey said. "Let's get the fuck out of this shower so we can go do something romantic and very, very dirty."

"If you insist," Jonah replied with a smile and another kiss. He reached out and grabbed a towel, with which he began to dry Casey's wet body. He rubbed and teased and caressed until Casey was thrumming with want.

"My turn," Casey announced, and he grabbed a second towel and dried Jonah with as much care and perhaps an even more insistent rubbing in certain areas.

The boys tiptoed naked from the bathroom to Casey's bedroom, and they giggled giddily when they had made the short trip without getting caught. They stood before the bed they had shared so many times as friends, and were now about to share, for the first time, as something more. Much more.

Jonah turned to his buddy. "Not sure how your mom would feel about this little slumber party if she knew about us."

Casey chuckled. "I think she knew about us before we did. Seems like she's fine with it. But just to be safe, let's not give her any details, okay?"

"Agreed."

Casey pulled open the covers of his bed and slipped between the sheets. He slid over to the far side and turned back to Jonah. He patted the bed next to him and said the words that had worked magic for him every time he had uttered them. "Come here."

Jonah smiled somewhat bashfully and sat gingerly on the bed, then swiveled around and lay next to Casey. His reserve evaporated in an instant, and he recklessly pressed himself up against his best friend. He put his arm around Casey, pulled him close. "Kiss me," he whispered.

Casey put his hands around the back of Jonah's neck, running his fingertips in slow, tingling spirals in the velvety short hair, cropped close by Woodley's only barber. He pulled Jonah into him, onto his open and waiting lips, and they kissed so softly and gently that Casey wondered how he had survived not having this feeling in his life before now. Far too soon, Jonah pulled away.

"What's wrong?" Casey asked.

"This is just... too...." Jonah's voice faltered, and he swallowed hard. "Too perfect. I dreamed of this for so long, but now that it's actually happening, it's so much... more than I imagined." He kissed Casey again, and again.

"What did you imagine?"

"When I used to lie here, watching you sleep, I would dream that something would wake you up suddenly, and your eyes would snap open. You would see me looking at you, and you would realize you loved me."

"And then what?" Casey asked. He had his arm slung over Jonah's side and was gently stroking up and down the ridged oblique muscles that swept around from his spine to his ribs.

"And then you would kiss me and whisper in my ear that you loved me, and then...."

Casey's eyes widened. "And then... what?"

Jonah grinned. "And then I would be so rock hard that I would have to slip out of bed and tug one out in the bathroom so I could keep myself from spooging all over you, that's what."

Casey mirrored Jonah's sly grin. "Show me."

Jonah's grin turned into an expression of alarm. "Show you what?"

"Show me how you would do it."

"You want me to... right now?"

Casey's grin widened, and grew even more devilish. "Right here, right now. Show me what I made you do."

Jonah's eyebrows shot up in shock, but Casey could also feel a surge in the hard cock pressed against his hip. He knew he had him.

"Do it," he growled. "Right now."

Jonah's hand slid haltingly down his body, but his eyes never left Casey's. "This is so... dirty," he whispered.

"And that's what makes it fun," Casey whispered back. He kissed Jonah again, just to remind him that he had promised romance as well. Then he kissed along his friend's cheek, soon arriving at his ear. "I love you," he whispered, his breath hot in Jonah's ear.

"Oh, fuck," murmured Jonah, as he wrapped his hand around his hard cock.

"Show me," Casey urged. "Show me what I made you do."

Jonah's hand slid slowly along the length of his penis as a sigh escaped his lips. It was the sigh that pulled Casey in.

"God, you are so hot," he whispered as he laid hold of his own throbbing member. He stroked in perfect unison with Jonah, their hands coming to rest against their hard lower bellies at the same moment, then sliding out to their flared cock heads in perfect coordination. "I swear, if I had ever woken up and found you doing this, I would have joined right in. You look so hot right now—your muscles are pumped up, and your nipples are hard, and that cock. How did I not know you had that monster tucked into your singlet?"

"Fuck," huffed Jonah. "You're pretty damn good at dirty talk."

"It's more than talk," Casey replied, and he pushed his own cock straight out from his body, touching it to the head of Jonah's hard cock, glossed now with precum.

Jonah moaned and looked down where the most intimate parts of their bodies were in contact. He pressed his own cock forward, sliding it along the length of Casey's. Casey felt the slippery, sticky transit of hard flesh against his own and joined Jonah in his moaning.

"Tell me what happened next," Casey breathed, desperation in his voice.

"I would whisper your name with every shot," Jonah murmured. "It was like a spell I cast, so you would know, magically, how I felt about you."

"Do it for me," Casey's voice rumbled, choked with a savage lust. "Do it so I know."

Jonah's gasped, and gave a small cry. Casey felt his hand stop moving, as if Jonah was trying to stop the inevitable.

In this he failed.

"Oh, Casey," Jonah sighed. He jerked as if shocked by electricity. "Oh, Casey, oh fuck, Casey, Casey," he chanted under his breath.

Casey felt the first rope of semen splash against his hip, hot and wet and powerful. The next two laced his own cock with strands of cum, and his hand slid freely along his own cock, slicked by Jonah's ejaculate. "Fuck, Jonah," he whispered. "Unh, Jonah, Jonah.... Jonah," he murmured, as his own load blasted across the six inches that separated them.

Their mutual spray spurred them on to a wild ecstasy of spasming orgasm; each blasted the other with widely scattered streaks of semen from chin to kneecaps. Years of pent-up tension, of attraction denied and completion deferred, broke free and made themselves known in each dripping streak of white passion.

They shivered with thrill and exertion. They were very wet.

Casey looked wide-eyed at his best friend, took him in from feet through privates, and on up to his panting face. "Kiss me," he croaked, his voice roughened by passion.

Jonah's face, as shell-shocked as Casey's by the passion they had unleashed, softened immediately into love-struck adoration, and he kissed his best friend without reserve because what did he have to hold back now? They had shared everything, knew everything now about each other, knew it and loved it entire. They kissed as the evidence of their furiously realized love cooled on their bodies.

"I think we might want to take another shower," Casey whispered. "You kind of made a mess."

"I've been saving up for years," Jonah said with an apologetic shrug.

"It was totally worth the wait," Casey replied with a smile and a kiss. "Now let's hit the shower—I have to get up in a couple of hours."

Jonah held his hand to keep him in bed a moment longer. "Promise me something," he said softly.

"Anything," Casey said, and he meant it.

"That this isn't a dream. That when we get up from this bed, the magic won't suddenly end and we'll go back to the way things were." Jonah sounded genuinely frightened by this prospect.

Casey smiled and took Jonah's face in his hands. "I promise you, nothing will go back to the way it was. We're different now. This is what we are." He gestured to their semen-streaked bodies. He laughed at the giddy obscenity of the scene they had made. "And now that we are, we can't go back to what we were before. As Nestor would say, we have no choice but to be what we have become."

Jonah gasped. "That's beautiful!" He looked at Casey with welling eyes. "I didn't think it possible to love you more than I did before. But now it feels like I've just begun." He kissed Casey again, with a desperate energy that gave Casey a chill.

"Now you know what I meant by 'I love you,'" Casey said. "And this is only the beginning."

They sat, lovestruck, for several long minutes, and then they rose, together, and walked quietly to the bathroom to wash up. And make out some more.

Lots more.

# CHAPTER SIX
# BOYS ON FILM

"OFFICER BRANDT, it's Chief Powell, from Woodley?"

"Woodley? Right. What is it, chief?" It was barely 5:00 a.m., and Brandt had been sleeping soundly next to Donnelly, who was still sleeping soundly.

"There's another video."

"Shit," Brandt muttered. This woke Donnelly up instantly; the loud clanging ringtone Brandt used had no power to disturb his slumber, but a half-spoken swear word had him bolt upright.

"I hate to impose on you, but do you think you could come up this morning and help us get a handle on this thing? This new one's a bit different."

"Shit, shit, shit," Brandt cursed, his hand over the phone's mic. "Sure, Chief. We can be there by, say, eight?"

"Ugh," Donnelly expectorated and then pulled a pillow over his face.

"That would be a great help to us, son. Thank you." The line went dead.

"What is it this time?" Donnelly asked from under the pillow.

"He said there's a new video. Didn't get any other details, but he sounded as mad as I've heard him."

"Well, that's saying something when it's Powell we're talking about," mused Donnelly, throwing the pillow off his head. He pulled back the covers and stepped out of bed. "I'll get the coffee going; you start some hot water in the shower. We'll meet in 5 minutes and pour both all over us, okay?"

Brandt smiled at his partner. "You're beautiful."

Donnelly rolled his eyes. "I'm still half asleep. I'm probably hideous."

Brandt shook his head. "You are rumpled and naked and your morning wood is making me drool a little," he said. "But duty calls, my love."

"Fucking tease," groused Donnelly. He grinned at his partner and stalked from the room with an extra swing in his hips that made the aforementioned morning wood dance like a sailor on shore leave.

After their shower and several cups of coffee, the men each packed a bag—the chances of running into complications in Woodley seemed high, and driving back and forth was getting a little tiresome. They would be able to stay in Woodley through Friday if they needed to. They hoped they wouldn't need to.

At just before eight they pulled into Woodley. Again.

"The rate we're commuting, we might as well live here," Donnelly grumbled.

"You just want to get your Frequent Flirter card punched by Malcolm," teased Brandt with a good-natured grin. He pulled the car up in front of the cafe.

"Morning, Malcolm," called Donnelly as they entered the cafe. The morning rush was in full swing; Malcolm darted back and forth behind the counter getting drinks and serving up scones and muffins.

"Gabriel! Ethan! Good to see you. But I imagine since you're in Woodley before 8:00 a.m., you're not here for fun."

"Got that right," answered Donnelly. "Gotta meet Powell at eight. Need some caffeine to power through it."

"Well, here you go," Malcolm said cheerily as he passed over two cups. "On the house. You guys are doing so much for Jonah and Casey—it's the least I can do."

"Thanks, Malcolm," said Brandt with a smile and a nod. "Casey in this morning? Everything okay?"

"Sure seemed so. Had a spring in his step for the first time in a while. Actually, I haven't seen him this upbeat since before wrestling season when he had time for a girlfriend."

Brandt and Donnelly exchanged a look but said nothing.

"Thanks again, Malcolm," Donnelly said as they turned to go. "We'll see you soon, I'm sure."

"Take care, guys!"

Brandt and Donnelly walked up the street, sipping and mulling over what Malcolm had said.

"So, sounds like Casey's walking on sunshine all of a sudden," Brandt observed.

"Be honest, now, Ethan. What was your first thought when he said that?"

Brandt looked around to be sure no one else was around to overhear. "That our boys had sorted out their… feelings for each other."

"Me too," Donnelly replied with a smile. "Let's hope it's good news, whatever it is."

"But first, the bad news," Brandt said as he held the door of the police station open for Donnelly to enter.

"Thank you for coming, officers," Powell said as he welcomed the men into the conference room.

Brandt had expected to see the Fischers, but there was only Coach Woody. That might be a good sign, or perhaps it was a really bad one. He and Donnelly nodded a greeting to the coach and sat down.

"I'll get right to it," Powell said. "Late last night several students reported receiving this video, forwarded to them from various classmates." Powell punched some keys on his laptop and then spun it around to show the officers.

The view was the same as in the previous videos, but the quality was much higher this time; the video was in color, for one thing, and was much sharper. Jonah's locker stood locked, and as the video began, several members of the wrestling team walked past and then stopped, as if saying a little prayer or offering their thoughts to Jonah. All of them were wearing towels, many of them set so low on their hips as to be nearly falling off. Then the fourth person to stop in front of Jonah's locker dropped the towel altogether. He stood like a statue, bare buttocks facing the camera, and then moved placidly on. This performance was repeated by several other teammates, some of whom were already naked when they entered the frame; some dropped their towel, while most kept theirs securely wrapped around their waists.

The video continued in this vein for over a minute, until one last wrestler entered the frame. It was Casey. He was naked when he walked on screen, and he bowed his head in front of the locker and then reached out and touched it with his right hand. Then he slowly turned around, his flaccid but still sizable penis fully visible. He touched his hand to his heart and then walked back out of the frame.

"Well, that's it," Powell said, snapping his laptop shut. "Every damn one of the wrestlers is on that thing, some of them naked. That Casey Melville boy was completely exposed. This is out of control, gentlemen. We need to discover who is responsible, or the entire team could be at risk."

"We checked our video sources this morning, after we got your call," Brandt said. "This new video has not been posted on the same site that the others were, so there's at least a chance it's just being passed around the school."

"We've thought that before, haven't we?" Powell snapped. His patience was wearing as thin as his hair. "This could destroy our entire wrestling program, and we're not going to sit idly by while that happens. I've asked all of the parents of wrestlers to come to the school auditorium today at noon to discuss what steps we, as a community, should take in light of this most recent development."

Brandt shot Donnelly a look. What Powell had described had all the hallmarks of a vigilante campaign.

"We'd like to be there, chief," Donnelly said with a calm Brandt knew he could not have mustered himself. "Some of the wrestlers may have mentioned some information to their parents that could be useful to the investigation. This would be an efficient way for us to cast the broadest possible net."

"Good thinking," Powell agreed. "The principal will speak, as will the coach here, and I'll say a few words. Then you can ask your questions. I've also invited some community leaders to participate. We really need to pull together on this. And we'd appreciate any help you can offer."

"We will do everything we can," Brandt assured him, and he and Donnelly stood to go.

"I'll walk out with you," Coach Woody said, rising with the men. "I've got to get to school now anyway." He nodded to Chief Powell and followed the men out of the conference room.

As the three walked down the street toward the high school, Coach Woody looked carefully around and then spoke in a low, quiet voice. "I didn't want to say anything in front of the chief, but that video is different."

"Seems so," Brandt replied.

"No, it's really different." Woody looked around again, spylike. "I think it was made by someone on the wrestling team. That's why I didn't say anything."

Brandt and Donnelly stopped dead in their tracks. "Why would you say that?" Donnelly asked.

"Did you notice that only some of the wrestlers were naked?" the coach asked.

"Yes," Brandt said. "Seemed to be about a quarter of them."

"Good guess. Seven out of thirty. Now," Woody continued, his voice even more conspiratorial. "You know how many of my wrestlers are eighteen right now?"

Brandt and Donnelly exchanged a look.

"Seven?" Brandt asked, squinting a bit at the coach—he was critical of this roundabout exposition.

"Exactly. The eighteen-year-old wrestlers are the only ones who got naked. What are the odds a spy cam is going to somehow magically record only legal nudity? No, the boys themselves are responsible, or at least they're in on it. No one else could have done it. You can't tell by looking at them—our heaviest wrestler is 190 pounds of stacked muscle, and he's fifteen. Our lightest guy is nearly nineteen because he failed a grade, and he's hairless. You'd think he was a fourteen-year-old... *girl*."

Brandt and Donnelly pondered this.

"You make a good point, coach," Donnelly mused. "Any idea why someone on the team would do this?"

Coach Woody shook his head. "No clue. But I thought you should know."

"Thanks for the information. It helps a great deal," Brandt said. "Do you think you can send me a copy of the video? I'd like to have our techs review it for clues as to how it was made or anything else we can get from it."

"Sure. Here," he said as he pulled out his phone. He clicked and swiped for about fifteen seconds and then stuck it back in his pocket. "There you go."

"Thanks. I guess we'll see you at noon."

Woody nodded, his face grim. "Yeah, that's gonna be fun." He managed a weak grin before turning and walking onto the high-school campus.

"Officer Brandt," Donnelly said, turning to his partner. "What do your keen investigative skills tell you about this new video? Did you notice anything prominent we haven't discussed?"

"Casey's penis was rather prominent," Brandt muttered under his breath.

Donnelly nodded. "And what observations would you care to make about that?"

"He's the only one who showed any peen at all, wasn't he?"

Donnelly nodded again. "And what inference can we draw from that?"

Brandt squinted at his partner. "Do you think Casey made the video?"

"It's the only thing that makes sense. It was staged perfectly, and his little tribute routine at the end was clearly designed to be a finale. Plus, once he turned around, he evened the score with Jonah—now everyone at the school has seen his dick too."

"Well, if you want to be precise about it, everyone's seen Jonah's erection. We didn't get that from Casey."

Donnelly considered this for a moment. "True. But then again, maybe the person who needed to be there to make that happen isn't in the video."

"Are you saying Casey's sending a message to Jonah?"

"Or he's sending a message about Jonah to the entire school. About himself and Jonah, that is."

Brandt considered this. "How about we head back to the cafe? Maybe Malcolm can tell us a little bit more about this new, improved Casey he saw this morning. And I'll send the video out for expert analysis."

"Going to have Walters look at it?" Donnelly asked.

"No, silly—Bryce and Nestor. If anyone can help us figure out if it's hit the web, it'll be those two porn savants."

"Perhaps we should get those guys on the payroll."

Brandt chuckled. "Can only imagine what *that* paperwork would look like!"

A QUARTER hour later, the officers were at a table in the cafe, sipping more coffee while they waited for Malcolm to finish up the last of the morning rush. Most of the tables were filled with the customary assortment of blue-haired matrons, all of whom could nurse a cup of coffee longer than they had their first-born.

Wiping his hands on a spectacularly splattered apron, Malcolm came to join them at their table. "Hey guys!" He took the chair next to Donnelly rather than the one next to Brandt. This did not go unnoticed.

"Hey, Malcolm," Donnelly said with a smile Brandt found a bit too genuine.

"I hear there's another video making the rounds. Is that why you're back in town?"

"What have you heard about the video?" Donnelly countered.

Brandt was delighted by Donnelly's deflection. It showed he was still more concerned with his police work than with impressing Malcolm with his involvement in the case. He also reflected for a moment on how much pointless effort jealousy required; he'd probably just be better off if he didn't bother with it.

"Casey's phone started buzzing with it this morning, just like it did on Monday with the other one—the one he calls the 'boner video.' This time it didn't seem to bother him as much, though. Probably getting used to it, poor guy."

"Have you seen any of these videos?" Brandt asked.

Malcolm immediately blushed a deep crimson, and his eyes darted from Brandt to Donnelly and back again, desperately. Then Donnelly nodded to him encouragingly, as if to let him know it was okay to admit it.

"As someone who's close to Casey, I figured I should probably see what all the fuss was about," Malcolm haltingly began. "So I asked around and was able to view them—just once—on other people's phones. It's not like I've got them stashed someplace or anything to look at over and over again. Would you like a refill?" His voice trailed off, having risen at least an octave during his answer.

Donnelly laughed. "Don't worry. We're not concerned about who's watching them. What we want to find out is who made them. Now, you saw the one that's going around this morning, right?"

Malcolm nodded sheepishly.

"What did you think?"

"As a film studies major, I was less than impressed with the narrative coherence. As a red-blooded man, I was... moved."

"Really?" Donnelly said with devastating insinuation.

"Gabriel, if you watched it all the way through and didn't feel anything, I am deeply concerned for you." Malcolm returned to his subject. "As Casey's friend, I say good for him."

"What?" Brandt leaned in to be sure he'd heard correctly.

"I say good for him." Malcolm looked at both men. "I just assumed Casey made the video—wasn't that obvious?"

"And why do you say that?" Donnelly asked.

"He's the final one to appear, and that thing he did in front of the locker? Well, like I said, it was amateurish, but it was heartfelt. And then when he turned around and gave up his last measure of privacy... well, that made it all clear. He was doing this to take the heat off Jonah. That boy would do anything for Jonah."

"Yes," Brandt said with a nod. "We've seen that."

"You said he seemed happier this morning." Donnelly continued his questioning. "Did he say anything specific?"

"It's funny," Malcolm replied. "It's more what he didn't say. Yesterday he had all kinds of questions about how I knew I was gay, and what it's like to come out. Today there was none of that. He just seemed so happy, and he said he had seen Jonah happy for the first time since this all began. He said how nice it was for Jonah to be staying with him, where he knows he's loved." Malcolm wiped his eye. "That kid, I tell ya. There's such a sweetness in him."

Brandt's phone buzzed, and he picked it up to read the message. "It's our"—his eyes darted to Malcolm—"video consultants. They say that they have found no trace of it on the Internet. They also would like to offer those who appeared in it a discount for their clothing store. They would be happy to provide any assistance required for proper measurement of their"—he leaned closer to his phone, squinting a bit to get the wording right—"muscular endowments." Brandt clicked off his phone and sighed at the ceiling.

"Never knew police work could be so sexy," Malcolm said with a laugh.

"You've never seen us do it," replied Donnelly with a wink.

Brandt just shook his head at his goofy, but undeniably sexy, partner.

Malcolm needed to prepare for the lunch rush, and Brandt and Donnelly needed to prepare for the parent meeting, so they spent the next hour working at their table in the corner of the cafe.

FINALLY, AT 11:30, they packed up and walked down the street to the high school. They stopped in at the office to check on the location of the auditorium, into which they strode a good fifteen minutes before noon. The place was packed. The Fischers were there, as were what looked like every parent of every wrestler. A good number of people in suits and ties were there as well—probably wrestling boosters from the business community, Brandt reasoned. The officers took seats at the front so they could get to the podium easily when it was their turn to speak. Chief Powell and Coach Woody sat several seats down the row from them.

Promptly at twelve, the principal of the high school stepped to the podium.

"Thank you for coming today on such short notice. We are all aware of the terrible blight that has struck our school, our wrestling team, and indeed our entire community. Let me assure you, we are doing everything we can to track down and punish the person or persons responsible for the gross perversion that has been visited upon these poor young men. To tell us more about the police efforts underway, here's Police Chief Powell."

Powell lumbered up the stage stairs and to the podium—the short trip winded him. "It's been said that on the Internet no one knows you're a dog. Unfortunately, that also means no one knows who's a pedophile who has unleashed his perversion upon the innocence of our fine, upstanding wrestlers. Until we are able to track every move made online by these disgusting deviants—something that we should be working for in every legislature in the civilized world, by the way— police will be stymied in their attempts to track down the criminal element that lurks online. To help us investigate, we have brought in experts in this kind of crime from the state police. Officers Brandt and Donnelly, can you come up here please?"

As Brandt followed Donnelly up the steps to the stage, he wondered what he could say that would provide any hope to this clearly aggrieved group. He and Donnelly had already decided not to mention their suspicion that Casey had made the final video, and with the full cooperation of the rest of the wrestling squad. They would want to be sure before saying anything, and they wouldn't have a chance to talk with Casey until after school was out and practice complete.

"Thank you, Chief Powell," Brandt said into the feedback-prone mic at the podium. "Officer Donnelly and I have been working for the past week to gather information about the videos—who made them, and why—and while we have little in the way of definite answers for you, let me assure you that we are committed to finding the person responsible and prosecuting them to the fullest extent of the law. Now, what would really help us do that would be to find out from you what your wrestlers have been saying about the experience. Have they mentioned any unusual occurrences, or have there been fights or disagreements in the past that may have resulted in bad blood or hurt feelings? We know Jonah Fischer has borne the brunt of the publicity over this situation, but he does not appear to be the sole target, particularly after this most recent video. It may simply be that his locker was the easiest to film, and what happened to Jonah could have happened to any of—"

A voice in the crowd distracted Brandt, but he couldn't make out the words.

"Excuse me? I didn't catch the question," he said, leaning over the podium, hand cocked behind his ear.

"I said, it could only have happened to someone who gets excited in the boys' locker room," one of the fathers in the rear of the room said, his voice a snarl.

Jonah's father shot to his feet and turned to the back of the room, face flushed with anger. "Are you calling my son a fag? Is that what you're doing, Jack? Because I will come back there and—"

"I think we will be most productive," Brandt shouted from the podium, "if we focus on the person making the videos, not the people in them." Mr. Fischer sank back down to his seat without taking his fierce gaze from the man who had insulted his son. "Thank you. Now, please, we'd like you to think carefully about whether your sons have said anything at all that might be relevant—even a casual remark at the dinner table about a conflict on the team. Any information you could provide would be helpful."

A hand went up in the room, held aloft by a young woman with a notebook in front of her. "Rachel Lawson, *Woodchuck Weekly*." She paused, apparently noticing his confused expression. "It's the student newspaper here," she explained. "I'd like to know why the Woodley police department is taking so seriously the filming of some wrestlers in the locker room, where there is very little presumption of privacy, when the filming of a female student in the privacy of a friend's bedroom six months ago didn't even get written up as a possible crime?"

Brandt was flummoxed. Donnelly stepped to the podium. "While we cannot comment on the work of the Woodley police department, from the perspective of the state, there is no difference between the two cases, and if we had been asked to investigate the previous video case we would have, using the same tools we are using now."

By this time Chief Powell had made his way back to the podium; he tapped Donnelly impatiently on the shoulder and moved in to reach the mic. "That is an impertinent question, young lady, and I would caution you to watch your tone. The situation you mention was completely different from the one we are discussing today. Those differences are obvious to everyone in this room except, apparently, to you. We will stay focused on the current situation, or you will be asked to leave." He retired from the mic.

Brandt stepped awkwardly back to the podium. "Does anyone have anything to add, or are there additional questions we can answer?" Brandt asked. There was silence in the room. "Okay. Please take one of my cards—you will find them on the table next to the exit in the back—and get in touch with me if anything occurs to you later. Thank you." He and Donnelly sat down.

Coach Woody passed the men as they descended the steps. He stood at the podium, regarding the crowd with what could only be described as a "game face."

"Parents," he began. "I know these videos have upset and concerned you. They have us all. But we cannot lose sight of what's really important here. Winning. Every day that your sons are distracted by these videos, and by the angry reaction to them among the community, is a day that's lost to us. A day on which we make no progress toward victory. Now, don't get me wrong. I'm not saying that we should ignore the videos. But I am saying that whoever made them did so with one purpose—to distract us from our focus on reclaiming the state championship title. As the officers said, we shouldn't focus on who's in the videos—they are victims, yes, but we victimize them all over again when we make a big deal about a few seconds of embarrassment. As for who made them, well, I know all I need to know about that. They were made by someone who wanted us to take our focus off victory." He looked out at the crowd, sweeping the room from one side to the other. "They must not be allowed to succeed!" The coach nodded emphatically and stepped away from the podium. Then, having taken two steps away, he lunged back to the mic for a final "Go Woodchucks!" Then he resumed his seat.

The principal stepped up to the podium again. "In times of crisis, we all turn to one place for help and support—the Lord. I have asked the pastors of our local churches to come today to share some thoughts on why this current situation might have happened, and what we can do about it. Gentlemen?"

A succession of clergy took the stage over the next half hour, and their tirades were horrifying to hear. Brandt and Donnelly were lectured that homosexuality leads inevitably to criminal behavior, which is why it should be criminalized in the first place; that tolerance for gays and lesbians is actually intolerance of religious freedom; that it is cruel to let young people even find out about homosexuality because they will be induced to try it, giving Satan an opportunity that he will ruthlessly exploit; and finally that homosexuality doesn't even exist, but is actually a name invented by the liberal media so they don't have to say "sodomy" as often. By the time the group wound up their angry blather, Brandt was running target practice exercises in his head, determining which pastors to pick off first should gunfire break out.

The final pastor to speak had an idea that struck Brandt as the worst by far. "Because this video situation has not only harmed the Fischer family, but the entire community, it's high time we reminded ourselves of the values that made Woodley great. That's why I am organizing the Rally to Restore Our Values, to be held in the high school gym Friday afternoon. This will be our chance to rescue the children of our town from the rising tide of perversion that threatens to drown them...." He continued in this vein for several minutes, but Brandt had already focused in on how bad this was going to be—for Jonah, for Casey, for all of them.

AFTER THE meeting ended, Brandt and Donnelly staggered out of the auditorium, laden with so much ill-reasoned homophobia that they hardly knew where to begin.

"First," said a visibly angry Donnelly, "how do they justify holding what is clearly a religious event at the school, in the gym, during the school day?"

"I'm still stuck on how all they wanted to talk about was the gays," Brandt said. "Someone's been secretly filming people, and putting the videos on the Internet, and the only issue they see with that is that someone somewhere must be gay and what are we going to do about it?"

They vented their anger all along the main street of town, until they arrived at the destination they seemed to have agreed on without speaking of it—the cafe.

"I think the best thing we can do is wait for Casey to come to work and see what we can learn from him," Donnelly said as they walked up to the door.

"I guess Malcolm won't mind if we grab a table and get some paperwork done until then. I'll even buy you lunch—handmade by your new crush." Brandt winked.

Donnelly, who had been reaching for the door, stepped back from it and stood toe-to-toe with Brandt. "Ethan, you know perfectly well you have ruined me for other men. No one will ever make me feel the way you do. You are the only man I have ever loved, or ever will. Got that?"

Brandt blushed and grinned. "Yeah. But it's nice to hear sometimes too. I love you, Gabriel." Brandt stole a kiss, then looked around furtively to be sure no one saw it. This reflex struck him as both necessary and infuriating.

They stepped into the cafe. "We're home!" Donnelly called. Malcolm, from behind the counter, laughed.

"Here for lunch, guys?" he replied. There was a line of a half-dozen people ordering lunch at the counter.

"No hurry," Donnelly replied with a wave. "We'll just grab a table and wait until the rush is over."

About half an hour later, Malcolm came to their table with plates of sandwiches and salads. "Here, gents. Trying some new sandwich ideas on you today. Let me know what you think."

"If we like them, will you name them after us?" Donnelly asked, grinning.

"You kidding me? To make a 'Gabriel Donnelly' true to the original, it would have to be a stack of lean beef served on tiny little buns. Who would order that?" He winked broadly at the men and returned to the counter.

"Okay, that was funny," Brandt said. "At least you two are getting more polished in your flirting." Brandt took a bite of the sandwich Malcolm had brought him. "Just so you know, I'd eat Gabriel Donnelly for breakfast, lunch, and dinner."

Donnelly fanned himself. "Is it hot in here, or is it just you?"

They spent the next two hours getting caught up on paperwork, until finally, at just after 4:00 p.m., Casey walked through the door.

"Did you see this?" he called angrily as he stepped into the cafe and flipped the door sign to "Closed." He was waving a bright-orange flyer.

"What is it?" Malcolm asked, coming around from behind the counter.

"It's a flyer for a 'Rally to Restore Our Values' this Friday. Looks like the people who honk at us about abstinence every year are coming back to scold us for—I don't know what. Getting naked in the locker room?" He looked at the flyer in disgust and crumpled it up.

"There's some folks who'd like to talk with you before you start work," Malcolm said, pointing to where the officers sat near the windows.

Casey looked over and instantly his expression of anger was replaced with one of joy at seeing Ethan and Gabriel waiting for him. "Hey, guys! It is so good to see you," he said as he jogged over to them. He pulled up a chair at their table.

"You're looking pretty spry for someone who's just starred naked in a new Internet video sensation," Brandt said with a smile.

"You know," Donnelly said, in a faux-serious tone, "Alfred Hitchcock appeared in every film he made, but only in a cameo role. He never would have stolen the final scene." He winked at the young wrestler.

Casey tried to arrange his features in an expression of embarrassment, or at least concern. It wasn't terribly convincing. He quickly gave up. "Man, you guys are good." He looked around the empty cafe. "Am I gonna get in trouble?"

"No," Brandt replied instantly. He wanted Casey to know he was safe with them. "You haven't done anything illegal—in fact, it was your careful adherence to the law that started us down the path of thinking you had made the video."

Casey grinned, pleased with the compliment.

"But we are interested in knowing why you did it," Donnelly prompted.

"I just wanted to find a way to take the heat off Jonah," he said with a shrug. "I started talking to some of the guys yesterday during a break in practice, and it turns out they all wanted to help Jonah too. So I stuck my phone in the empty locker across from Jonah's and we recorded it in about five minutes. Didn't really plan it out that much, aside from making sure the underage guys stayed covered up. That was actually harder than you might think. Some of them wanted to go full frontal." He laughed at the memory.

"But you did," Brandt said.

Casey nodded. "I wanted Jonah to know."

"Has he seen the video?" Donnelly asked.

"I don't know. I left him at my place this morning when I came to work at o-dark-thirty, and I haven't been in touch. He doesn't turn his phone on much to keep his parents from knowing where he is. I'll find out in a little bit when I get home for dinner."

An idea occurred to Brandt. "When you filmed your video, where did you set your phone?"

"I put it in Rusty's old locker," he said. "Russell Winslow. It's been empty since he left. He wrestles for Drummond now. He's pretty good."

"Do you know why he left Woodley?"

Casey shook his head. "I heard from somebody he got kicked out of school for drugs or something, but then I heard from somebody else that his family moved to Drummond for his dad's job."

"It looked to me like the same vantage point was used for the videos of Jonah," Donnelly said.

"So you think whoever it was put a camera in Rusty's locker?" Casey asked. "Seems like someone would have noticed it just sitting there in an empty locker."

"But remember that even though the first video didn't start getting passed around school until two weeks ago, it was posted to the web more than four months ago."

"Rusty was still at Woodley then," Casey said. "Why would Rusty want to film Jonah changing clothes? He could see that every day."

"Excellent question," Donnelly said. "It could be he was planning his move to Drummond already and wanted to have the footage on hand to distract the team when regionals started. There might be another explanation, of course. Anything about him you can think of that might help us? Anyone he was close to on the team?"

Casey furrowed his brow, working to recollect anything useful about the former Woodchuck. "He was a good wrestler," he finally replied, with an apologetic shrug. "He was pretty good friends with Max. I think they were in the same church youth group or something."

Donnelly nodded. "Well, we'll just have to pay him a visit and see what he can tell us. In the meantime, how's Jonah holding up?"

"He's good," Casey said with a grin. "Really good. We both are."

Donnelly and Brandt exchanged a look.

"Have you and Jonah—gotten closer?" Brandt asked.

Casey blushed bright red. "What do...? I mean…. It's…," he stammered then threw his hands in the air. "How do you guys do that?"

"You're dealing with professionals," Brandt said with a laugh. "Good for you guys, though."

"Yeah, it's good," Casey said with a grin. "I never knew it could be like that." He sighed. "Here's a question for you—did you guys start out gay, or did you just find each other?"

Brandt's eyes widened. "That's kind of a complicated question," he replied.

"No, no it's not," Donnelly said. "We were working a case that was really stressful and involved undercover work of an… intimate nature. At one point we were either going to make out or kill each other, and we chose the former." He looked at Brandt, a sparkle in his eye, before turning back to Casey. "I never considered myself anything but straight, and neither did Ethan. But we discovered we had grown to love each other, over the two years we'd worked side by side, and that adding in sex was more of a completion than a departure. It just made sense to us."

"Though it often doesn't to other people," Brandt added. "A lot of times people don't understand how you go from friends to lovers just like that."

"I understand it," Casey said. "I mean, I guess I do. It's kind of confusing when I try to think through how it happened. Jonah says he's been in love with me for years, like he's been gay all along. I've never even thought about another guy in a sex way—at all—and certainly not Jonah. But over the last couple of days, things that didn't make sense started to, and then suddenly—" He looked up at the officers and blushed deeply again. "Suddenly we're in the shower, making out," he added sheepishly.

Donnelly leaned in across the table. "Is that what you wanted to happen, Casey, or did you do it for some other reason?"

Casey pondered this for a moment. "It's what I wanted. Never knew I did, but suddenly it seems like Jonah's a bigger part of my life than I thought. Even after our day on Alta Avenue, I still don't think of myself as gay; I just kind of fell in love with another guy. Is that weird?"

"If it's weird, then we're weird too," Brandt answered. "Well, Gabriel's always been a little weird, but…."

"Thanks, partner," Donnelly said with a smirk. But then he blew a kiss across the table.

"Jonah says he only wants what you two have. After last night, I know that's what I want too."

Donnelly looked at him, an expression of deep concern on his face. "Woodley's a tough place for that," he said gravely. "You may need to keep it to yourselves until you get to college, or maybe even until you are out of school altogether. Jonah's parents looked pretty grim at the meeting today. I don't think they're going to suddenly decide to set a place at the Easter table for their son's boyfriend."

"Wait, there was a meeting today?" Casey asked tensely.

"At noon, with all the parents of the wrestlers in your latest video," Brandt replied.

"Oh, that's not good. Last time they did one of those, the prom was cancelled." He looked down for a moment, lost in thought. "I hope I didn't really fuck things up with that video. I was only thinking of Jonah."

Donnelly reached out and put his hand on Casey's. "You will never be wrong if you think of the people you love."

"Thanks. I really appreciate you guys and all you've done for us." Casey smiled at them, his worry about the parent meeting apparently allayed. "I better get some work done so I can get home to my... Jonah." He laughed as if the sound of that tickled him, then stood. "Can I get you a last coffee before I shut down the machine?"

"That'd be great, thanks," Donnelly said. Casey hustled off to the brass monster.

"I think we should pay Russell Winslow a little visit tomorrow before school," Brandt said.

"I'll call Drummond High and get an address," Donnelly replied. Then a thought seemed to occur to him. "Wait, does this mean we should spend the night here?"

"What do you think? Up for a night in the big city of Woodley?"

"Ugh. But it's better than driving all the way home and then back again. I'll check with Malcolm about where we should stay. I guess one more day in Woodley would be bearable."

"You guys'll be here on Friday for the rally, right?" Casey asked as he walked back to the table with their coffee.

Brandt and Donnelly looked at each other and shrugged.

"If I've learned anything from TV, it's that the criminal always returns to the scene of the crime," Casey continued. "Who knows— maybe something will shake loose at the rally that would be helpful to the investigation. Couldn't hurt, right?"

"Casey, you are the best junior detective I've ever met," Brandt said, nodding at his insight.

"Oh goody, two more days in fucking Woodley," Donnelly said. His voice dripped with sarcasm, but his grin told a different story.


"MOM? JONAH?" Casey called as he walked through the front door. It was nearly dinner time, but it didn't seem like anything was cooking, and there was only one light on in the house.

"In here," Casey's mom said from the couch, where she sat in the meager circle of light thrown by a small lamp on the end table.

Casey sensed immediately that something was very wrong. "Where's Jonah?" he asked, in a voice that was barely audible.

"Oh, honey," his mom said, shaking her head sadly. "He's gone."

"What?" spat Casey, furious and bereft all at once. "What happened?"

"It was after the meeting today. I took my lunch break to go to the meeting, but there was such hatred in that room—such ugliness—that I couldn't bear to go back to work. I called and let them know I was taking the rest of the day, and then I came home. I was telling Jonah what happened at the meeting when his parents drove up."

"How did they know he was here?"

"Honey, we live in a tiny town. Everybody knows everything. They asked if they could talk with him, and he said okay, and so I left them to it and went for a walk around the lake. When I got back, they were getting into the car, and Jonah was going with them. He'd been crying—a lot by the look of him. I made up a story about how I needed his help for a second in the house, and his parents waited in the car when we came back inside. I asked him what was going on, and he said he had to go with them. They told him they would do all kinds of awful things, like calling all of the university recruiters and telling them he wasn't going to wrestle, and that he'd never see his brother again. He just didn't have a choice!"

Casey was mute; even his sobs made no sound.

"I hugged him goodbye, and he whispered a message in my ear that he wanted me to tell you. He says he loves you, Casey, and he's sorry it had to end this way."

"End? What did he mean end?"

"His dad said they were taking him to an intervention of some kind, and he wouldn't be around for a while. Then his mom tried to pay me twenty dollars for housing him 'while he was lost.' That churchy bitch. I just looked at her money and told her I would always have a place in my home for Jonah. I made sure Jonah heard it too. Then they drove away."

They sat in silence for a long moment.

"I'm so sorry, honey," she said as she watched the tears run in long streams down his cheeks.

"I... I love him," Casey croaked out with great effort.

"I know, honey, I know." She stroked his hair and blotted his cheeks with a tissue.

"No, I mean—" He looked at her with an intensity that burned through the tears. "I mean, I really love him."

"I know," she replied, a sad smile on her face.

"You do?" he said, his voice high and young.

"Of course I do. Moms know. I've known about Jonah for a long time—the way he looks at you, especially when he thinks no one's watching. I've known forever. It's only been in the last week that I've seen it in you too." She laid a hand on his cheek. "I'm happy for you, honey."

Casey tried to say something, but all that would come out were more tears—of relief and joy, now, mixed with the sadness and loss.

"But it won't be easy," she said. While her voice was soft, it had an edge to it. "If you two want to be together, you are going to have a battle on your hands."

This was the call Casey had been waiting for. Suddenly, the hopelessness that had overwhelmed him cleared, and all that remained was resolve. He set his jaw and nodded.

His mom smiled at him. "I am so proud of you. If you have found someone deserving of the love you have to give, then he is worth fighting for."

"Jonah is worth fighting for." His voice was determined. "And I'm going to win."

DONNELLY'S PHONE buzzed as they were unpacking their few belongings at Woodley's only hotel. He read the message and gasped.

"What? What is it?" Brandt asked, startled by Donnelly's reaction.

"It's Casey. He says Jonah's gone. His parents came and took him away."

"Where?"

"To some intervention at their church. He says they threatened him into it."

"Shit."

"Indeed." Donnelly typed a flurry of text back at Casey. "I'm asking him which church." He turned to Brandt. "If it's someplace with a rep for shipping gay kids out for reeducation, we can start work on getting him sprung ASAP."

"We can't just go charging in and snatch him. He's eighteen, and unless we have evidence he was kidnapped, we can't do much. They may have blackmailed him emotionally, but that's not the same as force."

"I know. I'm going to check it out anyway. If there have been complaints before, we may be able to at least get a judge to bring everyone in to sort it out. Some of those church groups are brutal. They break down vulnerable kids to make them pretend they've turned straight. Gay kids already have a high suicide rate, but kids who get indoctrinated by those hate groups have an even greater chance of ending up dead." He turned back to the phone. "He sent me the name of the church, and now he says… that… he…." Donnelley set the phone down. "He says he told his mom about them, and she's fine with it. She told him she was proud of him."

Donnelly looked out the window, suddenly intent on the desolate highway beyond the hotel's parking lot.

Brandt came up behind him and put his hand on Donnelly's shoulder. "That's really great," he said, softly. He knew Donnelly's relationship with his own mother had always been difficult, and her own narrow religious views kept them from having any sort of relationship to this day.

Donnelly sniffed, then wiped his eyes. "Yeah," he said, his voice thick. "I'm happy for him. And I'm really happy for his mom. The Fischers are pushing their son away, and she's pulling hers closer." He put his hand on his partner's and held it tight for a long while.


THE TEXT to Brandt was just the first of hundreds Casey dispatched that evening. His mom hovered nearby, offering support, food, and—against her better judgment—coffee. Casey had never felt closer to his mom, and she glowed with happiness at being able to help.

# CHAPTER SEVEN
## PLOTS

THURSDAY MORNING came, and Casey was out the door for Malcolm's cafe before dawn as usual. He worked his morning shift, and then Malcolm wished him well on his calculus quiz—he replied that he felt pretty confident about it.

He never took that quiz. In fact, Casey Melville was absent from school that day.

THE WINSLOW farmstead lay about fifteen minutes out of the center of town, among the rolling hills that seemed populated exclusively by stubbly fields and scolding crows. Though he had switched schools, Rusty still lived in the far reaches of Woodley's town borders. He drove himself a half hour each way into Drummond every school day.

"I researched the church that Jonah's family belongs to," Donnelly said as he watched the landscape slip past. "It's pretty conservative. No surprise there."

"Find out anything about what Jonah might be going through, like a program of some kind?" Brandt asked.

"Nope. I couldn't even come up with a reference to an intervention of any sort in the past. Though they just got a new pastor about six months ago—super conservative guy fresh out of whatever school manufactures these... men of the cloth."

"So no legal avenues we could pursue to try to spring him, though that was always going to be a long shot," Brandt replied.

Donnelly sighed. "It just kills me that parents who say they love their kids will gladly turn them over to the worst kind of reprogramming—and often abuse. I would never let that happen to a child of mine, even if we end up raising a… *Republican.* I'd love them anyway."

"I guess all we can do is hope Jonah stays strong and gets through it. He's turned out to be pretty tough."

Brandt and Donnelly rolled up the long gravel driveway, trusting the last turn the GPS was capable of suggesting before it gave up. It now showed their vehicle driving through a completely blank, beige rectangle of land.

After nearly a mile on the pitted and rough driveway, they rounded a bend and saw the farmhouse. Brandt parked the car next to the porch steps, and they walked up to knock on the door. Before they could, though, it swung open, and they stood facing a young man in his late teens. He wore a T-shirt with the name of a band the officers had never heard of and an expression on his face they couldn't quite read.

"Russell Winslow?" Brandt asked.

The man smiled. "Call me Rusty," he said as he pushed open the storm door and waved the men into the house.

It was a simple place, decked out in what might be charitably called country decor. A mostly empty bowl of oatmeal sat on the table, a backpack on the chair next to it.

"Are your parents here, Rusty?" Donnelly asked. They had already gotten the Winslows' permission to talk with their son—not strictly necessary because he had turned eighteen the month before, but it was their practice to give the parents the chance to be present. Of course, Rusty wasn't a suspect, so their conversation wouldn't be an official one.

"They're out in the barn. Lambing season. They spend most of their time out there in March."

"So, we'll get right to it so you can get on your way to school," Brandt said, with an almost jovial tone and a winning smile. "You wrestled for Woodley until a few months ago, right?"

"Yes, sir, I did."

"And during the time that you were on the team, you had a locker across the aisle from Jonah Fischer, is that correct?"

"Let me think," he said, looking at the ceiling. "Y-yes, I think that's right."

"Right. So did you record videos of him changing for your personal use, or was there some other reason?"

"What?" Rusty paled visibly at the question.

Donnelly stepped in to take another tack. "Jonah's not pressing charges or anything. He would just like to know why you took those videos of him. Were you... interested in him?"

"Oh fuck no!" the young man blurted. He seemed disgusted by the very question.

"Then why take the videos of him?" Donnelly asked calmly.

"They weren't videos of him! I'm not some fucking faggot!"

Brandt seized on this admission. "Then why did you take those videos?"

Rusty's eyes darted from Brandt to Donnelly and back, as if searching for a way to answer this question that didn't involve Jonah's naked body. "I did it for Anna," he said quietly.

Brandt flashed a quick look at Donnelly, who shrugged. "Who's Anna?" Brandt asked.

Rusty closed his eyes and shook his head. "About six months ago a video was posted of Anna at a party. She was filmed while being molested by two of the guys on the wrestling team."

Brandt considered this for a moment, but still didn't see the connection Rusty was apparently trying to make. "And this relates to your videos... how?"

"I knew Anna. She was a friend of mine." Rusty paused, and looked down at the table for a long moment. "I felt really bad about what happened. So I did the only thing I could think of to help her—I set up a camera in my locker and shot some video."

"How would video of Jonah help Anna?" Donnelly asked, sounding genuinely confused.

Rusty looked at him with an intensity that made him startle. "It had nothing to do with Jonah-fucking-Fischer!"

Donnelly shook his head. "I don't understand."

"Have you seen the video Anna was in?" Rusty asked.

"No," Brandt replied. "Because they were all underage, the video isn't legal."

"Just about everyone in Woodley has a copy of it. You should take a look."

"What would we be looking for?"

"Stars." Rusty stood abruptly and reached for his backpack. "I gotta get going or I'll be late for school."

Brandt had more questions, but he couldn't force Rusty to stay and answer them—not unless they had a stronger sense of what his role was in the whole affair. "Sure," he said, careful to keep his voice casual. "If we have more questions at some point—"

"I've told you why I took the videos. How they ended up getting passed around, I have no idea."

"So, you never sent them to anyone?" Donnelly asked.

"Just to Anna," Rusty replied. "Now, I really gotta go." He walked to the door, and the officers had no choice but to accompany him. He shut the door behind them, strode to his car, and drove off without another word.

Brandt and Donnelly got into their cruiser.

"Why is it that whenever we talk to anyone in Woodley, I just end up more confused?" Brandt asked.

"This is one fucked-up little burg, that's for sure."

"I wonder if Powell can show us the Anna video?"

"I'm sure he can—the thing was all over the place last fall. I remember seeing a blurred version of it on the news."

"It's not the kind of movie I look forward to seeing, but I guess we need to." Brandt sighed and backed the car around to make the long trek down the driveway and back into Woodley.


DONNELLY DIALED Powell's number as Brandt drove back to Woodley.

"Chief Powell, this is Gabriel Donnelly. Fine thanks, sir, and you? Very good. We're still in Woodley following up on some things, and I wondered if we might be able to stop by and take a look at the video that circulated last fall, the one of a girl named Anna?" He paused, and looked at Brandt with a squint, as if he was hearing a response he hadn't expected. "We understand that the investigation is closed, but we think it may be connected in some way to the videos of Jonah Fischer. We'd like to see it for ourselves, if that's okay. Good. We'll be there in about twenty minutes." He set his phone down.

"What did he say?" Brandt asked.

"It was weird. As soon as I asked about the video, he got really short with me. Said the investigation on that had concluded, and they keep the video locked up because Anna was sixteen when it was shot."

"But he agreed to let us see it?"

"I think he knows we can find it other ways if we want to. Pretty much everyone in Woodley saw it, judging from the news stories about it. But he definitely didn't sound happy about it."

Half an hour later, they were back in the police department's conference room, awaiting the arrival of Chief Powell.

"You know, if this thing keeps getting more complicated, we might as well move to Woodley." Brandt winked at his partner.

"Keep joking, buddy. Move to Woodley and you can embrace lifelong bachelorhood."

"Good morning, officers," Powell said as he entered. He did not sound sincere. "Here is the department's only copy of the video you inquired about. I must ask that you not make a copy, nor that you let it leave the station. Is that clear?"

They nodded.

"Here is a standard acknowledgment of sensitive evidence." He slid a piece of paper to each of them. "Please sign and date these, indicating that you are aware you are about to view evidence that is illegal, and attesting to your belief that so viewing it will materially assist you in an ongoing investigation."

Brandt and Donnelly exchanged glances of surprise at Powell's grimly dramatic turn, but they signed and slid the papers back to him.

He set down a portable DVD player. "Here. Bring this back to my office when you have gotten what you need." He turned and left the room, shutting the door behind him.

"Wow," Donnelly said once the door was closed. "He's not happy about showing us this, is he?"

"Clearly not. Let's see if we can find out why." He turned on the DVD player and pressed Play.

The video was grainy, shaky, and only about twenty seconds long. It was taken from the viewpoint of a person kneeling on a bed; that person was clearly a male, as he was fully visible from the waist down. Below him on the bed lay a young woman. Her head was between his legs, and she was sucking the tip of his penis. At the foot of the bed another man was thrusting into her—he too was only visible from the waist down, as the frame of the video was centered on the woman. The only sounds in the video were the creaking of bedsprings as the man at the foot of the bed thrust back and forth, and the occasional moan made by the woman, who seemed less than enthusiastic about what she was doing. Then, abruptly, darkness.

Brandt turned to Donnelly, puzzled. "Observations?"

Donnelly thought for a moment. "She seemed... I don't know, bored? But then again the guy filming didn't seem that into it either."

"Why do you say that?"

"He wasn't erect at all. He was just kind of flopped into her mouth. The other guy was at least functional." Donnelly tipped his head and thought some more. "I can see why it wasn't possible to identify them from the video—no distinguishing features, except that they were definitely athletes. Super-ripped, not an ounce of fat on either one." He turned to Brandt. "What did Rusty say we were supposed to look for? Stars?"

Brandt nodded. "Let's try it again. Maybe we'll see stars."

They viewed the video again, looking for star shapes or patterns in the background, in any visible items of clothing, on the bed. They found nothing. Then, on the fourth viewing, Donnelly cried, "There!"

Brandt paused the DVD. "What did you see?"

"Go back a couple of seconds. Right where the guy jiggles the camera because he shifts his left leg a bit. Right... there!"

Brandt froze the playback and leaned in close to the screen. "What am I looking for?"

"On his hip, just above the hip bone. Look closely."

There, on the young man's hip, were three tiny stars arranged like Orion's Belt.

"He's got a tattoo," Brandt whispered.

"Now, why did Rusty tell us to look for that?" Donnelly asked. "What connection does it have to the videos of Jonah?"

"Well, let's take a look," Brandt said.

Donnelly pulled out his laptop and brought up the first video of Jonah, the one that had been posted online months before being passed around the school. They watched as Jonah prepared for his shower, returned from it, and finally dropped the towel.

"See anything?" Brandt asked.

"Not that I haven't noticed before. He gets ready for a shower, he comes back from a shower. There's not a lot of plot to follow."

"But what if it isn't about him?" Brandt asked. "Let's watch it again, at half-speed, and this time ignore Jonah. Watch the others who come through the frame."

Donnelly made it so, and they watched the wrestlers in slow motion as they entered and left the frame. "There!" he pointed to the slight and wiry form of another wrestler as he walked toward the showers with his towel wrapped around his waist.

"That may be him, but we can only see his right side. The stars are on his left hip."

"Maybe that's why the video jumps to after the showers," Donnelly said. "Watch for him coming back."

"There he is. And there are the stars." Brandt sat back in his chair. "Well, fuck me. This video was never about Jonah. It was about this other guy. He passes back through just as Jonah drops his towel."

Donnelly sat back as well. "So let's game this out. Why did Rusty say he made this video for Anna? Was it so she could embarrass this other guy as revenge?"

Brandt looked skeptically at his partner. "You've seen both. Does this seem like an equal violation? Would it even the score in her mind?" He shook his head.

Donnelly's eyes lit up. "But it would be enough to prove it was the same guy in the video."

"But did she think posting it online would accomplish that? No one even knew that it was Woodley, much less that it showed the same person who had filmed her. As revenge goes, this one's a loser. What was she thinking?"

Donnelly shrugged. "Let's call her and find out."

"You're brilliant, you know that?" Brandt exclaimed. He darted forward and kissed Donnelly.

Donnelly smiled and blushed.

"Let's get to the school and see if we can find a current phone number for Miss Anna," Brandt said as he closed up the portable DVD player.

Donnelly folded his laptop and stowed it in his briefcase. "I heard she moved out west somewhere. Maybe it's still early enough there for us to catch her before school."

Brandt nodded, and they walked down the hall to Powell's office. They knocked, and were admitted. Brandt handed him the portable DVD player.

"Find what you were looking for?" he asked.

"Perhaps," Brandt replied. "We have some more checking to do."

"It took months for this community to heal from that mess," Powell said, his voice laden with an odd mixture of anger and sadness. "I hope you're not going to dredge things up for no good reason."

Brandt studied the older man for a moment, trying to figure out what he meant with this somewhat cryptic warning. He decided to play it light until he had a reason to do otherwise. "Oh, I wouldn't worry about that. We just like to tie up all the loose ends. We're working on the footnotes now."

Powell's manner brightened immediately. "Oh, oh fine, then," he said with a broad smile. "Please let me know if there's anything else I can do to help you button things up."

Brandt nodded, and the two officers turned and left his office.

As soon as they were clear of the police department and walking toward the high school, Donnelly leaned in to talk quietly. "Something's got the chief worked up."

"He doesn't want us to look too closely into Anna's video, that's for certain."

"Why would that be?" Donnelly mused as they walked.

"Well, the obvious conclusion is that he knew who the wrestlers in the video are, and he didn't want their involvement in it to damage the chances of the wrestling team this year."

"But," Donnelly replied, "that assumes he realized that the Jonah video incriminated the shooter of Anna's video. But if that's the case, why would he involve us when the Jonah videos went public? Kind of risky to bring in outside help if you're trying to hide something."

"But by that point, what was he hiding?" Brandt asked. "Anna had already been run out of town, and no one had listened to her claims. That would explain why he was cranky when we suddenly asked to see the video this morning."

They walked the rest of the block in quiet contemplation and then arrived at the high school. A quick stop in the principal's office gave them the information they needed—a contact number for Anna's family. They walked back to their car in order to have a quiet place to talk with her.

THE SPEAKERPHONE rang three times, and then a woman picked up.

"Hello?"

"Hello, Mrs. Timmons?"

"Yes?"

"Mrs. Timmons, this is Officer Ethan Brandt, and I'm calling in reference to an investigation in Woodley. This is about the video that—"

"I know what it would be about. You bastards finally investigating, are you?"

"I'm sorry, Mrs. Timmons, but we were only brought in a couple of weeks ago to look into a separate incident, and we think it may be related to the situation with your daughter."

"The situation with my daughter is that we had to move clear across the country to get away from that mess, and it was nothing of her fault to begin with."

"I understand your frustration, ma'am. Let me assure you that I don't think there was an adequate response to your daughter's complaint, and we're trying to fix that if we can."

There was a moment of silence. "Day late and dollar short, officer."

"Mrs. Timmons, could we speak to Anna, for just a moment? There's some information we need in order for us to move forward with our investigation."

"I don't want her having to dredge up all of that mess now. She's finally getting past it."

"Wouldn't the best thing to help her get past it be for her to finally see all of the people involved admit what they did? I think that would happen if we could speak to her for just a few minutes."

Another pause.

"All right, but just for a few minutes."

The line was muffled as a hand was put over the receiver. They could hear a conversation going on, but could make out no words. A moment later a new voice emerged from the speakers in Brandt and Donnelly's car.

"This is Anna."

"Anna, this is Officer Brandt. Thank you for agreeing to talk with us."

"What is this about, please?"

"We've been looking into the case of some videos that came to be circulated around Woodley High School recently and think they may be related to the video of you that was taken without your permission."

There was a pause. "You've talked to Rusty?"

Brandt's eyes widened, and he turned to Donnelly in disbelief. "Yes," he managed to continue, "we talked with him this morning. That's why we're calling you."

"I figured this would all come out." She sighed, a more world-weary sound than someone her age should make. They heard a hand being put over the phone again, but this time they could make out Anna asking her mother to leave the room. After a moment, she took her hand off and spoke again. "Look, Rusty's not really to blame. I mean, yeah, he spiked my drink, but only a country boy like him would think it was enough to make me blackout drunk."

"Wait," Brandt interrupted. "Rusty got you drunk at that party?"

"Yeah, he'd been sweet on me for a while, but Rusty's kind of a doofus. He thought he'd get me liquored up and then have a shot. I got a little buzzed, but Rusty was shit-faced. After he puked up his guts into the kitchen sink and passed out, I ended up with those two bastards on video."

"Anna, did they rape you?" Donnelly asked, his brow furrowed with incipient rage.

"God, no. You sound like my mother. I hooked up with them because they were kind of cute, and seeing Rusty lying on the floor in a pool of his own sick made me want to do something to forget what a fucked-up night it was. I didn't even know their names."

"Were you aware that there was a camera?" Brandt asked after he had shaken off his surprise at Anna's response.

"Yeah, I saw he had it. I figured he just wanted a souvenir. Whatever. But when it started to get around, everyone started calling me a slut, and no one said anything about those two assholes who were trying to have sex with me. I wanted everyone to at least know who they were, so when I got a copy of the video, I sent it to the police. But they didn't even try to figure out who it was."

"So then you asked Rusty to film the wrestlers in the locker room, because that would give you proof of whose star tattoo was visible in the video?" Donnelly asked.

"Oh hell no. That was Rusty's idea. But I liked it, and he sent me the video he took. I gave that to the police too, and—big surprise—they never did anything with that one either. Claimed it proved nothing. That's when I knew I needed to get out of fucking Woodley."

Brandt's mouth dropped open again. "When did you give the police the locker-room video?"

"About two weeks after the video of me started getting around."

"And they never did anything at all with it?"

Anna sighed. "Not a damn thing. Said it was circumstantial, and they couldn't take it to court. I think they just wanted me to get the hell out of town and not embarrass the fucking wrestling team. So I did—my mom and I came out here to live with my aunt."

"And is that when you decided to put the locker room video on the web for everyone to see?"

There was silence on the other end of the line.

"Anna, is that when you decided—"

"I heard you," she interrupted. "I don't know what you're talking about. Once I saw the police weren't going to do anything—that video was fucking child pornography, for God's sake—I gave up. I never sent anything to anybody."

"So you don't know anything about the video being posted online? What about the other two videos?"

"Wait… are you saying there are more videos? Of me, or of those fucking wrestlers?"

"There are two more videos of the locker room."

"Whatever. If having videos of those guys walking around naked does some damage, great. I'm kind of over the whole thing—as over as I'm likely to get, anyway."

Brandt shook his head, trying to think of any other questions he needed to ask.

"Look, I gotta get ready for school. This has been fun. Let's never do it again, okay?" The line went dead.

"Just one time," an exasperated Brandt muttered, "I would like to talk to someone connected with this mess who doesn't make it worse by answering a few simple questions."

"At least we know what happened with Anna wasn't assault." Donnelly looked out the window and sighed. "Still, it sucks how it turned out for her. Of the three people on that video, two get protected by the entire town, and one gets run out of it. With all the progress we've made in the last generation, it's still the girl who gets punished for having sex."

"The wheels of change turn slowly," Brandt said with a resigned sigh.

Donnelly grunted. "Yeah, but they seem to be running backward in Woodley."

CASEY DIDN'T come to the cafe for his afternoon shift, something he had asked Malcolm to allow him to do; he also asked that he not mention it to Brandt and Donnelly. He didn't want to worry them, nor did he want them out looking for him—he had too many preparations to make. But by the end of the day, as he settled onto the sofa, exhausted, with a mug of hot tomato soup his mom had made for him, he was confident he had done all he could to gird for battle, the battle for the man he loved.

"You sure you want to go through with this?" his mom asked. "It could get kind of rough."

"I'm ready," he said. He leaned his head on her shoulder. "I'm really lucky I drew you in the mom lottery," he said.

"No, I'm the lucky one," she replied, whispering into the top of his head.

# Chapter Eight
# Rallying

Friday afternoons in the spring often saw boisterous rallies in support of the wrestling team; as regional competition was to begin next week, this rally was attended by nearly every student in the school. There was the usual round of cheers, fight songs, and inspirational speeches from the coaching staff and local boosters, who pledged support, both monetary and otherwise, should the squad emerge victorious.

At the conclusion of the rally, when the entire team had been introduced and applauded, the principal came to the microphone and motioned for quiet.

"Thank you, and good luck Coach Woody and the entire squad of wrestling Woodchucks!" He waited for the cheering to die down again and then resumed his speech. "It is now the end of the school day, and the official activities of Woodley High School have concluded. We will now begin the Rally to Restore Our Values, hosted by the pastors and leaders of our local church communities." He motioned to the aforementioned dignitaries to join him on the platform. "You may, of course, leave at any time," he mumbled into the mic, barely audible over the general noise of the entire student body packed into the gym.

"So that's how they do it," Donnelly murmured into Brandt's ear. "The separation of church and state in Woodley is marked by a half-hearted mumble no one heard. I'm going to make sure there's room in the final report for that little constitutional maneuver."

"I notice that no one left."

"Yeah, that's a shock," Donnelly replied bitterly. "People are usually so willing to go against the almost universal opinion of their peers."

The church leaders had now assembled on the platform and began to address the crowd. As the first pastor spoke about Woodley's tradition of traditional values, a flash of light attracted the officers' attention: one of the gym doors had opened. Instead of some lone atheist finding the strength to leave, however, four people entered. It was the Fischer family, all of them, and they walked silently to the seats in the first row of bleachers left empty by the group of pastors now addressing the rally.

"Well, that's a surprise," Brandt said.

"Not really. This whole circus is really for him—his parents, really. Get the whole town to funnel their suspicion of Jonah's sexuality into a values revival, and suddenly everyone's talking about Satan, not whether Jonah gets wood from seeing Casey in the shower."

Brandt turned to his partner, mouth open. "There are reserves of cynicism in you that still surprise me."

Donnelly chuckled grimly. "Tell me I'm wrong. I've seen all of this before. Remember, my mom freaked out about my older brother being gay years before it happened to me. I got to see the right-wing batshit crazy right up close."

"If it's any consolation, I still think my mom loves you more than me," Brandt offered.

"I should hope so. I've worked really hard to make sure she thinks I rode into your life on a unicorn. Wouldn't want to lose another mom."

Brandt squeezed Donnelly's knee affectionately. It was the most expressive gesture he could risk in their current situation.

It was clear as the rally continued that whoever planned it had worked out the strategy carefully; the first three people to speak were the warm-up, with a solid damnation routine that was based more in theology than demagoguery. They were followed by a brief head-fake toward moderation: a liberal rabbi from the next town over, then the Unitarian minister from Woodley's smallest congregation. At last came the big guns, and none bigger than the pastor of the Fischers' church, whose wide-ranging and frothy final-act performance threatened to bring the house down—literally. At one point he, in good televangelist style, got the crowd chanting and stomping in a manner that, he assured them, would make Satan take notice and seek out a softer, more accommodating burg than Woodley. Brandt worried about the structural integrity of the bleachers. At the end the pastor asked Jonah to join him on the stage.

Jonah walked to the platform with the desultory stride of a man walking to the gallows. He mounted the steps slowly and deliberately, but entirely without enthusiasm or even the appearance of hope.

"He looks miserable," Brandt murmured.

"He's part of a spectacle designed to erase him. The community he thought would hate him is applauding him. I'm sure that just makes it worse."

Jonah stood next to his pastor and turned awkwardly to face the bleachers. The young pastor in the expensive suit put his arm around him.

"Jonah, you are the hope of your team, and your school, and your community. You are strong in the love of your family and in the love of your God. There are some who have said that because a sleazy video shared online exposed you in the most despicable way that you must be"—here he turned to the crowd and leered like a mustache-twirling silent film villain—"a homosexual." There were gasps in the crowd. "And what do you say to that scurrilous accusation, that fruit of the labors of Satan? Are you, Jonah Fischer, a *ho-mo-sexual?*"

He pointed the microphone directly at Jonah. The young man blinked, then cast a wild glance around the gym: first at his family, and then over at the team, which sat in a line at the side of the platform clad in identical sweatshirts bearing the stylized woodchuck that was their mascot. Finally he looked directly at Casey, and he took a deep breath. Brandt slipped his fingers into Donnelly's, and they held tight while everyone waited for his answer.

"No."

A wild and raucous cheer rose from the entire assembly. Jonah's dad was standing, cheering and clapping.

Donnelly gave a disgusted grunt. Brandt's head swiveled to Casey, to judge his reaction to Jonah's answer. He seemed placidly unmoved. In fact, the entire team sat stony while the rest of the crowd cheered and hollered over the vanquishing of Satan with a single word. This mission accomplished, the preacher pumped Jonah's hand, pointed him back down the steps to the exuberant embrace of his family, and then sat back down at the end of the pastoral line.

"And now, the reason we are all here," announced the principal, "to support our wrestling Woodchucks, not just as athletes, but as God's creatures." More cheering. "I'd like to ask each of you fine young men to come up and say something about what this afternoon has meant to you. Please come up and share with us your thoughts— share with us what's in your heart."

"Ugh," exhaled Donnelly. "This is always the worst part. Having shoved salvation down your throat, they want you to spit it back up at them."

The first in the line of wrestlers stood and walked somewhat haltingly toward the microphone. He was one of the older wrestlers on the squad, which meant everyone in the gym had seen his ass—some probably had preserved it in freeze-frame screenshot for later recreational use. He walked across the platform, seeming to gain confidence as he did. He reached the mic and leaned down to it.

"Thanks, everyone, for coming today. Speaking as the co-captain, I can tell you the team appreciates it. And speaking to our captain,"— he nodded at Jonah—"let me say that we miss you, and we love you, and we want you to come back as soon as you can. In fact," he looked nervously at Casey but then seemed to take a breath and find his resolve, "I want to tell you, Jonah, that the entire team has your back." With that he stepped back from the mic and lifted his sweatshirt. He flipped it up over his head, revealing the t-shirt underneath. It was a skin-tight white shirt, and emblazoned across it in eight-inch black letters was "I AM JONAH FISCHER." He turned and went back to his seat, to the applause of the assembly. He was passed on the way by the next wrestler in line.

Having reached the podium, the second wrestler lifted his sweatshirt off immediately, and then approached the mic wearing his fitted shirt that read "I AM JONAH FISCHER." "What does this shirt mean? It means that no matter what you did, Jonah, or who you turn out to be, we are with you. Always."

He stepped back from the mic to somewhat halting applause, as if the crowd sensed that the rally was in danger of veering off message.

But the next wrestler was on his way to the mic, and no one seemed ready to stop him.

"You know," Donnelly remarked, "when people get T-shirts printed, they usually use cheap, baggy shirts. Those look more like something—"

"That Bryce would have chosen?" Brandt finished his thought. "Intriguing, isn't it?"

The third wrestler, a hulking slab of a man, approached the mic and took a deep breath. "I've listened to all you have to say," he began, looking to the assembled church leaders. "And to what you guys all cheer about," he said, looking out at the bleachers. "And I just have one question for you: do you people even know what friendship means? When someone you know and love does something you don't understand, or is facing an embarrassing problem, do you cut him off? Tell him that God won't love him if he doesn't change? You people sicken me." He stepped back from the mic and took off his sweatshirt. "I love you, man, no matter what these people say," he boomed into the mic. He tapped his chest and pointed at Jonah before returning to his seat.

The principal strode to the mic, clearly intending to cut this procession of subversives off before more damage was done. But someone got there before he did: Coach Woody.

"I'd like to say," he began, glaring at the principal before turning his back on him, "that I appreciate what each of you has to say, and the support you are showing for your teammate. I'm sure that Jonah—and we all—would like to hear from all of you. So please, continue." He stood aside, but stationed himself protectively between the principal and the mic.

One by one, the wrestlers came up to say a few words about Jonah, and to reveal their T-shirt proclaiming themselves to actually be Jonah Fischer. Some remarks were challenging to the very idea of the rally, and many more were simply more compassionate versions of the standard doctrine. But they all emphasized that they loved and accepted Jonah no matter what. By the time there were only three wrestlers left, Jonah was in tears, his mother was a mascara-streaked mess, and his father was a picture of befuddlement. He clearly had no idea what this all meant.

Then rose a pair of wrestlers, the last two in the line save Casey. They were the only ones to come to the mic together, and an anticipatory silence settled over the crowd.

"Oh, shit," whispered Donnelly. "You don't think those two are going to make an announcement of their own, do you?"

"I didn't bring any tear gas, so I'll have to say I hope not," Brandt whispered back. "I would normally applaud, but those two would get run out of town on a rail if they came out in the midst of this mess."

The smaller of the two wrestlers, so nervous he bounced up and down as he spoke, began.

"I'd like to say that I too am Jonah Fischer, but I don't deserve that."

A scandalized muttering exploded across the gymnasium.

"Six months ago, I did something that has haunted me ever since. I, and my friend"—he nodded to the wrestler who stood next to him—"have done some stuff we're not proud of."

Gasps erupted from across the assembly.

"And what's worse is that I filmed it."

Shouts and exclamations echoed from the rafters of the gym.

"Holy fucking shit," Brandt murmured. "What are the chances that guy's got stars tattooed on his hip?"

The taller of the pair leaned forward to the mic. "We never came forward and took responsibility for our actions."

Pandemonium reigned.

"Please! Please listen to me!" the shorter wrestler called into the mic. The din relented slightly, and he plowed ahead. "Now I know the damage a video can cause. Now I have seen the pain it brings to someone who did nothing to deserve it. And I am sorry. I will always know I caused such horrible pain, and I know that only because I saw Jonah go through it. But I hope that I have shown you, Jonah, that if you are honest, and you tell your story true, you can be free of the guilt and the judgment that has weighed on you. If I can do it, so can you. And only in that sense are we worthy to say to you that we"—here they both whipped off their sweatshirts—"are Jonah Fischer."

There was a stunned silence, followed by scattered applause that built gradually until it became a full-on ovation. The wrestlers stopped to say something to Coach Woody (Donnelly was sure he saw them mouth "I'm sorry") and then sat down.

"We should arrange to have a little chat with those boys after the rally, hmm?" Donnelly muttered into Brandt's ear.

As the applause died down, Casey rose. The room was instantly silent, as if the crowd expected even greater drama from this final wrestler. He approached the microphone, looked across the bleachers, and blinked. Finally, he took a deep breath, and began.

"Hey everyone, I'm Casey," he said, with a wide grin.

"Hey, Casey!" shouted out a few scattered voices.

"You may know me from such films as 'Woodchucks Gone Wild, Parts 3 and 4.'"

Raucous laughter erupted from all corners of the gym.

"Thank you, thank you very much." He waited for the audience to quiet. "It would be kind of redundant for me to say that I am Jonah Fischer, since if you've seen the videos you've gotten a pretty good look at how similar our... predicaments are." More laughter. "So I'll say something that I have said a million times over the last eighteen years." He took off his sweatshirt, and revealed a skintight T-shirt that proclaimed "I AM JONAH FISCHER'S BEST FRIEND." He looked down at the words blazoned across his torso. "But I am sorry to have to tell you that this is no longer true."

Widespread horrified gasping broke out.

"After all that has gone on over the past week and a half, I can no longer say I am Jonah Fischer's best friend."

The silence in the gymnasium was absolute.

Casey looked down at his shirt and shook his head. He lifted it off, revealing the athletic body underneath. Catcalls crackled across the gym. He pulled a second T-shirt out from this back pocket, and shook it out. He turned around and put it on facing away from the audience. Then he turned around slowly. "I AM," he read to them what was on the shirt, "JONAH FISCHER'S BOYFRIEND."

A stunned silence was followed seconds later by the eruption of such screaming and jostling that nothing could be heard for fully a minute. Casey stood strong, looking out over the crowd as if he had accomplished exactly what he intended to do.

Then, slowly, he lifted his hand toward Jonah. He reached out to him, beckoning. He leaned down to the microphone, and in a soft, low voice, said just this: "Come here."

Jonah, frozen, paled. He looked to his mom and dad, on his right and left, in a panic. From where Brandt and Donnelly sat, he seemed to be hyperventilating. He blinked hard and looked piercingly at Casey. Casey met his gaze, his hand still extended.

He wiped his eyes and stood. In the echoing silence of the gym he walked up the steps to the platform, never taking his eyes off Casey. From the end of the line of pastors, the leader of his own church rose, clearly intent on intercepting him. He might have made it, had the Unitarian minister not at that moment dropped the cloth she was using to clean her glasses. She pitched forward suddenly to retrieve it just as the pastor walked in front of her, effectively head-butting him right off the platform. He crashed to the gym floor with a thud. She apologized profusely, and almost convincingly; she did not, however, rush to help him up.

Without the pastoral impediment, Jonah finished his walk up to the microphone, where Casey stood waiting for him. They put their arms around each other and smiled at the assembled students and family. The rest of the wrestling team formed a semicircle behind them, in tight formation—no one would be able to reach them without going through that solid wall of muscle. Then Casey reached into his other back pocket and pulled out another T-shirt. He handed it to Jonah, who laughed and nodded. He took off his shirt—resulting in more catcalls— and then put on the one Casey had handed him. It read, across the front that clung to every muscle, "I AM CASEY MELVILLE'S BOYFRIEND." They stood together, arm in arm, and waved to the cheering bleachers.

It was when they turned to face each other, with a look in their eyes that clearly showed them to be lovestruck, that Donnelly whispered, "Oh, no." He went rigid.

Casey and Jonah inched closer together. They were going to kiss.

Donnelly and Brandt bolted up from their seats as Casey and Jonah moved closer to each other, closer to the moment that would bring the house crashing horribly down. As their lips neared, a scream went up from one of the fainter-hearted attendees of the rally; more joined her as they realized what was about to happen. Then stronger, deeper voices joined in, and the sound turned louder and more menacing. A rumble of impending danger filled the gym as members of the audience rose to their feet in indignation, some with faces reddened from yelling.

Brandt and Donnelly sprinted across the gym floor. They weren't going to make it.

Casey and Jonah's eye closed, and they kissed. It was a classic Hollywood kiss, no tongues or spittle, but one would think from the reaction that they were inventing sin itself by touching their lips together. There was shrieking, crying, retching, and it would be later reported in the local paper that three people fainted. Some townsfolk recoiled, others surged forward like a zombie horde, red-hot fury in their eyes. Camera flashes sparkled all around.

Brandt and Donnelly reached the boys, badges out.

"We're getting you out of here," Donnelly yelled over the din. "Follow me!"

He grabbed Casey's hand and pulled him off the front of the platform and in the direction of the exit he had scoped out as his escape route. Casey held tight to Jonah, and Brandt brought up the rear, making sure no one tried to grab on to them as they ran. The principal and Chief Powell climbed over tipped-over chairs, struggling to reach them; the pastor of Jonah's church, far younger and more fit, would have had a shot were it not for the unbroken wall of wrestlers who joined arms to effectively blockade Casey and Jonah's escape route. Angry students and townsfolk charged forward, shouting expletives and gesturing menacingly.

Casey looked over his shoulder at the Fischer family as they neared the door. Brandt turned to see Jonah's dad, purple in the face, screaming some decidedly un-Christian commands at his son. Mrs. Fischer stood stunned, but Sam, Jonah's twelve-year-old brother, was jumping up and down and clapping gleefully. Brandt turned back and saw Casey grinning as he ran.

In seconds, the four men were sprinting through the parking lot outside the gym in the brisk March air. Donnelly led them to their police cruiser, and they jumped in and pulled out of the lot before more than a dozen or so screaming, furious attendees of the rally had made their way out of the building.

Brandt turned around in the passenger seat to look at Casey and Jonah. "Well, I think it's safe to say Woodley will be buzzing about that rally for some time to come," he said. "We're so proud of you two."

Casey beamed. He looked at Jonah, who laughed and pulled him close. The boys celebrated their reunion with several holds that would not have been allowed in regulation competition. Brandt kept his eyes forward and let them enjoy being back together.

A FEW minutes later, Donnelly pulled the car up outside Casey's house.

"You know where I live?" Casey asked, amazement in his voice.

"I always prepare for every eventuality," Donnelly replied. "It seemed like a good idea to map some stuff out, just in case."

"Just in case of what?" Jonah asked.

"Just in case we had to break you out of your church intervention, for example, and needed a place to lay low for a bit."

"You were planning that? No way." Jonah shook his head in disbelief.

"I fully believe that my crazy partner here would have done just that, if he'd had the chance," Brandt said.

"You guys are awesome," Casey said, clapping both officers on the shoulder.

"Now, we shouldn't stay here long, because they are likely to come here first if they're looking for you," Donnelly explained. He turned around and spoke to the boys. "I'm thinking we might want to give Woodley a cooling-off period. Why don't you go in and gather up what you need for the weekend."

"The weekend? Where are we going?" Casey asked.

"It's a surprise." Donnelly smiled broadly and waggled his eyebrows. Brandt, as well as Casey and Jonah, burst out laughing.

The young men hopped out of the car and ran into Casey's house.

Brandt swiveled his head back to Donnelly, and he was all business. "You should call your guy at the university."

"My thought exactly. It'll give the guys something to distract them from the memory of being chased from their hometown by angry villagers." Donnelly replied. He picked up his phone and dialed.

A few minutes later, the young men returned to the car, bearing two duffel bags (both had "MELVILLE" stitched on them, as once again Jonah was left with only the clothes on his back). Donnelly pulled out of the driveway and pointed the car toward the highway that would take them back to the city.

"Did you leave a note for your mom so she won't worry?" Brandt asked.

"I made sure he did," Jonah answered.

That is exactly what Donnelly would have done, thought Brandt with a smile.

"So," Casey asked. "Where are we going?"

"We'll go to our place tonight," Brandt replied. "And then we've arranged for you to spend Saturday and Sunday at the university."

"I just talked to the wrestling coach there about you two," Donnelly said, "and he'd very much like to meet you."

"He probably won't want to now, though," Casey said, looking down at their matching T-shirts.

"Actually, that's one of the reasons he's interested in you. The university lost a lawsuit a couple of years back about the way it treated gay and lesbian students. The state supreme court decided that Section 28 of the civil code required equal treatment, so they had to make some changes. Now they have a great program to support gay athletes, but so far the wrestling team hasn't been able to recruit anyone who's out."

"Wait, they want to recruit us because we're...?"

"They want to recruit you because you are a couple of amazing wrestlers. But the fact that you are a couple, well... that's a big plus."

Jonah looked at Casey, and kissed his hand as he held it tight. "I can't believe this," he said softly. "An hour ago my life was over."

Casey's eyes gleamed with mischief. "Jonah Fischer, are you a *ho-mo-sexual?*"

"Fuck yeah," Jonah answered without hesitation. The boys giggled gleefully.

In the front seat, Brandt took Donnelly's hand and held it tight.

IT WAS twilight when they arrived at Brandt and Donnelly's house. Casey and Jonah had collapsed together in the back seat, exhausted from their respective ordeals of the last couple of days. Brandt and Donnelly took their duffels into the house, and Brandt ordered Thai food to be delivered while Donnelly went out to wake the boys. They stepped groggily into the house but revived as soon as they realized they were safely out of Woodley and back to a place where they could be themselves.

Brandt showed them to the guest room, which was larger and more completely furnished than the one at Bryce and Nestor's. It did, however, seem to lack a drawer full of lube and condoms. They returned to the living room, to find Donnelly setting out drinks and some appetizers to tide the boys over until the food arrived.

When they had settled in, Donnelly raised his glass of sparkling water and said, "To Jonah, who came back to us, and to Casey, who nearly staged a riot to make it happen."

The boys laughed and drank and hugged and kissed.

A knock on the door announced the arrival of dinner, and once again the boys proved what everyone says about the appetites of eighteen-year-olds. Donnelly refilled plates as often as needed, and Brandt put on a movie.

As they snuggled together on the couch, Jonah turned to Casey. "This is… normal." He smiled. "All that drama, the entire town going batshit crazy over us, and this is all I wanted—for us to be together and eat dinner and watch a movie and be normal."

Casey grinned, and kissed his best friend. "I would happily be run out of any town in the country if it meant I could end up with you, doing this."

Brandt shot a glance at his partner. "You're going to cry, aren't you," he whispered.

"They're just so cute!" whispered Donnelly in return, a catch in his throat. "Think about how many more years of happiness we could have had if we'd started that early."

"But we weren't gay then," Brandt reminded him.

"I would have been gay for you no matter when you came along," Donnelly said and kissed his love on the nose.

"You sweet talker, you," sighed Brandt and laid his head on Donnelly's shoulder.

At the end of the movie, Donnelly stood and announced to the boys that it was time for bed. "You have a big day tomorrow. We'll have breakfast, and then take you to the university. So off to bed with you… and try to get at least a couple hours of sleep," he said with a wink.

A FEW minutes later Casey and Jonah were once again sitting together on a bed—but this time was different. They weren't questioning, uncertain boys groping their way through the unknown territory of their attraction. Now they were a real couple, and they and the whole of their hometown knew it.

"I can't believe you did all that," Jonah said softly. "You practically set the school on fire. I don't think Woodley's ever going to be the same."

"I would have done anything to get you back," Casey murmured.

"Even after I stood up in front of God and everyone and said I wasn't gay?"

"Jonah Fischer, that was the first lie you've ever told in your life. You are terrible at it." Casey giggled and kissed him on the cheek.

There was a soft knock on the door.

"Come in," they said in unison.

Donnelly opened the door and poked his head in. "You guys decent?"

"For about ten more seconds," Casey said with a snicker.

Donnelly laughed. "I'll take just that long to say goodnight and to let you know you should look in the box on that nightstand. See you in the morning."

"Goodnight, Gabriel," Casey said. "Thank you for everything."

"Goodnight guys. Try to get some rest, okay?" he said with a wink and pulled the door closed.

"Okay, I have to look," Jonah said excitedly and lunged for the nightstand. There was a wooden box sitting on top of it, and he gingerly lifted the lid. He burst out in giggles.

"What? What is it?" Casey demanded.

Jonah held up a small bottle of lubricant and a package of condoms, with the expiration date highlighted on the box. "They're more orderly about it, but there's a little Bryce and Nestor in our troopers."

"They've really been amazing."

"We'll have to find some way to thank them." Jonah closed the box and turned to Casey. "But first I'm going to spend some time finding ways to thank you." He pulled the boyfriend shirt off over his head and slid his pants and boxers to the floor. Flipping back the covers, he slipped into the bed, then lay back on the pillow and raised one arm over his head. He looked at Casey with a smolder. "Come here."

"THEY'RE SETTLED in for the night," Donnelly said as he closed the bathroom door behind him. Brandt was at the sink, washing his face. Donnelly stepped behind him and slipped his hands into the waistband of Brandt's new underwear—a gift from Donnelly, direct from the new stock at Grindstone. He whipped them down Brandt's legs, leaving them to pool at his ankles.

Brandt stood upright and reached for a towel. "Probably not a good idea to be walking around naked with impressionable youth in the house," he tutted at his partner.

"The only impression those youths are going to make is by grinding each other into our guest room mattress," Donnelly murmured as he traced Brandt's muscular buttocks with his fingertips.

Brandt spun around, his ass pressing against the cold porcelain of the sink. He put his arms around Donnelly. "You were amazing today."

"Just doing my job," Donnelly replied modestly.

"Actually, your job should have prevented you from doing several of those things, strictly speaking."

"Strictly speaking, protecting those boys from a God-crazed mob is the most important thing I can think of. If I couldn't do that, then I'd be turning in my badge on Monday."

"Good God, you're sexy when you get all Chuck Norris about gay rights." Brandt kissed him and ran his hands on his back from neck to ass and back again. "I'm proud to be the only person in the world who can fuck with Officer Gabriel Donnelly and live to tell the story."

"You just said the magic word," Donnelly replied with an eager grin.

"Chuck Norris?" Brandt asked, a sly smile playing on his features.

"Bed. Now."


CASEY CRAWLED over the bed, naked, and lay alongside Jonah. He rested the side of his head on Jonah's pectoral, his nipple within nibbling distance. They lay there, breathing together, for several minutes.

"This has been an amazing day," Jonah said as his fingers gently stroked his best friend's arm. "When the sun came up, I wasn't sure I would ever see you again. Now look at us."

"You were up at dawn? What were they doing to you?"

Jonah was silent for a moment. "It was awful. I don't think I can really describe it." He gathered his thoughts, then continued. "It was like they had shaped God into a club they were going to beat me with until I told them I was straight. And the whole time they kept telling me they were doing it because they loved me and just wanted what was best for me."

Casey lifted himself up on his elbow so he could look Jonah in the eye. "If that's love, then I think I'm doing it wrong."

Jonah smiled. "Everything you do is right." He kissed Casey tenderly. "But how did you get all the guys to do it along with you today?"

Casey grinned. "It was pretty easy. At practice on Tuesday, I told them I wanted to make a video that would cheer you up. They were all over that. A couple of the guys wanted to go full frontal, and I had to talk them out of it. Then when I told them what I was planning for the rally, they were completely on board. They felt really bad about what was happening to you."

"So they didn't care that I had a boner?"

"Funny thing about that. They were more concerned about how I felt about it. Their attitude was that if I was okay with it, they were okay with it. And I pretty much told them I was okay with it—really, really okay."

"Did you tell them that we were…?"

"I hinted at it pretty hard, I guess."

"But we hadn't done anything yet," Jonah said, his eyes wide.

"The fuck you talking about? After dancing in front of a train, snuggling by a campfire, having gay day with Bryce and Nestor, and enjoying naked cuddle time in the Bedroom of Many Condoms, you think I had no idea where things were going? There was no way I wasn't going to drag you into that shower and have my way with you, mister."

Jonah laughed at this exasperated exposition and pulled Casey to him. They kissed, softly at first and then more urgently. Then Jonah broke their kiss, and looked into Casey's eyes with a seriousness that startled him. "Casey, I need to tell you something."

Despite all of the wonderful things this day had brought, Casey felt panic rising in his chest at Jonah's tone. He tamped it down the best he could. "What is it? You know you can tell me anything."

"I've never… had sex. Of any kind. With anyone."

Casey exhaled a relieved sigh. "Oh, that. I know. You didn't have to tell me."

"But didn't you think I might have… you know… with some girl or something?"

"I guess you might have. But remember the first time you jerked off, and you couldn't wait to tell me? And the first wet dream you had—the sheets were probably still damp when you told me all about that. You told me when you measured your penis, and how long it was. I figured if anything as momentous as losing your virginity happened, you would find a way to let me know. Like maybe by putting it up on the billboard out by Highway 9."

Jonah laughed along with Casey, but he quickly grew serious again. "But you have, right? Had sex, I mean?"

Casey nodded. "Like a dozen times."

Jonah hesitated, but then he asked, "How was it?"

"Remember when you started driving, and it took months before you could get the car into your driveway without running over your mom's flower border?"

Jonah chuckled. "Man, she was pissed about that. But if I went too far on the other side, Dad would get pissed because there wasn't enough room to get the truck out of the garage."

"But after those first few months, you got the hang of it, right? And your mom's peonies were safe?"

Jonah nodded, but his brow was creased as if he had no idea where this was going.

"That's pretty much the way it is with sex. I think you need to do it, like, a hundred times before you feel like you know what you're doing and you're not going to mess anything up. And, just to refresh your memory, I've done it a dozen times. I was nowhere near any good at it."

Jonah squinted at his buddy. "That's not what I'd heard."

Casey's mouth dropped open. "What did you hear?"

"Bethany said you were the biggest she'd ever seen. And Alyssa told someone that you were an amazing cuddler. And…."

"And what?" demanded Casey.

"It's kind of dirty," Jonah replied.

"Even better! What else did you hear?"

"Someone said—I never found out who—that you came more than anyone she'd ever been with. That the condom was shaped like a light bulb, there was so much cum at the tip."

Casey's scandalized laughter filled the room.

Jonah, though, grew serious once again. "Are you sure you want to do this?"

Casey startled. "Do what?"

"Be here with me. You've been pretty successful with girls. No one seemed to have any complaints. Are you sure you want to give that up?"

Casey took a breath, and looked Jonah right in the eye. "All of those things are true, I guess. But I can't really take credit for the size of my dick. And being a good cuddler means I can sweet-talk them afterward to cover up how nervous I was during the sex. And you know what happens when I shoot—I did it all over you!" He leaned down and kissed Jonah's chest. "I can do all of that with you, and I'm never nervous, and I don't have to worry about doing it right, and it's just easy and... right. I'm not going to run over your flowers, is what I'm trying to say."

They shared a laugh, then Casey continued. "Being with you is everything I ever wanted. Yeah, I have a few more miles on me than you do, but it's not much and it doesn't matter. We're starting this together. There's nowhere I'd rather be, and no one else I'd rather be with."

They kissed, again and again, proving to themselves the truth of Casey's words.

"Now get ready," Casey growled. "I'm going to cuddle you so hard."


DONNELLY OPENED the bathroom door and checked to be sure the guest room door was still closed. He waved to Brandt, who did a cartoonish tiptoe to the bathroom that made the semiboner Donnelly had incited bounce crazily before him. Donnelly followed behind, stifling a chuckle, and once they had reached the bedroom, he kicked the door closed behind them. Then he lunged. He caught Brandt completely by surprise, crashing into his naked back, throwing him forward onto the bed.

"Oof! Fuck," Brandt groaned. He adored the sweet, gentle side of his partner, but he craved the wild animal he sometimes became at night.

Donnelly pounced on him, straddling him and kissing the back of his neck as he wrenched his own clothes off. He kissed his way down Brandt's spine, gaining speed toward his ultimate goal—Brandt's exquisitely rounded ass. Once he had arrived at the point where those globes of strength and power rose from the twin dimples that anchored the muscles of Brandt's back, Donnelly took a great mouthful of Brandt's left buttock and slid his teeth along the smooth, downy skin. He bit into the right glute as well, with a nip strong enough to make Brandt shiver.

Donnelly chewed a line from the indented outer edge of Brandt's right ass cheek all the way to the center split. Brandt ground his pelvis into the sheets. Donnelly knew him so well. He could keep Brandt on the edge where pleasure spiked into pain without going over the line. Too far over, anyway.

Donnelly kissed the very top of the cleft between Brandt's buttocks and then kissed a little farther down. As he made his way, he applied a gentle tension with his fingertips to pull the firm cheeks apart. A little farther on, however, more assertive traction was required; with a grunt he pushed Brandt's legs apart and settled his body in the vee they formed. This served to further separate Brandt's buttocks, and into the small gap between, Donnelly launched himself.

Brandt groaned and writhed as Donnelly's tongue invaded his ass, but Donnelly seemed unsatisfied with the access he had gained. He pressed his fingers into the space between his cheeks and Brandt's, and wrenched them apart. Brandt's anus twitched at the exposure and in anticipation of what was to come. Through this most intimate portal Donnelly roughly jammed his tongue, making it as thick and long as possible. He pressed and sucked, nibbled and shook, until Brandt's breathing was ragged and quick.

Donnelly groaned when he finally released his hold on Brandt's ass and came up to catch his breath. He grabbed hold of Brandt's right leg and lifted it, rolling his partner over onto his left side; he nudged the leg forward so Brandt's knee pressed against his belly, and Donnelly had free access to chew his way from back to front. This he did with noisy, slurping suction and insistent nibbling of his teeth. Brandt knew where he was going, and he held on to enjoy the ride. Donnelly inhaled Brandt's balls in one swoop—a move that had shocked him when Donnelly first tried it, but now he enjoyed immensely. Then Donnelly threw Brandt's right leg the rest of the way over, rolling Brandt onto his back. His hard cock jabbed the air, dripping the clear fluid produced by Donnelly's ministrations.

Donnelly wrapped a hand around Brandt's sturdy member and spread the precum around the head with his thumb. He swooped down on it, taking in the first four inches at once, and holding it there while his tongue—Brandt always loved this part the most—danced around the head. He sucked and swirled for several minutes, until Brandt reached for the bottle of lube by the bed.

Donnelly looked up at Brandt, lips still wrapped around Brandt's cock, and raised his eyebrows. "Now?" he was saying with his eyes.

Brandt answered by handing Donnelly the lube bottle—it was his way of saying "Right the fuck now."

Donnelly pulled off Brandt's cock and flipped open the lube bottle.


CASEY AND Jonah's kissing grew more and more passionate, until they could no longer ignore certain physical ramifications.

"Dude, your dick is drooling on me!" Casey exclaimed.

Jonah giggled. "You always do that to me."

Casey looked at him with eyebrows up. "Always?"

"Oh, man. Sometimes when we're in the weight room, and I'm spotting you on the bench? Fuckin' faucet in my shorts."

"You are so sick! And awesome." Casey laughed and looked down at the slick spot spreading from the head of Jonah's cock. "I've never touched one," he said quietly.

"You've touched your own—I watched you!"

"Yeah, that was amazing." Casey looked back down at Jonah's engorged—and sizable—cock. "But I think I'll try something new tonight."

Jonah held his breath as Casey reached down and brushed his fingertips along the length of his cock. "Oh, fuck," he exhaled. "You're the first person who's ever touched it."

"The world doesn't know what it's missing," Casey replied. He wrapped his fingers around Jonah, felt the weight and girth. "Oh, dude," he groaned. "You are so much thicker than me."

Jonah's eyes widened. "Really?"

"I can barely get my fingers around it," Casey replied. "But I'm going to try!" He began stroking gently, not yet confident that what felt good to him when he jerked off would feel good to Jonah. "Hey, toss me some of that lube," he said.

Jonah reached over and pulled the bottle out of the box. He handed it to Casey, who flipped the lid and squeezed some into his other hand. Rubbing them together briskly to warm the lube, he then resumed his strokes, now slicked and crackling.

"Oh, Casey, fuck," moaned Jonah, his eyes rolling back in his head.

Casey, stretched out alongside his best friend, watched his face as he picked up the pace of his stroking. Jonah's face flushed, and he writhed under Casey's ministrations. Casey leaned forward and sucked one of Jonah's nipples into his mouth. Jonah jumped as if shocked by electricity, and his cock surged in size and, amazingly, firmness. Casey suspected it wouldn't be long.

"Jonah," he whispered into his ear. "You are all I want, and I love you more than you can ever know. I want you… I want you to come for me."

Jonah's back arched off the mattress, and his hands flailed wildly. Casey gripped harder and stroked faster. He could see the full range of changes showing on his best friend's body: nipples hard, ridged abs flexing and stretching, balls pulling up. It wouldn't be long.

"Casey," he croaked. "I love you." Jonah gasped and his body went tense from head to toe. The first blast of semen exploded from his cock and flew over his head, striking the wall with a splat.

Casey gasped and kept stroking. The next three shots also flew over Jonah's head and were followed by six or eight pearly ropes of cum that laced his entire torso from throat to belly button. Casey slowed his pace, and he ended with a few gentle squeezing strokes to coax the last drops of semen from the deep-crimson head of Jonah's cock.

He released his grip and let Jonah's exhausted penis come to rest on his heaving lower belly. He gave it a few last tickling strokes with his fingertips. He looked into Jonah's flushed, glowing face and smiled.

"That was... amazing," Jonah panted. He brought his hand up to Casey's face and stroked his cheek. "I'm so glad it was you."

"We've been heading here all our lives," Casey whispered, nuzzling into Jonah's hand on his cheek.

They kissed and tickled each other for a while, and then Casey figured he should get something to clean up with. He pulled on his discarded boxers, which were grossly distended by his long-standing erection, and went to the bathroom for a washcloth—and something to clean the wall. When he returned, he lovingly mopped up the ample evidence of Jonah's excitement.

He settled back into bed next to Jonah and sighed. "I'm so happy."

"I'm so gay," Jonah answered back with a giggle, "and now I'm the only one in this house who has never touched a dick. No fair."

Casey cleared his throat ceremoniously. "Jonah Fischer: I, Casey Melville, hereby grant you exclusive access to my penis. Hell, my entire private area, up to and including those parts that, quite honestly, I still have a hard time thinking of as sexual. Be that as it may, I put them all at your disposal, though I warn you I'll want them disposed of at least three times before we go to sleep." He saluted smartly, because that's what this momentously silly speech seemed to call for, and then burst into giggles.

"Challenge accepted, Mr. Melville. Prepare to beg for mercy."

Casey wasn't sure what wrestling moves Jonah used in the lightning attack that followed, but he was never so happy to end up on his back.


DONNELLY SLIPPED his fist slurpily up and down Brandt's erection, spreading the lube evenly across its considerable girth and length. He then took a squirt of the shiny gel and applied it to his own ass, slipping a finger in to be ready for what was to come.

He straddled Brandt's legs, braced around his hips, and reached behind to grab the slippery pole he was about to mount. He touched its wide head to his anus, and Brandt sighed in contentment. This was what he wanted more than anything in the world. Donnelly pushed back, as Brandt knew he would, and Brandt pushed up, as Donnelly knew he would, and they joined. Donnelly gasped—as many times as they had done this, the intrusion of Brandt's substantial cock head through his tight ring of muscle still sent goose bumps over his entire body.

Brandt watched avidly as Donnelly slid down his fleshy pole; his descent was achingly slow and unbearably hot. Finally, Donnelly's wide-spread ass came to rest on Brandt's pelvis, and he took on the weight of the man he loved. This was without question his favorite part—the look of utter contentment on Donnelly's face as he felt the entirety of Brandt enter him. He would rest here for a moment, as if he needed to sort through the sensations crashing through his body, before motion could commence. But motion was what Brandt craved, and he waited anxiously for Donnelly to begin his slow transit upward, where he would nearly—but never—surrender the tip of Brandt's rock-hard cock.

Slowly, Donnelly began to move, but he wasn't gradual tonight. Tonight he hesitated at the very tip of Brandt's cock, and then he brought himself down hard, impaling himself on the intruder. He touched down only briefly before rocketing up, and there he began the cycle again.

Brandt gasped and groaned, straining to absorb the aggressive fuck rhythm Donnelly was pounding out. He was more than up to the task. He shifted his hips slightly and thrust his pelvis up when he knew Donnelly's prostate was in range.

Donnelly's growl was like that of a bear that smells honey just out of reach in a treetop hive: deep, rumbling, and dangerous. Again and again Brandt stabbed at his prostate, pressing it, milking it, until Donnelly's cock, rock hard against his heaving belly, emitted a steady crystalline drip of fluid. Then the shudder began, the clearest sign to Brandt that Donnelly was going to have an orgasm without ever touching his cock. His bounces became shorter, more focused; the muscles in his ass began to spasm; Brandt felt his prostate grow and tense and solidify, and he knew it was time.

Donnelly froze at the precise point that Brandt's cock applied the greatest pressure to his gland, and his whole body twitched while the orgasm Brandt had driven into him exploded out. He looked down with peaked eyebrows and pleading eyes to his cock, which had taken on a life of its own. It bobbed madly, and at the highest point of each bounce it shot out an arc of white, a jet of pure pleasure. Brandt felt splash after splash laid across his body, coming to pool in the valleys between his plated ab muscles.

It was what Donnelly always did next that got him every time. Having emptied every drop of semen from his body, he would look dreamily into Brandt's eyes—and then somehow tighten down his ass so that Brandt's cock was suddenly squeezed along its entire length, milked from base to tip all at once. The effect was instantaneous and urgent. Brandt simply had no choice but to try to hang on as Donnelly's ass forced the orgasm upon him. He grabbed his lover by the hips, right where that sexy V-line descended to his cock, and held him firmly in place while he bucked like an angry rodeo bull thrashing the last rider of the day. Donnelly, the imposing and muscular trooper, bobbed like a demented doll on Brandt's dick while his ass filled with the hot spunk it craved.

Donnelly pitched forward, glossed with the exertion of his virtuoso performance, into Brandt's arms. Sweat-slicked and panting, they kissed, and caressed, and reveled in the exhaustion that only love can bring.

JONAH STRADDLED Casey and raked his fingernails down the sides of his lover's ribcage. The combination of tickling and stinging intoxicated Casey, and he writhed, hoping this sensation would never end. Jonah, though, clearly would not be deterred from his goal of finally getting his hands on a dick other than his own. He lifted himself off Casey and slid neatly down his body; he stopped only when he was facing the object of his quest.

Casey watched as Jonah's hand slowly approached. Until now, no man had ever touched Casey's cock, and Jonah had touched no man; then, in the blink of an eye, all that changed. Jonah wrapped his fingers around Casey's achingly hard prick. As his fingers slid along its length, he looked up at Casey, joy in his eyes.

"The skin is so soft!" he exclaimed, wonder in his voice.

"Well, I occasionally massage lotion into it. You know, for softness."

Jonah grinned at his best friend. "Tell me, honestly, did you ever—even once—think of me when you jerked it?"

Casey blushed and looked away.

"Oh my God! You have to tell me." Jonah's kept up his stroking, a move he surely suspected would provide motivation for his friend to talk.

Casey closed his eyes for a moment and then looked down at his best friend in the world. He owed him the truth.

"There was one time. This was just after I'd discovered how to find good porn online, and I was watching a lot of it. I found out I was kind of an ass man—the curve of a smooth pair of cheeks would put me over the edge every damn time." Casey sighed dreamily, then snapped back to the present. "Anyway, we swam at the lake a lot that summer, and you brought that stupid pool float that could barely hold air— remember that?"

Jonah laughed. "I loved that thing."

"You would float around for hours while it slowly leaked and you sank lower and lower into the water. Once it had deflated enough, only your head and shoulders and ass would be out of the water. So this one time I catch sight of you out of the corner of my eye, and all I see is the mound of your ass rising up out of the water and curving back in. My stupid dick decides that an ass is an ass, and it goes full bone in like a second and a half." Casey laughed. "And then, because I'm so fucking horny, I just stare at you for like ten minutes while you float around on the lake. And it hits me—your ass is beautiful, every bit as beautiful as the asses I was jerking it to on the interwebs every night. Fuck. Good thing I was already in the water, so you couldn't see me. There was no way I was going to get out of that water until I got rid of my boner, so I just went at it. Right there in the lake."

Jonah was entranced. "So you closed your eyes and thought of porn to finish the job?"

Casey was suddenly serious. "No." He took a deep breath before continuing. "I looked at you. I saw the water drops on your ass as they caught the sunlight and glittered like diamonds. I watched you clench up those muscles when you tried to hike yourself up on your sinking raft. I looked at you, Jonah. I saw you as I stroked. It was all you. And when I came, I was still looking at you."

Jonah's mouth was hanging open. "Why didn't you tell me?"

"What was I going to say? 'Hey, buddy, you know what's funny? I pleasured myself while looking at your ass.' Yeah, that's kind of a high-risk move. So I did what guys do—I buried it. I haven't thought about that day since. Now, of course, it's kind of hot to look back on. But that's only because of where we are now. Back then it would have been... awkward."

"That is about the sexiest thing I've ever heard," Jonah murmured. "But this," he nodded down to Casey's cock, "is about the sexiest thing I've ever seen. And it's about to become the sexiest thing I've ever tasted."

It was Casey's turn to gasp. "You're not really going to... are you?"

"Try to stop me. I have legal claim to these parts, you may recall. I'm going to do what I want to them."

"Fuck," Casey moaned, and laid his head back on the pillow. He gave himself to this moment, to this man.

Jonah lifted Casey's cock away from his belly—a challenging task, given that when erect it slapped right up against his abs—and looked intently at it.

"Do it, man," groaned Casey, who had lifted his head again and was watching Jonah with terrified anticipation. "Suck me, Jonah. Suck me, please?"

Jonah looked right into Casey's eyes as he brought his penis to his lips. He opened his mouth, and his tongue darted out, flicking at the tip. A chill shot through Casey, and he feared he might come right then from that little bit of stimulation. But Jonah apparently had plans to do much more. He licked his lips and opened wide.

Hot. Wet. Tight. These were all the sensations Casey registered in that first moment, and they combined to push him immediately to the very edge of orgasm. There was no slow build-up, no gradual increase of sensation. Everything he needed to exist as a sexual being was in Jonah's mouth, and his body responded.

"Jonah!" he called, to warn his friend he was about to come. But he was unprepared for the manic fibrillation of the muscles deep inside him that are only called into action when there is sperm to unleash on the world. Unleash they did.

Casey's ejaculation was a steady stream of semen—no breaks between blasts for him, not when the stimulation was so new and so intense—and it overwhelmed Jonah instantly. He coughed, sending Casey's spunk everywhere, while still more flowed into his mouth. He pumped with his hand—he had probably learned that trick watching porn—but he still tried to keep his mouth on the erupting head of Casey's cock. It was a losing battle.

Finally the storm subsided, and Jonah slowed his pumping and swallowed what was in his mouth. Most of Casey's load had flowed immediately back out and down his prick, to pool at the base of his cock and coat his balls.

Casey finally lifted his head, and looked down, panting, at his best friend; Jonah's reddened face was spattered with cum. "You're a mess," he said with a smile. "And I love you for it."

Jonah grinned and tried without much success to wipe some of the cum off his face. But his glow said all that Casey needed to know: this is what Jonah had wanted, maybe for as long as he'd had sexual thoughts, and now that he had achieved it, it had been everything he had hoped for. He reached down to the side of the bed for the washcloth Casey had brought in; he used it to wipe his face and then darted out to the bathroom—naked, scandalously—and returned with it rinsed and warm. He wiped up the considerable pools of semen Casey had blasted out all over the place.

"I guess what they say about you is true," Jonah said as he mopped up.

"That I'm a handsome rake who will win your heart with his devilish charm?"

"No, that you cum like a volcano. Is there any place this stuff didn't land?" Jonah burst out laughing.

"You're one to talk. At least I didn't paint the walls like you did."

"Only because my tonsils got in your way."

Casey conceded the point. As he wouldn't be able to get another erection for at least four minutes, he lay back on the pillows and looked at his friend, his lover. "Come here," he said, and with great joy in his heart, he wrapped his arm around the man he had come to realize he loved.

BRANDT AND Donnelly lay quietly in their bed, limbs intertwined haphazardly.

"Sounds like they're settling down in there," Brandt observed.

"They're eighteen," Donnelly replied. "Give them five minutes and they'll be at it again."

"Ah, youth," Brandt said dreamily. "You did show them where the condoms are, right?"

"Of course. But I don't think they'll be doing anything requiring a condom for a while. You know what the first times are like. We just rubbed up against each other for a few minutes our first time, and that was a life-altering experience. They'll need some time to work up to butt stuff."

"I love it when you talk that way," Brandt said, sleepily.

"I love you every minute of every day," Donnelly replied, and he seemed quite pleased with his rhyme. "Now get some sleep—we need to get up early to cook enough bacon for our wrestlers." He paused, listening. "Sounds like they're starting to work up an appetite as we speak, in fact. Good for them." He kissed Brandt good-night.

# CHAPTER NINE
## COLLEGE LIFE

CASEY'S EYES admitted the first light of day far later than usual, but the exertions of the previous night had exhausted him to a degree that even wrestling practice didn't. He blinked hard to bring the room into focus, and the first thing he recognized was Jonah, watching him.

"Morning," he mumbled, and he was rewarded with a smile that made his heart light.

"You're still here," Jonah whispered, stroking the side of Casey's cheek.

"Where else would I be?" Casey put his hand on Jonah's, brought it to his lips for a kiss.

"I must have woken up a dozen times last night. Each time I was sure I would be in an empty bed."

"I'll keep saying it until you hear me. You will never be alone." Casey lifted his head up and kissed his best friend. "This is where I want to be."

Jonah smiled and ran his fingers through Casey's hair. "We should probably get up. I smell bacon. I wouldn't want to keep Ethan and Gabriel waiting."

"You had me at 'bacon,'" Casey murmured with a grin.

They got up and pulled on some of Casey's clothes from the duffels.

"Good morning!" called Donnelly as they entered the kitchen. He was hard at work producing an epic breakfast.

"Morning," the boys answered in unison.

"Coffee?" asked Brandt, who already had mugs in his hand.

Casey reached out a hand and made a noise like a zombie smelling fresh brains. Jonah laughed and took a mug as well. Then Casey dropped in a shocking amount of sugar and took a long slurp of the black liquid.

"Oh, that's the stuff," he said with a sigh. "Now, how can I help? I'm pretty good in the kitchen, if I do say so myself."

"No! You two sit," Donnelly replied, shooing the boys out of the kitchen with his spatula. "Judging from the sounds coming out of that guest room last night, I'd be surprised if you got twenty minutes of actual sleep."

Jonah smiled and blushed as they sat at the table. "Sorry if we kept you up."

"Oh, we were up anyway," deadpanned Brandt as he perused the paper. He lowered the page and winked at the boys. "You rather inspired us."

"Is that what all the racket was?" Casey joined in with a laugh. "It sounded like someone was fighting off a bear attack."

"Kinda felt that way too," Donnelly cracked from the kitchen.

"This is amazing," Jonah said when the general laughter died down. "Talking like this with you guys. I feel normal for the first time in my life."

Casey erupted into laughter again at this. "So 'normal' is being turned into an Internet sex object against your will, imprisoned by your parents, and chased out of your hometown by an angry mob?"

"I guess it has been an eventful week," Jonah said with a shrug as he sipped his coffee.

"I get what you mean, though," Donnelly said. "When you're straight, making jokes about people having sex, and being able to sleep with your partner, and having your relationship accepted by other people is automatic. But the threat of not being considered normal is one of the most powerful weapons our society uses against gay people."

Brandt nodded. "And only once you accept that some people won't think of you as normal anymore can you start to build a new community of people whose idea of normal is the same as yours."

"Plus Bryce and Nestor," Donnelly added, rolling his eyes and grinning.

"Oh, man—those guys are awesome," Casey said. "They helped me so much with the rally. Did you see those shirts they got for us?"

Brandt looked at Donnelly and nodded his acknowledgment of his partner's sartorial instincts. "Gabriel suspected Bryce might have had a hand in that."

"He was really great. And all he wanted in return was a picture of us wearing them. The guys wanted to do it wearing only the shirts, but I told them we should keep it clean. I have the picture on my phone. I should send that to him." Casey pulled out his phone and started typing.

"Actually," Brandt said, "I think Bryce can get the picture right here." He folded back the newspaper and there, on page three, was a photo of the rally. Under the headline "Rural Rally Raises Ruckus" was the wrestling team surrounding Casey and Jonah in the moment before they kissed.

"Oh, my parents aren't going to like that," Jonah said under his breath.

"Have they liked anything you've done in the last two weeks?" Casey asked. Contempt for the Fischers dripped from his words.

"The article doesn't go into a lot of specifics, but it does name you both, and the writer takes a decidedly... celebratory tone about the stand you took for gay rights."

"Yep, Dad's having a heart attack right about now." Jonah sighed and looked down. Clearly the situation with his parents was weighing on him.

"Breakfast is ready," Donnelly announced, bringing two large platters of bacon, eggs, and pancakes in from the kitchen. "We can obsess about the tabloids later. First, we eat."


AFTER BREAKFAST Jonah went into the bungalow's only bathroom to take a shower, leaving Casey and the officers to enjoy their third cups of coffee.

"How's Jonah doing?" Brandt asked, once they could hear water running in the shower.

Casey smiled, but it was a smile that carried a larger measure of worldly maturity than Brandt was used to seeing. "It's like he's two people right now. One is really sad about how his parents have treated him, and the other is like a kid on his first trip to Gay Disneyland. He's really, really happy and really, really sad at the same time."

"He's really, really lucky to have you," Donnelly said warmly.

"Oh, I'm the lucky one," Casey replied. "I had no idea this is what I wanted until I saw how brave Jonah was in the face of that homophobic shitstorm. It finally gave me the courage to think about how much he means to me, and always has." Casey thought for a moment. "Here's something I don't really understand, though."

Brandt and Donnelly both nodded expectantly.

"Jonah's been feeling pent up and scared and basically in denial about being gay for, like, ever. So all this stuff that's happened lately kind of forced him to be honest about it, which is great. But I never felt any of that. I was pretty happy dating girls, and I think I was pretty good at it. No complaints, if you know what I mean." He winked at Brandt and Donnelly. "So, here's my question: am I really gay?"

Brandt smiled at the question. "Casey, you would be amazed how many times I asked myself the same thing when my life was crashing down around me. I had never—never—even thought about another man that way until Gabriel. And it wasn't easy to admit those feelings were developing, either."

"But sometimes," Donnelly interjected, "you find love where you weren't expecting it—and sometimes it has a penis." He made a shocked face and then laughed. "Conservatives would have you believe that everyone is born straight, and a few sickos go haywire and have sex with other men. But humans are much more flexible than that."

"I think what we're trying to say," Brandt summed up, "is that you fell in love with your best friend, and that's awesome. So if you need a label, I'd stick with that one: awesome."

"You guys... I tell ya, I feel sorry for people who don't have someone like you in their lives. You kind of rescued us from what could have been a really awful situation. I feel like we somehow managed to come out of it way better than we went into it."

"We're happy to help," Donnelly said. "I think you'll find that there is a lot of support out there for you, as well as a lot of people who will be critical of how you're living your life. The trick is to figure out who's who."

"And speaking of who's who," Brandt added. "We've been meaning to ask you—who were those two guys who spoke just before you at the rally yesterday? The ones who talked about the other video?"

Casey nodded. "That was Max and Trevor. I'm really proud of them for speaking up. I mean, what they did was shitty, but at least they see that now."

Jonah poked his head out from the bathroom. "Case, you coming?"

"If you'll excuse me," Casey said to Brandt and Donnelly, "I need to jump into the shower and have awesome unlabeled sex with someone." He bolted from the room. The bathroom door swung shut and ecstatic giggling commenced, as well as some giddy splashing.

"Another cup of coffee?" Brandt asked. "They may be a while."


IT WAS nearly noon by the time the foursome drove onto the campus of the university, the largest in the state. Casey and Jonah piled out of the backseat with their duffels and looked around at the dorms surrounding the parking area. They had been on the campus before— the state championships were held here every year, and the Woodchucks had earned a spot in the tourney every year since the mid-60s. But this time they looked at it with new eyes. This might be where they would spend the next four years of their lives. Their lives together, Casey said to himself, and he smiled.

"The liaison person is supposed to meet you here right about now," Brandt said, checking his watch.

The wrestlers had an appointment to meet a gay-athlete outreach coordinator before the scheduled meeting with the coach later in the afternoon. As if on cue, the door swung open, and a tall, well-muscled young man scanned the area quickly and recognized the ones he was supposed to meet. He jogged over briskly.

"Jonah? Casey?" he asked, and when they nodded he advanced with his hand extended. "I'm Reese. It's great to meet you." He turned to Brandt and Donnelly. "And these must be... your... older brothers?"

"I'm Officer Ethan Brandt, and this is Officer Gabriel Donnelly. We've been helping Casey and Jonah sort a few things out."

Reese's eyes widened. "Are you the ones who broke them out of Woodley?" he asked in reverent tones.

"You've heard of that, then?" asked Donnelly, wincing a little.

"Of course!" Reese replied. "I've been following the whole blow-up there—my high school faced them at wrestling regionals several times, and the rivalry was pretty bitter. It was really cool to see those guys getting behind you that way. I thought that Woodley was pretty conservative."

"Yeah, it's still pretty much a redneck backwater when it comes to gay stuff," Casey said. "But the guys on the team stand up for the guys on the team, right?"

Reese nodded. "That's the way it works here too. How about I take you to the room you'll be staying in, and then I'll show you around?"

"We'll swing back by tomorrow afternoon," Donnelly said. "We need to get you guys back to Woodley so you can get ready for regionals."

"Sounds good," Jonah said, "though it's going to be kind of strange to be back in Woodley after the way we left."

"The Woodchucks want another state title more than they fear a boner in the locker room, so they'll probably roll out the red carpet for you guys once they've had their cooling-off period," Brandt said.

"Welcome would be a nice change," Jonah said with a touch of sarcasm. "We'll see you guys tomorrow."

Donnelly hugged both boys as if he were their father dropping them off at college, and then the troopers got in their car and left the boys to their visit.

"Come on in. We'll get you settled in one of our elegantly appointed dorm rooms," Reese said with a wry grin. He led them into the building marked Hurley Hall. "This is known as the athletic dorm. Most of the athletes who play for the university live here their first year. They used to group all of the Section 28 couples together in one of the ancient firetrap dorms across campus, but starting next fall they're going to house the athlete twenty-eights here with everyone else. Makes for stronger team unity to keep everyone together."

Reese told them about the facilities as they climbed the stairs to the third floor of the building, and then he led them to a door about halfway along the hallway. "Most of the rooms here are doubles, but some are set up as triples. Since my room is over in the other dorm, I asked them to put you up in one of the triples so I could stay with you overnight—kind of a university-sponsored slumber party."

"Why are you in the other dorm?" Jonah asked. "Aren't you an athlete?"

"Yep, and I play a real sport—lacrosse," Reese replied with a wink. "I'm in one of the Section 28 rooms with my boyfriend, who plays football."

"Wait—what?" Casey asked. "You're gay?"

Reese nodded. "That's kind of why they asked me to help recruit the star wrestling couple," he said with a laugh. "Calvin and I are going to move here next year. They're making us gay-athlete RAs."

"And won't Calvin miss you tonight while you're sleeping here?" Jonah asked.

"Yeah, not so much. He's out this weekend on a recruiting trip for the football team. They send him out when there's a gay player they really want." Reese laughed. "Actually, they send him out even when there's a straight player they really want. He's kind of amazing that way. No one's straight around Cal." He saw them eyeing the less-than-romantic sleeping arrangements. "When they set up a room for you guys in the fall, they'll take out the bunk and bring in a double bed."

Casey and Jonah dropped their duffels on the bunk bed. "And the other guys in the dorm are okay with this whole thing?" Jonah asked.

"It's going to sound kind of strange, I know—I come from a pretty conservative town, and a very conservative family—but the university is really committed to equal treatment, and they make it pretty clear to athletes and everyone else that they need to grow up about how some guys like dick."

Casey turned to Jonah. "I like this guy."

Reese laughed. "All right, shall we take a little tour?"

They left the dorm and walked over to the sports facility, where they toured the training rooms, workout areas, and finally the locker room.

"Remember, our boy here can't be trusted in a locker room," Casey warned as they entered.

"The stuff I read mentioned something about a video in which his excitement was visible, but I was never able to find that online." He glanced at Jonah. "Not that I searched all that hard for it or anything."

Jonah laughed. "It's okay. After the workout I got last night I'm pretty sure it won't be a problem."

Reese's eyebrows shot up, but his facial expression seemed to indicate that he could guess what Jonah was referring to.

They walked down the central aisle of the room, and found it to be as nicely appointed as the one back in Woodley. As they returned to the corridor, Reese checked his watch. "Oh, we gotta get you over to the coach's office. I told him I'd be by with you before three, and it's two thirty already." He led them back out to the hallway and up a flight of stairs to the offices of the coaching staff. He knocked on the door of the head coach for wrestling and was invited in by a gruff voice from inside the room.

"I'll wait for you guys down the hall where the couches are," Reese said as they entered the office.

As soon as the coach saw who was at his door, he sprang to his feet and strode over to the young men. "You must be Jonah and Casey from the hallowed halls of Woodley. Great to meet you!" He shook their hands and motioned for them to sit in chairs at his desk.

"I'm Dirk Sawyer, and I run the best wrestling program in the United States."

"Wait," Jonah said. "You're Sawyer the Destroyer?"

Sawyer laughed and nodded. "The one and only."

"They still talk about you in Woodley." Jonah sat back in his chair, a look of amazement on his face. "I can't believe I'm actually sitting here with Sawyer the Destroyer."

"That was a lot of years ago—nice to know they still remember."

"Your name comes up a lot when they give us the safety lectures," Casey said. "I think they just like talking about that guy's leg."

"Like I always said, it was broken when I got there." Sawyer held up his hands and shrugged.

"This is awesome," Jonah said.

"But we're here to talk about you two joining my wrestling program. I've been following your careers at Woodley, and I'm very impressed. You would make great additions to my squad. Now, what will it take for you to agree to come to the U?"

Casey had hoped for a warm welcome, but he had not expected a sales pitch. "Well, I'm sure you know the economy in Woodley sucks donkey right now, so money for tuition and stuff is going to be really important for us."

"I hear ya," Sawyer replied. "And I want you to have no worries on that score. You two are among the top wrestlers in the state, and the only ones I am aware of on the top-ten list who haven't chosen a college. I can't offer a full ride to all of my wrestlers, but to bring you two here, it won't be a problem."

"Do you mean for the first year only?" Josh asked. "Or all four years?"

"All four, including any time that you might be sidelined due to injury. We don't walk away from our athletes if they are unable to compete."

"Wow" was about all Jonah could say.

Casey cocked his head to one side and looked somewhat critically at Coach Sawyer. "You haven't talked about the whole mess in Woodley. It's gotten pretty ugly, what with the videos and all."

"Casey, I've been following the situation pretty closely. I have to say that your bravery has impressed me greatly. And Jonah, your resolve in the face of such horrible exploitation has been amazing to watch. I think you both have acquitted yourselves admirably throughout the whole controversy."

"That's good to hear, but there's still the issue of our being... you know... a couple." Casey would need some time to get used to describing himself and Jonah that way. "Is the rest of the team really going to be okay with it?"

"Why don't you ask them yourselves? We do a Sunday pick-up practice at noon, to get the men back in the gym at the end of the weekend. Come by and see what you think of the squad. But I can assure you they would welcome you to the team without reservation. They know I'm trying to recruit you, and they are excited as hell at the prospect of adding a couple of Woodchucks to the team. What those Woodchucks do in their spare time is their own business." Sawyer smiled confidently. He went on to describe the squad's practice schedule, training regimen, and other details the boys needed to know. He wound up his talk as the clock neared three thirty. "So, I have to ask—what's it look like for us, right now?"

"I'd say really good," Jonah said, beaming.

"I'm ready to sign up," Casey agreed. "Can we give you a final answer once we've met the team and had some time to discuss it?"

"Of course. And I'd be happy to talk with your parents at any point, if they decide they want to pick up our conversation. It ended rather abruptly."

"You talked to my parents?" Jonah asked.

"Yes, several times. But then last week they called and told me you weren't going to wrestle in college, and that you were going to be going to another school. I think it was a Christian college somewhere. I'm really glad you decided to give us a second chance."

Jonah looked nonplussed. "Me too. And don't worry about contacting my parents. I'll be making this decision, not them."

Sawyer nodded. "Good to hear. I think student athletes who make their own decisions make better ones, and they stick to them."

"Well, we should get back to Reese," Casey said, rising. "Thanks for your time, Coach Sawyer."

"It was my pleasure, men. If there's anything I can help you with, please don't hesitate to call. And I'll look forward to seeing you tomorrow at noon."

Jonah and Casey nodded and took their leave. A few doors down the hall they found Reese, reclined on a sofa in a common area. He sprang to his feet.

"How'd it go?" he asked.

"Good," Jonah answered. "Almost scary good."

"He wants us to scrimmage with the team tomorrow," Casey added.

Reese smiled. "I told you, he's desperate for some hot Woodchuck-on-Woodchuck action."

"We'll try to keep it clean on the mat," Casey said with a laugh.

"Wrestlers." Reese rolled his eyes. "Now, next up is a campus tour, so let's get moving. Oh," he said, as they started walking toward the large buildings at the center of campus, "we have several choices tonight for activities. First, the Campus Pride organization is doing a rally to support gay candidates in the next election—kinda dry political stuff, but their post-march dances are usually pretty hot. Second, it's drag night at the club in the student center. But you came with duffels and not gown bags, so I'm thinking that might be a 'no.'" Casey and Jonah shook their heads.

Jonah asked, "What would you be doing tonight if we weren't here?"

"I'd be at Balls Out—it's a sports bar near campus—watching the basketball game."

Casey and Jonah fist-bumped.

"Yeah, let's do that one," Casey said. "I was hoping to be able to catch the game."

"I had no idea there were gay sports bars," Jonah said, shaking his head.

"Oh, it's not technically a gay bar," Reese said. "The guy who owns it thought the name sounded, I don't know... extreme? And then he wonders why most of his customers are gay. It didn't start as a gay bar, but you wouldn't know that on a Saturday night."

Casey turned to Jonah. "I think I'm going to like college."

"I think I will too," his best friend agreed.

AFTER THE game, Reese brought Jonah and Casey back to their room. They brushed their teeth down the hall in the large bathroom and then settled in for the night. Casey and Jonah sat in the lower bunk on one side of the room, and Reese sat on the futon that was tucked under the other bunk bed.

"So guys, what do you think?" Reese asked.

"This place is amazing," Jonah replied. "After all the shit I've been through in the last week, I can't believe I'm here."

"How about you, Casey?"

"If Jonah's happy, I'm happy. I kind of figured I would end up here anyway—my family donated a metric ass-ton of money back in the last century sometime, and part of the deal was that descendants get in. But to be able to wrestle here—that's pretty awesome."

"Excellent. Looks like I don't have to give you the hard sell," Reese said with a smile.

"What would that involve, exactly?" Casey asked with a wink. "I may be having second thoughts."

Reese threw a pillow at Casey, which bounced back and forth among the three for a few minutes.

"So I know you guys have a workout tomorrow at noon. Would you like to come with me to the early service at my church, and then we can carbo-load in the dining hall before you meet up with the team? The church thing is entirely optional, of course—just thought I'd throw out the offer."

Casey looked somewhat nervously at Jonah.

"I've never had a Sunday without church," Jonah said, after a pensive moment. "But my pastor kind of went apeshit homophobic avenger on me this week, so I might just want to go off the God grid for a while."

Casey turned to Reese, brow furrowed. "So, you go to church regularly?"

Reese nodded. "Calvin and I were raised in a church that sounds a lot like the one Jonah's been in. They were all about love and communion until we came out. Then they slammed the door on us pretty hard. But there's a church here that's awesome—mostly students, and they welcome everybody. I think you'd like it. But again, entirely up to you."

"I've never been to a church thingy—"

"A service," interrupted Jonah.

"Right—one of those thingies—in my entire life." He looked at Jonah and smiled. "But if Jonah's up for it, I'll come along."

Jonah seemed to ponder the question for a moment, then nodded. "Sure, why not? Maybe one thing in my life won't have to change."

"Great! I'll set my alarm for seven, and we can shower and get over there for the 8:00 a.m. service—sorry, Casey, the 8:00 a.m. thingy." Reese laughed. "Then we'll hit the breakfast buffet downstairs and get you to your practice. Sound like a plan?"

The boys nodded.

"Now, you just have to decide who gets to be on top," Reese said with a wink as he climbed the ladder to the top bunk.

"You kidding me?" Casey cried. "I could have lost this boy a half dozen times this week. No way I'm letting him out of my sight."

Jonah turned an apologetic face toward Reese "I promise we won't keep you up or anything."

"Heh, no worries," Reese replied. "I sleep like a rock. You two have fun," he said, then turned over and laid his head on the pillow.

Casey and Jonah, exhausted from their day, snuggled together on the bottom bunk and fell right to sleep.


THE THREE boys entered the church just before the service began, hair still a little damp from their showers (they had been the only ones in the shower at that hour, and had spent perhaps a little too much time splashing each other). The church was an airy, sunlit building across the street from the university campus, and the pews were filled with college students. The minister at the front, a large black woman with rainbow vestments, held forth with a compassionate and inspiring sermon on community, with specific reference to upcoming service projects the church was organizing.

After the service, Reese introduced Casey and Jonah to a large group of his friends, and even Casey began to feel more comfortable with the idea of attending church thingies.

Their breakfast excelled in the foundation of dorm food—carbs, and lots of them. Covered with maple syrup. The boys ate joyfully and then headed for the practice gym back at the sports center.

Coach Sawyer had arranged for clean uniforms for Jonah and Casey to wear for practice, and they walked into the gym to be surprised by the applause of the wrestling team.

"Um, what the hell?" Casey leaned over and whispered to Jonah.

"Not sure," Jonah replied. Both of them simply responded with a smile and a nod, like a couple of prom princes.

"There they are!" shouted Sawyer. "Good to see you, men. Now, there'll be time to get to know our Woodley Woodchucks at the end of practice. For now, let's see what they can do on the mat."

The next hour saw the boys from Woodley in constant action; some members of the team seemed to go easy on them, perhaps out of deference to their widely publicized shitstorm of a week, and others seemed to be trying their mettle. A sweaty time was had by all.

Sawyer passed out water bottles at the end of practice—Jonah and Casey would add these university-logo bottles to the sweatshirts, coffee mugs, and key chains the admissions office had loaded them up with—and formally introduced everyone to the new recruits. The university wrestlers seemed pleased to meet Jonah, whose reputation as a champion wrestler far preceded him, and they asked some questions about his technique. But they all clamored to talk with Casey, whose role in supporting his friend had made a significant impression. Several asked questions about how to support friends or roommates who were, or who seemed to be, gay.

"My best friend kind of hinted he might want to be more than friends," one said. "I'm not into it, but I don't want to hurt his feelings. What should I do?"

Casey had never intended to be the poster boy for gay allies, especially since he was an ally for about three days before becoming

Jonah's boyfriend. But he was glad to see so many of the wrestlers wanted to be supportive, so he tried to help.

"I would tell him," Casey replied, "that you're flattered, and you appreciate the attention, but you're just not wired that way—it's you, not him. Then offer to fix him up with one of your single gay friends."

"What if I don't have any single gay friends?"

"Then," Casey replied with a giggle, "you need to get out more."

"Okay, guys, I'm sure you have homework to do," Sawyer announced. "Let's hit the showers and get on our way."

Jonah and Casey were swept along into the locker room with the team. Shoes and socks went flying, and singlets were dropped into a big hamper on the way to the showers. The shower room was large and open, dotted with poles running from floor to ceiling, each sprouting five shower heads. As they entered, water began flowing from several of the groups of shower heads, and the wrestlers gathered around them and began soaping up and talking loudly.

Casey leaned over to Jonah, who was rinsing in the stream of water next to him. "You know what's great?"

"What?"

"No one cares." Casey gestured around to the rest of the team. No one was hiding their nudity from them, or acting in any way anxious or upset.

"I wish it could be that way in Woodley," Jonah replied with a not-very-hopeful shrug.

"I think it will be. The guys were pretty angry about the way the school and your parents were treating you. I bet it'll be fine."

"We'll see." Jonah shook the water out of this hair and went to grab a towel. Even these were provided for them, by a smiling staff member.

"Yeah, I could get used to this kind of treatment," Casey said as he came up behind Jonah and took a towel from the attendant.


THEY STOOD waiting for Brandt and Donnelly in the same parking lot where they had been dropped off the day before.

"It was really great to meet you," Reese said. "What are our chances of snagging you for the team?"

"I'm ready to sign up now," Jonah said. He turned to Casey, eyebrows up as if to confirm. Casey nodded. "We both are," he said, turning back to Reese.

"Awesome. I'll let admissions know, and they'll send you the paperwork."

"Can you have them send it to Casey's house? That way I won't have to worry about my parents getting it before I see it." Reese nodded.

"Plus you'll be living there, right?" Casey said to Jonah.

"Can I?" Jonah asked.

"Of course. You know that! My mom will be ecstatic to have you back in the house." He looked teasingly at Jonah. "And so will I," he added with a saucy wink.

Brandt pulled up near them and honked. "Ready to go?" he called.

"Yep!" both boys replied, and with a handshake for Reese, they climbed into the car.

Donnelly turned to the backseat as soon as they closed the doors. "So? How'd it go?"

"It was awesome," Jonah replied immediately. "Kind of gives me hope that whatever happens in fucking Woodley, I'm going to be okay once I get here."

"Seems like a great place," Casey added. "We met the wrestling team and they were like, 'we don't give a shit about y'all shaking your money-makers on the Interwebz' and just wanted to wrestle and then talk about how they could be even better about supporting their gay buds. It was kind of epic."

"Excellent!" Donnelly cried, clearly relieved that all had gone well. "I assume we're going to drop you both at Casey's house?"

The boys nodded and then turned to each other to talk about their time at the university.

They arrived at Casey's house by the lake just before 6:00 p.m. Casey's mom invited Brandt and Donnelly to stay for dinner, but they had decided to stay in Woodley for the night to get an early start tomorrow on some remaining questions they needed answered and so wanted to get settled in back at the hotel. They stood on the driveway, saying goodbye while she put dinner on the table for the boys.

"We'll swing by the cafe tomorrow afternoon and give you an update," Donnelly told Casey. Then he turned to Jonah. "You going to be okay at school tomorrow?"

Jonah nodded. "After seeing what college is going to be like, I can handle a few months of people whispering about my boner—and my boyfriend," he replied with a laugh, throwing an arm around Casey. "Assuming we haven't been suspended for causing a riot." He turned to Casey. "I guess we should check on that."

"You kidding?" Casey replied. "There's no way they would suspend their star wrestler the week before regionals. Or you, for that matter," he added, with a mischievous grin.

"We'll see who comes out on top," Jonah growled as he mussed Casey's hair.

"Get a room, you two!" Brandt scolded. Then he looked over at Casey's house. "Oh, I guess you did. Well then, have at it."

"Nice to know we have your permission," Casey said, grinning. "We'll see you tomorrow."

The officers drove off toward the highway, and the boys headed into the house for dinner.

A little later, as they sat at the table, Casey's mom began a conversation she clearly was anxious about. "So, boys," she said, having steeled herself with a deep breath, "I want you to know that I am completely supportive of your… relationship."

Casey beamed. "Thanks, Mom. That means a lot to me—to us." He turned to Jonah, who could only nod, fighting back the tears suddenly welling in his eyes.

"Now, if Casey were dating a girl, and she were going to spend the night, she would of course sleep in his bed, and he would sleep on the couch. But Jonah, you may be staying here longer than that, and of course I'm delighted to have you here. I don't think it's practical to change the sleeping arrangements we've become accustomed to over the years. So, here's what I propose. I will let you two continue to share Casey's bed under two conditions."

Casey nodded, afraid that if he even breathed he might jinx it, and his mom would change her mind. This was going very well for him and Jonah, and he wanted desperately for it to continue to do so.

"First, that I don't hear anything—not a sound, okay?" she looked at them, eyebrows raised, and they nodded their agreement readily.

"All right. Second, that no matter what you do, you do it safely. Casey, I've put some stuff in your sock drawer that you two absolutely must use if... you do the things... that require you to... use that stuff. Got that?"

Casey blushed furiously, and Jonah couldn't drag his eyes up from the tabletop.

"Casey, we had this talk when you started dating girls. Do we need to have the full conversation, or can we agree to this right now and save ourselves time and embarrassment? Because I printed pages and pages of stuff off the Internet about this, and I will go through it all with you point by point if I have to,"

"No!" Casey blurted. "No, you're absolutely right. We will be safe. I promise."

She nodded. "Thank you very much. Now, I have to open again tomorrow, so I'm going to head to bed. Do you two have homework to do?"

Casey and Jonah shook their heads.

"All right, then. Don't stay up too late, okay?" She rose and kissed them both on the forehead before heading to her room.

The dishes in the Melville house had never been cleaned and put away as quickly as the boys did it that night. They locked up the house and retired to Casey's bedroom, easing the door shut behind them. Casey made a beeline for his dresser and pulled open the sock drawer.

Inside, his mom had tucked two packages of condoms—one a standard-issue store brand marketed by the chain drugstore she worked for, and the other a brand name in "extra-large" size. Casey held this latter one up for Jonah to see. "Looks like she's seen your video," he said, grinning.

Jonah blushed. "Funny. But I think you're bigger."

"There's only one way to settle this," Casey said, with the swagger of a sheriff in an old western. "We draw our weapons and see how they stack up."

"We'll settle this like men," Jonah snarled.

"I don't think women would have the same... oh, I see what you're doing," Casey said, with a chuckle. Then he turned the macho back on. "Yes, like men," he growled.

Jonah unbuttoned his jeans and slid down the zipper; Casey mirrored his movements, and soon their jeans were puddled around their ankles. They took a couple of shuffling steps closer to each other.

"If this is gonna be a fair fight," Casey drawled, "we both gotta be hard."

Jonah sneered at him. "Done." He whipped down his boxers, and stood with his fully erect cock bobbing out in front of him.

"En garde!" Casey cried, and pulled down his boxer briefs; his own hard-on swung wildly before pointing directly at Jonah.

"Now we just need a ruler," Jonah said.

"Fuck that," Casey replied. "I have a better way." He stepped directly in front of Jonah, mere inches away from him. He grabbed his best friend's penis, and pulled it down from its near-vertical inclination.

Jonah looked down, apparently surprised at Casey's frank handling of his privates. "Pulling on it isn't the same as measuring it."

"Just watch," Casey murmured. He grabbed his own cock with his other hand and pulled it down so it lay directly on top of Jonah's.

"Ohhh," Jonah replied in a half moan.

Casey gripped their stacked cocks firmly and squeezed them along their lengths. He looked down at where his touched Jonah's belly. Then he switched them around so Jonah's cock was on top; it didn't quite reach Casey. He looked up at Jonah. "I guess I've got the longer barrel," he drawled.

"But I think mine's a larger gauge," Jonah replied, gripping their cocks himself. He moved them side by side, and it was clear that his was broader.

Casey looked down at the girthy member next to his. "There is no fucking way that is ever going inside me, just so we're clear," he said, looking Jonah in the eyes. "I'll do whatever you want to it, but not that."

"Who said I wanted to stick it up your stinky butt?" Jonah said, a sly grin flickering at the corners of his mouth. "I was thinking something more like this." He spat a huge glob of saliva directly onto Casey's cock and then covered it with his own. The two erections now slid along each other easily.

Casey's eyes rolled back in his head, and he moaned at the sensation of their slippery, hard flesh gliding against each other. He snapped back to full attention immediately and brought his hand up to his mouth. He spat into his palm and then wrapped it around their two steely-hard penises. It was Jonah's turn to moan and tip his head back in sensual overload. Casey's pelvis began to twitch and rock, imperceptibly at first, but his thrusts gained in strength and momentum as Jonah's hips began to swing in a carnal harmonic. They thrust into, at, and against each other for another minute—that was all they could take.

"Gonna," breathed Casey, looking into Jonah's eyes.

"Me too," whispered Jonah, and since he had two free hands he wrapped them around Casey's neck and pulled him in for a kiss. Their tongues engaged in the same frenzied friction as their cocks.

Casey's back arched and he broke their kiss with a moan. The first spasm of orgasm sent a hot wet splat onto Jonah's lower belly; in response to being painted with Casey's semen, his body wrenched into an ejaculatory spasm that forced a groan from his mouth and a thick rope of white from his cock. They bucked and wriggled against each other for a full minute, tugging every drop from their still-hard cocks and smearing it all along their lengths. Then, when they could no longer bear the touch of each other on their cum-sensitive glans, Casey released his grip and they fell into a passionate, elated kiss. Their bodies collided, hard muscle and soft skin united in twitchy friction.

It was the drip-drip-drip onto the floor that brought them back to the world. Jonah looked down at the puddle their mingled semen made on the wood floor, then back up to Casey. "Oops. We didn't use condoms."

They burst into delighted giggles as Casey reached for a handful of tissues to wipe up their spill. "We should get cleaned up," he said, looking at the glistening torso of his friend. "You're kind of a mess."

"You're the one with the sperm hose, and I'm a mess? Holy crap, Case, you soaked me!"

"You got a few shots in too," Casey replied, rubbing Jonah's load all over himself. "Getting sticky here—we should git."

"Lead on, pardner," Jonah said with a drawl and a swagger.

They showered—for the third time this very long day—and slept soundly.

# CHAPTER TEN
# TRYING FOR NORMAL

"MORNING, MALCOLM," called Donnelly as he clamored through the cafe's door at six Monday morning.

"Gabriel! Ethan! What a way to start the day." Malcolm walked to the counter from the back of the shop where the clattering of pans told that the day's baking was being finished up.

"Morning, Casey," Donnelly called back to the kitchen.

"Hey guys," Casey replied, wiping his hands on his apron and coming out from the back. "You're up early."

"We took one sip of that horrid stuff the hotel calls coffee and knew we had to come here for the real deal."

"Coming right up," Malcolm said as he worked the levers on the espresso monster.

"Guys want a scone?" another voice called from the back of the cafe's kitchen.

"Is that Jonah?" Donnelly asked, cocking his head.

"The one and only," Jonah replied as he came up to the counter, outfitted in one of Casey's aprons. "I'm trying to help, but my first attempt at scone making was kind of lame. Want to sample the damage?" He held out a small tray of clearly unsalable baked goods. They looked tasty enough, but were not formed in any way one might recognize as scone-like.

"Never one to pass up bakery seconds," Brandt said brightly as he scooped up a particularly eccentric raspberry attempt. He took a bite and groaned. "Oh, wow. It's like my partner here—not much to look at, but so sweet on the inside."

Donnelly shot him a playful dagger with his eyes. "Keep it up, buddy, and we'll see if you get anything sweet inside you tonight."

"My, my," Malcolm said, fanning himself delicately. "The way you two flirt."

Donnelly winked at Malcolm, which Brandt made a great show of ignoring.

"You guys ready to get back to school?" Donnelly asked.

"I guess so," Jonah replied. "It sucks to still be in high school after touring the university and seeing what next year is going to be like. Plus, there's the whole 'walking into a seething pit of homophobia' thing. That's bound to be a ton of laughs."

"I'm sure everyone's forgotten about the whole video thing," Casey said, his voice full of wishful bravado. "It'll be business as usual. You'll see."

"I sure hope so. I just want to win the state championship and get the hell out of here."

"But first, we need to finish screwing up all of Mal's baked goods. Come on," Casey said with a tug on Jonah's elbow, "maybe we can find something back there you haven't already dropped."

"Getting a little bakery hazing this morning?" Brandt asked Jonah.

Jonah nodded and shrugged. "But it beats lying in bed alone worrying about what's going to happen at school today."

"Whatever happens, I'm sure you'll be fine," Donnelly said. His voice was deeper, but it was tinged with the same wishful tone as Casey's.

The cafe staff returned to their work, and once Brandt and Donnelly had polished off the defective baked goods, they too were on their way.


"I'M SURE it's going to be okay," Casey repeated as he and Jonah walked down the street from Malcolm's cafe toward the high school.

"I wish I could be as confident as you are," Jonah replied, his already grudging pace slowing even further as they neared the school.

"Even if it's bad, we'll face it together. What's the worst that could happen?"

Jonah stopped walking altogether. "Seriously? After everything we've been through, you still have to ask that? The past two weeks have been one worst thing after another. It's like we're never going to hit bottom."

"But we've also had some good things, right? Look at what's happened for us." He took Jonah's hand—a risky move in downtown Woodley—and looked into his eyes. "I wouldn't change a thing that's happened to us if missing any of it meant that we didn't end up together."

Jonah smiled for the first time since they'd walked out of the cafe, and it made Casey's heart light. He nodded, and they continued their walk, though they dropped each other's hand.

They were just around the corner from the school when they saw a couple of their wrestling teammates coming to meet them.

"Hey, guys," called Casey as they approached. "What's up?"

Their friends just shook their heads. "It's not good," one of them said. He was the one who had spoken up about friendship at the rally on Friday.

"What's not good?" Jonah asked, paling.

They were joined by three more wrestlers. "The rally kind of set some people off," their friend replied. "Today might be a little rough for you. Sure you don't want to take another day off?"

Casey shook his head. "We're not going to hide," he said defiantly. "If people have a problem with us, they're the ones with the problem, not us."

Another group of wrestlers appeared; nearly the entire team was present now. The co-captain—the first one to speak at the rally— nodded grimly at Casey's words and then to the other wrestlers. He led the pack, and the others arrayed themselves around Casey and Jonah like a protective detail around the president.

"Guys, do you really think this is necess—" Casey broke off abruptly as they rounded the corner and stepped onto the high school campus. Everywhere they looked there were flyers and posters with one image on them—a photo of Casey and Jonah, taken at the moment they kissed at the rally. There was a heavy black X crudely scrawled over the image.

There were numerous different messages proffered by the posters as captions to the crossed-out photo: "Adam and Eve, not Adam and Steve," as if the picture had been taken at their wedding in Eden; "Woodley, Not San Francisco!" screeched many of them, followed by several dense paragraphs of angry text; and many opted for the simple clarity of "DISGUSTING!"

Jonah stopped walking, and seemed to go limp. Casey, overwhelmed with trying to take it all in, walked on for a stride or two, but then stopped as well. Their protective perimeter halted, glaring outward from the two in the middle.

Casey turned to Jonah, intending to ask him whether he wanted to continue into the building, but the look on his friend's face stopped him cold. Jonah was looking up at the steps leading into the main entrance, his face pale, his mouth open. Casey turned to see what he was seeing.

At the top of the steps stood a group of thirty or so students, each of whom carried a sign denouncing in the strongest possible terms homosexuality and a number of conditions they deemed to be related (these included bestiality, incest, pedophilia, and—somewhat puzzlingly—polygamy and gun control). These were their general grievances, but the signs made clear that they viewed Jonah and Casey as local representatives of the entire world of perversion.

Casey turned back to Jonah, trying to tamp down the defensive anger rising in him. "Those are just a bunch of puritans who are trying to use us an excuse to shame everybody. I don't think I even know any of them. They're just being assholes."

Jonah shook his head. "I know them. All of them. They're the youth group from my church. I'll bet they made the signs together at yesterday's social awareness hour." Jonah spat bitterly. "My dad probably helped them spell the big words."

The team co-captain put his hand on Casey's shoulder. "This is what I was talking about. There's going to be more of this kind of thing, all day. Sure you don't want to turn around?"

"The school can't let them do this all day." Casey looked over and saw the principal coming toward the wrestling group. "See? I bet he's coming to tell us to wait a couple of minutes while they break up the group."

"All of you," he said, pointing to the wrestling team surrounding Casey and Jonah, "get to class."

The team did not move.

"And you two," he continued, pointing to Casey and Jonah, "you shouldn't be here at all."

Casey was never one to back down in the face of capricious authority, and he did not do so now. "We go to school here."

"Not this week you don't. I have not filed the paperwork to formally suspend you because I assumed your shame would keep you away until the mess you caused settled down. It appears I was wrong."

Casey nodded. It was easy to agree with him when he was admitting he was wrong.

"So I will make it official. Casey Melville and Jonah Fischer, you are hereby suspended from Woodley High School for a period of five days for intentionally and maliciously disrupting a school function."

Casey smiled, but quickly stifled it. "And what school function would that be?"

The principal grunted and narrowed his eyes. "You know perfectly well what happened at the rally on Friday afternoon."

Casey turned to Jonah. "Do you remember the wrestling rally on Friday?"

Jonah shook his head.

Casey turned back to the principal. "We don't know what you're talking about."

The principal looked at all of the wrestlers. "You were all there. Are you telling me that none of you remember what these two did to disrupt the rally? Do I need to suspend all of you to improve your recall of recent events?"

Casey shook his head and frowned as if searching his memory. "Ah! I think I remember now—are you referring to the T-shirts, and the speeches, and the kiss?"

The principal fixed him with a deadly, sneering look. "Yes, those are the events I am referring to."

"I see the reason for our misunderstanding. You said we had disrupted a school function—that's what caused the confusion. What we disrupted was a nonschool function. You said it yourself. If you're going to try to suspend us for something we did at a religious thingy, then I should have no difficulty getting a lawyer to explain to you how the separation of church and state works."

The principal seethed, his eyes nearly disappearing into narrow judgmental slits.

Casey continued. "Jonah and I are here to finish our education. We will abide by school rules while we're here. That means we won't even touch each other, despite the fact that when straight couples maul each other in the hallways no one says a word. We'll play by the rules, and we expect you will do the same. Now, if you will excuse us, we have a calculus class to get to."

The group stepped around the principal, toward the steps where Jonah's friends from church were awaiting their arrival. When the wrestlers reached the bottom step, Jonah tapped the co-captain on the shoulder and nodded up the stairs, indicating that he would take the lead. The co-captain stepped aside, and Jonah mounted the steps—followed closely by the group.

Jonah approached the apparent leader of the picketers. "Daniel," he said in polite greeting.

Daniel forced a reptilian grin. "We missed you in church yesterday," he replied in low, even tones. "Faggot," he added in a whisper.

Jonah's face hardened into an expressionless mask. "Very Christian attitude you have there, Daniel. Now, as nice as it is to chat with you, I have a class to get to."

"No." Daniel's face was as devoid of emotion as his voice.

"Step. Aside." Jonah's reply carried an unmistakable, if unspoken, threat.

"I won't let you defile this school with your perversion."

Jonah stared at his former friend for a long moment, then turned around to the group of wrestlers. "There seems to be some kind of blockage on the steps."

The team advanced on the group holding signs. They so overmatched the picketers in size that the way was cleared for them without any contact between the parties. The wrestlers, having broken through the line, stepped apart as if they had rehearsed this choreography; they formed a channel through which Casey and Jonah walked into the school. Once they were safely in the hallway, Jonah and Casey turned to address their teammates.

"Thank you all so much," Jonah said, his voice thick. "I can't tell you what this means to me."

"Hell, I can," Casey chimed in. "You guys came through for us again. I know not everyone here is super excited about me and Jonah being together, but you're helping us because that's what teams do. And we will repay you, not just with our thanks, but with the long line of asses we will kick on the way to the state championship."

The team cheered and then walked with Casey and Jonah to their calculus classroom. "Let me know if anyone gives you shit," the co-captain said.

"I'm sure we'll be fine," Casey said. "They were counting on us turning and running. You guys helped us stand our ground, and now they know we're not going to be intimidated by their stupid signs about sex with animals. We can get back to falling asleep in class like usual!"

The group broke up, and Casey and Jonah went into the classroom to take their customary seats. As they sat, they exchanged a glance and a nod to reassure each other that they really would be fine. They needed to believe it.


"MAX, TREVOR, thanks for agreeing to talk with us," Donnelly said as the boys entered the meeting room the high school had allowed the officers to use for this interview.

"Thanks for getting us out of history class," Max replied with a grin.

Trevor didn't seem to share in his buddy's good spirits. He sat and looked politely, but somewhat sullenly, at the officers.

"We have a few questions about the video you made with Anna."

The smile evaporated from Max's face; his expression now matched Trevor's. "Not proud of that. I know it was a really stupid thing to do. I fully intend to apologize to her once I find out where she moved to."

"I'm sure she would appreciate that," Donnelly replied. "The ethics of making the video aside—and I recommend in the strongest possible terms that you reflect on your role in the utter destruction of that young woman's life in Woodley—we have a question for you about Russell Winslow."

Max looked up from his contrite staring at the tabletop. "What did Rusty say?"

"What do you think he said?" Donnelly asked.

Max looked down again. "He was really pissed at us for moving in on him that night. But he was really stupid about it. She wouldn't drink the stuff unless he did too, and he was too dumb to switch out the alcohol. So by the time she's... loosened up a little, he's off puking up his guts. So my man Trevor and I decided to help out the little lady."

"Do you hear yourself?" Brandt interrupted. "You don't even realize you're talking about a human being, do you?"

"Wait," Donnelly said. "We haven't even gotten to the part where he sends the video around so the school can see what a stud he is."

"We didn't do that," Trevor blurted. It was the first thing he'd said since entering the room, and it caught the others by surprise.

"You didn't send the video to everyone you know?" Donnelly asked, looking at Max. "Is that what you're telling us?"

Max shook his head. "I would never have sent it to everybody I know. I only sent it to one person. I wanted him to know that we'd won." He looked into Donnelly's uncomprehending face. "I sent it to Rusty so he would know he'd been beat." Despite the bragging words, his voice was meek and miserable.

Brandt took a breath and squinted at the boys across the table. "Do you mean to tell us you sent the video only to Rusty?"

They nodded.

"No one else?"

They shook their heads.

"Why should we believe you?" Donnelly asked pointedly.

"Have you seen the video?" Max asked.

The officers nodded.

"Then you know that I'm as exposed as Anna was," Trevor said, desolation in his voice. "Everyone's panicked about Jonah's boner, but that video shows mine in action, and"—he heaved a great breath, as if trying not to cry—"everyone can see it's about four inches long. Why would I want that to get around?"

It was Max's turn. "And if you've seen the video, I don't really have to explain to you why I wouldn't want anyone to see it."

Brandt and Donnelly looked blankly at him.

"You said you watched it." They nodded. "Then you saw that even with my dick in her mouth, I didn't get hard. Why would I want that broadcast?" Max started to cry. "Everyone who saw that can tell right away that... that I—"

Trevor put his hand on Max's shoulder, and Max crumpled, sobbing, his arms covering his head on the table. "What Max is trying to say is that... he's gay."

Max sobbed for a good couple of minutes and then tried to pull himself together. "That night," he said, wiping his eyes with the tissue Donnelly handed him, "was supposed to be my big debut as a straight stud." He rolled his eyes. "Stole somebody's girl, had sex, got it on video. It was desperate and stupid, and I ruined her life and almost ruined my own too. I sent it to Rusty right after I took it, but the next day when I'd sobered up, I saw what it really showed about me, and I just about... well, I came this close to ending it all. So when the video started making the rounds, I just shut the hell up and hoped no one saw it was me." He sighed. "Thought it had all blown over. But then this thing with Jonah came along, and I had to clear the air. Seemed like it was time. If he can be honest, so can I." He looked down again. "But I think I have a lot more to make up for than he does."

Donnelly held his hand to his mouth, shaking his head sympathetically.

"We're sorry to put you through this, guys," Brandt said. "You seem aware of the complete shits you've been, and you're going to do better in the future, and that counts for something. If you want, I'll check with Anna to see if she would be willing to talk with you."

The boys nodded.

"You should get back to class. Thanks for your time." Brandt watched as the door closed behind them. He sighed and slumped forward, face in his hands. "Every. Fucking. Time." He pounded the tabletop. "Ask a simple question, and bam! Down the fucking rabbit hole again."

"Everyone's suffered in this," Donnelly said, rubbing his face. "Every single person. Anna gets run out of town. The entire population crashes down on Jonah and riots when Casey tries to defend him. Max nearly gets outed as gay and Trevor gets outed as having a small dick— not that they should be ashamed of either. The only person in this whole mess who doesn't come out of it wounded is Rusty. He seemed like kind of a bumpkin, but apparently he's a criminal mastermind."

Brandt nodded. "He punishes Anna for not falling into his drunk-ass arms at that party, and then he gets to embarrass Trevor and Max at the same time. Sweet deal for him—but what a colossal bastard asshole. I think we might have to come up with some way to lay the blame where it belongs."

THE HIGH school cafeteria at lunchtime—even on its better days, it is one of the most unforgiving social milieus known to man. Today was orders of magnitude worse. One side of the hall was occupied by the churchy group that had attempted to repel Jonah and Casey before school; the other was the domain of the wrestling team and its sympathizers, and at their center sat Jonah and Casey.

When the twentieth person passed by their table and muttered "Faggot!" or some variation thereof, Casey looked up at Jonah. "The ambiance in this restaurant isn't what it used to be," he sniffed. "They'll let any rabble in these days."

Jonah smiled for a second or two, but then looked back down at his tray of haphazardly prepared, lowest-bidder provisions.

"It's better than after English, though, I will admit that," Casey continued.

"What did they throw at us?" Jonah asked.

"I think it's called glitter-bombing. But they don't seem to realize that it's generally what gay people do to conservative assholes, not the other way around. Especially because they used pink glitter."

"You still have some on your forehead," Jonah said, pointing. "I would help you with that, but I heard from my student government contacts that our dear principal is looking for any excuse to kick us out of here, and if I touched you that would just about make his day."

"It can wait. I checked in the bathroom, and I also may have some glitter in a hard to reach spot. You can help me with that after school," Casey said with a wink.

"Right about now I just want to go home and never leave until we move into the dorm. Think your mom would go for that?"

Casey looked at his friend with his eyebrows peaked in wonder. "Did you just refer to my house as 'home'? Because that's awesome."

Jonah smiled. "Well, seeing as the entire town was there to witness the complete implosion of my family, I think we have to face up to the fact that your house is all I've got now."

"What if they've been trying to contact you, but your phone's not on?"

Jonah pulled his phone out of his pocket, and set it on the table. "It's been on since we got back from the university. Nothing."

"They'll come around," Casey said, but his glum tone didn't make him very convincing.

The bell rang, announcing the end of the lunch period, and the entire wrestling posse stood as one.

"There go the Queens of Woodley and their merry band of faggot lovers," sneered one of the glitter bombers.

"Have a ssssuper day, you sssstallionsssss," called another with a mocking sibilance.

"So I get thrown out of school if I touch you, but what about if I touch them?" Casey muttered. "You know, just to rearrange their faces a bit?"

Jonah shook his head slowly.

"Great. I'm surrounded by Christians and I can't do anything about it because you're being Christlike."

"Just let it go—they'll get tired of it after a while."

"I hope so. I'm pretty tired of it already." Casey took a deep breath and tried to think positively. It almost worked.

AS BRANDT and Donnelly pulled into Drummond, a town almost exactly like Woodley the next county over, Russell Winslow was being escorted from his afternoon English class by the school's principal. Brandt had called to advise her that they needed to speak with Rusty about an ongoing investigation. As they had visited the school previously to talk with the wrestling coach, she understood the gravity of the request.

"We've spent the better part of two weeks poking around this area," Brandt said as he stepped from the car, "and I don't think I could tell these towns apart. Drummond is basically Woodley, but with the high school on the other end of Main Street."

"And no cafe," Donnelly groused.

"We'll be sure to drop in on your boyfriend Malcolm when we get back to Woodley," Brandt replied with a roll of his eyes.

"All right, then," Donnelly said. "I guess I can soldier on."

They entered the high school, and were directed to a conference room next to the principal's office. Rusty was waiting in a chair outside the door. He did not seem happy to see the officers.

"Mr. Winslow," Brandt greeted Rusty as the three of them entered the room. "Good of you to make time to speak with us today." He shut the door behind them.

"Didn't really have a choice," he replied gruffly.

Brandt smiled genially, as if Rusty had just commented on the fine weather. It was Donnelly who began the questioning.

"Now, Rusty, you should know that you are not being charged with anything, and this conversation is not an official interrogation. We just want to find out what happened with these videos. Is that clear?"

Rusty sighed, but when he saw that they weren't going to continue until he responded, he nodded.

"We've talked to Anna." Donnelly let this statement sink in.

Rusty shifted in his seat.

"She told us some interesting information about that video," Donnelly continued. He stared at Rusty for a long, uncomfortable moment.

"And what was that?" Rusty finally asked when the tension of Donnelly's silence appeared to have gotten to him. "I already told you I made that video for her."

"She told us that she sent it to the police."

"I imagine she did," Rusty said, no inflection in his voice.

"We assume Chief Powell wasn't the one who started passing around a video of Jonah in the locker room, so we're wondering why you did."

Rusty was instantly agitated. "I told you it wasn't a video of Jonah! It was a video of Trev—" He stopped himself before he could finish.

Donnelly sat back again. "Ah, yes. Of course. It was a video of Trevor. And Max—the star of the show. Or should I say, stars?"

"Excellent detective work," Rusty muttered. "After I told you what to look for."

"We actually did do some detective work, you'll be happy to know. We talked to Max and Trevor just this morning. And they told us pretty much the same thing Anna did—that you are the only person they know of who had a copy of the video." Donnelly paused and let this sink in.

Rusty's breath seemed to be coming in more rapid bursts now. He swallowed hard and closed his eyes for a moment. Then he seemed to pull himself together. "Yes, I saw all of the videos. But I wasn't the only one who had them. Anna probably sent out the locker room video to everyone she knew, and Max and Trevor were such slut assholes— they wanted everyone to know what they did."

"You know as well as we do that Max and Trevor had a lot to lose from that video getting out. They wanted to piss you off, and it was a stupid and mean thing they did sending it to you. But you sending it out to everyone—now that's a way to get back at all three of them at once."

"You can't prove that."

"No," Brandt interjected. "The phone companies don't keep that kind of record. But you know who keeps better records? Websites that host videos, particularly if those videos might involve people under the age of eighteen. Because, as you may or may not be aware, uploading that kind of video is a felony. What do you think about spending the next two decades in a federal prison? I may be wrong, but I think twenty years is longer than the life expectancy of the average woodchuck." He paused, and looked at Donnelly. "Or wait, what was that other name for it? Oh, right," he said, turning a frighteningly harsh gaze on Rusty. "Whistlepig."

Rusty jolted as if his chair had been electrified.

"Yeah, I thought so," Brandt said with a nod. "You know, a warrant for child porn gets a very quick response. We could have the proof we need within the hour...." He reached for his phone.

"I didn't upload that one." Rusty blurted, panic in his voice. "Just the locker room ones. No one's under eighteen in those, at least not that you can see anything on." He gulped. "The one from the party I only sent to a dozen or so people, but I was seventeen at the time! I never posted it online."

"Okay, so we have our Whistlepig," Donnelly summed up. "Now, I want you to tell us why you did it, Rusty."

Rusty was shaking, but he managed to speak after several false starts. "I was really pissed at Max and Trevor for taking Anna. And I was kind of mad at her for going with them. I wanted them to get in trouble for it, so that's why I sent out the video."

"Okay, so that's why you sent out the party video," Donnelly replied. "What about the locker room ones?"

"Well, the police weren't going to do anything about it, so I wanted everyone to see who did it. I wanted Max and Trevor to get in trouble."

"Why post it online, though?"

Rusty looked up at Donnelly as if he were talking to a particularly stupid child. "I wasn't going to send out a video of guys in a locker room. Everyone would think I was a fag."

"But sending out video of two guys having sex with a girl is okay?" Brandt asked.

"Well, duh—there's a girl in it." Rusty shook his head as if amazed that any simpleton off the street could get a badge.

"That still doesn't explain the other two videos," Donnelly said. "You put up the video of the locker room that showed Max's stars tattoo to get him in trouble, but the other two videos were posted within the last two weeks, and they don't show Max at all."

Rusty sighed and looked down. "After what happened at the party, the entire team stood behind Max and Trevor—hell, even the police were behind them. So I decided to get the hell out of there. I came here to finish my senior year and tried to forget about fucking Woodley. But when the locker room video finally got around the school, all anyone cared about was poor little Jonah." Rusty made a disgusted face.

"Wait, I thought you said this didn't have anything to do with Jonah," Brandt said.

"It didn't—not at first. But once I saw what happened with the video, I went back to what I'd shot in the locker room, and I found other stuff I could use. And it worked." Rusty seemed almost proud of the uproar he had caused. "For a while, anyway."

"It worked... how?" Brandt asked. "What were you trying to do?"

"Jonah and I wrestle in the same weight class. For four fucking years I was in that guy's shadow, and it meant I would never have the same shot he had at scholarships or a championship."

"I don't understand," Brandt said, looking from Rusty to Donnelly.

Donnelly nodded. "Most wrestling competitions are dual meets, where two schools compete against each other. Each school can only enter one wrestler in each weight class. That means either Jonah or Rusty could compete in that class—the other would have to wrestle up one class, which is a whole lot harder."

"And that asshole Coach Woody would always put his special little Jonah in and make me wrestle up. I got pounded, and he got the glory. That's why I left Woodley. And that's why I uploaded the other videos. I'll get to wrestle Jonah at regionals, and we'll finally see who's the better wrestler."

"But that's hardly fair. Your videos turned his life upside down—they've distracted the entire team."

"Oh, now I'm supposed to care about what's fair? After years of being dicked around? Huh," Rusty scoffed.

"Let's just add up all of the people whose lives you've made worse so that you could make yours a little better, shall we?" Donnelly said. "Anna had to move to the other side of the country to get away from the reputation you established for her by making the party video public. Jonah's been through hell, Casey too, and Max and Trevor—though not innocent in all of this—were exposed in ways they never imagined. The entire team is having to prepare for regionals under the cloud of scandal. And still you think this is fair?"

"Looks to me like a lot of people made bad choices and didn't like the consequences." Rusty shook his head.

Brandt leaned in again. "What choice did Jonah make?"

"To get a boner for his buddy," Rusty said, his singsong voice contrasting with his disgusted frown. "Not going to cry about that. He deserves what he's got coming."

"Charming," Donnelly replied sarcastically.

"I think we're done here," Brandt said dismissively. "I would strongly recommend, young man, that you destroy any additional footage you have kept of the Woodley High School locker room. We won't be as quick to let bygones be bygones should any more videos show up. As difficult as you've made Jonah's life by posting them, that's nothing compared to what would happen to you if we identified you publicly as the guy who brings a spy cam into the locker room to get video of naked guys. Understand me?"

Rusty nodded glumly. "Not gonna matter now anyway. Regionals and state is all I care about—the Woodchucks can go to hell without any more help from me."

"Sounds like the positive attitude of a champion to me," snarked Donnelly as he stood. "Best of luck at regionals."

"WELL ISN'T our young Mr. Winslow a model citizen?" Brandt muttered as they put as many miles as they could as quickly as possible between themselves and Drummond.

"At least we finally know how all of those videos got around. And I don't think we'll be seeing any more of them."

"Small consolation to Jonah," Brandt acknowledged. "It's not like his family's going to welcome him back just because we know why the videos were released in the first place. That train has kind of left the station."

"Do you think we did the right thing back there? There are charges that could be brought against him."

Brandt looked at his partner. "I know, but when I think about the way that would play out, it doesn't seem like the best for everyone. We told Rusty we weren't charging him, so nothing he's just told us is admissible. He says he sent the party video out, but there's no proof of that from the phone records, and it wasn't his video to begin with— Max sent it to him in the first place, so that's going to bring him into it as well. The locker room videos are a stronger case, but again we don't have proof from that creepy website, and with no underage nudity in the locker room we don't have leverage to get it. Plus, bringing this into court means Jonah and Casey could become a national story, which makes their lives even harder. There may be some justice in it for Anna, but I wonder if an apology from Max and Trevor might not go a long way toward healing those wounds."

"Officer Brandt, you are showing some flexibility! Thought you only did that in the bedroom," Donnelly said with a chuckle. "I just hope the first day back went well for Jonah and Casey. There are a lot of Rustys in that school."

IT WAS late afternoon when Brandt and Donnelly returned to Woodley. They drove directly to Malcolm's cafe, hoping to slip in before closing time. Casey was just about to flip the sign to Closed when they walked up. He swung the door open wide.

"Oh, man, it's good to see you guys." Casey pulled them both into a hug.

"Tough day?" Donnelly asked.

"If today is as bad as it gets, we'll be okay. If it gets any worse, Jonah's going to pull the covers over his head and not get out of bed until college."

"What happened?" asked Brandt.

"How long ya got?" Casey answered, the corner of his mouth tucked up in a world-weary hint of a smile.

"Pour me some coffee and I'll listen for hours," Donnelly replied, taking a seat at a table near the counter. Brandt sat next to him.

"Do I hear the long arm of the law approach?" cried Malcolm from the kitchen. He hurried up to greet them, wiping his hands on his apron. "How are law and order progressing, gentlemen?"

"This is Woodley," Brandt said. "Despite appearances, law and order are in complete disarray."

"So," added Donnelly, "business as usual."

Malcolm nodded sympathetically and began working the levers of the espresso monster, coaxing coffee from it in the midst of great steamy clouds and metallic pinging and whirring.

"How was practice?" Donnelly called to Casey over the din.

"'Bout the only normal part of the day. It was great to just get on the mat and work after all of the crap we walked through during the school day. Once you're on the mat, all of that other stuff just falls away. I think we're going to be in great shape for the first round of regionals on Friday."

"Whose ass are you going to kick?" Donnelly asked.

"Trash talk from a guy who hasn't wrestled in more than a decade," Brandt remarked. "Classy."

Donnelly fixed him with a withering gaze.

"We're gonna start by wiping the floor with Drummond," Casey said. "Rusty's about the best they've got, and Jonah was always able to take him out during practice. I like our chances."

"Coffee," called Malcolm as he approached with two mugs.

"I better get back there—gotta get as much done as I can before Jonah gets here to 'help,'" Casey said with a grin.

"Jonah's coming?" asked Donnelly.

"Yeah—Coach Woody wanted to talk with him after practice, but he said he'd be here after that. Shouldn't be long." Casey walked back into the kitchen, and from the sounds echoing out of it, he got right to work.

"Those poor boys," Malcolm said, joining them at their table. "Casey gave me a quick rundown of the horrors they put up with today."

"There's no homophobia like hometown homophobia, I always say," Donnelly grumbled.

"Sounds like the rest of the team really came through for them, though. Lunch hour apparently saw the God squad and the wrestlers about to re-create *West Side Story*, but things calmed down a bit after that. They just had to walk past a prayer vigil on the front steps after school, where half the school gathered to pray for them to 'heal from sodomy,' which sounds like something you would only have to do if you didn't use enough lube."

"Fucking Woodley," Donnelly said as he lifted his coffee cup.

The door jangled.

"Hey, Jonah! Good to see you," Brandt called.

Jonah walked over to where the three men were gathered. "Hey guys."

"What'd Woody have to say?" Malcolm asked.

Jonah brightened a bit. "He's being really awesome about all of it. He's like, 'focus on competing, and don't let the other stuff get to you.' We talked about strategy, and he showed me the brackets for Friday. Looks like I'll be facing my old buddy Rusty." He paused. "Hey, why the look?" He had caught Donnelly flashing a glance at Brandt.

"Just that... well, it turns out that Rusty's carrying quite a grudge about never getting to wrestle in his weight class at Woodley," Donnelly explained. "He told us that's why he sent out the videos—to intimidate you before regionals."

Jonah stiffened. "It won't work," he said, a steely resolve in his voice. "I'll take him out."

"Good man!" cried Malcolm, clapping Jonah on the back.

"I'm going to go help Casey in the kitchen," Jonah said as he stood.

"There's an apron behind the door, and you know where to find the broom, on the off chance you drop something…," Malcolm said as Jonah walked off to join Casey.

The happy sounds of the Casey and Jonah reunion echoed through the cafe.

"God, I love those boys," Malcolm said. "Just listen to the joy they've been able to wring out of this awful experience."

"They deserve all the joy they can get," Donnelly said wistfully. "They still have some challenges ahead."

# CHAPTER ELEVEN
# REGIONALS

EACH DAY of that week saw the conditions at Woodley High improve for Jonah and Casey. The organizers of the protests against them soon tired of being ignored, and fewer people each day turned out to wave signs with antigay slogans splashed across them. By Friday morning the customary sleepy calm had nearly been restored to the school.

The first round of regional competition would be held in the afternoon at Woodley's gymnasium, the site of the previous week's religious rally turned near riot. Jonah and Casey spent their lunch hour helping Coach Woody make final preparations for the tournament.

Competition was to begin at 4:00 p.m., and by 3:30 the bleachers on both sides of the gym were nearly full. It seemed Woodley's entire student body was in attendance, and the Drummond side was almost as populous. Warming up on the side mats, the Woodley Woodchucks and the Drummond Demons worked out their prematch jitters on one another.

"Hey Case," Jonah called. "Look who's here."

The home team had a "special guests" section of the bleachers set aside for family members and invited dignitaries. As the boys' families currently totaled one person (Casey's mom was already there, waving madly to them), they had invited some others to come. Brandt and Donnelly were currently making their way to the stands, as were the other special guests: Bryce and Nestor. Casey and Jonah waved to the foursome as they made their way to the reserved seats.

"Nice of them to come," Casey said as he handily threw and pinned his warm-up partner.

"I'm glad Ethan and Gabriel made time to be here—but I think Bryce and Nestor would chew off an arm for a chance to watch a wrestling tournament."

Casey laughed. "I'll see if I can tear off someone's singlet, give them an extra thrill."

The young men turned their attention back to their warm-ups.

"So, this is a gymnasium," Bryce mused wonderingly as he looked about. "The lighting is harsh, but the view is"—he peered through his opera glasses—"divine."

Donnelly laughed. "You've never been in a gym before?"

"Oh, honey, no. Certainly not with the lights on. But I've always been an athletic supporter, in my own way."

Brandt, chuckling, turned to Casey's mom, sitting next to him. "How have the boys been this week?" he asked.

"They've held up well. I'm damned proud of them," she answered. "Jonah was still pretty hung up on his family, but as the tournament got closer, he focused more on that. Plus, I think they're getting more sleep the last couple of days—settling in like an old married couple." She laughed at the domesticity of her son and his best friend.

The draw at the beginning of the tournament had the competition start with the weight class above Jonah's—which meant that he would wrestle last. The early rounds of the wrestling were fairly quick. The higher weights went first, followed by the low weight classes, and the Woodchucks had a strong roster at both ends of the range. Casey's match saw him put down his Demon with ease, something that surprised even him.

"That was awesome!" Jonah said as Casey returned to the bench, sweaty and panting but victorious.

"He made a huge mistake early on," Casey said, drinking from his water bottle and catching his breath.

"I saw that—his head was down and you were able to spin on him before he even knew where you were."

"No, it was before that. Right after the whistle, he goes, 'Come at me, faggot.' So I'm all, 'Hell yeah, I'll come at you,' and then I just took him apart. It was like I could see the whole match from above—I knew how he was going to move before he did. It's like a faggot superpower, man!" Casey grinned and then chugged down some more water.

Jonah leaned close and spoke directly into his ear: "I want to tear that singlet right off you."

Casey blushed and giggled, but then waggled his eyebrows and winked. "You're going to make me bust out of it on my own, keep talking like that," he replied.

FINALLY, AFTER all of the other wrestlers had competed, Jonah's weight class was called. He stepped out onto the center mat, where Rusty Winslow stood waiting for him. The two adversaries eyed each other warily, but they entered the ring like sportsmen. The referee was about to blow his whistle when Rusty raised his arm.

"What is it?" demanded the referee.

"Challenge," Rusty said.

"What's going on?" Brandt asked Donnelly.

"Rusty made a challenge. That means he thinks Woodley violated the rules somehow."

The wrestlers and the referee approached the officials' desk, and the coaches of the respective teams jogged over as well. Their conversation was animated on the Woodley side: Coach Woody was red in the face, and Jonah was clearly worked up as he protested something that was not audible in the bleachers. The Drummond coach seemed as stunned as the people in the stands, while Rusty looked blandly on at the spectacle he had caused.

Finally, the official for the tournament took the microphone from the announcer. He stood up and faced the crowd.

"The Drummond wrestler has made a challenge. His claim is that Woodley has violated the state wrestling charter by entering a known homosexual into competition. The officials are consulting the charter now. Competition is suspended until a ruling can be made."

"What the fucking fuck?" Brandt exploded. "How is that even a possibility? What do they need to look up—whether it's 1958?"

"Calm down, Ethan. The state wrestling charter is as old as the hills. I'm sure it's been updated since the nondiscrimination act was passed. They probably just don't have the latest version."

Bryce turned to Nestor. "I love the costumes, but the plot feels too retro. Do you think there's a bar in the lobby?"

"We would be rude to leave when they are still so muscular," Nestor burbled in reply.

"This terminology is all really new to me," Casey's mom said, turning to Brandt and Donnelly. "He called Jonah a known homosexual. But Casey already wrestled—does that mean he's not considered a known homosexual? He calls Jonah his boyfriend, and that's pretty well known by now. What more would it take?"

"It's just Rusty being an asshole, if you'll pardon the expression," Donnelly replied.

"Pardon it? I've been using it myself," she returned with a laugh.

The officials were busy consulting books and sheaves of paper brandished by the coaches on both sides. Finally someone from the IT office brought out a laptop, and they turned their attention to researching the question on the state wrestling association website. Finally, after ten minutes of fussing about, the official stood and took the mic once again.

"After consulting the most current version of the rules available, we have no choice but to grant the challenge by Drummond. The match is forfeit, and the final score for the tournament will now be calculated."

There were gasps on all sides of the gymnasium. A shocked silence settled in, and the coach and wrestlers began to retreat from the officials' desk. This was the end of Jonah's chance at a championship season.

"Stop!" rang out a voice from the side of the gym. All heads turned to see who had shouted, but the man took no notice of the hundreds of startled faces. He strode purposefully to the officials' desk, a phone at his ear.

"Dad?" Jonah cried out. He took a step back, but then walked haltingly toward the desk.

Mr. Fischer's voice boomed out across the gym. "I'm on the phone right now with the president of the state wrestling association. He says that according to the rules issued last month, no wrestler may be disqualified on the basis of sexual orientation… or gender identity, whatever that means." Into the phone he said, "Thanks, Leo," and then hung up. "According to the rules, you must let Jonah"—his voice broke—"you must let my son wrestle."

"See, this is just the kind of plot twist I was waiting for," Bryce said in a stage whisper. "Thank goodness we decided to stay through the intermission."

"The performance art—so rewarding," Nestor agreed, patting Bryce on the knee.

The noise in the gymnasium rose steadily as this latest development sank in. Mr. Fischer pointed to the laptop screen and finally turned it toward himself and clicked away, apparently running a gantlet of navigational difficulties to arrive at the latest version of the rule book. The official took off his glasses and nodded. He stood, and once again took the microphone.

"We stand corrected. The latest version of the rules under which this tournament is conducted clearly requires that we allow even…." He sighed here, his distaste evident. "Even known homosexuals—and *females*—to compete." He paused here to allow a shocked susurrus at this last bit work its way through the crowd. "The match previously halted will now be resumed. The challenge is denied."

Jonah shook his head in wonder as the Woodley team—and the whole Woodley bleachers—erupted into cheers and clapping. Rusty screamed and gesticulated at his coach, but he had clearly heard enough already and simply pushed Rusty toward the ring. The referee waited for calm before allowing the match to start—he waited a good while.

Mr. Fischer took a seat in the guest area, in front of Brandt and Donnelly (and, though he didn't look to his side, next to Bryce and

Nestor). He didn't acknowledge the presence of anyone around him, so focused was he on Jonah.

Donnelly turned to Brandt, eyes wide with wonder. Brandt could only shrug.

The match between Jonah and Rusty would go down in wrestling lore across the entire northern part of the state. It was quite literally a grudge match, in ways that few spectators fully understood. The competitors grappled with each other with such force and determination that Brandt feared he'd hear a bone snap before it was over. The score ratcheted up wildly, with neither wrestler pulling ahead more than a point or two before trading the lead.

Jonah was ahead by two at the end of the first round, Rusty by one at the end of the second. If the first two rounds were a festival of taut violence, the third round was open warfare. Jonah and Rusty went at each other as if possessed. When the whistle blew, the score was tied.

The referee walked to the officials' table and took the mic handed to him by the announcer. "Sudden victory round!"

Brandt looked to Donnelly for explanation.

"If the score is tied at the end of the third round, there's an additional one-minute round. The first wrestler to score a point wins the match."

"I'll say this for Woodley—it always brings the drama."

"Tell it, sister," Bryce said with a snap.

Mr. Fischer's head swiveled to the side, his expression one of pure confusion. But the match drew him back immediately, and he started yelling encouragement to Jonah once more.

THE WRESTLERS returned to the ring. Both were clearly exhausted, but their resolve was written on their faces. They crouched, panting, awaiting the referee's whistle. When it came they fell at each other like a superhero and his nemesis in the final minutes of a summer blockbuster. The gym echoed with the sound of their grunting effort, their desperate grappling. Despite their frenetic, angry thrashing, neither wrestler was able score any points.

As the final seconds were ticking down, they were at a stalemate, locked together but still standing. Rusty growled into Jonah's headgear, "Do you thrash this hard when Casey fucks you?"

When Jonah later watched the video of his match, he would remark that he had no memory of how he ended the match. He executed a flurry of expert moves that resulted in the scoring of not just a match-winning point, but five of them once all of the falls and reversals were scored. To cap off his victory, a penalty point was taken from Rusty's match score because of his taunt.

The Woodley crowd was on its feet as Jonah's arm was raised in victory at the end of the match. Casey ran out to the mat and hugged him—as did the rest of the team, once they got there. They bounced up and down as a single mass of boisterous humanity. Completely obscured from the spectators' view, Casey gave Jonah the briefest of kisses—a down payment, both knew. Then, suddenly, the crowd of wrestlers stopped bouncing up and down; they retreated to the bench as if evaporating. Casey turned to see what had driven them off and saw Jonah's father approaching.

Casey whispered to Jonah, "Remember who you are." Then he went to hug his mom, who was coming down from the bleachers.

Jonah looked at his father, as if trying to understand his change of heart. "I didn't think you'd come," he said.

"You've been working for this all your life. Did you think I would miss it?"

"I didn't think you wanted me anymore."

His dad sighed and looked down at his shuffling feet. "Jonah, I didn't know what to do. All I ever wanted was to raise you and Sam to be good men. To see you wrestle... well, I worked my ass off at it, and on my best day was never half as good as you. You always made me so damn proud. And then all of a sudden, it's like I don't know you anymore, like you became something I never—" He shrugged and shook his head, out of words that were up to the task.

"Dad, I—"

"Wait." Mr. Fischer held his hand up. "Let me finish. When I saw you here today, surrounded by your team, it was like nothing had changed. I could see the kid I've known since he was a minute and a half old. And then when they weren't going to let you wrestle… well, I couldn't let that happen. Not to my boy."

"That was really awesome of you to do," Jonah said.

"Honest to God, Jonah, I had never read that wrestling charter. Did you know that until a couple of years ago you couldn't wrestle if you were more than one-sixteenth Chinese? Or if you spoke German? Or if you were Jewish? All this stupid crap in there meant to exclude people. That's what they were trying to do to you—to my son! And then it hit me: that's what I'd been doing to you too. And I'm sorry." He paused and cleared his throat. This was obviously hard for him. "Now, I can't say I understand what you're going through, or what this thing is between you and Casey. That's going to take a while for me to get right with. But I promise you, I will try. I want us to be a family again, Jonah."

"Thank you, Dad. I really appreciate it. It's going to take me some time, though. It's been really hard the last couple of weeks, and I… I'm going to need some time."

His dad nodded. "I understand."

Jonah looked up, struck by an inspiration. "How about this—can you and Mom and Sam come to this new church on Sunday? I went there last weekend when I was touring the university, and it's really great. It's kind of a drive, but it'd be worth it."

His dad smiled. "I've been thinking it might be time for a new church," he said. "I don't think ours is very… welcoming."

Jonah was deeply pleased. "Say hi to Mom and Sam, okay? And tell Sam I know a great place for waffles after church."

"Will do." His dad reached out a hand. "I'm proud of you, Son."

Jonah grabbed his father into a hug. "I love you, Dad."

"I love you too, Jonah."

"Swing by Casey's on Sunday around eight, okay? We'll go to the late service."

"It's a date." His dad smiled and couldn't seem to resist ruffling Jonah's hair before he turned to go.

"Well, that looked promising," Casey said, running back up to Jonah.

"It's a start," Jonah said. "Feel like going to Reese's church again? Dad agreed to give it a try."

Casey shrugged and then nodded. "You'll make an honest man of me yet, Jonah Fischer."

They hugged, and in a sea of men in singlets hugging, no one thought anything of it.

"Hey, I invited everyone over for dinner. Ethan and Gabriel are going to pick up some groceries with Bryce and Nestor, and we'll cook up a storm. Should be fun, right?"

Jonah beamed. "Looks like I'm going to end up with two families—the one I was born with and the one I've chosen. I'm the luckiest guy in the world."

"That's not what makes you the luckiest. Getting to sleep with me, now that makes you the luckiest." Casey laughed. "Well, second luckiest, after me."


THE MELVILLE boathouse had not witnessed such a raucous group of sociable souls in decades. Nestor, Casey, and his mom were in the kitchen clanging and whisking away, while Bryce sat on the couch regaling Brandt with what he viewed to be the highlights of the tournament—an estimation of the endowment of each of the wrestlers, based on the relative topography of singlet bulges. Donnelly and Jonah stood on the porch overlooking the lake, which reflected a nearly full moon.

"Your dad was kind of a surprise guest star today," Donnelly said, handing Jonah one of Nestor's hot, exotic drinks.

"It was amazing and weird and just about too much to take. I was already pretty much tensed up to where I could snap pencils with my butt, and then there's the challenge, and then he shows up. Thought I was going to hyperventilate and pass the fuck out."

"Things look like they're going to be okay with the family?"

"Honestly, I think my real family is in there." Jonah jerked a thumb over his shoulder at the rowdy group in the boathouse. "But I'm open to it. I just don't think we'll ever be as close as we used to be."

"Well, that was going to happen anyway, with you going away to college and all."

"Yeah, I guess I wasn't expecting it to happen so soon, or so suddenly." He sipped his drink. "Do you have a good relationship with your dad?"

Donnelly sighed. "My dad's long gone. Died when I was three. Mom was always religious, but she turned pretty hardcore fundamentalist after he passed, and that's why she basically disowned my brother when he came out as gay."

"That sucks. She probably lost it when you came out too."

"Wouldn't know. She won't talk to me. I haven't had any contact with her since Ethan and I got together. Luckily, there's my sister Chris, or I wouldn't have any family at all."

Jonah was quiet for a moment, swirling the liquid in his mug. "Gabriel, can I ask you a personal question?"

"Of course."

"Do you still go to church?"

Donnelly leaned against the railing of the balcony, pausing before making his answer. "No, I don't. I was raised in a very strict church, but once I saw what it did to my brother, I didn't believe in what they taught anymore. I still had to go, because my mom forced me to, but I would just kind of tune out. Once I was out of her house, I promised myself I'd never go back."

"Huh," Jonah said in reply. "I feel like I almost lost my family because of the church we belonged to, so I'll never go back to that. But last weekend the guy who was showing us around the university offered to take us to his church, and it was pretty great—even Casey seemed to enjoy it. It made me feel like I didn't have to lose everything I believed just because my family ended up with an asshole pastor."

"That's great."

"I asked my dad if he would go with me on Sunday, and he was up for it—the whole family's going to come." He paused again, shifting his weight from side to side. "Do you think you might like to come too?"

Donnelly, startled, looked at Jonah with his eyebrows up. "You're asking if I want to go to church?"

Jonah nodded. "I understand if you don't want to, but I thought I'd ask. It's really helped me to feel like I could have a new relationship with my dad."

"Jonah, you are a very mature young man. With all that you've been through, you are still thinking of other people." Donnelly smiled. "I'll consider the church thing. It's been a long time."

Jonah smiled, and they stood and stared out at the placid surface of the lake for a long while.

"FIRST, I'D like to say thank you to my good friend Nestor," Casey's mom began, her glass lifted. "He has taught me three new dishes and several new words, most of which I can't use in polite company."

"You are being too kind," Nestor murmured modestly.

"And to the lovely Bryce, who finally figured out how to make those awful curtains work. What did you call those things you used to make the tiebacks with?"

"Cock rings. I never leave home without a couple. One never knows when one will need to practice restraint."

She nodded her appreciation. "And to Gabriel and Ethan, who have helped us all through a very trying time. I can't thank you enough for all that you have done for Casey and Jonah."

"Just doing our job, ma'am," Donnelly replied with a nod.

"And last but not least, to my beloved son and his beloved. I am so proud of both of you—you are a great couple of sportsmen, and a great couple. May you be happy all the days of your life together."

There was general acclamation—and the odd call for them to get back into their singlets, which was politely ignored.

AFTER THE guests had departed for the city, and Casey's mom had gone to bed, and the dishes had been washed and put away, Jonah and Casey sat on the couch in the living room drinking the last of the fragrant spiced tea Nestor had made as an after-dinner drink.

"One step closer to state, my friend," Casey said, raising his glass to Jonah. "Plus, vanquishing your nemesis has got to feel good, right?"

Jonah chuckled. "You make it sound so dramatic. There were times in that match where I was spitting distance from having my ass handed to me. I could tell he had gotten some different coaching in the last few months. He had some new moves."

"But they were nothing compared to your moves," Casey murmured. "And now I've got some new moves I want to show you." A sly grin made his meaning clear.

"Are you asking me to come to bed?" Jonah asked primly.

"Hell no," Casey replied. "Stay right where you are. Once Mom closes that bedroom door, she's tucked in for the night. Just do me one favor?"

"Anything," Jonah answered.

"Try not to moan too loudly," Casey said with a wink. He took Jonah's glass of tea leaves and set it on the table at the end of the couch. Then he slid over to Jonah's side of the sofa and threw his leg over, straddling him. "I fucking love you, man," Casey groaned, as he brought his lips to Jonah's.

They kissed, and Casey's hands were everywhere on Jonah at once. He slid down Jonah's body, kissing his chest through his T-shirt, massaging the powerful pectoral muscles. He lifted Jonah's shirt and kissed his navel, and then the thin line of hair that led down into his shorts. Casey slid to the floor and then grabbed the waistband of Jonah's basketball shorts and the boxers beneath.

"Lift up," he ordered, tugging at the garments.

"Right here, in the living room?" Jonah protested.

"Fuck yeah, right here. Like I said, Mom never comes back out. Now lift."

Jonah cast a wary glance over to the bedroom door but did as he was told. Casey stripped the shorts and boxers down in one smooth motion and then yanked Jonah's feet up off the floor, landing his bare ass back down onto the sofa. The shorts and boxers went flying, and Jonah was naked from the waist down. Casey pushed his legs apart and settled himself between them.

"You are… beautiful," Casey said softly, wonder in his voice. "I look at you, and I see everything I want in the world." He gazed up at Jonah. "Thank you for being so patient with me."

"What do you mean?"

"You waited for me all those years. I think most guys would have gotten tired of lying awake all night wishing for their dreams to come true, but you held out, and waited for me to finally realize what we could be. I never imagined I would be here, but now that I am, I can't imagine being anywhere else."

Jonah looked down at his best friend. "I love you, Case."

"I love you, Jonah." Casey beamed up at him. "Now, you may want to put a pillow over your face, because you are about to get something very special."

"And what would that be?"

"Casey Melville's first blowjob."

"Oh, fuck," Jonah sighed, his head lolling back.

Casey wrapped his hand around Jonah's cock, which had been bouncing at him, hard and dripping, since the shorts came off. Casey lightly ran his fingers up and down it, really examining it for the first time up close. It was, as he had said, beautiful. And it was connected to the man he loved. And it was going into his mouth.

He leaned forward, and kissed the tip. Jonah sucked in a sharp breath and groaned it out. Pleased, Casey ran his tongue across the broad head of Jonah's cock, tasting the sweet, delicate fluid that was dripping from it. That was when it hit him—he was tasting another guy's dick. Every homophobic taunt, every mocking gay stereotype he had ever heard, clattered through his mind, but they were no match for his love for Jonah and the rightness of what he was doing. He smiled, deeply thrilled at the pleasure he was able to give just by being here, doing this, loving him.

He licked his lips and tucked them around his teeth. He knew from the few halting, half-hearted blowjobs he had received that just about anything felt good when applied to an erection—except teeth. He was determined that this would be the best one Jonah had ever gotten, but then as he made this vow, he realized it would also be the first one

Jonah had ever gotten, which kind of took the pressure off. He leaned in, and Jonah entered him.

"Oh my God oh my God oh my God," Jonah murmured, his ecstasy finding voice in an endless looping blasphemy. His hands gripped the sofa cushions, crushing them under the force of his abandon.

Casey delighted in seeing the taut landscape of tendon and sinew that raised itself in stark relief under Jonah's smooth, pale skin. The muscles he knew so well from the wrestling mat were directed to other ends now, reaching for joy rather than domination. His heart light, he turned to the matter at mouth. He had done some research over the past few days on technique, and he had learned well from a porn starlet named Iphelia Johnson, whose instructional videos he had studied quite closely. This is how he knew, for example, to wrap his hand firmly around the base of Jonah's cock and to pull his mouth off and let the saliva that had collected drip down over the entire member. This slicked up his fist and made the head of Jonah's cock much easier to slip smoothly past his lips.

Casey sucked and swirled and bobbed like a pro, and Jonah was powerless to resist the onslaught. Not that he showed any signs of wanting to—his abs tensed and flexed, his pelvis began to thrust, and Casey could feel him start to breathe more quickly. The penis in Casey's mouth somehow got even larger, threatening to close off his throat, but he took a deep breath and kept plunging it in and out, all the while stroking firmly at its wide, hard base. The loose skin below the shaft tightened as Jonah's balls drew up in preparation for the final act; Casey was afraid of bumping them too firmly on the downstroke, but Jonah seemed only to writhe more energetically when he made contact, so he kept the length and vigor of his pistoning stroke.

Jonah laced his fingers in Casey's short, thick hair. "Oh, fuck, Casey, oh fuck, oh fuck—" His already tight buttocks tensed even more as he thrust frenetically into Casey. Jonah's hushed moaning grew to a fever pitch in a plaintive register, and then with one great surging breath, he froze. Motionless, joints locked, muscles frozen in leveraged extension, he drew no breath.

Casey could taste victory in the ever-increasing flow of precum that filled his mouth with Jonah's sweet essence. He doubled down, increasing his pace and the power of his suction, and soon his efforts paid off. He felt Jonah thrash three times, and then the taste changed as his mouth was filled with a new, thicker fluid. He knew what would come at the end of a blowjob, he knew full well what the result would be, and yet when it happened, it was completely new. He swallowed, because there was no way he could get Jonah's massive—and now massively swollen—cockhead out of his mouth in time to do anything else with it. So he drank him in. The most intimate part of his friend was now inside him. Life itself entered him.

He slurped and sucked and swallowed, and then as the tensions began to ebb from Jonah's body, he licked and kissed and ran his lips over this magical flesh until Jonah pulled on his shoulders and brought him up to be kissed, and kissed, and kissed.

"That was perfect," Jonah sighed as they snuggled together on the couch.

"I think we're perfect together," Casey murmured back, finding his special spot on Jonah's chest.

"Promise me something," Jonah whispered.

"Anything," Casey replied, as he always did.

"That when we've become what we're going to be, we'll still be together."

"Always," Casey swore. "Always."

# CHAPTER TWELVE
# COMMUNION

THE CHURCH was filled with a bright golden light, filtered through windows high on both sides of the building. Jonah and his family arrived early; he wanted to introduce them to Reese. They made introductions in the entry behind the pews; the Fischers met Reese and his boyfriend Calvin with the genial grace Jonah had made a condition of their being invited here. Jonah's younger brother Sam, an avid lacrosse player, laid hold of Reese and never let go. The entire group moved to a pew together.

For his part, Casey was happy to see Jonah reconciling with his family on his own terms, not theirs. He was still a little reserved about the whole church thing, but he felt confident that if Reese and Calvin were comfortable here, he could be as well. When he saw those two holding hands, he laced his fingers with Jonah's and was rewarded with a sweet smile. He turned to the back of the room when he heard some latecomers slipping in as the opening music played.

"Jonah," he whispered. "Look who's here." Casey tipped his head to the back of the church.

Jonah turned back and saw Brandt and Donnelly sliding into a pew at the back. He smiled at Donnelly, who smiled back.

"IT'S NICE to see the Fischers reunited, isn't it?" Donnelly whispered to Brandt as they settled into their seats.

"It sure is. Seemed for a while there like it wasn't going to happen."

"Almost enough to make you believe in miracles?" Donnelly gave him a playful bump with his shoulder.

"Actually, it's enough to make you believe in the power of obstinate eighteen-year-olds who bend the world to their will. Those two turned out to be a force of nature, didn't they?"

Donnelly nodded as the minister took the podium. The day's message was about family—Casey told them later he suspected Reese had something to do with this but would never admit to it—and the importance of defying anyone or anything that would turn family against one another. Jonah's dad was crying freely by the end of the sermon, as was his mom. The service ended with a call from the pulpit for volunteers to help build a house for a family in need the following weekend.

The entire group of friends gathered outside after the service, enjoying the sun despite the cool mid-March temperature. The Fischers wanted to hear from Brandt about how the investigation had concluded, and he explained to them about Rusty Winslow and his role in the entire affair. Casey talked sports with Reese, Calvin, and Sam.

Meanwhile, Jonah chatted with Donnelly.

"Looks like you've got the whole gang here," Donnelly remarked.

"Well, everyone except Bryce and Nestor," Jonah replied. "I invited them, and Bryce seemed really excited about a church that serves mostly college students. But when I told him there aren't any altar boys, he seemed to lose interest."

Donnelly burst out laughing.

"But, hey, thanks for coming today," Jonah said more seriously. "It's really good to see you here."

"Thanks for inviting us. I thought a lot about what you said, and you're right—I shouldn't reject the whole idea of religion because of how my mother scarred me with it. I don't know if we'll make it a regular thing, but it feels so... normal. Plus, it's fun to watch Ethan when people start talking about God—the whole idea makes him a little crazy."

"Well, as long as you're having fun," Jonah replied with a laugh. "Now, I promised my little brother waffles, so we should probably get going."

"Have a good time. And best of luck, Jonah. You and Casey are my heroes—you stuck to your guns, and you stuck with each other, and you made it all work out in the end. You should be very proud."

"Thank you, Gabriel. And I hope we'll still see you—though maybe not every single day, and certainly not in fucking Woodley."

They laughed, then shook hands, then hugged each other goodbye. Jonah and Casey made the rounds of the group, bidding everyone a fond farewell, and then retreated to the Fischers' car for their waffle mission. Jonah's dad seemed eager to talk about the house-building project the church was working on the following weekend.

"Hey, want to take a little walk?" Donnelly asked Brandt as they left the churchyard.

"Sure. This was always one of my favorite parts of campus," Brandt replied. They walked along the wide avenue of trees, the lawn just starting to wake from its winter rest. A few sleepy squirrels plied their trade beneath the maples that were starting to bud.

"I've been thinking," Donnelly said as they walked, "and this morning made me think more seriously."

"Um, good for you? Thinking is important."

"Shut up—I'm being serious," Donnelly replied with a giggle and a slap across Brandt's shoulder. "Being back in church for the first time in years, well—it made me remember the things I used to think about while being scolded about how damned I was."

"And what was that? Ice cream? Large-caliber firearms?"

"Nothing like that. I used to imagine my wedding day. Don't laugh—guys are allowed to think about their wedding! Anyway, I would imagine myself at the front of the church, looking up the aisle, waiting for my bride to appear. I never got as far as imagining what she would look like. Probably a sign of something, right? But I would think of how it would feel to be up there in a tux and all nervous and stuff, with the eyes of everyone in the congregation on me, and it seemed like the most glamorous, terrifying, and wonderful thing in the world." He paused, and they walked on. "So today, that all comes flooding back. And I realize that I'm never going to be standing there waiting for my bride, because I have you. And you are more wonderful than anything I ever imagined." He nodded and continued walking without another word.

Brandt smiled at him. "We've spent nearly every waking hour together for almost three years, and for the last six months we've spent the nonwaking ones together as well. You'd think I'd know everything there is to know about you, but you still manage to surprise me. Who would have thought?"

"Thought what?"

"That you spent your youth planning a dream wedding."

"That's not the point of telling you that story." Donnelly's voice was warm, but growing serious.

"What was the point, then?"

"It wasn't a story about the past—it's a story about the future. Our future." Donnelly stopped walking and turned to face Brandt. "Ethan Brandt, will you marry me?"

Brandt gasped and took a step back when he felt his knees start to buckle. He took three rapid breaths, and his lips moved as he repeated Donnelly's words, checking to be sure they meant what he thought they did. He looked into Donnelly's eyes piercingly, weighing what he had just said. All of this happened in a rush of about three seconds, which was all it took for Brandt to form the words: "Yes, I will marry you." He shook his head, unconvinced that what he had just said made any sense at all, but Donnelly's excited squeal and vigorous hug let him know his meaning had come through.

"I love you so much," Donnelly murmured into Brandt's ear as he bounced.

"I love you too, Gabriel. I will always love you."

They hugged until they could hardly breathe and then only partially released each other.

Brandt, who could hardly stop laughing with delight, finally caught his breath. "So, do we elope, or do we engage our wedding planners?"

"Oh, God, Bryce and Nestor?"

"Of course. You know if we plan a wedding without them, they'll only pitch a fit and then seduce all our caterers. We'll end up with no food and bad music. Better to get them in on it from the beginning."

Donnelly nodded, but his eyes were a little unfocused. "So, we're really going to do this?"

"Damn right. It'll be easy—simple plan, simple ceremony, simple party after, perfect for our simple lives. What could possibly go wrong?"

"You should know better than to challenge the universe that way. Let's just say that no matter what goes wrong, we're going to be married and be happy for ever and ever."

"That's exactly what we'll do. No matter what."

Under the clear blue sky of a March Sunday morning, they glimpsed the shape of their future together.

It would be perfect, no matter what.

XAVIER MAYNE is the pen name of a professor of English who works at a university in the Midwest United States. Versed in academic theories of sexual identity, he is passionate about writing stories in which men experience a love that pushes them beyond the boundaries they thought defined their sexuality. He believes that romance can be hot, funny, and sweet in equal measure.

The name Xavier Mayne is a tribute to the pioneering gay author Edward Prime-Stevenson, who also used it as a pen name. He wrote the first openly gay novel by an American, 1906's *Imre: A Memorandum*, which depicts two masculine men falling in love despite social pressures that attempt to keep them apart.

Please visit Xavier Mayne's website at http://www.xaviermayne.com.

Brandt and Donnelly Capers from
XAVIER MAYNE

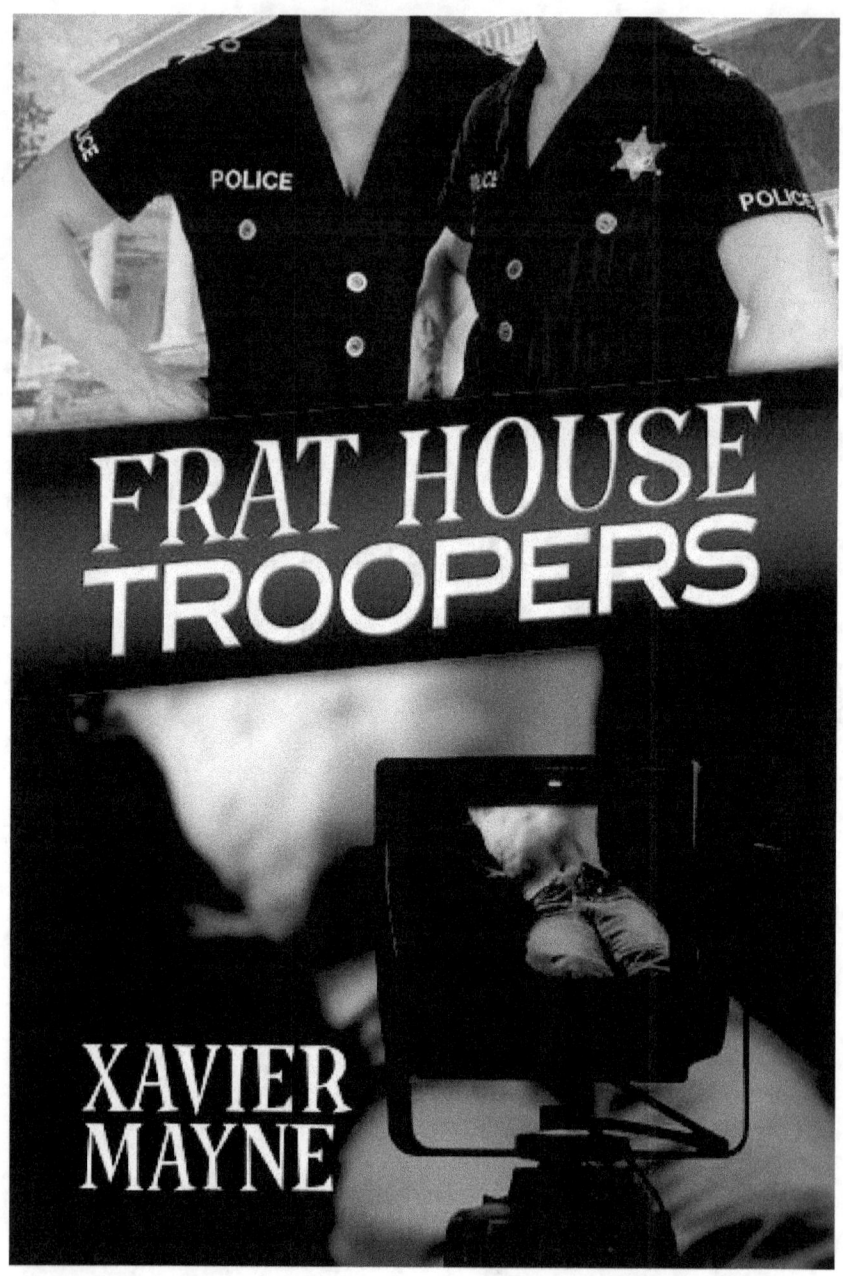

FRAT HOUSE
TROOPERS

XAVIER
MAYNE

http://www.dreamspinnerpress.com